The Siege of Salt Cove

BY ANTHONY WELLER

NOVELS

The Garden of the Peacocks

The Polish Lover

The Siege of Salt Cove

TRAVEL

Days and Nights on the Grand Trunk Road:
Calcutta to Khyber

Being a firsthand account of

its cowardly assault

and

heroic defense

THE SIEGE OF
SALT COVE

Anthony Weller

W. W. Norton & Company

NEW YORK   •   LONDON

For information about permission to reproduce selections from this
book, write to Permissions, W. W. Norton & Company, Inc., 500 Fifth
Avenue, New York, NY 10110

Manufacturing by The Courier Companies, Inc.
Book design by Brooke Koven
Cartography by Jacques Chazaud
Production manager: Amanda Morrison

Library of Congress Cataloging-in-Publication Data

Weller, Anthony, 1957–
The siege of Salt Cove / by Anthony Weller.—1st ed.
p. cm.
ISBN 0-393-05886-7
1. Bridges—Design and construction—Fiction. 2. Government,
Resistance to—Fiction. 3. City and town life—Fiction. 4. Bridges,
Wooden—Fiction. 5. Massachusetts—Fiction. 6. Aged women—
Fiction. 7. Inventors—Fiction. 8. Secession—Fiction. I. Title.
PS3573.E4569 S54 2004
813'.54—dc22

2003026073

W. W. Norton & Company, Inc.
500 Fifth Avenue, New York, N.Y. 10110
www.wwnorton.com

W. W. Norton & Company Ltd.
Castle House, 75/76 Wells Street, London W1T 3QT

1 2 3 4 5 6 7 8 9 0

for
Steve Gottlieb
and
Eddie Lazarus

friendship beyond measure

I want to marry a lighthouse keeper
And keep him company
I want to marry a lighthouse keeper
And live by the side of the sea
I'll polish his lamp by the light of day
So ships at night can find their way
I want to marry a lighthouse keeper
Won't that be okay?

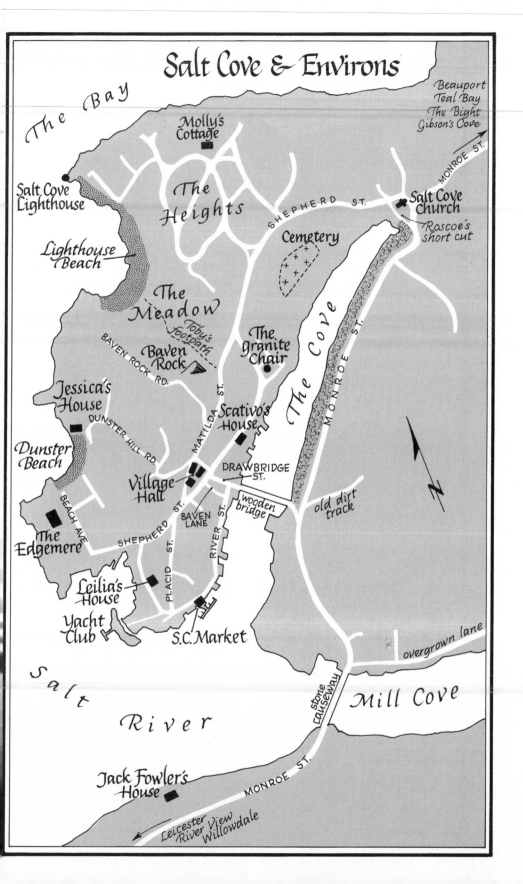

The Siege of Salt Cove

1

Jessica Stoddard

I AM LIKE A beached whale, with none of the disadvantages of size. No one walks around me with pity or dismay; I am stranded only by the inexorable motion of tides that I might have swum harder against a little earlier in the day. However, I am the one nobody notices. I hear and see everything. As historian of the Siege of Salt Cove, a witness to the heroic defense of that village by its beleaguered, vastly outnumbered inhabitants, and of the strange fate of our reluctant leader, Toby Auberon, I may be trusted. At my age I have nothing to lose by telling the truth.

When the siege began—long before any blood was spilled and the vicious armored vehicles rolled up—I was the first to realize these were illustrious, important events. I took notes, I wrote down what people said and what they thought, I knew this might all mean much to posterity. I see now, a full year later, that no one else could have spoken to everyone as I did, could have recorded what it was like for a small, insignificant coastal place, no more noticeable than the nail on your last toe, to stand up to the greatest power on the face of the planet, and hold its attacker at bay. Led, I must add, by a genius. There goes that foghorn again.

And where, you ask, am I stranded, and for how long? Why, for as long as it takes. Not that I mind.

The village of Salt Cove, whose history you can easily ingest if you consult the scholarly sources I will remember to list at the back, occupies a lumpy peninsula of granite outcroppings, bare meadow, and rock-enclosed beach about five miles from the old fishing port of Leicester, a quarter way round Cape Sarah, an hour north of Boston. Some claim Salt Cove was named by an explorer (Jonathan Mabb, sandbanked for a week, 1628). Another legend holds that the village was named by a child in the first wave of settlers, who quickly set the tiny place up as a center for shipbuilding and fish curing. I like to think it was a child.

The peninsula lies at what would, to a more superstitious society, be a sacred confluence of waters, the meeting of river and ocean. We are given snowy winters, muddy springs, incandescent summers, and potluck autumns. My people were from around here, but hard labor vanished in the village itself a generation after they arrived. The stonemasons and fishermen who could still afford property in Salt Cove after the war were by then working elsewhere on the cape. Now we have perhaps three hundred year-round Salines (*not* "Saltines," as several journalists insisted) and double that in summer. Many such fair-weather Sals—expecting another July and August beach holiday, then head back to civilization—got caught against their will in the siege, and had a more problematic summer than they expected. Ask me, an old lady of three score and thirteen with several healthy appetites, if I really care.

The moon must be in klutz, I'm dropping everything today. Including this pen.

To resume the march of history: it all began on a rain-swept March evening, when the year-rounders who manage the destiny of Salt Cove turned out for the most important of our three annual meetings upstairs in the creaky Village Hall. My job was to get there early and, while Mitch was turning the heat on, go over the minutes of the last meeting. People like to clomp in just in time to get a good seat, even though all the wooden folding chairs are equally uncomfortable and even those Salines going deaf can hear well from anywhere in the big hall.

I often wonder how different the village would've become without that hall, which was like our collective unconscious. Not because it was old, white, and musty, and overlooked sibling buildings that were once upon a time the schoolhouse and fire-brigade barn, but because its walls were hung with paintings from my childhood and before, Salt Cove as it then was: the mailman in blue cap on his rounds, his leather shoulder bag large enough to hide a body in; the lane winding away behind the Granite Chair to the cove; a trio of old salts mending lobster pots by the wooden bridge, when they should've been mending the bridge itself; my grandfather at work on his masterpiece, the dry stone wall limiting the former Elmo estate, with my father attentive beside him at fourteen, a decade before graduating from the state law school that would vindicate my grandfather's calluses. Or—your favorite, my darling—Dunster Beach at dusk, with the changing shacks still in place on the ledge above the pearly expanse.

We would come to these meetings and feel that this was the village, the one in the paintings, that we were striving to preserve. People say Salt Cove is a place where the old won't die and the young can't live, but our cemetery is full, and you don't have to be all that alive to be walking around shooting your mouth off. Those paintings, which people pretended to notice anew before each meeting started, reminded us how long the village had looked as it does now, how little its skin had changed, most of all reminded us of our perpetual responsibilities.

"Say, Jess . . ." Mitch Wapping was saying, with a retired conscientious hand steadying his forehead as if he'd forgotten something that truly mattered. "Do you think . . ." His voice trailing off like a balloon while I wondered if there were any point in my interrupting him, *It's Jessica, thank you, I know you can afford two more syllables,* as if I hadn't told him countless times.

"Yes, it is too hot in here," I said.

"That's not it. I forget what I was going to ask you."

"I need to look over my notes, Mitch."

"Oh, that's it," he said. "I remember now. Jess, I feel strongly we should have a new procedure for putting motions before the meeting."

"I don't think so," I murmured, stirring my dossier papers noisily and thinking it was always the men with little power in their lives who turned into control freaks when they retired, strategizing how to run the village while carving decorative duck decoys. Or lopping down age-old trees for a temporary view.

"Well, Jess, I've thought about this a lot."

"I'm relieved to hear it."

"Just letting you know. I'll be putting in a motion to change the rules of procedure." He was fiddling with little scraps of paper in a flannel shirt pocket. "Got my reasons right here."

Don't lose 'em! "You go right ahead, Mitcheroo." The hall was filling now, with plenty of mud satisfyingly tracked in. Here were Roscoe Hughes, the septic-tank and land-clearing specialist, and Billy Fagles, who worked Roscoe's backhoe; Jack Fowler and a recent young wife, daughter of the big house he'd roofed just off-cape; the two sets of Smiths, one ex–Pan Am, the other still in insurance in town; the divorced woman who'd bought the red-shuttered cottage in the Heights and who a few people later swore was an ex–porn star (well, you boys should get so lucky, I wanted to say). There was also the short fellow with a flag of long, messy hair who'd lived for three years in the lighthouse, renting it from the Coast Guard since they'd made the mechanism entirely automatic; we gathered he had some arrangement to be there every day of the year and keep an eye on a generator if the power died. That was Toby Auberon.

I often think the most crucial moments of our lives have, in fact, neon signs all over them, like downtown Las Vegas, if only we can open our eyes. I do not believe I'm imagining things when I say I felt the twinge of continents shifting as my glance passed over Toby—"a little rat of a man," as one weekly newsmagazine greasily referred to him just before I canceled my long-standing subscription. Reporters initially made him sound like one of our regular Leicester bums. You might've put him in his late thirties (forty-two, to be accurate, just at that seven-year pillar of cataclysmic changes in a man's life, you'll notice). You might've concluded, like one British journalist, that living alone in a lighthouse had "dulled his sartorial concerns," as he reminded me with a laugh three fateful months later, while I was trying to persuade him to wear a suit for the television cameras. "From Sartoris," he added, thinking I might not know the word. "The Greek god of fine menswear."

To many he looked like just another town drunk, but the truth is that a) he was a teetotaler, and b) he was bleary-eyed from staying up all night, every night, hard at work on his ongoing project, which it took me months to pry out of him and which he describes in his own idiosyncratic notebooks—paradise found, multiple volumes—entrusted now to my safekeeping. He was very small, about five feet two, and also very smart. He was lying when he shrugged off his education; I have confirmed via a few telephone calls that in fact he graduated summa cum laude from Stanford and thence from their law school. Why he misled us is still a mystery, though I believe he'd come to enjoy seeming unremarkable, disguised by anonymity and size. He was like a lithe burrowing creature: compact, nimble, with the ability to slip into rooms or even under doors so no one noticed he was there or gone, and with the aimless charm and meticulous gestures of, let's say, not a rat but a field mouse.

Sometimes he pulled his hair, the hue of dishwater, back in a rubber-banded bundle; sometimes it flowed in dishevelment off his shoulders. Because of this and his Wild Bill Hickok mustache, most of our mature year-rounders assumed he was high all the time, smoking opium and burning joss sticks in the lighthouse. But they would grudgingly admit he'd kept the foghorn and the light going round the clock in the bad November storm of '01 that surprised everyone, and there'd not been a single wreck along our coast on his watch.

This was totally wrong, of course, giving him credit where no credit was due. As he demonstrated to me one sunny summer day in the thick of the crisis, there was little he could do with an entirely computerized, digitalized lighthouse controlled from a hundred miles away except admire it, and dust every now and then. From that high up the sea looked like blue stone.

The most significant thing any of us knew about Toby Auberon was that none of us really knew him, much less thought about him. He was on hand to help if there were some village activity; he was very good with wiring and had repaired the lights for our village fair one Saturday the previous August when everything shorted out. Someone learned then that his father had been an electrician in Sierra Madre, California. He did some clearing regularly in the Meadow, the tract of communally owned scrubland spread over several granite hills above Lighthouse Beach. But he had no visible means of support, and we all imagined he scraped by on the shards of a small family inheritance, like several others in our village. Or else—as a few upstanding Sals whispered—sold drugs, offloaded from South American freighters he signaled in with the lighthouse using a secret code on foggy nights, their cargo later transferred to dealers' skiffs. Often I went for moonlit walks by myself in the Meadow, a habit since childhood, and Toby's own lamps, spiraling up the body of the lighthouse, were always blurrily on, no matter how late.

No matter how early I got to these meetings it was never early enough. People were always chattering in my face while I was trying to get organized, especially those who imagined these were my sole moments of identity because I sat onstage in the public eye, perched in a folding chair beside a rickety card table, writing down whatever I thought might be of use four months later at the next meeting. "All set, Jessica?" they'd say gleefully, as if I were supposed to cackle back, "All systems go, Bernie! Ready for liftoff!" You pass seventy and they look you over (if they notice you at all) and think they're doing you a favor by offering any lame comment that comes into their heads. They don't realize you take the aerial view by then: with neither cruelty nor kindness, you see them as ants that time will eventually step on. So you go along with them a little, humoring your fellow ants, just enough to stop them from labeling you a grouch, and hope the day will never come when you'll be drooling in some nursing home, missing the attention.

The hall was almost full by now, nearly a hundred of us. Even with everyone talking, the rain was still loud on the roof like somebody doing typing exercises, which surely meant we'd bring up getting it reshingled this summer. The president of the Village Hall Association—a squat schoolteacher named Italo Simpkins who'd lived here more than a decade and taught high school physics over in Beauport, nine miles away on the other side of the cape—gave me the customary salute I relished, and we both took the stage and waited for the other village officers to follow. I uncapped my pen and Mitch, shambling into one of the chairs arrayed on my side of the podium, peered past me and muttered, "What's that guy from DPW doing up here?

Bad news, Jess, I bet you a buck," which for him was a dramatic wager.

"Find out soon enough," I said, and (as I am doing right now) turned over a blank page.

The DPW—the Department of Public Works—was five miles away in Leicester, under whose jaundiced municipal auspices our village found itself, like the cape's other tiny villages: Gibson's Cove, River View, The Bight, Teal Bay, and Willowdale. Everything but the tourist trap of Beauport, in fact. "Town" on Cape Sarah meant only Leicester, a threadbare port that had lost the fishing industry but not its resemblance to paintings Edward Hopper did during my adolescence—a Depression-era Ford that belonged to a stonemason friend of my father is still parked in one of Hopper's street scenes.

Because of what befell Salt Cove, people would soon be noticing and partly blaming Leicester. During the siege a national commentator would describe the town as "like a lost, almost poetically dysfunctional family," which tells me he spent too much time at the theater. This was malicious, irresponsible reportage: all of us on the cape loved Leicester for what it was, despite what it was not, which is the only wisdom I have garnered that has not altered over the years.

But as Leicester was the town that regulated our public services, we villagers felt shoved under a ragged umbrella that couldn't keep the rain off. The single road around the cape was awful, and when the Commonwealth of Massachusetts finally got the whole area sewered after years of tearing up the roads, Leicester—"the City of Leicester"—never properly repaired them. They looked held together with duct tape; only our mechanics and used-car salesmen profited from all the potholes. Each village had fought in its own pipsqueak clamoring voice, with dozens or low hundreds of votes, and gotten nowhere, as did even our eventual united front, riven by petty disputes.

So no one from the Department of Public Works was welcome on that stage. Our taxes had gone up, our roads were worse, our gardens had been torn apart and cobbled together with beach sand masquerading as quality dirt so several Leicester contractors with cousins on the city council or in the DPW could make more money. Meanwhile, those few houses by the ocean that were the actual problem got easements for avant-garde waste systems, because the sewer the rest of us didn't need couldn't reach them due to the lay of the land. We were all still furious.

"This meeting will now come to order," announced Italo in his science teacher voice, shuffling his hands together in discomfort. He was nursing a cold and I made a mental jotting to take some soup to his wife Myra the next day. "Let it be noted that we find ourselves gathered on yet another unseasonably dry, warm March evening." (Rueful chuckling in the hall. I made a show of writing all that down and had a success with those whose eyes were on me.)

"We have with us tonight a guest from the state Department of Public Works. Now, now"—Italo held up his calm stubby fingers—"since he drove all the way from Leicester"—(a more grudging response this time: it took all of twelve minutes to get here)—"let's hear what he has to say. Chester Cairns, the village of Salt Cove welcomes you to its spring assembly and yields you the floor."

Doom, in the form of a rumpled, blond, pasty-faced fiftyish guy named Chet, taking off his glasses and rubbing his eyelids as he stood up, had arrived. I felt a rumbling in my blood at that instant, I swear on my father's soul I knew my life was about to change; I could almost swear I gazed out over the assembled multitude during the same instant, that my eyes passed over Toby Auberon, seated on an old church pew against the back wall, and our eyes met. Then the trapdoor of the future closed again and I was asleep once more in the present, swaying where I sat.

This guy Chet standing at the podium looked no more of a threat than a basted turkey, but I suppose your authentic assassins rarely do. He was apocalypse camouflaged as a cog of state bureaucracy. When he fussily cleared his throat and tapped the microphone unnecessarily—since it wasn't turned on, and didn't work besides—then introduced himself as an engineer, we all sat forward and thought: At last, they'll be fixing Shepherd Street, which is the only way for cars onto the village's peninsula. In my notes for the meeting I wrote down his name, *state engineer?* and the phrase *Road repairs!* which I had to scratch through as soon as he uttered his first deadly yap.

"Some of you may recognize me, since I recognize you. I've been out here in Salt Cove on different days with other members of my team, colleagues from Boston. Maybe you noticed we had a surveyor one morning. And we've, ah, concluded—this won't surprise anyone—that there are some very real problems of entry and egress." (*That's right, too many damned birds,* a few of us were thinking.) "Specifically, the wooden bridge over the cove, which"—he consulted a spiral notepad—"which has been there, one way or another, since 1821." (*1817!* someone shouted from the back. Mildred, I'm sure.)

I wrote down that he'd gotten the date wrong.

"Let me briefly summarize its history. The first wooden bridge was used only for foot traffic, and burned down in 1828. Was then rebuilt, considerably wider and sturdier. It lasted, with frequent repairs, until 1919, when it burned again during a Fourth of July celebration. At this point it was rebuilt wide enough to allow not only pedestrians and horse-drawn carts as before, but also that newfangled contraption, the automobile."

He waited for us to laugh, thinking he had us in the palm of his evil hand. We were hoping he'd get to the point, or at least say one thing we didn't know. (I kept wondering if Mildred, whose painstaking book on the history of Salt Cove was obviously his source, might stand up and yell, "Plagiarist!")

"This is the bridge," he went on, and I wrote down every syllable, "that survives in a considerably dilapidated and, I should add, treacherous condition. It is one of only two uncovered, all-pedestrian wooden bridges left in the entire United States." (A few gasps; none of us knew that. I noted his claim and scribbled *verify*.) "The last cars crossed it in 1969, when iron posts were put up to block each end. The chains went up soon after. The wooden safety barrier down the middle, to stop pedestrians from leaving the walkway part and falling through the missing planks in the traffic part of the bridge, went up in '73. Almost," he intoned gravely, "a third of a century ago."

Mitch shot a here-it-comes look at me.

"Now," said Chet gently, the smiler with the knife, "I don't need to tell any of you what this old bridge means to the character of Salt Cove." No, do go on, tell us, I murmured. Just then a flashbulb went off up front, I saw it was that young photographer for the *Leicester*

Daily News, and I thought, They know already what he's going to say, everyone knows but us.

Let me interrupt myself and say what this bridge has meant to me. More than mere handmade beauty, its lengths of wood fitted imperfectly together like a child's kit; more than the vision of something vulnerable exposed to all the harm the seasons can throw at it. It is uneven underfoot, far from amenable in most weathers, but the fact that it's always been there as long as anyone has known our village is reassuring. I see it as the best truce possible between the natural cove that Indian tribes would've known (I see them crossing in canoes by night, their torches held high; I can even smell their tobacco) and the unnatural aspects of man living here now. I believe every Saline finds it meaningful mostly because when you walk across it alone, this public loveliness belongs entirely and privately to you, at least for those brief minutes.

I have seen philosophers and poets speak of every human being as, ideally, attaining a condition in which all our souls extend bridges to one another so we can walk across and make contact and grow less alone and more fulfilled. I cannot say I have been more successful than most in this way, though I have tried. I do not believe that many of us have a natural gift for bridge building or bridge walking. Each person is so complex the only means to get anywhere is total immersion, you jump from the bridge and dive in the other's territorial waters. Together you each go swimming in the other person. Yet who wants to risk being wrong by constantly diving in to investigate?

The fact is, most of us do not conjure the fascination needed to attract another's soul in our direction. It takes a great deal of allure to make another person jump.

When I was younger I had my affairs but there was no one in whom I inspired much of a bridge, much less a dunking apart from the obvious, and there was no one who made my soul want to leap very far. I have liked living here, somewhat stranded no doubt in this other time and place apart, because I was on a crooked peninsula of my own all my life, parallel to the mainland but never touching except at the narrow point of departure, and with only an increasingly shaky wooden bridge leading across to me as the years echoed by. That image in old movies of calendar pages flipping over faster and faster does not do justice to the drawl and rhapsody and demise of each day. It hurts because it makes them all look equal, but truthfully, out of our whole lives, how many days can we recall as individual, if we had to say what happened on them? A rare hundred? A low thousand? And the few we remember as different are all the time we have.

Yet with only a weary unsafe bridge that led creakily to me, or from me, supposedly connecting me across a narrow, solitary cove with everyone else, it is no wonder my soul has found its own private ways of doing things, which are still a source of endless delight, a solace for what surely lies ahead, a reminder of all that has sung, despite this gulf, across a happy, useless life.

"But I'm afraid," said Cairns from the DPW, "we all have to acknowledge a situation that is, frankly, dangerous. And has been dangerous for some time."

2

Toby Auberon

GIVE ME TEN minutes in a court of law and I'll tear this clown to pieces. Ten minutes, Your Honor, that's all I ask.

"But I'm afraid," the man from the DPW was saying, "the time has come to take steps. We have to acknowledge a dangerous situation." Cairns paused to let his sermon sink in and blinked solemnly, as if this were going to hurt him just as much as it would the people of Salt Cove. "My team of engineers and surveyors found no less than fifty-three planks ready to break out of a total four hundred sixty-one, another twenty-seven that qualify for failure, and another thirty-four showing significant rot."

Forget it. Five minutes. That's all I need to eviscerate this guy. Why doesn't somebody speak up? Doesn't anybody else see what's going on? Is everyone up past their bedtimes?

Imagine: he and his band of merry men were out there for days doing their stress tests and reaching their official conclusions and none of the villagers even got suspicious. Probably thought they were tourists from Boston, up for a day of sightseeing, enchanted by the ramshackle bridge.

"In other words, out of a total four hundred sixty-one crosspieces of wood making up your bridge, one hundred and fourteen are seriously rotten. When we examined the pilings, some of which appear to be originals from the second bridge of 1828, the news was even worse. Part of this is due, no doubt, to the extreme storms of the last few winters. As many of you may not realize, when water in the cove freezes around the pilings, a surface layer of ice gets shifted by tidal force. It's like a dog gnawing away at a bone, on every single piling. The truth is, we don't understand why the bridge hasn't collapsed already, and it could do so at any moment."

I can't believe—no, I can believe far too easily—what I'm hearing. I can't believe I'm even at this meeting; this is exactly what I came all this way to avoid. I should've stayed in Rio. I could be sitting in front of a steak at the Bar de Arnaudo right now. Or I could've tried the South Seas. Palm trees, balmy breezes. Or even gone back to California. Unreliable electricity in each one, but an inventive man learns to work around it.

In Mesoamerica a thousand years ago they'd have settled this the civilized way: their king against our king, on public view under a glaring sun, whacking a heavy rubber ball with hips, knees, and elbows, no cheating with hands or feet, both players high on hallucinogenic enemas administered by nubile girls, home court player with a huge advantage, plenty of betting from the crowd, loser dies. By decapitation, if he's lucky. Still want to discuss the bridge, Chester?

"As you can see," Cairns went on, pouring my fragrant Brazilian *cafezinho* down the drain, "this puts the city of Leicester in a very difficult position. Should some accident occur—say your daughter's crossing the bridge after school and it tumbles down and she's paralyzed for life—well, the city would be legally, which means both financially and morally, they tell me, responsible. That's millions of dollars right there. I'm sure you'll understand why I've advised both the city and the state, in my report, not to run this risk any longer. So as of tonight, the bridge is officially closed."

In the stunned silence someone called out, "We can't even walk across to catch the bus?" and then there was uproar. The village leader Italo stood up, eyes bulging, astonished as they all were, but at least he had the presence of mind to call for quiet so this government hench-man could go on.

I nearly stood up to say something; I nearly stood up to vamoose. Instead I sat there, painfully reminding myself why I'd left the law in the first place, how I'd made a pact to stay single-minded about what I came here to do, and taken a vow never to get involved. Hadn't I learned that lesson over and over, the hard way? Just look what hap-pened the last time, a few thousand miles away—make that countless times. Nope, you should never try to help; certainly never try to inter-fere with the practiced entropy of human affairs.

"Signs went up on both sides of the cove tonight, while we've been in here," Cairns said, and this behind-their-backs duplicity nixed any hope of reasonable discussion. "Saying that anyone who walks across does so at his or her own risk."

There was a collective sigh, as the villagers all thought: *Fair enough, Chet, I'll take that bet, nothing to worry about.* But I knew the weasel was far from done.

"We recognize there's no way, short of armed guards, to physically prevent someone from going across." He smiled as if everyone saw what a joke the attempted denial of liberty was. "Hell, if we put up a wall of barbed wire, kids would just sneak around it. We both know that. And the lawyers—I guess we all know what to do with the lawyers—insist a sign just isn't good enough. Suppose it's a five-year-old kid who hasn't learned to read yet, and he's showing off for the other whippersnappers, and gets himself killed? So both the city and the state have concluded that, as soon as possible, meaning later this spring, the wooden bridge across Salt Cove will be demolished."

I guess we all know what to do with the lawyers? Keep talking, sun-shine, and you'll talk me out of retirement.

3

Jessica Stoddard

I WAS WRITING FEVERISHLY, my heart ticking away like a stop-watch, as the death of our bridge was pronounced. It is pretty peculiar to see an entire hall of people go through a moment of befuddlement as they ask themselves what they really just heard. I remember I put down my pen because my hand was shaking so much I could no longer hold it, trying to write Cairns down as fast as he was speaking and getting to what he was going to say before he got there, so I had to break off. Even now, not that it is the fault of that horrific man with the face of a breakfast bun, I find I get the shakes if I have to write something that bothers me. Oddly enough, it is sometimes the only way I know what bothers me.

"You can't do that," said Mitch breathlessly as if to himself, right beside me, and everyone was saying exactly the same thing. A voice in back yelled, "Go work on Cape Cod, you dingleberry!" and got a laugh. Billy Fagles called out, "It's our fuckin' bridge, you asshole, keep your paws off it!" and got a rumble of assent. I thought, That's telling him, just wait till we all get audited.

You could hear people saying, *Demolish, dream on,* and feel the mood switch in seconds from fear to defiance to confident mockery. Cairns had been expecting this; he waited it out before holding up his hands, quieter and terse now, so we had to pipe down and listen.

"Fact. It takes seven minutes longer for a fire engine, or ambulance, or police car, in any number of emergencies, to come down Monroe Street along the far side of the cove, do the sharp turn around the village church at the head of the cove, get onto this peninsula, and reach the heart of your village. Those truly precious minutes can mean the difference between losing a life and saving a life. Not to mention between losing a house and saving a house."

"We'll burn!" someone shouted.

Cairns ignored him. "I understand there hasn't been a fire here in years. What this means, mathematically, is there'll be one soon. Just ask yourself how you'll feel when your neighbor's house is going up in flames and you know the fire engines had to go the long way round the cove to get to it. And hit a bottleneck at the church since there was a wedding, and half of Shepherd Street was lined with cars. All of that instead of just cutting straight across a functioning bridge that could actually support the weight of a fire engine and save your neighbor's house by getting there a hell of a lot sooner. And save the house next to it. Which might be yours."

He paused to let this penetrate, and my heart dwindled. I felt sure that if someone would only hurl an obscenity at him it would be like a fearless talisman that could shatter the dire future he was conjuring up before us.

"Next door is what used to be your very own Salt Cove Fire Rescue, into the last century, because it was impossible for any unit to get here from The Bight or Willowdale in time. Back then the bridge, even as a drawbridge, functioned better than this one, because any emergency vehicle in existence could get across if a fire broke out. And it was passable up till 1969, when my predecessors made it essentially only a foot bridge. But for the last thirty-five years you've been living in a fool's paradise. It's not 1910, and you don't have a fire brigade. You realize how easy it would be for one house to set fire to another? Not to mention the Meadow. Supposing that caught fire and burned all the way down to the beach? And spread through the trees to the houses on both sides? That kind of hilly terrain, plenty of bush, a wind off the sea, that's like a recipe for an urban interface wildlands fire."

We were all seeing it: the Meadow aflame. I was watching from the beach below—not far from Toby Auberon, perched desperately in the lighthouse set on rocks astride the far end of the sands.

"You people need to be realistic," said Cairns. Chester the Realist addressing his foolish flock. "Suppose your wife has a heart attack. Like my own dad did. I've seen how quickly the damage gets done. Seven minutes can make all the difference—" We saw him swallow and his jaw deliberately tighten. "All the difference in the world. Believe me, I'm not saying you don't need a bridge across the cove. Of course you do. Just not a thing that's like some rope contraption for your bow-and-arrow men down in the Amazon jungle. You think I enjoy these test results my men are giving me? I don't like them any more than you do. But you need a bridge that works. And what you have now is a pretty postcard."

Well, he had our attention. Leilia Milne, a bantamweight wrestler of a woman who'd been cherished by her husband Harold (one of our cape's very best surgeons), and who'd cherished him alike through forty years in the village, stood up and put her cancerous hand on his shoulder; I saw him pat it. She said, "Statistics? Crap. I was trained as a mathematician, and I'll prove on a blackboard that your reliable numbers can be misinterpreted more ways than you know how to count. You're trying to frighten us that just because there hasn't been a fire here for decades, there are plenty coming? Big deal. Fifty years from now there'll be another gap of no fires. It evens out in the end. If all it takes to preserve the bridge is lose a house or two, Harold and I will burn ours down and move into the shed out back. When he was doing his residency in Everett we lived in an apartment that was even smaller. Think I'm kidding? You give us till the weekend and you can come watch the bonfire. Big house, big smoke. Then you can take your damned statistics back to your Boston drawing board and leave our bridge alone."

I have probably abbreviated the flow of her reminiscences. Cairns wasn't sure how to respond and had the sense not to try. Way at the back, Roscoe—whose late father started the family business of land clearing and septic tanks and property maintenance for the summer people—took his pipe out of his maw and adjusted his loose jacket around his belly, every inch the brawny, dissolute sea captain his great-grandfather was during the era when the mariners of Leicester ruled the North Atlantic. Roscoe said in a keel-hauling whisper that could wake old maids in their beds, "No sense demolishing. Most of them pilings still sound. Tested every one myself, last summer."

"That's simply not the case," said Chet from the DPW. "My team—"

"You wasn't there," said Roscoe dismissively, and tapped his pipe hard on the bench pew for emphasis—seated beside Billy Fagles, his right-hand man, with Mildred, our village's self-appointed historian, on the other side. A strange, stalwart trio if ever there was one. I recall noticing that Toby Auberon, in the corner, looked as if he might've fallen asleep.

"If this state," Roscoe whispered, "wants to build us a bridge" (he made it sound like a threat, not an improvement), "it can't be done from scratch. It won't look right. You reinforce first. If you know how to read boards."

"We have, uh, actually, looked into that possibility," said Cairns. "With all due respect to whatever conclusions this gentleman reached on his own, my engineers concluded that for a safe wooden bridge we would have to start from scratch. The problem is that a wooden bridge, in this day and age, is much too costly. The estimate we got for a structure capable of carrying cars and people the two hundred seventy feet across the cove is over eight million dollars."

Nothing makes people sit down and shut up like money. There was an unearthly silence as we all tried to take this in. (Mildred told me later, "Jessica, the only thing that came into my head was, Gee, I don't have eight million dollars.") Then, defending us, you heard the rapid clack-clack-clack, like anti-aircraft fire, of Roscoe's pipe against the wood of the bench. He said derisively, "I know a couple of brothers. The Harris boys, down River View. Carpenters. They'll do the job for fifteen hundred, you let me ask 'em."

People were laughing again, a little hysterically, because we were all wondering what the government must have in mind for our village.

I was trying to make out the clamor in the rows below the stage, and Italo, our elected leader, was futilely calling for order. I felt as if reality were breaking apart. The world I'd grown up in, the village universe portrayed on the walls around us and which we'd come out on a chilly wet evening to sleepily maintain, was being rent in pieces. It was as if someone had marched up to the painting by the door and torn the wooden bridge right out of the canvas.

I was trying to write it all down and realizing how much I didn't want a safer wooden bridge, even a wider new one that honored our ramshackle old one. It wasn't a question of allowing rescuers in faster, or helping you to get away smoothly. It could also lead you out to all the wrong places, plus it let in danger. I didn't want strangers coming here so easily; to someone old they are a threat. I thought of my elderly friend up the hill whose niece was forever trying to trick her, Wisenheimer meets Alzheimer, into falling down the well of managed care, and only a dinky splash at the distant bottom. When you're young and beautiful they kidnap you into marriage like Helen of Troy, when you're my age they cart you off to a nursing home or worse.

It still upsets me that at that moment I didn't rocket to my feet and loudly say all of this in a clarion voice, because I knew it was the truth.

One of the Smithson grandchildren got up, still wearing his dreadful sincere suit from work; I remember when he was a boy in white, playing tennis on the seaside court with a sagging net where there was a granite quarry in my grandfather's day. Now he was a grown man from some bank in the city, with a young daughter and a petite wife who wasn't at the meeting. I'd see them walking on weekend afternoons, gleaming with pleasure at living in the village, their lives already utterly devoted to homemaking, as if they were from my own generation. He stood up like a bottle frothing over, more earnest than Gandhi, and shouted at Cairns, "Don't you get it? We don't want people coming here. We don't want to make it any easier. When the bridge carried cars we had people constantly driving across to look at the cute harbor. My folks always told me how bad it was. Now those same people drive past because they can't figure out how to get here. That's the way we like it. No one's asking you to live with us, you know." He looked astonished at the violence of his own outburst, but when most of us made assenting noises he smiled sheepishly and sat back down.

Onstage, I could sense what few could—how little effect this was having on our guest. His dumpling looks hid his shrewdness; he was expecting everything we'd said, and more. He knew there was nothing we could do, especially in a hurry, cowed as we were by having lost the sewer battle.

I was the only person, writing down accurately all he said, who saw the pattern in his words as he hopped from point to point like a wayfarer leaping across a river from stone to stone, taking us from hello all the way to the bridge is going down, a new one is going up. This insidiousness is why I dislike organized religion so much, why I have never been a churchgoer even within the village, where to miss the weekly trotting of the homilies is a social sacrilege. I do not like the way the stories have their little meaning enclosed in them like a motto in an Oriental cookie, while the story itself is utterly without interest unless you winkle the moral out. I do not think life needs help from the ardent professionals to be full of meaning. I do not like the way they insert the simplified explanation with a string attached saying *Pull Me*, so people can conveniently tug out the answer and feel satisfied. I do not trust melodrama outside of old movies, I do not find that the secret in the skull is so easily read, I do not need to remember God to look for meaning in my day, and I do not believe in the string.

Italo Simpkins—a regular churchgoer, or he would not have been elected president of the Village Hall Association—said, "Mr. Cairns, I'm not quite sure if you're representing the city's interests here, or the state's."

"I'm representing your interests." People muttered *No, you're not*, naturally. "I'm working with the city at the moment, but I answer to the state. It's the state which has the power to enforce a decision."

"You can see what the mood is here, I'm sure," said Italo. "I'm going to move that we put this matter to an initial vote—"

"I guess I haven't made myself clear," Chet said irritably. "We're not asking you to vote on anything. We're informing you of where the city Department of Public Works, under explicit orders from the state, stands on the issue of the bridge. We'll give you a firm timetable next week for the demolition. We've estimated a month. What we need to address is the new bridge. Jim?" He nodded swiftly to the foot of the stage and a lackey in a baseball cap handed up a large poster board, which Chet uncovered.

"As you can see"—he held it up to reveal some architect's computer-generated sketch—"we have a preliminary design. There'll be tender offers, of course. The bridge would be a concrete structure, a continuation of the forty-eight-foot roadway down from Monroe Street on the Leicester side of the cove, and from Drawbridge Street on this side. There'd be five sets of large concrete pillars in pairs supporting the bridge, which would accommodate two steady lanes of traffic, each wide enough for fire engines or garbage trucks, with pedestrian walkways on both sides. This bridge would arch, and thus be much higher than the present one. The arch would allow sailboats that now cannot pass under to make their way to the inner part of the cove by the church, and even tall masts would be able to get through at low tide—"

"There's no water back there at low tide!" someone yelled plaintively, but we were all staring in horror at his modern highway bridge that spanned our cove and joined us efficiently and hideously to the rest of the world. I saw Cairns's chain-mail watch strap as he held up the computer sketch of our future and I thought, You can't trust the aesthetic judgment of a man who wears a wristband like that one.

I did not even try to convey the enormity of the sketch in my notes, I just jotted down *highway robbery* and felt sick.

"My father," I muttered to Mitch, who wasn't listening, "would've found a way to sue that man. To sue the city, I mean." I realized that Cairns was not the villain here, he was merely an agent of evil, sent to do the bidding of a larger concern. It'd never struck me that our bridge could be a threat to anybody, but apparently it was, or even an opportunity for others to get rich.

"So what's the cost of your fancy bridge?" someone called up.

"Four million dollars," said Chet coolly. "I promise you, there are even cheaper versions if you don't like this one."

He hadn't forgotten that we'd called him a dingleberry.

I said earlier that Toby Auberon had fallen asleep in a corner. By now he'd roused himself and I suspect he was never asleep at all, just biding his time. We were to learn in the hard months ahead that he was a master at letting the enemy give away their strategy before making his own move.

My intention, of course, is that this account should be as historically accurate and responsible as I can make it, but we know from Thuycidides that to write an unopinionated version of the past is not humanly possible and I do not expect to better my distinguished predecessor. However much I would hate for the casual reader, fascinated by the most courageous American revolt of the early twenty-first century, to find this volume tarnished by friendship, the fact remains that without Toby there'd have been no revolt by our village. Salt Cove would be simply one more tiny place that, before a governmental onslaught, rolled over on its back, legs in the air, and said cheese or whatever the expression is.

I cannot therefore pretend that this is history without the prejudice of personal association, or that I am not taking sides. Sometimes bloodstained events which seem ominous to the outside world are shot through, for the participants, with moments of extreme affection alongside the desperation and violence. We villagers were classified at times as mutineers, or members of some cult, and lumped with astral wackos and imbibers of poisoned soft drinks. Nothing could be further from the facts—as these individual histories of the siege, gathered by me with no little toil, will show. Perhaps it is vanity, but I would not wish for what we achieved to vanish from the erasable pages of history. The world remembers the *Bounty*, but who recalls His Majesty's frigate *Hermione*, a few years later (1797), whose crew dismembered the captain, butchered nine other officers, and handed the ship over to the enemy? I would hate for us to end up equally forgotten by that fickle mistress, posterity.

To us this March evening, though, Toby Auberon was still the disreputable guy whom no one really knew, who lived alone in the lighthouse but was always ready to help out. Our dogs liked him; he seemed harmless.

And, misleadingly, he looked unsure of himself, since he was scruffy and small rather than scruffy and a big bully. I have often noticed that people draw conclusions more from the expense of a person's clothes than their comfort within them. We make assumptions about what else they possess rather than wondering who else they might be; we confuse the soul with a clothes hanger.

In fact Toby dressed entirely appropriately for someone who inhabited a lighthouse and worked away at a large-scale project that occasionally got him dirty. He did not look like our Zorro, nor as if he'd even washed that day. I learned later from an eyewitness that every morning at first light he liked to go swimming from the brooding, jumbled rocks which were his front garden, and he tried to time his swim so he came out of the water precisely as the sun rose. In winter he might only stay in the sea a few seconds, so it was truly a matter of perfect timing. His timing was always extraordinarily careful, even at the end.

Thus I shouldn't be surprised there are so few mentions in his journals of what was to bloom between us, alongside the tanks and secret messages, the unexpected tragedy and devastation that would soon engulf our village.

Amid all the hubbub he stood up in the corner and winced to himself, as if his back were creaky, and wiped the back of one hand on his Wild West mustache. He said cheerily, "Hey! My name's Toby!" and everyone turned and probably thought disdainfully, *Now what?* Those of us who knew he was originally from California reminded ourselves that it all added up.

"My name's Chet," said Cairns with manufactured amusement, and it occurred to me he might even have hidden political aspirations. We will see if the decades prove me right, or if he survives merely as a bureaucratic footnote who deserves to be sewing his own trousers.

"I'm not talking to you yet," said Toby casually, and I thought, *Ah ha.* "Mr. President, may I be yielded the floor for a moment?"

"Go right ahead," said Italo, at a loss for where to steer a meeting that'd foundered on the rocks. This was, in hindsight, the moment when the natural steersman took the wheel from the amiable but clueless first mate.

"Can everyone hear?" said Toby. "I want to talk about a rat I know."

More people turned in their chairs at this.

"Most of you are probably aware I live over in the lighthouse. You won't be surprised to learn that when I moved in there was a rodent problem. Proximity to the water. Neglect. The fact I had food. Now, I'm kind of an old-fashioned guy. I don't like sharing my psychological space with rodents. So I got rid of most of them. They were faster, but I was smarter.

"Eventually it got down to just one, upstairs where the big lamp is. I don't live up there, the rat does. Kind of a mangy old scoundrel. He's not afraid of me, never was. I tried everything I could think of. Tried shutting him in to starve him out. I tried reinforced mousetraps. I tried slingshots. Tried high-frequency noise bombardment. I tried poison. I even tried borrowing someone's cat which I didn't feed for two days just to encourage the hunt.

"I don't like to lose, but over several months I realized this stubborn old rat had an advantage. He'd been there longer, and nothing I was going to do would ever convince that rat to see eye to eye with me. So, after a long period of frustration, I just gave up. He stays out of my way, I stay out of his way. He won because he knew he didn't have to budge. He knew I wasn't going to crawl into the walls and invade his territory, which he ultimately controlled no matter how much I strategized, no matter what I did."

"You're saying this village is full of rats?" said Cairns lightly. He was one cool customer, all right. "You said it, I didn't."

"I'm saying," said Toby patiently, as if explaining the world to a child, "that my rat had a conception of beauty, of the proper life, that he was not willing to yield on or compromise whatsoever. Look around you, Chet. It's not just our bridge that's made of wood. Most of our houses are made of wood, too, growing almost supernaturally on hills of granite. With trees busting out only where the rock says okay, I'll let you. Everything you see in this village is made of either stone or wood or earth—from our glass windows to our clay chimney bricks to the lighthouse to the slate roofs on the older houses. To the stone walls that let me know when I've set foot on my neighbor's land. This is how we face up to living next to the sea, Chet. With materials hacked out of the earth. Your steel beams and concrete pilings, your highway bridge that looks like part of the interstate, they just don't have anything to do with us."

I was writing so fast I thought my hand would crack, but I wrote it all down, verbatim.

"Maybe to you they're beautiful. Not to us. Look at the people here. A lot of us don't even know each other's names, and we wouldn't get along if we did. But we do all agree on what's beautiful, and that's why we live here. I'm trying to warn you, in the nicest possible way, that you won't have any more luck with us than I had with my rat. It took me a long time—and I'm trying to save you time—but I finally figured out that the only sensible move was to leave it alone."

Chet Cairns looked officially pissed off. (I'm sure he is a perfectly adequate husband and father who treats his children well, but I never got to know him in this capacity.) He said, "If the city and the state both decide that a bridge is structurally unsound, and can't be repaired, as my engineers' report indicates, they can close it down. And they can demolish it. They have so decided, and that's where we are now. I don't imagine the federal government would do anything but back the City of Leicester and the Commonwealth of Massachusetts on this matter. Outside of raising the eight million dollars for a new wooden bridge, much less at least another couple of million to put in escrow for future maintenance costs, you're going to end up with a bridge like the one we propose. That's how we build bridges in the twenty-first century. It's that simple. And it's for your own good."

"Well, I'm no lawyer," said Toby Auberon, lying through his mustache, "but in that case I think the village would have no choice but to secede."

4

Billy Fagles

Hoo boy. Hippie on the warpath! Everyone talking at once. Slime Lips from the Pubic Works Department says he made his point, good night ladies, drives off shitting cinder blocks in a '98 maroon Windstar. Then the Roscoe and I crack a couple of brews and us and a few others march down the hill like that mob in *Frankenstein*, original version and still the best. With the tubby photographer from the *Daily News* in front of us, shooting his flash all the way. Nailed his older sister twice, just out of high school—Denise or Darlene, I forget. Talk about your Roto-Rooter suction. Don't think he recognized me. Before I went with the beard and weights.

So we get to the bridge and the official warning turns out to be some pathetic little sign, just so the mayor don't get sued if I fall off. It's on a wood post and we all stand around looking at it under the streetlight, and old Dr. Hengerberg says, *Gentlemen, that post is on the edge of my property.* So the Roscoe gets really pissed off like I've never seen, he says to the tubby photographer, *I hope you got film,* and he kind of surrounds the sign like a bear, and the photographer starts yelling, *Other side! Other side, I need the bridge in it!* They switch and before you know it that sign is hasta la vista history, baby. Funny as a bastard.

We're out there taking turns and I show Roscoe how you can play it like a guitar, got them old Pubic Work Blues again, Mama! Then, well, the question comes up of how flimsy is it, and someone, might've been me, breaks it in two across his leg. But first we do the pic that ends up on the front page, maybe a dozen of us and the sign upside down so you can see the bottom cracked off. *Salt Cove Defiant!* is the headline, the next afternoon.

They wrote down what I said, too. Some reporter. It's a lousy government, one bystander was heard to commentate. Actually it's a lousy butt-fuck government of obsolete cocksuckers is what I said. The hippie is with us and you can see him on the edge of the pic trying not to be in it—too late for that—and itsy-bitsy Eyetie Simpkins from the Village Hall saying, *I wish more people would come down the hill, then we could call this a quorum action taken by unanimous agreement.* Eventually it started raining again and everybody went home and I thought, Shit, that's the end of a good night out, wonder how old Denise or Darlene is looking these days. Caught *Stagecoach* on the ancient movie channel, not a total loss. Always wondered about that stuff with John Wayne secretly being a communist. You never know. Still like cowboys and Indians around here if you ask me. And the next morning Roscoe is in a crappy mood cause he's smart enough to see we ain't solved nothing.

Very next day after lunch trying to do over the fence for the yellow house over on Baven Lane we get the paper and they say the Pubic Works Dept. is pissed off at us, also the Leicester City Council, especially our village rep who wasn't even at the meeting last night since she lives up Gibson's Cove. A strange oversight, one bystander was heard to mutter. But she's annoyed too, she says, that she and all the other city council persons had no warning from the Pubics or anyone else this was going down. The newspaper says the mayor officially did not know, but I say maybe unofficially he did, and the Roscoe goes, like, *You think he don't know? You think he don't know before anyone? Don't listening to that guy make you want to fart, Billy?* Then he lets loose with the Greek love call just for emphasis.

Not that it matters much. The bottom line, as I try to point out to the Roscoe, is that it really don't count what anyone in Leicester says or thinks. Thirty-eight miles from Boston by road, half that by water, we might as well be living on the surface of the frigging moon, trying to throw rocks.

So no one in the state office of Pubic Works in Boston is available for comment even a day later. No surprise, since they must have took one look at that photo and figured we was ready to attack with the torches and pitchforks. The funny thing is now it all just seems like a picnic, that night. We got angry, we tanked a couple of brews, we marched down to the bridge and pulled up a sign, I figure that's the end of it, they'll get the message. Like when the Indians shot the first settler, they figured that's the last we see of them guys, not imagining paleface got a prefab Fort Apache waiting back on the *Mayflower*. Never would've guessed that night was the beginning of a small war.

The Roscoe even talks to one of his buddies down at the DPW, and he says they're bullshit about this guy from Boston driving up then all of a sudden telling everyone what to do. And those same engineers already looking over a wharf in East Leicester on the Neck. So this trouble is all coming out of Boston—Roscoe says Leicester Pubic don't give a flying Wallenda if the Salt Cove bridge floats away, just so we don't bother them. And most of the guys down there thought what we did to that sign was funny as a bastard. Personally they don't mind if we send them state engineers to the Red Cross.

But the day after the newspaper comes out, when we ain't looking, another sign exactly like it goes up again.

5

Italo Simpkins

[Dictated]

March 27

Editor, Opinions page, *Leicester Daily News*:

As president of the Salt Cove Village Hall Association, the institution by which local problems have been settled for well over a century, I must take exception to your editorial of Wednesday criticizing in unfair terms certain members of this community.

The destruction of the sign warning people not to cross the bridge was not "irresponsible and illegal" as your pundit wrote, nor was it "an experiment in anarchy." As a scientist I abhor the incorrect use of technical terms; I will prove that nothing either experimental or anarchic occurred.

No, the sign itself was irresponsible and illegal. Did anyone consider the traumatic effect it would have on schoolchildren crossing the cove to be picked up by their morning school bus? Not to mention residents who use the bridge to catch the Cape Sarah Transport Authority bus to work?

Fortunately, the Village Hall Association chose unanimously to remove the sign shortly after it was put up by state engineers, and without any prior notice to us, I might add. That removal, once voted on, was duly enacted.

I regret that some unforeseeable and unavoidable harm came to the sign in the course of a delicate removal operation conducted at night during a rainstorm. I should mention, however, that the sign had been installed on private property without permission from the owner.

It is unrealistic, immoral, and outrageous of the city and state to imagine that they can, by secret administrative fiat, decide through a fog of bureaucratic blunders ~~assisted by your newspaper's garbled opinions~~ that

a) our bridge is unsafe, and too costly to repair

b) therefore it must be destroyed, then replaced

c) with a modern monstrosity whose like Cape Sarah has never seen.

A first-year student of logic will tell you that a) is not a closed system from which b) and c) are necessary and limited results.

If any politician imagines that, the year before an election, bringing up such a matter would do him ~~or her~~ any good, he ~~or she~~ is woefully mistaken.

Can the anonymous author of your editorial "Village on a High Horse" not imagine that a more polite, sensitive broaching of the subject would meet with a friendlier response? We are all in favor of improvements and repairs. In point of fact the Salt Cove wooden bridge, one of the entire cape's architectural beauties, has had to be substantially rebuilt in bits and pieces, if not totally replaced, at least once every century. ~~No doubt this is why the bridge failed to win Historic Landmark status thirty-five years ago, when we were forced to close off the vehicular portion for safety concerns.~~

Doubtless the bridge is ripe for another overhaul. I would remind your readers that repeated letters from the Village Hall Association requesting state assistance for repairs have met with nary the favor of a polite reply. Our village wants to improve our pedestrian bridge. Under the right circumstances we might even favor light automobile traffic as well. We are, nevertheless, opposed to a bridge that is not made of wood.

As president of the VHA, I have written a letter to the Massachusetts Department of Public Works as well as the Leicester City Council, requesting a meeting to discuss the bridge issue in a spirit of camaraderie. We in Salt Cove are willing to let bygones be bygones so long as the needs of our village are addressed and our voices heard. We will not, however, be trampled ~~needlessly~~.

Respectfully yours,

Italo Simpkins

[J. Stoddard, sec'y]

6

Toby Auberon

WHAT HAVE I gotten myself into?

As one who lives for the ding-ding and the chunk-chunk, a few balls down the gobble hole are to be expected every now and then. I wouldn't have guessed the entire community could be sucked in and whirled under, however. Democracy caught with its pants down, but this should come as no surprise. Even so, hard to imagine a more congenial location for the work at hand, which goes well—a mostly original design for the captive ball feature—despite the new bridge anxiety.

Points here in my favor. Year-round, I daily enjoy:

1. Unobstructed vista of the horizon, with sea filling about 180 degrees of the view from the rocks near the lighthouse entrance, and about 320 degrees as we spiral upward to the top.

2. Sonic vista filled with waves lapping, gulping, crashing, gargling. A soothing undertow of sound, as contrapuntal and suggestive as Bach, plus you get it free. Though I wish there were fewer seagulls, with fewer complaints.

3. Olfactory vista crammed with the smell of the ocean, more

diverse than people notice. It could make a popular perfume, especially for those on their deathbed. *"Enjoy an aroma before the loam-a."* One solace of dying might be to bow out with bottled fragrances of the sea in your final nostril gasp.

4. I am left alone. If people are curious, they keep it to themselves. I doubt this is the famous New England social distance. More likely a feature of village life, adjusted for local cultures, the world over. It's an essential human need to want all the gossip, the juicier the better, about everyone. At the same time, to have all your questions answered spoils the fun. Thus, in a very small place, a healthy push-and-pull is maintained between the essential knowledge and the essential mystery of each person. They leave me alone because I'm not a threat, nor intriguing enough to bother with. Which is fine; if I had to explain what I'm doing here I'd have moved away long ago.

5. Both the lighthouse and my lease are fundamentally strong, thanks to the initial builders of 1873 and to my scrutiny of the rental agreement. *GET A GOOD LAWYER* should be framed in every kitchen in America.

6. Funds remain sufficient, due to constant frugality. I lack nothing; the Leicester library is excellent; I eat well though I have no one else to cook for.

Points here not in my favor:

1. I miss steady sunshine. Any image of a palm tree, no matter how kitsch, brings on bouts of nostalgia. Also, the lighthouse remains difficult to keep toasty even with my two rotating black heaters. Not much fresh air on the lower levels either, except in summer.

2. No women. I would like a woman for every possible reason a man can want a woman. The fact is, I get lonely some days—which nudged me to the village meeting last week. Not to meet somebody but merely nod to people and have them nod back, though I feel most alone when least alone. Hard to get anywhere with heterosexual conversation at the Leicester bars if you aren't a sports fan; my natural camouflage does not inspire sane, beautiful women to poke around in the underbrush to see what measure of man is there concealed.

3. Issue of whether I am "wasting" considerable life and intelligence. A discipline produces a disciplined mind. An obsession does not.

4. Muscle strain from the spiral staircase. My design for a dumb-
waiter proved unwieldy. What I need is a grunting manservant with a
heavy accent and a tireless back, who would live on grubs in the cellar.
If I had a cellar.

I feel I am accomplishing great things, more than anywhere else
I've lived—Rio de Janeiro is a lusciously difficult place to remain
undistracted in—but I need to do better, and whether it's the place's
fault or my fault doesn't matter. As a doubly reformed ex–federal
prosecutor and ex–public defender, I'm no longer stuck trying to
assign blame, or avoid it. Easier to admit my own guilt outright.

Yet my nights up top are productive, thanks to the bracing salt air.
This winter I've taken to sleeping twice a day in four-hour spurts,
both A.M. and P.M., from 3 to 7. Since I'm at my best right after I
wake, I now get two chances a day. It means giving up my dawn swim,
at least until summer, but I have swum a lot of dawns by now.

Most crucial, I've found that the darkness hours—when those of
us who stay up all night ensure the continued existence of the world
by keeping an open eye on it—are natural for the work at hand. It's
highly problematic during afternoon glare to assess how effective the
combination of lit and unlit bumpers is; seeing the Machina aglow
and on the go-go is not the same. Yet in the early morning—with a
milder, unexcited sun bathing the lighthouse's upper levels—I can
evaluate my ideas from the night before. Night is the creator, day the
judge. I have always felt amply repaid by the night.

No one has ever lavished the hours, days, months, years that I have
on such a complex game system. Its significance as an allegory for
death and life, sacrifice and renewal, with an ever increasing difficulty
factor for keeping the balls in play, will be obvious as the score
mounts, even to those who see the elaborate beauty of the table itself
as mere decor and miss all the symbolism of a Mayan ball court and
its underworld. No fortunate Bally man fifty years ago, working on a
design team, had to compete as I do. I am up against an entirely new
mode of thought that has entered the world since the first bagatelles
of two centuries ago: I am trying to turn back the clock, to exchange
the visual illusion of a computer game for the actual world of ball and
machine, to replace the up-to-the-minute with the supposedly obso-

lete. But I'll resurrect this version of life yet, and leave it to dance till the last ball drops long after I'm gone. And who knows? Maybe I'll even grow rich in the process.

Which brings us inevitably to this recent salvo from the government. If the state proves determined, nefarious, and organized enough to destroy the bridge because it no longer "functions properly," there's no reason to suppose they'll stop there. The next item on their numskull agenda for improving, uglifying, updating, and erasing what makes my adopted village special will doubtless be this lighthouse—i.e., my home, laboratory, general headquarters. Its history closely parallels that of the bridge, from the wooden version of the early 1800s destroyed by fire, rebuilt by public subscription, burned again, and remade in a larger, more solid form.

As a physical entity my lighthouse is as solid as the rocks on which it rests, and though the climate here is damp, in terms of leaks and cracks the building is as dry as a white bone in which I am the marrow. It has never suffered the seasonal ravages the bridge has, even under assault from the worst winter storms I've witnessed, through crashing winds and seas incoherent.

Still, eventually someone in power will decide that the beacon system can be made more streamlined, compact, and computer-perfect, and set about circumcising what's now outmoded. Even though I am uninvolved with its function as a lighthouse, when the beacon replacement work is slated to be done I'll be kicked out or else find myself in a complicated legal battle which, though I could possibly maneuver through, having lived here for three years, would prove an arduous and time-devouring interruption.

So this offensive by the state must be fought on all fronts. The wooden bridge, even without historic landmark status, can act as a lightning rod for public affection and support in a way that replacing a beacon mechanism, while booting out the tenant, never could. It is a fight the village can win and must, for both our sakes.

What we need is a plan of defense, since the state has a plan of attack. How else to explain that man's smugness the other night, under his varnished professional concern? Some government jobs attract sleepwalkers, others pull in predators. What I don't see is the state's motivation. Public Safety asks for a new bridge, so Public Works designs it, yet there must be more to it than that, even if the slumbering media don't think so. There was a similar fiasco down on the other cape last year, the crumbly old seawall that collapsed and pulverized someone out walking her dog. But just because the government was right that one time doesn't mean there's no story here, and no guile.

Since we already have a road into the village which every motor vehicle uses and pedestrians besides, the bridge is only an extra route people take at their own risk. A sign stating this, and a fifth of their budget applied to repairs, would solve the problem. After all, it's not an anaconda-infested swinging rope bridge, it's simply got several planks missing and a few weak pilings.

Therefore their so-called justifications were meant only to distract. From what? The "choice"—between their four-million-dollar monstrosity, or an eight-million-dollar bridge like ours—swept aside all discussion of, say, a one-million-dollar repair. Predators are sometimes incompetent, but they are never generous.

Rain all morning. Lousy weather for finishing the captive ball feature. I could defy the warning sign and risk my life by crossing our bridge, while it still exists, to catch the jitney into Leicester and do some research at the town hall, to see what lies behind the zippered stares of the state knuckleheads. Then start preparing a defense. This is now a village under siege.

I should know better than this. I do know better. So much for learning from prior mistakes.

Important to remain inconspicuous. Maybe draw up a defense strategy but stay totally out of the mayhem. Let someone else handle it. No point in becoming a nuisance, in giving the state any reason to want me out of here.

They can always play the trump card of the state's police power to protect against public danger. The inherent clause in the social compact that they invoke whenever they want to fuck someone over. So we'll have to argue that a repaired bridge would be just as safe. And that to replace wood with anything else would be a huge catastrophe for the environment, starting with the general quality of human life followed by the food chain. Dig up study after study showing how modern materials will crush a highly fragile ecosystem that's been used to wood pilings for countless generations of fish, seaweed, and microorganisms. Food-chain them to death.

I do know better than this. The last thing in the world I need is to get wrapped up in another pointless struggle. It is utterly futile to try to make people better, to improve their lot; it's a zero-sum game, what's won in one place is lost somewhere else, somewhere out of sight, and you're better off just staying home and getting on with your own machinations so you can pack up and move elsewhere in good time. Anyway, there's no longer a sleeping giant here to awaken, a *vox populi*. I learned far too well in my twenties and early thirties what happens when you try to help, when you try to fight with any integrity for someone besides yourself. You lose all personal momentum, you make enemies all round, you don't win, and you wind up beheaded. And full of rage for nothing, a rage like a smeared stench that takes years and years to leave you, to wash off your skin.

Good, I have learned something.

And yet the prospect of anything but a wooden bridge across the cove—a handmade solution to an ancient transport difficulty—seems criminal, even barbaric, and fills me with fury. That old, despised, chastising friend.

This morning I received a note, shoved under the door while I was asleep, from a woman I don't know. Probably one of those elderly ukelele ladies in the village, the cookies-and-tea duennas in the little Salt Cove library on Monday afternoons. A Jessica with complex handwriting that I found illegible, something about the bridge. I should've kept my mouth shut the other evening.

I see problems, only more problems. What is the essential truth to cling to? Day in, day out, it is the quiet emptiness of things I find most strange, a nothingness abetted by the sea shifting outside my door, the caw of competing crows as I stride through a fading village. No, my solitary truth is this: *Build a better pinball machine, and the world will beat a path to your door.*

7

Jessica Stoddard

I WAS NOT SURPRISED that I received no reply to the note I slipped under the lighthouse door. I have known for a long time that my handwriting is hard to decipher; my niece tells me constantly, as if it is proof I am just around the corner from the Happy Hunting Grounds. This is why I'd already taken to typing my handwritten Village Hall notes into a small computer I instructed her to buy for me. It is easy to use (thanks to my grandfather I've always been manually inclined) even though I have no need to communicate with strangers for electronic chats about television programs of yesteryear, muffin recipes, or obscure sexual practices. Nor do I wish to buy anything. Instead I try to keep the floodwaters from rising.

So no word from Toby Auberon. In retrospect, when I consider all that arose between us, the call-and-response pulsation in the blood, the heliotrope unfolding toward the sun, the lustrous panorama of secret emotion like some ornately embroidered silken robe spread out on a bed, I feel by turns terribly fortunate or in terrible distress—or, right now, amused that he lumped me, however briefly, with all the dotty old witches of the village. We had another important meeting coming up, an emergency referendum; I told myself to damp down the twitch of raw delight when I reread my notes from the last one, that sense of conspiracy all great lovers share, as if they alone know a revolution is simmering in the streets. Of course this time, my darling, a revolt actually was stewing away, though none of us—not even I, not even you—realized it yet.

I must try to keep this impersonal, to remember that the historian, a mere human witness, becomes, thanks to the productions of time, the anvil on which the shape of events is hammered out for future generations.

Early the morning of the next meeting I was roused after a fitful night by Mitch banging my furniture on the veranda. (Most people knock.) By now four days had elapsed without a reply from Toby. From my bedroom window, through the curtains I made one summer from mosquito netting, I could lie in bed and watch the ocean fill a similar view to that from the lighthouse a half mile up the coast.

I went downstairs in my robe, shut off the computer which was winking on my dining table, put on some coffee, and let Mitch in. He knew by now to remove his shoes like a Japanese. He said, "You're going to want to fix up that iron table before summer."

"Maybe. Maybe not."

"I told you the same thing a year ago."

"I heard you the first time."

"You should take better care of this place, Jess. You can afford to."

You might assume the paint was peeling off my house. Wrong; I needed one window puttied, and that old table resprayed, unless I donated it to our summer village fair. Otherwise my property was seaworthy and could—certain people told me this repeatedly—be sold as is. Mitch is one of those retired gnomes who, on his hands and knees, measures his grass with a ruler to know when to cut it. A mind is a terrible thing to waste, even a male mind.

He said, "I talked to Italo. There's two state guys going to be there tonight. The paper got it all wrong. Turns out the reason is matching funds."

"Tell me more, Mitch." He was so happy at being the first to let me know, just as he still got excited at imparting knowledge to his wife, Anita, whom I like. I admire her colorful taste in cardigans and it's she who insists they rent a cottage in a different European country for six weeks each winter. I always saw hers as a difficult vocation, concealing so assiduously how much smarter she is than her mate.

He went on in his cicada way. "See, if the state throws thirty million this year into improvement of decrepit roadways—like our bridge—they get matching money from the feds that goes into a discretionary fund. To do whatever they like. Maybe they use it to fix up the governor's driveway. Or pave the whole coast. On top of that, Toby Auberon told Italo he should look into getting a writ to restrain the state from destroying the bridge."

"I didn't know they were friends."

"Can't say they are," agreed Mitch. "Funny guy. Never heard him say much before the other night. 'Hand me those pliers,' I heard him say that once. Not surprised there's a rat in the lighthouse. Probably a whole gang of them."

"He sounds like a fascinating rat, though," I said.

"I'm surprised they rented the place to him. Might spill his whiskey on the wrong wire some night."

"I really meant the rat, Mitcheroo."

"I offered to buy that place, you know. Wrote the Coast Guard a letter. I said, 'Let me take it off your hands. Keep the light up top, I'll take care of the bottom.' Thought I'd make it a woodworking shop. Never even wrote back."

Mitch had dreamed of buying many houses in the village; I suppose his fantasy was to move a few hundred yards up the road. I have seen these afflictions overcome many men after retiring, as if males have a kind of pharaoh-itis buried in the genes that asserts itself when they feel the stale breath of oblivion upon them. There are no more pyramids to be built, so they move to what they see as the ideal tomb. I am always ready to suggest they go on a long journey by tramp steamer instead, but no one ever asks me for advice.

I said, "Mitch, what would happen if the government really won? If they tore down our bridge and put up that thing in its place?"

He looked almost bashful when cornered into confronting the very worst possibility. "Me? Well, maybe I'd jump off it first. I don't know."

"Seriously."

"Seriously." He nodded to himself. "I was up all night thinking about it. All night, all week. You don't see the bridge from up here, where you are. In Upper Salt Cove." He chortled at a term few besides us had ever heard, not for decades. "I see it when I step outside for my morning paper. Anita sees it from her side of the bed just by turning over. In my den the window is mostly that bridge. Why do you think I bought our little house? All day at work in Boston I'd sit surrounded by shipping reports and dream about coming home to that window. What would I do? I haven't decided. Buy another house, I guess."

"Another house? Where?"

"Maybe next to you. Though I wouldn't be as happy up here. Maybe just cut my own throat. Better than letting them cut it for me."

"You don't think you'd get used to it?"

"Why should I, Jess? Got used to plenty in my life already. How the cargo business changed. How the world we always knew changed. Why d'you think Anita and I don't travel some places we used to? Reached my limit last year. Like somebody flipped a switch. I said, Okay, from now on, they adjust to me, or I stay home. So you see—" He paused, startled at having told me this much. "I intend to fight them any way I can. And we need all the allies we can get."

I had not thought very clearly about what I might do. Move to Paris? I am too old to move to Paris. There is a photograph down at the museum in Leicester which shows the last schooner gliding through the Salt Cove drawbridge around 1895 (I will reproduce the picture in an appendix, assuming the publishers do not take out my appendix). People knew then that it'd no longer be a drawbridge, they were seeing an inexpressibly lovely sight for the last time. All week I'd been feeling that we were living that moment again in the twenty-first century: witnessing this ramshackle wooden bridge on the verge of extinction, like some graceful bird with great wings extended protectively around our cove so we could walk across its back throughout its last dying weeks, days, hours.

I was trying every time I walked over it to take my time, to memorize the sensations of it swaying underfoot, the pang of the spring breeze whipping past, the creak it made at an invisible gesture of the tide beneath. They worry about every obscure plant or animal becoming extinct but look the other way when some man-made thing vanishes from the face of the earth. No one will ever know again the morning sensation of finding fresh milk on the doorstep in a bottle, on some day far in the future the last person who remembers the harrumph of a paper grocery bag being opened will die, as surely as the last man who fought in World War I will soon croak. I was wondering if it was wrong that the extinction of an insect in the jungle meant less to me than the extinction of our bridge. After all, this place is one of the few incarnations of beauty that I have seen survive, persistently beautiful, for my entire life. I had no children; my niece Sarah tolerates me; I created nothing; the beauty that I do believe in I have no wish to see extinguished before I check out. Afterward, it's not my problem.

I said to Mitch, "I'm with you. I'll fight however I can. I don't know if I could live here and look away, though. Tell myself sooner or later it would happen anyhow."

"Sooner or later," he grunted. "Three little words. The biggest excuse anyone ever thought up. Say, what you got going on that computer?"

I looked over and realized I hadn't shut it off after all. I did so and was glad he hadn't seen what I was writing.

"So what can we expect tonight?" I said.

He grunted. "They're calling the meeting a referendum. More hogwash from the government."

"Whenever people in power want to frighten you, they talk about money."

"We'll have to hire our own engineer, to show they're exaggerating the costs of repair. We'll all have to chip in for that. Then prove their estimates on a modern bridge are real low, which is their whole plan. Since what they're after is matching funds, see? If theirs is more reasonable than ours, it's likely to get approved. Then it turns out more expensive than they promised. I figure if we keep putting them off, maybe they'll find somewhere else to improve."

Mitch was clairvoyant about the meeting in most respects. That night we first listened respectfully to what the two fellows from the state had to say. (You should always listen more to your enemies than to your friends; they are more likely to be right.) They were a bit apologetic, a bit cold, and reminded me of the front paws of a lion, which do not budge for any man. Cairns was at the meeting, but he didn't say anything and wouldn't look me in the eye. One state fellow used the allegory of suicide, as if by trying to preserve our "gimcrack" bridge we were drinking poisoned Kool-Aid en masse. Pass me the hemlock, I hate to survive. I note the following exchange:

ITALO *"We understand the state is trying to get matching funds. We agree our bridge is in tough shape. If you repair it, the money comes straight out of your budget. But if you replace it, you get to take earmarked money and double it by magic into extra cash you can then spend any way you want. So isn't it all really about creating mad money?"*

STATE #1 *"I don't know where you're getting this."*

ITALO "The Boston Globe. *And the Internet."*

STATE #1 *"That's like saying you heard it from someone in a bar. That's not reliable research."*

ITALO *"I did a lot of research for my doctorate sitting in a bar. Are you saying there are no matching funds connected with a new bridge?"*

STATE #2 *"Let me butt in here. You people don't seem to understand that if we build you a new four-million-dollar bridge, that's all taxpayer money. Now let's say it turns out matching federal funds are available. Your bridge then ends up costing taxpayers only two million. That's how we look at it."*

STATE #1 *"Whereas if we repair your decrepit bridge, make it safe for another five years if you're lucky, or till the next giant winter storm, it winds up costing taxpayers eight million bucks. There's six million right there that doesn't go to schools for your children."*

WOMAN IN AUDIENCE *"Or a summer house for the governor!"*

STATE #2 *"Or a better road around the cape. I personally don't want to have to explain that to the other taxpayers in the great state of Massachusetts. I don't see why they should have to subsidize—to fork over a wad of extra cash because a few of you hate the bridges everyone else likes. Sorry to be so blunt."*

MAN IN AUDIENCE WHO DIDN'T IDENTIFY HIMSELF (IN FACT,

JOSHUA PARRY) *"Well, I work for the IRS, and if that's how the guys in your office juggle figures, I look forward to auditing your private tax returns next month, sir."*

I wanted to say in my biggest voice, "It's still a bargain for so much beauty," but I was too busy writing.

It went on this way, with the government fellows being polite but relentless and us persuading ourselves we were being resourceful, letting them know where we stood. Anyone who has ever watched local officials pretending to listen, masturbating at their own self-importance, can imagine the rest. My father, a first-rate lawyer despite a tendency to give his clients the benefit of the doubt when it came to settling their bills, always told me never to pay attention to the cant and rant of a situation, as he called it. All that mattered was what was signed at the end of the day. And for us, as I saw it, nothing had changed.

Oh, we'd made our dramatic gestures, we'd had our referendum, but now it was April 9, and the government intended to destroy the bridge the second week of June. We could hold meetings until Christmas, but unless we got a lawyer to handcuff the state master plan, none of our talk mattered a tinker's cuss.

After the official monkeys left we took some steps. They now seem laughable considering what we were up against. We established a legal defense fund. Bob Herbert, who lives over in Willowdale but whose father was still here, in the family house on Shepherd Street facing the Civil War memorial, headed it up. (He said offhandedly that we'd talk about his fee later, but enough of us protested that he had to get paid for his time that he caved in.) We managed to pledge about $1800, a lot for a bunch of Yankee tightwads like us. Bob agreed to draft a writ requesting a stay of execution on the bridge. It struck me that that'd been what Toby suggested, only he kept mum at the back this time.

Harvey Wilfong, who has an ad agency in the city, offered to write a press release and make sure the Boston media who mattered all got it, plus a follow-up phone call. He felt sure that with the media on our side—he is a robust man with a white-bearded grin, a carnival barker voice and a winning way of making fun of his girth—we'd get the state to back down.

I wasn't so sure. It seemed to me (and of course I was the one proven right, I foresaw much of what was to come—even you) that a community which most folk on Cape Sarah regarded as privileged by virtue of being separate on its own peninsula, and having no grotesque aspect, would not arouse much sympathy once the state started brandishing their figures and rattling their bureaucratic sabres. Plus our bridge was in far worse shape now, which meant even less original and hence less worth preserving, than back in the sixties when it got unfairly turned down as a historic treasure; pretty soon we'd just given up trying to raise money to repair it for cars, and limited it to being used only as a footbridge. So much of what goes wrong in life comes from waiting too long to act.

In the end we agreed that if we gave in to a modern bridge, even with the stipulation that we had to approve the design, then all would be lost. Our only viable defense was to protect the wooden one. So that was that.

Though I have striven in these pages to be objective and impersonal, you should know that nothing seemed more personal to me. Scant wonder I can barely hold my pen. However, I would hate for posterity to dismiss this as only the ravings of a prejudiced insider. (By the way, my two years as a young nurse in the Korean War are carefully recounted in my diary, which I donated ages ago to the Leicester Library local authors collection.) But no matter how much we remember, we are all reducible to a few essential images vividly imprinted on our souls' eyeballs. They add up to our lives for us; to someone like myself, of a natural lyrical bent, they are what I hold beautiful, the beauty that holds me in its sway. One such was our bridge. You take my point.

Let me interject that, contrary to most people around these parts, snoring away with their minds buttoned up in pajamas, their imaginations in slippers beside a sputtering fire, I like modern art—it's the old stuff I mostly can't stand. I am an elderly (not my word) child of the twentieth century with her toes wiggling in the twenty-first, and I always find it unbearable that 90 percent of the painters who ever lifted a brush on Cape Sarah pretend that art history stopped around 1850, which is about when it starts for me. The tyranny of the received idea, of course: they are like muddy serfs howling to be kept enslaved forever, terrified lest a genuine glimpse of life liberate them into the hard work of seeing the present world for themselves and themselves alone.

I would naturally have no objection to a bridge across the cove designed by Frank Lloyd Wright, a contemporary of the village's most recent houses. Yes, I am well aware of the reports of his death. My point being that I do not favor a concrete bridge whose construction date is 2004 but whose true date of design is a very crude 1972. Better a graceful 1890 than something barbarous masquerading as new.

I also firmly believe that a government, composed all my life of ever more arrogant and less qualified people, will, given the option, choose something ugly over something beautiful out of a willful duty to not do anything exceptional. Every time the Leicester DPW has had a simple task in Salt Cove they have (as I heard my niece mutter over the telephone one day, interlocutor unknown) fucked us royally up the ass. You might think this not a turn of phrase worthy of a Thuycidean endeavor—but you get my meaning, doubtless a very mean meaning. How else to describe the inept edging for several roads like a long black molasses canker sore, so the rainwaters gather and undermine the gray lanes I grew up on? No, one should leave no aesthetic decisions to such an unconsidering government.

Let me sing of the bridge I know, the bridge across which so many of my hopes and disappointments have strolled over the years, this bridge lashed by rain, thumped by blizzards, seared under a surprising summer sun. Think how few are the works of man that have so many lives and idle conversations barnacled to them. No wonder it has all but worn away.

I was eight or nine; the year probably 1938. I remember being allowed to stay up on drowsy summer nights when my father and mother had people over for bridge—I thought the game was called that because one regular set of friends walked over the bridge to get to our house. In midsummer the air here can seem tropically dense and lush after the thin airs of February. It stays light till very late, from my house you can hear the sea slapping at the rocks on Dunster Beach below. They would all sit in the large breezy room in wicker furniture my mother exchanged from the cellar every May for our padded winter armchairs. They'd drink their highballs (I wondered what a lowball was), the man was a lawyer like my father, I have forgotten his first name, the wives were close. The Naddies, they were called. I'd sit on the wide porch in a swing loveseat, holding my knees, staring out at the far shore and up the river towards Leicester's lights, and remember the stories my grandfather told me of the days when it was quicker to get here by boat from Leicester than even by the trolley service around the cape which shut down when he was a boy.

And I was still on that porch ten summers later. I'd sit out there by myself, content to have a little sister—my dear, long dead Jennifer had arrived unplanned just after the Battle of the Bulge began—and think how good it was to be alive, with plenty of chocolate now after the war, not as in England where I had a pen pal who complained so much about rationing that I dropped her. (*Mustn't grumble,* she'd write, and grumble away.) How I could hear, coming up from the cove and over the hill, the tremble and clatter of motorcars trundling across the wooden bridge. You could tell whether the driver lived in Salt Cove or was only visiting by how confident or hesitant he sounded in the fifteen-odd seconds it took. For years I had fantasies of setting up a tollbooth on the other side, wearing a black mask to conceal my identity, making off each night with the profits filched from gullible summer outsiders ("tenderfoots," I called them) before the alerted authorities came swooping after me on a raid. Just in the nick of time I'd slip noiselessly through the trees coasting up the cove, to make my hidden way back to the village, hooded by darkness.

Of all I knew those summer nights, very little that is not sea or landscape is left. My parents and younger sister are all decades gone; I am the only long lived family member on either side, and I will not pass that on. The houses by the water have changed their identities due to new owners. A photograph would argue with me that much remains, but this would be a lie. The altered sounds of the world have altered it so, the buzz saw of constant voices, the hum of radios replaced by the stereofied din of exploding grapeshot, the trees grown up like a fungus with splotches of houses where once there were none. The rumble of the bridge is gone but not the bridge.

I find myself dreaming more and more of the child I was, hugging my ankles on this porch, hugging my escapades in darkness to myself. I tell myself that the lives we lead are not our lives; it is the lives we imagine, which hurtle through our dreams, that in the end feel like the lives we really led—because they are the ones that changed the least over the years, were the least vulnerable, the most unfettered, the ones in which we were free to be most ourselves. So long as the bridge that once clattered with motorcars is still there, it still has the capacity to clatter through my memory; and the entire vista of night sea, the drowsing body of the land like an animal curled up contentedly in sleep, is as I know it should remain.

If I were not an old lady (the words are mine now) with a weakening grasp of who I might be, a limited repertoire of beauty I can summon up out of a limited will, I would not persevere so much with that local array of matchsticks across my insignificant cove. And perhaps I have reinvented it all backward. Perhaps what means the most to me is not the faint past but this siege one year ago and the unexpected stranger who came my way, Toby Auberon, to protect me, under the guise of protecting a village. Oh impenetrable mystery, let me salute you as I cap this pen at last and turn over in bed to sleep.

8

Nancy Eckerman

ON LIGHTHOUSE BEACH this morning at seven, backpacking the baby who'd been up for hours already, I found a driftwood man three inches long, perfectly formed, like a man wearing a hood. Shoulders hunched, arms at his sides, his coat draped to his knees, one leg longer than the other so that, propped in the window, he looks as if he is leaning dangerously into a high wind. Not the dilapidated gray driftwood often is but a healthier brown, like a deeply tanned cork. He looks indomitable, this man with the silhouette of a hero who can survive any weather, any misfortune, any sea of shipwreck.

I found him in a rock crevice as you descend from the Meadow right onto the beach. As if he'd been walking himself, except he fits right across the palm of my hand. From now on he shall be the man of my dreams.

Life here has been a riot in the year since the baby. The sudden death of Grandma E. leads us to expand our house-hunting horizons; Nancy and Jon buy beyond their means and walk into remodeling hell. Dissertation put on hold, with luck I'll get back to it when Jeb reaches kindergarten. At last I understand, with the perspective of motherhood: in this day and age nobody, not a single person, gives a damn about a seventeenth-century Spanish poet. Not even over in Spain—what do they care if Quevedo never finds his ideal translator? I might as well be some Neanderthal watching the rest of the tribe getting on with evolution, not ready to admit things are headed radically away from me.

Since coming here I've learned that all I knew up till now is irrelevant. Irrelevant to motherhood, to making a house work, to making a marriage work. Every week I feel more like a fly pinioned in a spiderweb of gossip.

I realized this last week, four months to the day after the contractor moved on and we moved in. I was out walking the baby in the aftermath of a storm which had cleared to a beautiful thunderstruck light. The owlish older man in that small house past the Village Hall was standing outside with his hands in his pockets, looking at the sky, and nodded to me conversationally. Mitch something. "Hey, I saw your lights were on at three in the morning," he said. "What're you doing up so late?"

Feeding Jeb, I could've answered. Writing up my notes on a study of village voyeurism. I could've smiled: Why, sucking off my husband, how nice of you to notice. What were *you* doing up so late?

But I don't want to know. I don't want to know their special family recipes for mulled cider with cinnamon, I don't want to know who owned the house twenty years before we did, I don't want to hear the saga of the ladies' sewing circle—defunct, I'm sure, since the discovery of marijuana and videocassettes. I don't want to know who just went into hospital for a hip replacement, I don't want to know who's sleeping with whom. And I most of all don't want to have to answer questions like this one. Or why my husband is still awake and on the computer at 2 A.M.

What I need is an art cinema up the road, I need more hours in the day, I need to know that utter strangers—and this rarely happened in Philadelphia—are not spying at my windows in the middle of the night. These people speak more humanely to their dogs than to their neighbors.

I wondered how much was visible from the street, if I could be glimpsed stepping into the bath.

I said coolly, "Try having a baby, you can't remember what you were doing ten minutes ago," and immediately regretted it. Too much shooting from the hip, as Jon would say. The man probably has grown kids and knows a hundred times what I do, and I could hear the remark reverberating from mouth to mouth around here. Only on reflection did I realize he was trying to do me a favor in his backhanded New England way, trying to warn me that I should put up denser curtains if I want privacy. A Peeping Tom wouldn't have told me, after all. Or maybe I'm simply giving a village busybody the benefit of the doubt.

Then he bent my ear about this exhausting bridge. He was like a little hopping Jiminy Cricket, galvanized into activity. I could feel Jeb stirring in my backpack, and wanted to get him home before he woke up. I said, still irritated, "You don't really think anyone's serious, do you? They're not going to put up a suspension bridge, who'd be that crazy?" Then, without meaning to be insulting, I added, "Surely that's just small-town paranoia."

He peered at me with dismay. "Property values around here will drop like crazy. You watch. What'd you pay for your house?" Before I could answer vaguely he rattled off the exact figure as if it were an experienced guess—public record, no doubt, but still unbelievable. He added, "I bet you're paying what? Fourteen hundred and change in taxes every quarter?" (Of course he was dead on, I had to look it up when I got home.) "What we're going to see, if that bridge comes in, is the market value of all our houses drop like crazy. And our property taxes go right up. They're high as it is. We'll end by paying for the new bridge, don't worry about that. And just try to sell your house three years from now when it turns out they've ruined Salt Cove with the ugliest bridge in Massachusetts." He was chortling in disgust. "No, sir, they rob you blind at both ends. Rob you naked."

I didn't know what to say to this and the baby was waking up, but I felt a stab in my abdomen, like I was being gutted for money. That evening I told Jon, and as usual his response was ineffectual, a pathetic echo of my own. "I can't believe anyone around here will let that happen. This village must have friends in high places. Say, I had a great idea for a self-help Internet company today. Ready? *Feeling lonely? Suicidal? When the tide's going out, let us be your final surf. Don'tJump.com.*"

"This man told me the court turned down flat the village lawyer's request to put off destroying the bridge. Ruled that it's the state's choice. Some local judge conveniently appointed by the governor. So nothing's changed. It was very eerie, the way he was talking. Like in the Bible—a plague upon the land, flocks of locusts, crops dying, animals coming down with strange diseases. I'm sure his generation sees it that way."

"That's from living through several wars. They read it all as destiny. They don't realize there are plenty of behavioral characteristics you can control in human nature. You click them on, you click them off."

"Well, you can't click off the suspension bridge in his mind."

"It's difficult for that generation. They can't admit property values will inevitably go up as the place becomes more accessible. Faster access, more information, greater market. Not that we have to like it."

"I'm not so sure." I had lost most of my trust in Jon's business acumen; he'd sworn to me that moving here, to work eighteen hours a day for a tough, second-wave, Internet start-up located improbably in Leicester, was brilliant. So our private life was at the mercy of when they chose to go public.

"People just don't understand," said Jon, taking our sleeping son from me, "that it's not whose gun is bigger. It's whose bluff is bigger. It's all Vegas now. If the village can stare down the players in the capital, and keep upping the ante, those guys will back down."

It's whose prick is bigger either way, I thought, and if there were anyone whose looks I liked in the village you would have something to worry about, except you wouldn't worry. You're lucky this is the end of the world and no one passes through here on the way to anywhere else, because I am looking for a tall, dark, handsome stranger, and I don't give a damn about the white horse he rode in on, only that he doesn't wake the baby.

"If the village tried bombarding the state," said Jon, still parsecs distant from what I was thinking, "with an electronic petition, with hundreds and then thousands of e-mails every hour, all telling them to back off, they would. It's not hard to do."

"Come on," I said. "They wouldn't even have the staff to read them."

"No kidding. They wouldn't even have the staff to erase them. But if the e-mails have similar titles, like *Leave the Bridge Alone*, or *Lose Our Bridge, Lose Our Vote*, and start coming in from all over the state, even all over the country, they'll figure it out."

"Jeb," I murmured to the baby, "your father's a political strategist." And not a Francisco de Quevedo, I thought, feeling like a prophetess of our doom.

> *Shake your head, mistress. Loose your hair*
> *In an unexpected hurricane of pure fire*
> *So that my heart, hungry for beauty,*
> *Can ride like storm-waves its expected desire.*

The transcendent question, nearly four centuries later—worth mysteriously more than any doctoral degree—still being whether my beloved Spanish poet's mistress was a redhead. Like me.

9

Scott Mahren

THE WILY SCATIVO here—Scativo on a roll again, everybody out of the way! Avoid that black-and-blue, you know what's good for you! Chump change, buddy, that's what makes the world go round. They don't realize that's not how it gets decided in the end.

The Wily Scativo has no need of chump change. He soars over all and sundry like a peregrine falcon, fastest creature on earth, look it up you don't believe me. The wily one begins his day by squashing his first cup of coffee, contemplating whether to grace his followers by shaving this morning, call it noon to the rabble, maybe time to go cash another royalty check, well-earned from inventing one of mankind's great labor-savers, when suddenly the knock fraught with meaning comes at the door, not the black-and-tans this time but that gay chump from the church. With a slab of paper under his arm, clearly for the old W.S. to sign. And I'm thinking Hey, he's human— wants an autograph just like all the others.

Not that Scativo ever refuses to grant a John Doe or even an audience to a fan, unless he happens to be drilling for oil or laying cable with another fan at the time. So I welcome the autograph hound, polite as ever.

"You've certainly got a lot of videos and DVDs, Mr. Mahren," he murmurs once I let him in and offer him a cup of Joe. Not even a smile when I put it like that. And not entirely comfortable either, once he steps round the Himalaya of films I'm getting ready to return, with the idea of sitting on my sofa—a collector's piece, at least in those four colors. Evidently he's not the interior designer kind but the regular guy weightlifting kind, though I incubate his handshake easy. Guy needs to work out a little more.

"Eight thousand two hundred books in the basement," I say. "Dry as a bone. Range of subjects. Don't need to collect the cinema, though. Rent 'em, watch 'em, got 'em. Store it all up here." I tap on the wily cranium like Cagney tapping an egg. "Shot by shot."

He mutters nervously, "Your, uh, overdue charges must be immense."

"The Wily Scativo is *never* overdue," I say loftily. As if I don't know what day of the month it is! Go on to explain the virtues of renting by mail, plenty of time to dissect technique, narrative angles, where you put your cameras. Never heard of such a dissection, he says. Slightly unusual sexual orientation an excuse as always for lack of genuine curiosity about the world.

Or maybe I just get bored easy—call it one of the penalties of greatness. Ask him to come to the point.

"Well, Mr. Mahren—"

"Scativo, if you please."

"Scativo, then." Adds a little inflection like I might be Italian, do I look Italian, you twink? But no, I feel pity; I leave his chump inflection unassailed and let him sip his Joe. He starts to explain the bridge issue, I know all about the bridge. I explain that not a single deal goes down, not a single thought flits through anyone's mind but the Wily Scativo doesn't hear about it first. Who knows what evil seeps through the hearts of men? The Scativo knows.

I love to see the gasp and astonishment clouding people's gaze when they realize they're in the presence of a titan. It proves they aren't as stupid as you think. For the record, I always insist on the opposite. "Mankind," (this is a direct quote, first uttered back in 1993), "lets the chump in all our hearts get the better of the hero," and you can set that one in stone, baby. *Thou shalt not fold like a cocktail napkin* is my First Commandment, and one day the W.S. is going to issue a leatherbound, gold-embossed, signed numbered commemorative edition of all twenty-three personal rules and ratchet up a new tax bracket. Tell the people what they need to know and they'll turn out in droves, and the Wily Scativo is nothing if not a drover—that is, he who drives cattle to market.

None of this is what our pal from the church particularly wants to hear at this slope of the morning, early afternoon rather. Give him credit for being able to get to the point. "Our village has got a problem," he murmurs.

"No kidding, buddy." Tempted to add, on a more personal note, *Not as big as your problem would've been in prison.* But contrary to popular myth, after his great invention (Patent No. 5,689,076, dated 2/14/94), yours truly never, repeat never, spent time in the Big House. Nor has he ever resorted to the Hershey Highway for amusement. The universe is full of beautiful women; I am a core star in that universe; the rest is simply gravity.

"Our petition," he pushes on, "will be more persuasive if we can get everyone in Salt Cove to sign."

"Good thing you've started with me, then. Got a petition of my own under way, too. Dig a hole deep enough, and they'll all jump in, eh? Artist buddy of mine used to swear by that."

Watch him flinch as he has to explain that in fact he's collected many other signatures already. Saving the best for last, I say, and he has the sense to agree. "We really would like to have you on board," he adds, so I give him the coveted autograph, complete with all the trademark flourishes.

"Think this petition is actually worth the trouble?" I ask. Being a lifelong student of human nature, I'm genuinely touched at how people concoct an alternate vision of the future, hopeful enough to clobber the difficult present on a cold night. Just to keep themselves crawling down the road without having the nerve to ever change anything. Hope is the biggest lamest fucking excuse on the planet, I tell him with a thousand-watt smile, you think every nun doesn't know that deep down?

Guess he's got a thing about nuns. Gives me the usual rigamarole people armed with only petitions and no real ammo hand out. They don't realize that democracy as the guiding ethos of this country died off a long time ago, a victim of sheer size, and that to people in power the rabble are a necessary nuisance, no more threatening than a back-yard, a horde of fools and robots who need occasional tending but can basically be told and sold anything if you know what you're doing; a little weed killer goes a long way. And the more silenced they become, drugged by the opiate of instantaneous electronic miscommunication, the fewer you need to vote for you before you have a majority. The rest are so busy raising their voices they never shut up long enough to real-ize no one's listening. But they'll buckle too, they'll shout themselves hoarse and go back to watching reruns they can't even remember they've seen before. This nation's attention span, I tell the chump with the petition, was cut off at the knees two generations ago. And you think a signed piece of paper is going to threaten the state?

What you need (and I emphasize *you* because the Wily Scativo lacks for nothing as long as the royalties keep wafting in) is someone who can march down to the State House, locate the governor's office without a map, push his way past the large-breasted receptionist to the inner sanctum, yank the man by his moronic power tie, and turn him upside down till he squeals in terror and promises to do whatever you tell him. (Don't want to put too fine a point on it, but using an African-American, if you can find one around here, always adds a useful element of fear to the situation and gets you to *yes* that much faster.) Otherwise you're wasting your time with your petitions and letters to the editor and all your legal farina. No one in power ever gives up anything, least of all money, unless you put a gun to their heads—figuratively speaking, I add, just to relax him—and any threat of a few hundred votes from this village is a farce.

He's irritated by this, natch, since I just called him an idiot to be walking around collecting signatures. I figure Moses got the same lukewarm reception when he read out the Ten Commandments, and my ancestors were around for that announcement of bad news too. Gets up to leave and at this point a moan issues from Pamela in the bedroom. Groaning for the Wily Scativo to come back to the gold mines, and I mean only golden, baby, in the most natural way. Our visitor's eyebrows perk up and I explain she's a young film student, studies hard, applies herself, but definitely of legal age, in case anyone's wondering.

Her evident sincerity makes an impression—man, if he only knew—and the natural curiosity of a fan-to-be gets the better of him. "What's *your* petition for, Mr. Scativo?" he asks, knowing he can find an excuse not to sign if he has to. "Since you don't believe in them, if I understand you correctly."

"Social principles," I answer, giving him my most earnest stare. "No man shall be granted a marriage license until he purchases a certain invention that pays, by the way, for all this," and I draw his attention to my unsurpassed view of the bridge, this house having been set in 1787 at an auspicious spot by one of the more successful shipbuilders in Salt Cove.

"You're an inventor?" murmurs our chump from the church, and at this moment another moan of pure lust—enough to make a Buddhist monk drop his begging bowl, robes, and vows—comes from the bedroom, and I do my best to shoo the guy out. By now he's more intrigued than ever. "What did you invent? Do I know it?" as I'm cranking the doorknob.

"The Mahren Pedal," I say. "Standard issue in restaurants and on high quality commodes. Available in many reasonably priced models, too. The discreet pedal that allows a man to swiftly lift the seat on a toilet by a gentle action of the right foot before taking a whiz, then lower it back into place after the last splash. The noblest invention of mankind after the bicycle, and a preserver of marriages the world over."

And bless my soul if he didn't warm the cockles of the Wily Scativo's heart, nearly as much as Pamela did a minute later, when he cried with unfeigned exuberance as I slammed the door behind him, "We've got one!"

Over and out.

10

Chet Cairns

Memo re Salt Cove meeting #3 [Password required for entry]

1. They still don't get it.
2. They never will get it.
3. Recommendation: immediate action.
   a. Once several pilings have been removed, present bridge is rendered unrepairable.
   b. After they see how rotten it is, more of them will change their minds.
   c. Easier for them to give up if we've wrecked it.
4. Enlist television support.
   a. Positive story on WXWD about new bridge. Interview w/ locals in favor.
   b. Negative story about dangerous bridges elsewhere. Consequences re Wisconsin accident 1989, Alabama 1992, etc. Photos of dead kids always a plus.
   c. Continue to smash historical argument. Present

bridge of no antique pedigree whatsoever. Junk held together with spit and glue.

d. Save reveal of Env. Non-Impact only for when absolutely necessary.

e. Lowell "restored" mill collapse in 2002. No lessons learned?

5. Speech by Leicester fire chief. Could offer to co-lead fund drive.

6. Speech by someone in Boston re public risk. Larger issues, etc. ("Think global, act local.")

7. Fund drive for new bridge around Cape Sarah, whether they like it or not in Salt Cove. Ungrateful to not go ahead once public has contributed.

a. General smear of villagers as stuck-up elitist snobs.

b. Children fund-raising door-to-door. Prize for most collected.

c. Try elderly rest homes as well.

d. Get Leicester Bank & Trust and Cape Sarah Savings to start a bridge fund. Point is publicity, not actual money raised.

8. Important to amass weight of public opinion against them.

9. Real estate agents could argue new bridge will raise property values.

10. Threats not yet stated:

a. Render present bridge unusable, offer to leave in semi-demoed condition unless they cooperate.

b. Threat of earmarked funds not available a year from now.

c. Corollary of price going up, etc. Threat to raise taxes to make up difference unless done now.

d. Threat of village reputation/animosity within greater Cape Sarah community. Editorials, etc.

e. Insurance companies raise rates for houses out of reach of immediate fire engine/ambulance response? Investigate.

11. Personally I do not care if they go along with the new ~~bridge. The old one will collapse on its own soon enough.~~

12. When you asked me to take charge you never mentioned possible long-term backwash for me personally. At some point it may not be expedient for me to be associated with this, unless you're willing to drastically change your plans re Cape Sarah.

13. In that case I may wish to pull the rip cord and bail from this project.

14. Important to have a successor in mind as right-hand man who can be fed to the wolves as necessary.

15. If you ask me, the old bridge looks better.

11

Jessica Stoddard

WHEN OUR FIRST request for a stay of action, on legal letterhead courtesy of Bob Herbert—an avid windsurfer even at fifty, who was often out among the whitecaps in a wet suit, like a windjamming seal in a spring gale—anyhow, when our plea for an injunction was turned down by the state, Italo told me he was calling an emergency meeting for the following Monday, May 26. I readied my papers, and when that morning rolled up, I did what I'd put off with schoolgirl bashfulness for many weeks. I decided to go to the lighthouse and introduce myself to Toby Auberon—no response, not even a polite *Leave me alone, please,* having come from my initial sally of a note, which (I know now from his journals) he had indeed received.

One of the strangest, most relentless aspects of life is how often we feel that some innate balance exists in the world which has gone off-kilter, and needs to be set right. We meet someone and sense a potential best friend, but either the generations are wrong, or perhaps the other has all the friends he or she needs. This has happened to me, and probably to you.

Likewise, we spy someone up close yet so unapproachable as to seem perpetually afar. Take the gentleman I watched once on a ferry-boat (*feribot*, as I recall) crossing the stirred-up Bosphorus, on a bold trip I made to Istanbul, ancient city of the world's desire, when I was forty-eight, just after my father died. I believe he may have been a Spanish gentleman, a financier from Madrid with literary leanings, though I only supposed this from the style of his hat. Behind him lay the unruly panorama of immemorial centuries, the jam-jar domes of mosques, the hypodermic minarets, a wind that made me shiver glancing off the vexed waters separating Europe and Asia. I can see it all vividly: the weather today makes me remember. There goes that foghorn again.

Had we been standing next to each other earlier in the ten-minute crossing, had my childhood Spanish been learned with more confidence, perhaps he'd have offered me his coat (draped, roué-style, off his shoulders) for the duration to keep me warm. Perhaps a little idle conversation, thrown like a wish for good luck into the teeth of the wind, and one thingum would've led to another, or at least to a thimbleful of mint tea, as they drink it there, then an exchange of addresses, a deepening contact to follow. For a duration.

I remember feeling all through that evening that a secret gyroscope in the world had been revealed to me, yet I'd failed to meet this man. The gyroscope was slightly off, and needed a gentle nudge from either the gentleman or myself, although the timing of my father's death at seventy-seven, and of my journey, had conspired to bring us this far. Yet it was not to be, and I know that no amount of reinvoking that day, that watery shimmer, brings any of it back except in passive memory. This is why I resolved, on that (I am not ashamed to admit) tearful evening in Istanbul, to always give the gyroscope of the world a nudge whenever I felt the teeter and totter were out of whack with what I sensed the equilibrium should be.

Which brings us back to Toby Auberon.

I shall try to do justice to the sunlight of that morning, when I went for the first time into his lighthouse and woke Toby up. The great fiction of memory, of course, is the sentimentality we ascribe to weather: nothing dramatic ever happens on days when the climate is anticlimactic. But it really was one of those illuminated May mornings, full of derring-do, for which our cape is justly legendary, the Byzantine-blue sky pouring forth its serene dazzle on the pagan confusion of the coast, over tumbled rocks and ragamuffin trees, the barren slope of the Meadow, most of all the enamel sea sliding up to that white candle of a lighthouse with its dark green foreskin on top, its thick stubborn body and single eye—yes, I know what I am doing, Sigmund, down boy, down—and soon I was walking across the broad, low-tide expanse of Lighthouse Beach (Robinson's Cove on the very earliest maps), and recalling the glass-plate photograph from over a century ago that I keep framed in my hall, of a ghostly lone woman in stays and bustling skirt, wandering this same pale strand near the fire-doomed wood forerunner of the present stony beacon.

The lighthouse is approachable two ways—either via the road that winds shoreward through the forested Heights, past several dozen houses, until you come to the former lighthouse keeper's cottage, now owned by a family called Meiden who come only in August; or else you can, like me, cross the sun-stunned beach, clamber over some rocks hidden in deep marsh grass, skirt several brimming tide pools with the odd stranded crab or upended gelatinous jellyfish, and scramble across a few more barnacled and kelp-bearded rocks.

Either way, you reach a plank walkway leading to the white lighthouse. Its white door is indistinguishable from any distance, and there is apparently no way in. This is why such beacons always look impregnable and beyond reproach, this is why I keep dropping my pen.

The body of the lighthouse is dotted with those thick, translucent glass bricks that admit light but not reality, much less any detail. If Toby wanted to see anything he had to climb to the beacon level with its unobstructed view; from below, in his living quarters, he received the world surreally blurred. I believe he found this creatively liberating. One of my personal projects, once this is done, is to follow his example with my own ground-floor windows, assuming no one tries to stop me.

Unlike the most crucial lighthouse of all, the one in your mind's eye, Salt Cove's does not taper but rises straight, a full 28 feet in diameter at the beacon area (which resembles a crown) just as at the rocky base. This meant not quite 24 usable feet in diameter inside, allowing for the thick wall, as Toby's living area. The height is 62 feet up to (but not including) the beacon level, but Toby's problem was how to make use of this space, which was all vertical. Essentially he had only a ground floor. As I was to learn, he'd solved the problem with characteristic ingenuity and boldness.

As I slipped on the last jumbled rocks I wondered if I was as unwelcome as I feared. After all, I don't much like people dropping in on me, though they hardly ever do, with the exception of Mitch or my niece. I wondered whether he was even home. From the rocks a few steps got me onto his gangplank, then to his door. I knocked.

No answer. The door was so heavy I only achieved a halfhearted thump when I pounded. At last I heard a faint groan, as if suspended in midair.

"It's Jessica!" I called out. "Jessica Stoddard! From the Village Hall!"

No more groans. Without any breeze, I could hear someone moving inside. Surely this was only my whispering imagination, or a trick of the sea. Perhaps he thought I was selling something; in a way, I was. It struck me in a desperate flash that, as there were stone walls edging the lighthouse property, I could tell him I was researching my grandfather's backbreaking labor of a lifetime.

"There are 253,000 miles of stone wall in New England," I'd offer. "More work in those than went into the Pyramids of Egypt." *I know where the Pyramids are,* I heard Toby saying, and that conversational gambit crumbled. I knocked again, and heard a grunt from barely over my head. In ensuing months I'd become accustomed to such noises just above me.

Then I got a brainstorm, remembering with teenage excitement his rousing speech at our first fateful village meeting.

"I came to see your rat!" I called out.

The white door swung inward slowly, for he had to squeeze back against the spiral staircase that was the spinal column of the lighthouse. I felt as if I were the fortunate archaeologist first looking into Tutankhamen's tomb: that much profusion and life. Of all the marvels I saw, I did not see him. Then he spoke, from just beyond my line of sight.

"There is no rat." Laconic, as if touched despite himself. "There was never any rat. Come in, if you want."

It was like entering a highly complex seashell, and finding the whorled world within more capacious than you could've imagined. I record my impressions here as a hedge against posterity; historians would give their wooden eyeteeth, no doubt, for a detailed description of George Washington's military headquarters by the Potomac, or Alexander's final tent.

Toby had (he liked to say) made do, but in fact he'd utterly transformed the small lighthouse interior into a bachelor pad. He'd built open mezzanines, balconies of planks, every seven feet going up—being so small, he never felt constrained. On the lowest level were a ship's galley with small stove, fridge, cabinets of condiments, an armoire, some clothes hanging on pegs, a filing cabinet. The next three levels up was the library, the bookcases packed tight with volumes, ranged all round the lighthouse; oddly enough, I spied a whole stretch of law books, recognizable even from below, sprouting weary yellow markers. Even from a mere glimpse I could appreciate the carpentry skill it must've taken to make the shelves conform so neatly to the feminine curve of the sole wall, for it had no beginning and no end. I couldn't see what was on the other levels above, but I assumed there was a bed eventually. What I did not see was a place to sit down.

As the door shut he stepped out from behind it. He was in a worn baby-blue terry-cloth bathrobe with golden fleur-de-lis over his heart. The insignia, aha, of the Hilton La Jolla. His gunslinger's mustache was a mess, as was his hair. I wondered where the bathroom and shower could be.

"What do you mean?" I asked. "That story you told, about the old—"

"Rat? I've never seen any rats in this lighthouse."

"That was all a fabrication? Just to make a point?"

"A parable," said Toby. "Doesn't have to be true."

I did not know what to say to this. I had not figured him such an actor, an elegant deceiver. "I came to give you some news," I said. "Italo's called an emergency meeting for tonight."

"Right." He yawned. "Sorry. It's a little early for me."

"I thought you always get up at dawn to swim."

He blinked. "Where did you hear this?"

I said unconcernedly, "People see everything around here. I bet there are folks I've never met who know my bra size. We're snoops, you know that."

"I guess I do know that." He ran a hand through his hair. "So what's the point of this meeting?"

I explained that since the initial writ had been denied, we were now at a crossroads. "Bob Herbert's approached the state court of appeals, but he isn't optimistic."

Toby snorted. "That's just three hack judges in the governor's pocket. Their job is to rubber-stamp everything. They won't even open the appeal. They'll just send back the preprinted postcard denial. By return mail."

He turned out to be right, in fact, as we were to learn that evening.

"How come you know so much about it?" I asked.

He shrugged. "I read the papers, like everyone else."

"Well, no one's sure what more we can do, legally."

By this time he was making some fancy coffee with a gizmo like a plunger in a glass beaker. The tropical aroma, fresh from jungly hillsides, swirled around the intimate space. Toby said, "Can I offer you some? Direct from southern Kenya. No? Well, if all else fails we'll have to go to war."

I still believe he was joking at that moment.

"Seems excessive," I murmured, as he sashed the bathrobe tight once again. "I must say, it's a revelation to see this place. You read a lot."

He fiddled with the plunger. I realized I'd outstripped the bounds of privacy, and it was all I could do to resist pushing past him and hurtling up the staircase to see the rest of his organized lair. But at my age it's not wise to hurtle, especially up a steep spiral of narrow steps. Perhaps this is what the ascent to the next incarnation will be like, with *Don't look down, you might fall* resounding in one's soul.

I said, "Why should anyone have to go to war just to keep a harmless old bridge? It leaves me sick at heart, right to the core."

"Exactly," he said. "But you have to escalate if you want them to back off. Always raise the stakes. Force the other fellow to give up."

"I thought that was our strategy."

"Not yet it hasn't been. We can't threaten any votes. They aren't frightened we might win a lawsuit. Bad publicity might worry them if it were really dirty. But it's a little late for that."

"You'll be at the meeting?"

He took a reluctant swallow of coffee. "Of course."

"I'll be there," I said, "taking down the minutes. That's my job."

"I know, I've seen you."

"It's been almost seven years now. Since I retired from the Leicester library system."

"You certainly write very quickly," he said, and I wondered if I gave an impression of haste and clumsiness, a person fumbling with pen and paper, or of grace and speed, of events being smoothly transformed into words that would summon them up again much further on. Sometimes lately I wish I could turn off this blasted music in my head.

"Most of what people utter is utter hogwash," I said, not sure why I was speaking so frankly, and thinking that perhaps it was because he was still clad only in a bathrobe. "I write it down anyway. It may mean something later." I paused. "And you, Mr. Auberon, what do you do with your valuable time?"

"We haven't met, have we," he said, somewhat tenderly, and for an instant I wondered if he felt tinges of what I did. Then I felt only pathetic for how rapidly I dismissed this notion, while reminding myself of my vow that night by the Bosphorus so many decades ago, to never again shrink from giving the half-kiltered gyroscope of the world a nudge. I put out my hand to him.

"Jessica Stoddard, delighted to meet you." We shook and I asked, "Do you have a chair?"

"I'm so sorry." He fiddled with straps along the wall, and unfolded what became a billowy canvas seat that he evidently kept tied out of the way. I sank into it as if I were back in the late sixties—an exuberant decade for me—or else below decks on a yacht. I said, "Perhaps I'll take that coffee now," and watched him get it for me. "Black, please," I added, tempted to say *like my devilish heart*.

He frowned as he handed it over, uncertain which cards in his hand (and you always held all the powerful cards, Toby) to turn over.

"I don't do much of anything with my time," he answered at last. "Just try to keep the ocean from coming in the door, mostly."

I took a swig. "I do not believe a word you're saying."

"Not one word?" He smiled. "I should never have told you about the rat. Let's just say I have my hobbies. Like everyone else."

"Many people around here think your hobby is smuggling, Mr. Auberon." I made it clear with a wink that I was not among them. "They suspect you of being in the illicit drug trade."

"As opposed to the licit pharmaceuticals industry? Well, maybe I am."

"Maybe you're not," I said drily.

"What else do they think?"

"Some say you have more than a mild drinking problem."

"That's correct. All my drinking water is bottled. What comes out of the city pipes isn't fit for human consumption. I never use it for my cannibal feasts. Was that what you meant?"

I swung my heels and rocked in the canvas seat. "You know it wasn't. What do you think of all the figures they've given us on the cost of a bridge?"

"Totally unreliable. The question is whether anyone's willing to cough up big money to repair the bridge we've got. If every household in Salt Cove had to pay an extra three thousand in annual taxes for the next twenty years—assuming we got a low-interest loan—would they? I'm not sure they would."

I shook my head. "People around here hate to spend money. They guard their cash like it's their virginity."

He raised a single eyebrow. When I was a girl I used to practice this feat in the mirror but I never succeeded, I could never isolate the proper muscle. "Then some people are going to have to lose their virginity in a hurry. If we go to the state with money on the table it'll be harder for them to press ahead."

"And what if we don't?" I said, looking all around, trying to memorize how he lived so I could write the details down when I got home.

"First comes the bridge. There'll be other plans, inevitably."

"Such as?"

He rubbed his neck. "Even though the village is zoned for residential use only, any multiple-family dwelling, even from a century ago, can get turned into condos. There could be plenty of those. Or suppose someone buys the Salt Cove Market and turns it into a tiny inn, right on the harbor? A zoning board might not object."

"I never considered that," I muttered gloomily. And I knew none of us had; all this was unthinkable.

"Maybe the old Edgemere gets bought out and renovated as a luxury hotel, not just a summer boardinghouse with one toilet per floor. Then we'll hear talk about the Meadow being prettified for tourists. Plus there's the entire other side of the cove, from the bridge back to the church. What if there were pressure on the Salt Cove parish to sell off all that empty land?"

"They never would."

"If you say so. But a new bridge and a horde of cars might change anyone's values. It happens all over the world, it can happen here. People turn greedy once the place they've protected all their lives looks really different. *Why shouldn't I make money, since everyone else is?* You wait and see."

I said with clairvoyance, "I imagine this lighthouse might even come under attack. They talked about shutting it down twenty years ago. They could sell it off, and ship it out to Nevada as a tourist attraction."

He gazed at me. "I hadn't thought of that."

But I knew he had.

He said, "I'd hate to leave. Living in a lighthouse focuses the mind."

"So does the prospect of being hanged tomorrow morning. One of my father's favorite expressions. He was a lawyer."

"I set out to be a lawyer," said Toby Auberon. "Gave it up."

Now we're getting somewhere, I thought.

"For heaven's sake, why?"

"I guess I wasn't ambitious enough," he said. "Or, maybe, dispassionate enough. Or maybe I just got interrupted by happiness."

"I still don't believe you."

"Let's say I discovered the joys of smuggling arcane drugs. Can I get you more coffee?"

"Fill her up," I said wickedly. "Right to the brim." He did so, and I thought: I bet the view is dreamy from up high, by the beacon. "I don't suppose you give guided tours of the light itself."

"Not allowed to. It's written into my Coast Guard lease."

"They'd never find out."

He said, "Sorry. It's an agreement I signed willingly, so I stick to it."

I realize now that he didn't trust me to keep my mouth shut; he thought I would kiss the beacon and tell, so to speak. Well, I was the one who'd reminded him what gossip-driven chatterboxes we all were. Beyond that, his real reason was not wanting me to see what he was doing on the mysterious upper levels over my head, past his books, past where he slept—which is what I wanted to see. I'd have seen everything on the way up to the light.

"As the daughter of a lawyer," I said, "I respect your attitude. Though I'd love to see how the beacon works."

"There's not much to see. All the mechanisms are hidden." Then he looked at me curiously, as if wondering whether what he was about to say would be wasted on me. "Besides, I'll end up feeling too much like the *A Bao A Qu* if I start taking everyone up."

"What's —" And I mangled the pronunciation of what I thought I'd heard. (It took real sleuthing, but I finally tracked down the source of his tale, an obscure 1937 work on Malay witchcraft. The copy from Toby's library is now, I am sad but proud to say, in my possession.)

"The *A Bao A Qu* is a who, not a what," he said. "Or maybe it's an it, since it's definitely not a he or a she. You might call it a creature, but it's more like the sketch of a being. And it lives in a stone tower that overlooks a perfect vista of the horizon. With a circular stairway of very worn steps in darkness going up, and no windows.

"Now the people who live near the *A Bao A Qu* shun the tower. They have no idea that where they live is so exquisite, because none of them ever tried to reach the top and see the view. But every now and then a wayfarer passes across the landscape, and attempts to make his way up the tower. Or else a pilgrim who's journeyed there deliberately."

"The *A Bao A Qu* lets them in the door?" I asked, and by now, because I am a good listener, I got it right.

"I don't know." He looked a bit peeved that I'd asked him a question he couldn't answer. To his credit, he didn't just invent something to mollify me. "Anyway, the wayfarer or pilgrim starts up the stairs, going round and round and up and up, and from the very bottom he's followed by the being. When it's alone, which is most of the time, it sleeps almost invisibly on the lowest step. But as soon as the visitor starts his climb, the *A Bao A Qu* comes to life. It has a slightly blurry skin you can virtually see through, and as it awakens a glow comes to life inside it. So the visitor's path is lighted by the glow of the creature following him so closely."

"What's its shape?" I asked.

"It doesn't have a shape near the bottom. It's an amorphous, sluggish blob. That's the whole point. It acquires its shape gradually, as it climbs the stairs with the visitor. And in the tale the being feels a kind of mournful familiarity toward him, because so many generations of pilgrims have come to the tower and tried to make their way up. At every stair, as they climb together, the being's glow changes, and grows stronger, more iridescent. And his form becomes more defined, like a body. The idea is that if the visitor can reach the highest step, he'll attain perfection. And be able to gaze out on that limitless view, all the way round the horizon of the most beautiful landscape on earth."

"And if not?"

"Well, that's it. He never does. Over the centuries only one visitor ever made it to the top, but that was a long time ago. And when they each turn back—I suppose they realize they've failed, and just can't go any farther—the creature collapses. Its glow diminishes very suddenly, its form fades, it begins to lose consciousness and gives a soft moan. Then it tumbles all the way down to the bottom stair, where it waits for the next person. So it goes on, always following, then suffering when each visitor can't make the final move into the perfect."

"I get it," I said. "A creature of endless hope."

"That's just how I see it," said Toby Auberon.

"I wonder which one managed to reach the highest step." I noticed that one wick end of his mustache was drenched with coffee. "I'd think the story would make you want to usher a wayfarer like me up your stairs. Doesn't the creature yearn and yearn to achieve its shape one more time?"

"You missed the point," he said. "I'm not the creature. I'm the visitor, who's now so determined that he's actually living in the tower. Trying to make his way up, every day."

"In that case," I said, "I'll be the amorphous one."

Glowing from within, I thought, lighting your way.

12

Molly Mellew

So I GET THIS JINGLE and it's an Indian dealer with a gallery in Santa Monica, not the curry kind but the Geronimo kind, and he says, Got your photos, we checked out your work on your site and we're really impressed, especially the designs in silver and lapis. So I'm thinking, Hey, at last, a little solid recognition after years of basically apprentice eating it, and people mostly not appreciating what they're buying, so I'm like, Cool, Geronimo, state your terms. Since I really don't care that much if he wants an excessive cut or not, it's just time I got into the right venues on the Coast, where people are a lot more ready for the type of beauty I'm selling.

So he offers me a percentage I can live with and we're talking how many bracelets, how many earrings, maybe an anklet or two though I think those could really fly, rings, necklaces, the whole caboodle, then he says, You know, your face looks familiar. And I've been using a picture of me wearing this silver and turquoise star, so now I'm thinking uh-oh, here it comes, but no, it's just the usual flirt thing. That's a flow it works to go with over the phone because for some reason guys really get into the idea of knowing what you look like when you don't have a visual of them, and he's pulling the whole horse-and-buckskin Indian thing which I've got to admit does kind of turn me on. At the same time I figure Big Running Deer is probably not very fast in the old moccasins but just your usual jewelry tweep, half dweeb, half twerp, probably employs a great-looking nephew with an Appaloosa bod to run the shop and dial the women customers.

So I go along with the flirt flow and he's saying do you ever make it out to the Coast and I say nope, used to live out there but I moved away a few years ago, lucky I didn't say I was in the movie business or he'd have figured it all out eventually. At least around here no one knows they have Clitemnestra, the nineteen-year-old star of *Puss in Boots, Gypsy with a Prong, Uncaped Crusaders, Babalicious,* and *My Groin's Accustomed to Your Face* living in their midst twenty years later. No diseases, either.

I smile and smile at some radically overweight Leicester white-bread selling overpriced kitsch mugs and porcelain figurines to people she goes to church with, everyone acts like she's some fine upstanding member of the community because they never realize how they're all getting ripped off. But she'd be the first to condemn me (if she only had a clue) for spending a few years getting laid for a living just because I used to like making it on camera. Happened to me in Oregon, in Florida, in Montana. Some people never evolve.

So anyway it's turning out a totally realized afternoon for me. I package this primo stuff for Ca., three months' work, ship it out registered insured priority from that tiny post office down in Teal Bay. Back here for my run, got the gray sweats on to hide the merchandise even though it's eighty-two thanks to global warming. Then I head smack into some kid who wants to hand me a circular. About some emergency bridge meeting. I mean, as if anyone's serious about putting up the Golden Gate here, but a hundred yards long? And this kid, he's probably about eleven, he's looking at me with dinner-plate eyes like I'm, I don't know, a Hi-Ho or an Eskimo Pie or something. One day maybe he'll rent *Hullabaloo in the Igloo* and get a shock. And he says, can you believe it, "I like to watch you run, lady."

It's just ridiculous how young they start trying to dial you. And how many different lives you almost get to lead.

13

Toby Auberon

SPRING, AND THE HUM of the weed whacker is heard through the land. A visit this May morning from that woman, Jessica something, who left me the unreadable note. Handwritten junk mail is so rare these days. Seems intelligent but rather lonely, but then everyone seems lonely the more you talk to them.

And this evening the dreaded meeting took place. My hope was that my cynicism would prove unfounded, the crisis would resolve itself and the planets gently resume their orbits. As usual, my worst fears turned out correct and my most optimistic hopes mere breakfast cereal. We are in real trouble here.

The state brutes didn't even bother to show up: an old tactic. Our rep on the city council made a brittle speech (everyone made speeches) about how we shouldn't give up using the proper channels, she'd see the mayor personally the next day. A lot of syllables, sound with no genuine fury, signifying nothing. She doesn't live here and is only one more elected official who wants to be elected again to work with her fellow councilors, all "honorable men." We villagers just aren't worth getting angry about. An enormous drawback that Salt Cove has to share its rep on the Leicester council with two other villages.

The lawyer, Bob Herbert, has gotten nowhere. As I predicted, our appeal was turned down without being read. The bridge demolition is to start June 9, the Monday barely two weeks hence. These people have no sense of the hierarchies, that they have to go after some other authority. The lawyer seems honest, well-meaning, a few years older than I; just the right man to execute a will. But not a skilled hand-to-hand fighter. He tried to explain his pessimism—boy, do I concur—about a writ of Cert. to the state Supreme Court. Everyone argued, since an uninformed opinion means as much as an informed one. This is democracy, more than half the people wrong more than half the time.

There is a deep feeling in this country that if you speak up loud and clear, something will happen; if you express your feelings, something will happen; if you exercise your right to free chitchat, something will happen; if you let the world know you exist, something will happen. In fact nothing will happen, except you eventually grow weary of being reminded how ineffectual you are. A corollary to the schoolboy lesson you're fed—how what makes this country great is being able to say whatever you like—is that in a place where everyone can say everything, it's hard to make anything you say matter. All our elected officials know full well that after a while, people get tired of throwing a ball over the wall and not ever having it come back.

This is partly why years ago, after getting reamed in court trying to defend a boatload of illegal Vietnamese who'd duped me into presenting false evidence, then being jacked up on charges by the same prosecutor's office I used to work for, I quit my chosen profession and decided henceforth to let the world come to me. It has yet to do so, but on the other hand I haven't issued an invitation. And if all the creation I can muster results in not a peep out of a distracted globe, so be it. If it results in a cavalcade of sultry brunettes in fishnet stockings who can discuss the Popol Vuh after making love, I won't complain.

Sat at tonight's meeting feeling of many minds. I know, if I were the village's lawyer, what I'd do next, but I can't imagine their lawyer ever trying it. Should I? I know from bitter experience that this is usually a waste of time, it's precisely why I left the law, and I'm a year behind already on the Machina. Not to mention the next project, a book on "the little brother of war," the Maya and Aztec ball game, still languishing as field notes. To get caught up in the bridge dispute could be one of the hugest mistakes of my life—a vast statement—which for the past eight years has been a concentrated, virtually successful effort not to get involved. In another year the Machina Excelsior will be done and I can move on if I'm forced out.

Man changes not at all, learns nothing, myself included; what begins as politics ends as mysticism. I felt, sitting at the back of that village meeting, apparently the token hippie, in reality a lion in a den of Daniels, that I was simultaneously present at a gaggle of bickering eighteenth-century nincompoops in the original colonies and, equally annoying, two millennia earlier in ancient Rome. I told myself to keep my mouth shut, walk away, get back to work on my design for the left drop target. But instead—like a resurrected Lazarus ball on a vintage Gottlieb machine—I stuck around.

When people are in a crowd with a cognate, if vague, purpose, it is significant how few can assert their individuality, while most are pulled by dumb gravity toward an expression of the mass in each of them, ready to agree to opinions or actions that, one on one, they'd never go along with.

First, a gent I've seen walking a black Labrador stood and announced in a blustery voice, "The fact of the matter is, this is the state's way of letting us know their opinion of us. They think we're people they can just push around." My fellow villagers all yelled *Hear hear, Joe.* "All politics are local," the gent went on in a retired school principal croak and everyone yelled for that, too.

After cries for Susan Thayer, our conciliatory rep on the Leicester city council, to proclaim this, proclaim that, we went back to buggering Leicester. Italo gave a stirring speech about all not being lost, thanks to our petition sent down to Boston last week with 328 signatures including a few summer residents, plus another 36 supporters in nearby villages.

People cheered the petition, swelling with pride that something effective had at last been done. "Two weeks and a day from now," Italo concluded irresponsibly, "our bridge will still be there." Right, buster, I thought; going, going, gone. "Our next step is to start a fund drive for the money to repair it. So no one can accuse us of freeloading, or doing nothing." After six weeks of pointless blather, now that the clock's run down they feel mainly offended.

I've met you all before, I wanted to say, *out in California twelve years ago, you're mostly older than I am, how come you're still so profoundly naïve? Haven't you ever paid attention, not once? Didn't you wake up every now and then as the predators rolled right over you? Or was it just comforting to know that at least you weren't dead yet?*

At this point I lost it. I'd been simmering for over an hour; probably I should've just slipped quietly out the door, bayed twice at the moon, and gone home. Beside me the enormous Roscoe had been efficiently cursing each successive speaker under his breath with a bizarre catalogue of bestial practices. He may be a type of genius, as not everyone can keep this up for an hour. He didn't help my sense of futility. A season from now I'd be cursing myself as a layabout who merely sat there, nursing grievances long past while tragedy slammed away with a full agenda. How would I feel in July when the bridge was gone, dismantled like rotten toothpicks, and the steel girders were arriving on flatbed trucks?

With extreme reluctance I realized I had no choice. No one else was going to say what was needed to impel right action. As I stood up to speak, in the lull of lemmings congratulating themselves that all would probably be just fine while they plummeted off a precipice, I caught the gaze of Jessica, seated on the stage scribbling down every syllable of the melee, poor thing, and I could swear she breathed a sigh at the sight of me with my hand raised. I even thought—and my eyes may be worn out from working too many nights—that she winked at me.

"Speak up, you damn hippie, half them bastards are stone deaf," hissed Roscoe. At the podium Italo announced, "Toby wants to say something," and looked a tad relieved.

I waited until people turned in their seats, then got straight to the point while a little voice said, *Congratulations, nitwit, what does it take to convince you?* Well, if I didn't convince them, my defendant was going straight to the electric chair, without any last-minute reprieve from the governor.

"Ladies and gentlemen," I said, "I'm confused. Two months have gone by. Nothing has changed in the state's position, or in their schedule. We've tried unsuccessfully to wield the power of public opinion, the force of legal argument, and the threat of our combined voting weight. Despite what we'd like to believe, we've gotten nowhere. We fought them, and we lost."

At this point people started grumbling and growling, but when I put my hand up for silence I got it. "I'd love to believe our petition is going to make a big difference. But if the state doesn't even consider it worth sending someone to attend this meeting, clearly they see any request from us as just the buzzing of flies they can swat any time they like. You see, they want us to write them begging letters. They want us to spend the next two weeks offering them proposals, and sending them e-mails, and making phone calls, and complaining to our mayor—and not realizing that, without a court order in our favor, none of that adds up to more than a few more dead flies in the window. And on the ninth of June, we'll watch our bridge get torn apart. Roscoe's explained to me just how quickly they can do it. Then we're lost."

He hadn't, but I heard him grunt with approval behind me. I had them now: the bearer of bad news always gets listened to. Just ask any priest.

"It doesn't have to be that way. There comes a time in the affairs of a people when they're forced to decide what really counts. Does this bridge matter enough that we're going to form a human shield to protect it? And not allow the engineers to break through our lines and destroy it? That's one option. If we want publicity, we'll get it that way. How far are we willing to go? Up till now all we've done is generate a bit of paperwork. Suppose we park a few cars at both approaches to the bridge, how easy would it be for them to get their equipment in? It might be impossible, unless they attack from the river.

"Now it's hard to imagine a naval battle for the cove. Still, we have to be prepared for the state trying to get around any steps we take. People might get arrested, or have their cars impounded, for blocking state workmen. It'll be an unbelievable nuisance. But we have to be ready to physically stop them from wrecking the bridge if we want them to go away and stay away. Otherwise, no matter how much mail we send them, they'll do whatever they want.

"Meanwhile, we've got to persuade them that the nuclear fallout, the horrible publicity, will be so absolutely devastating that they back down. This is going to take time. Only a federal judge will give us that stay of execution. They've got life tenure to protect them from the rabble howling for their impeachment. State judges are just politicians in black robes. But with a federal district court on our side, I'm confident" (though I wasn't at all) "we can make the state see eye to eye with us on money for repairs. Or maybe we end up compromising on a new wooden bridge. But for now, we've got to protect this one for dear life. Or we'll have a monstrosity that belongs in New York City insulting us every day."

As soon as I shut up everyone started talking at once. Mostly worried about getting thrown in jail or losing their Toyota or standing out there all night long. And what if it started raining. When people talk about the weather they usually mean something else. Behind me Roscoe said with a snort, "Look what you started. The hippie wants a sit-in."

"Believe me," I told him, "what I want is a stand-in."

Italo was yelling for order. I realized I no longer felt shaken up but relaxed, even giddy—final remnants of the lawyer in me, I suppose. *Why is this man laughing?* People quieted down, and Italo said from the stage, "Toby, I'd like to believe our petition means more than that. But I'm afraid you may end up being right."

"Of course he's right," said Roscoe in a scornful rumble that could bend steel plate. "If I'm standing there, you think anyone's coming through? Let me tell you, nothing's getting through."

And it won't be your end of the line they trample, I muttered to myself, not when there are old ladies to run roughshod over. But his remark elicited roars of approval. Roscoe was looked on as the village's massive destructive force, whom people called when they needed trees uprooted or a slab of granite blown up, a septic tank pumped or a ditch excavated. He hauled problems off one's property or simply dynamited them. I saw now that he had an enormous attractive force as well. He was seen as indomitable, unafraid of trifles like a backed-up waste system. With the new government sewers in place, he'd lost a lot of business; he had plenty of personal reasons to resent the state's intrusion, and want to pop open a tall, frosted bottle of revenge. If he were behind a strategy, it would succeed.

A fellow up front—cannon fodder in two weeks—yelled, "Isn't there any alternative to being arrested or losing our cars?" and got drowned out.

I said sharply, very loudly, "Sure there is," and people stopped chattering to listen. I now see this was a bad sign.

"One way is to let the state know our intentions. That we'll have the news media in place, and there's no chance they'll come out looking good. This is also the moment to each contribute twenty bucks to the Leicester Policemen's Fund. It'll end up money well spent.

"Look, the state thinks it knows exactly how far we'll go. They're not afraid. I don't see why a new bridge means so much to them, but it does. So we have to convince them we'll go a lot further than they will. We have to make them fear us."

"Why should they?" someone piped up amid the murmur of assent.

"Because our hearts are pure," I said, and no one snickered. "At least when it comes to this. Because everyone likes an underdog. Because no one much likes them. And because we're going to persuade them that if we have to end up fighting a pitched battle on the bridge, or blowing their boats out of the cove, we're just crazy enough to do it, we'll go right ahead while smiling at the news cameras. They may not get the message at first. We may have to explain it to them several times. But they'll end up being afraid of us, I promise you."

It all sounded very convincing, though I wasn't sure how much I'd believe in the morning.

This was the moment when, had the universe followed my plan, I'd have sat back down and listened approvingly while everyone else spun versions of my theme and I could comfortably recede into my bench beside an obscenity-spouting Roscoe. Instead—without asking me whether I minded, or might even be traveling abroad sometime soon and hence unavailable—he stood up and very loudly berated the efforts of the Village Hall Association until now, methodically derided the city, state, and federal governments in ascending order of size, dishonesty, and gross malfeasance, then finished by suggesting that what was called for was a Special War Room and a commander in chief, that neither Italo nor Bob Herbert could be expected to do everything, and thus we needed someone who for the next few weeks could devote himself ("Or herself," I muttered to no avail, seeing just where he was headed) to staving off the enemy. The human need for an enemy must be hard-wired into the cells; I'd have argued that the enemy here might not be the bullying state itself but rather the destruction that a stumbling, cretinous bureaucracy could do unless you caught a stick in the spokes in time. But if the village needed an enemy, they needed a hero too, and before I could slink away Roscoe had nominated me, the motion was enthusiastically seconded and voted on, the ayes had it, the nays had all the backbone of a dishrag, and I was anointed to lead them into battle.

Several ideas struck me on the way home, after the handshakes, the claps on the back, and the understanding that we'd meet, a dozen volunteer ringleaders, on Wednesday at Jessica's house. As always I walked back across the Meadow. It was a starlit night of uncommon serenity, with many stillnesses and many brilliances happening at once, not only the stars in a dense violet sky but also a shimmering moonlight that made the water into a sheet of corrugated aluminum. When I came down the broad tumble of hillside after the massive hump of Baven Rock—like a ball descending a well-designed play-field—the expanse of the Meadow resembled a long swell of undulating land, a rhythmic wave surging in darkness, cresting and crescendoing where the illuminated beach met the illuminated Atlantic.

I gave a cry at the sight, for there at the end of it all, perched on its own bumper of rock, was my white lighthouse, my home, lit up as if suffused from within by electric moonlight, its voltage pouring forth on top with the beacon flashing out to ships at sea, its foghorn ready to bellow out a voice of safety that anyone could understand. I felt, more acutely than ever: That's mine—knowing it didn't matter that I rented it. Nor was it only mine, for I belonged equally to it; and if the job of my adopted house was to act as ships' protector, maybe its sense of duty (for all lighthouses are alive) had reawakened in me.

So be it, then.

I have several options, but a sudden flight to parts unknown, like the last few times, is not one of them, much as I'd like to refuse the voice of the people. However, I am not at a point in the Machina Excelsior where I can lay aside my work for a month. The next few weeks, until this threat dissipates, will merely mean less sleep.

Apart from the little I told Jessica, which made me sound like a law school dropout, I don't think anybody here knows my background. Though Bob Herbert must suspect. He and I need to have a private talk.

It occurred to me while crossing the Meadow that if the populace of this village knew I spend probably every other waking hour designing, devising, and constructing the greatest pinball machine ever created, they might not be so willing to put their trust in my hands—although they have unwittingly made the right decision, for all the wrong reasons. Still, without Roscoe to brute them around, undoubtedly most are having second thoughts.

Important not to give away more personal details than necessary. If they line up two weeks from now and dare the flatbed trucks to run them over to get at the bridge, if it's a rumpled hippie (as they see me) who can convince them just as easily as the ghost of Justice Holmes, it's all the same. As soon as the bridge goes on the endangered species list, I'm back to the Machina full-time, and—just as I vowed a decade ago, but henceforth I'll keep my vow—I stick my neck out for nobody.

Less sleep, then. The Excelsior must remain relentless. As I have proven in my journals, anyone living in a lighthouse is up against the notion of foot-hours of sleep. An equation can be arrived at of

$$\frac{a}{b} \; x \; c \; = \; d$$

where **b** represents the height of the person expressed in inches, **a** the number of inches of bed space that person sleeps in measured from a bed's diagonal corners, **c** the number of hours when rest occurs, to arrive at **d** as a calculation of total foot-hours of sleep. Thus if I'm to get less shut-eye, I'd be better off in a bigger bed. This is true; I can't explain why, but it is, just as moonlight on the ocean is always beautiful. The argument is not susceptible to proof.

Even better for this nonexistent bed would be my naked dark-haired friend, resplendent in boots, followed by her tawny blonde comrade in arms. Old friends are best, I find, even if you haven't seen them for years. In memory they are as resolutely wicked as ever, and since all experience ultimately exists only in my imagination, for me they pout on, temptresses offering themselves as solace one at a time through my every dawn falling-to-sleep when the ocean salt is still on my skin and I find myself questioning whether I'm mad to devote all my energy, savings, and limited patrimony to this life. Or else visiting me—I am still young enough to dream—in intramural twos and threes, lolling and rolling around with the utmost camaraderie, enthusiasm, and catholic purpose.

Sometimes I wonder, too, if they are secretly thinking of me at exactly the same time, hundreds or even thousands of miles away, and so many years after we last made love. Perhaps this is why they come into my mind, because I am coming simultaneously into theirs, amid lives doubtless filled with husbands and children. Appeased in their destinies, I hope; they were all women who deserved good fortune. I bless them from a distance and wonder if they remember the wilder days of their youth as fondly as I, if all love's grudges have been banished, if waking up some mornings they do not slyly remind themselves of that insolent afternoon in a sudsy bathtub, that searing twilight by the hedge of an upstanding park, that hurtling morning on a rattletrap foreign train. I lie back, my remembered loves, and the greedy years do not dim your ardor one gasp, the body's blessing. It must be that some telepathic equivalent of e-mail, even more immediate, has always existed via our minds and our minds alone: m-mail. How could we prove it, except to contact each other and ask if we were stroking the same lubricious thoughts at precisely 7:18 A.M. last Friday? Because, old friends, I know you can feel me thinking about you, and I believe I can feel you thinking about me. There goes that blasting foghorn again.

The Machina Excelsior will render all this lascivious joy moot, mere personal history that fades against the public luster of a limitless triumph. (I am not speaking commercially; I have ceased caring. The ladder I hope to climb is among my treasured fellow craftsmen, those doddering, dying wizards and hobbyists in their eighties, plying their bagatelles in the basement and recalling the long vanished golden era of that game of the gods, pinball.) I need not list the deficiencies of the life around us, that seems always so full of disappointing objects which exist in perpetual shadow, and whose secret being is hardly ever realized. No matter what we do, they never awaken into the allegorical life which we all agree is the richer life we seek. Our objects follow us like whipped dogs through our daily routine, but where is the special object, the talisman that works the opposite way, that pulls us reliably into the other life which is truly the life we crave?

Ladies and gentlemen, I give you: the Excelsior. A machine that allows you, the player, to navigate a silver ball through the gates of doom, the lamps of perception *(Special when lit)*, the traps that lie in wait, the bumpers that keep you alive and dancing, the flippers that fling you back at the moment of utmost peril, always with gobble holes and deadly bleeds, slingshot kickers and thumper bumpers and (my favorite) tall posts illuminating the sea of constant treachery. This has nothing to do with those computerized game-constructs that burp back at you like television cartoons; mine is more elaborate, more humane. A person, a silver ball (or the option of several at once) pitted against my devious two-level board, with a world above and an occasionally revealed world below, where a danger instantaneously becomes an ally and vice versa, just like life itself. You are never the plaything of my game. You can lose, and try again, and the Machina will remember where your skills lay, and alter its strategy. Life gets harder, you make it up as you go along, you make your own skill, you make your own luck. It is my cosmos you glide through, or are defeated by, but in the lower level of my afterworld there is always the benediction of another ball, another try, another life. I personally do not believe in reincarnation, but my game does. The lighthouse I live in is nothing less than a giant bumper post, part of the game that exists outside the game.

In other pinball tables over the years, the fortunate player has plied his wits amid the imagery of circus performers, harem princesses, stock-car races, sailors on a spree, soldiers on furlough, casinos, barnyard animals, rocket ships, battlefields, short-order chefs, south of the border or west of the Pecos, on express trains or with jungle elephants and tigers, with Hef and the Playmates or King Arthur and his knights, in a Paris music hall or a Venetian gondola, an ice revue, a bullfight, on the rings of Saturn, a paddle wheeler, an around-the-world flight replete with smiling stewardesses—sorry, flight attendants—all the harmless fantasies that decorated the backglass and got him playing again after *Special when lit* was replaced by *Game over*. No game has ever had a profound design to match the allegory suggested by the infinite vagaries of a silver ball and the fate of one's play. Until now.

Play the Excelsior. Remind yourself how it feels to be alive. Watch the progress of your singular, rolling soul as it descends through ever shifting labyrinths of the cosmos, through paradise and purgatory and hell, yet refuses to die, but is ever resurrected and sprung again, shot sprocketing back into play. *Why is this man laughing?* Because my game is never over.

14

Sarah Joad

JUST WHAT I NEED, a dimwit old aunt on the warpath. One day Jessica's making cupcakes for the library tea and the next she's General MacArthur. Like I'm supposed to sit here and listen to her give speeches about establishing a beachhead and how she'll fight them on the seas, she'll fight them in the air. She'll fight the hospital nurses is what I predict.

All I am asking for if it's not too much trouble, excuse me for even breathing, is a chance to take it easy for a little while. Call it an extended coffee break. They don't warn you a degree in communications means nothing, since every moron thinks he knows how to communicate. They knew but wouldn't let on they knew that everything they taught us would be obsolete in a few years. That the old rules, which we paid decent money to learn, would no longer apply. Some geek physicist working for the army invents cyberspace, nothing better to do so he asks himself where all the lost things end up, then comes along with a way to send them there deliberately and find them again. What a jerk. And before you know it, while I'm in Rochester freezing my buns off, trying to keep the checks from Aunt Nun coming in with a B- average, before you know it there's this big tree growing in the cybergarden, everyone instantaneously communicating with everyone else like they've all got something to say.

So it's every cyberbranch in bloom, branching off to other branches and multiplying round the clock. Even though it's mostly a bunch of propeller-heads arguing about which episode of Gilligan was better. And I'm still standing there with a doofus look on my face trying to decide which skirt to wear for the interview, how to project myself personably, the ten rules of clear speaking, the six maxims of selling an idea over the telephone, the fourteen inexorable laws of good advertising, the eight bullet points of effective consulting strategy, meanwhile that damned tree keeps branching and blossoming day and night. No way I'm going to catch up.

What I really need is for her to take a hike and let me get on with it. Another stroke, another few IQ points down the drain, and we can escort her over to Seaside Solutions. Let her discuss Helen of Troy with the orderlies while I discuss renovation with the architects.

I'm a grownup, I can admit we're both victims here, that's exactly what already slammed into me—the new rolling over the old like a bulldozer. Do not pass Go, do not collect what's rightfully yours. The sad part is I got taught ancient, useless ideas. By who? By the same conspiracy that just stacks up to more people protecting their own skins. So I was history in my chosen fields before I even realized my chance was gone. It happened to me, it will happen to you, Miss Stoddard. One minute you're a healthy dinosaur, the next you're asteroid gravy.

Now the television industry still strikes me as having plenty of options. Not that anyone with clout wants to hear your ideas, even after eight years in the cable industry at a local level. The trouble is even now it gets too general, they're always trying to reach everyone in America. I say: Why not just get incredibly specific? Instead of a channel showing all sports all the time, why not one showing only beach volleyball? Surf hunks and bikini babes, follow the bouncing ball all the way to the bank. Or why not a channel for, I don't know, baseball card collectors? The country's big enough.

Well, talk is cheap, listening is expensive, as *mi amigo* Raymond says. The message is time's up, auntie. You aren't satisfied with any of the younger generations? As personified by yours truly? Congratulations: you're the one who blew your chance to contribute, you're the one who made it harder than it ever had to be. You're the one who sat there for years staring out at your view and telling yourself all's right with the world and it's nothing to do with you. So what if your niece's parents suddenly get butchered by a faulty left front tire and it's up to you to take over administering the tuition?

Here's the evening news: everything that happened to the world is your fault, and no one else's. It sure wasn't mine. You had sixty years of peace in this country and you squandered it perfecting cruise control, you spent it maintaining those tired old-boy politicians in their velvet slippers and monogrammed bathrobes sucking on imported cigars next to their leathery wives, so much smoke rolling out of their mouths and ears you can't even see their beady little eyes. These are the people you've got deciding the future in this country, and when some top-secret army physicist invents a whole other dimension and someone else finds a way to charge twenty bucks a month to rent you a key and a locker there, those guys are still in their slippers by the fire, they aren't crazy, they just throw another log on since they own the forest anyway. Try explaining this to the Virgin Queen, see how far you get.

What we have here is a failure to excommunicate. Family problems? Everyone has family problems. The only thing called for is what Raymond calls "progressive action." And what might my dear departed parents think? Let me wipe away the tears; by now I have to assume they like the view from heaven. Make Seaside Solutions your loved one's next-to-final solution. No one lives forever, and no one lives at home forever, especially not the old and the gaga. They'll all be chatting away together on high soon enough.

15

Italo Simpkins

Dear Jessica,

I took a few notes at your house last night and thought they might help in writing up the minutes. Don't let me clutter up your gears, however. I maintain total faith in your ability to swoop like a falcon on what matters amid the hurly-burly of loose talk. I must say, your lighthouse crony has a most logical mind. (Myra was wondering, by the way, if he has a lady friend?) Toby's argument, after brainstorming with Bob Herbert, seems the following:

Having now been denied our latest writ by what calls itself with no irony the Supreme Judicial Court of Massachusetts, we do still have a few hewable lines of legal defense to present before a federal district court. The strongest being to claim federal interest by citing the Clean Water Act—i.e., the many adverse effects of a new bridge on the natural environment. Not just polluting waterways and marine life, but also the scenic vista of Salt Cove harbor.

As for trying once more to get the bridge designated a historic landmark, Toby drafted a "pleading" letter for Bob to overnight to the Dept. of Interior, citing a bridge in Oregon. Toby did seem rather miffed that no one approached the feds on ecological grounds sooner.

The longer this gets delayed, the more the court of public opinion will sway to our side. For now we have only this weekend and next week to win a stay of execution. On the following Monday, the wrecking ball hits our bridge. Or maybe those explosives they're constantly seizing from terrorists at airport security, who knows.

Their most aggressive argument, besides the hypothesis that the bridge could fall down, is that emergency access to the village is limited by the very nature of a foot bridge. As Toby emphasized, the state can always exercise "police power" if they decide there's a serious threat to health or safety. This depends, I pointed out, on how serious one's definition of *serious* is.

We've got on for years with ambulances and fire engines entering the village the long way round. It's easy enough for the state to concoct scenarios where those few extra minutes make a life-or-death difference. (I'd like to persuade a judge that eating nonorganic produce is statistically more dangerous for the same household than a few extra ambulance minutes.) But in the context of Cape Sarah, where loads of people live in the woods down inaccessible paths, or off coastal cul-de-sacs where the fire brigade would be virtually passing the slopping buckets of water hand to hand, to carp about a few minutes of delay seems ludicrous.

On a personal note, what lifted my spirits was Toby's sturdy belief that our best chance is a sense of public outrage, which can be nurtured. If photos appear in the paper showing villagers, especially older ones, barring the state wrecking crew from the bridge, the images will get picked up by newspapers and TV around the country, sent all over the Internet, and it'll become very touchy for the state to actually do anything. As he says, we shouldn't wait for Doomsday Monday to enact such dramatic scenes. We can erect our photo-op barricades right away.

A similarly concrete threat *(Vive le pun, Jessica!)* is that the new bridge ushers in an equally insidious upscale development. Houses split up into six-way condos, like the abandoned boat shop by Roscoe's headquarters last year. It even sounds remotely possible for a developer to turn, say, a rambling house like yours back into a seaside hotel, as I recall your niece Sarah mentioning it was a century ago. But I agree with Toby, this undercurrent of general threat only aids our cause, and gathers a huge swell of emotion in villagers.

When I teach physics I am careful to explain Newton's third law of motion, commonly rendered as every action resulting in an equal and opposite reaction. Frankly, I've never found this true in human affairs. People have a frightening capacity to absorb waves of attack, to take thud after thud from life and not react at all. You can argue that a reaction occurs at unseen levels; that these people die younger, get cancer, erupt in hives, or break down emotionally from within. But I've come to believe that what distinguishes humanity from the rest of the apparent universe is how much that fundamental, classical law does *not* apply. Unlike leopards, marmosets, trees, sine waves, unmapped galaxies, and the lint on my coat, people just do not react.

When I was younger I saw the world as things linked by lines of force. I have come to see it instead as myriad crisscrossing lines of force which very, very occasionally manifest themselves as things. This is the only explanation I can muster for why people react so seldom to anything. I don't mean this as an unkind judgment. If force is simply passing through them, if they are just an efficient conduit of it, if we are all mere bumps on the pathways of force, there is no reason for us ever to react with anything more than a shiver or shudder as the jolt of force passes through us and onward.

However, I do think that people should aspire to the condition of an ordinary subatomic particle. We *should* react, not live in perpetual hibernation.

Thus what the state perceives as a gentle nudge regarding

our bridge is for us like being brutally hit by a train, and we need to hit them back just as forcefully. It is crucial that we morph ourselves, in their terms, from a sleepy village into a fierce locomotive hurtling right at their ugly kissers.

I think of myself as a man of peace. But when the very character of a place beloved to me is under siege, I become a man of war, and fight back.

I anticipate, as always, your gracefully phrased and carefully typed version of Wednesday's meeting. I like the team we've assembled and I thought it very considerate of you to make those gingerbread cookies. (I wonder if you saw your friend Toby sneaking a fat napkinful into his pocket. Evidently a man of foresight. I also wasn't surprised to learn he managed to graduate from one of the smaller California law schools before having radical second thoughts.)

I look forward to our next conclave Monday night, and what results there may be of Toby going to visit the Army Corps of Engineers.

I regret that, as president of the Salt Cove Village Hall Association, I have not been effective up until now. I'm afraid it boils down to my being a man of science. Better at observing, measuring, researching, experimenting, and theorizing than at actually making something happen in the cosmos—which already behave, as Haldane puts it, not only more queerly than we suppose but than we ever *can* suppose. . . .

And perhaps the result of all this, as Toby suggested in passing, may be a broadsheet signed by every man jack of us, openly defying the government. Perhaps we must become traitors to our country's bullying laws to remain loyal to our village.

I will leave you (it is already late and I have enough coffee in me to float a frigate) with a motto I kept propped on my desk all through grad school to keep me going, the famous cable that Field Marshal Foch sent to his French superiors in the First World War:

My center is giving way,
My right is in retreat.
Situation is excellent.
I am attacking.

16

Henry Wilkes Jr.

PUBLIC NOTICE!

I am looking for thirteen men,
all brave and true, with special abilities,
who are ready, able, and willing
to lay down their lives to battle the dreaded
Zazinas from the planet Nocturon
in the hidden folds of tesser-space,
thus saving our entire solar system,
including the beloved planet we call Terra,
from the upcoming invasion
and who are not afraid to embark
on a six-year mission, no matter what the odds.
I, your fearless captain, have reserved for myself
the shapely company of our first lieutenant,
the superb Molly Mellew, who owes me her life
for rescuing her from the evil tentacles of Dr. Analyd

in a previous adventure, as well as from
the mishap with the faulty airlock on Luna XVI.
I may be contacted at my temporary local address
where I am currently repairing both shield guns
of the cruiser *Stellar Maiden* every afternoon.
Messages may also be left with my wisecracking robot,
Carnahan, or with my mom.

17

Roscoe Hughes

ALL RIGHT. HERE'S what you asked for. Don't say I didn't warn you.

If you want to block a road you block it with a truck, sideways. Why?

It stays blocked.

Harder to get around.

Harder to tow away.

You also chain up the wheels and padlock the chains. Why?

Harder to remove.

Harder to cut through.

Harder to tow away.

Heavier the better. So maybe the truck I got in back of Zeke's, over Tristram Point. If I can get it here. Inch it in sideways at the Monroe St. side of the bridge, down the incline. No one getting it out of there we do it right, they'll need a frigging crane when I walk off with the keys. Public property, so fuck them. Once I let the air out of the tires they might as well take out a mortgage on the sucker, cause it's not going anywhere.

That leaves the Drawbridge St. side. Maybe Billy's truck except I can't afford to tie it up here. Like I'm the only bastard in the village owns an extra truck. Not like I don't need every single piece of equipment. I got a living to make. You want to rent the use of my truck for a day it's usually $75 p/h and that's including Billy. Plus this roadblock would be 24 hours a day. So every day I leave it there to block those sons of bitches it's $1800 out of my pocket. Not that I give a flying rat's ass.

Don't ask me to block with one of the earthmovers, they're too easy to climb across. Anyway, there's nothing to stop them from just blowing out the bridge pilings. That's sure what I'd do.

Why use explosives?

Better for demolition.

Easily portable.

No back talk.

But since this is the government maybe they don't allow it. Probably they got some plan to pay some shitheads to pull down the bridge plank by plank so it costs more and keeps them working overtime then charge the taxpayers double. Probably they got some puffy-ass engineer consultants sitting around in deck chairs arguing about which plank to pull off next. Then they got ten forms to fill in for every square foot of planking. Meanwhile it's us paying, then we're the ones get screwed. Like some dumb joke. Except.

No one's laughing.

I'm sure the fuck not laughing.

Maybe after I get the truck in place that I got up at Zeke's, if I got five minutes to kill I'll put Krazy Glue inside the emergency brake, they'll never get that son of a bitch to release. Then I'll slather a tube of the stuff right on the handle so that government goombah grabs it, he splats himself with miracle formula, now he's glued to the damn emergency brake which is glued right in lock, then they're going to be trying to lift that truck out by crane with the guy wriggling his little legs and hoping they don't drop him, just like that commercial they used to show with the blonde chick getting lifted in the hard hat. He won't be smiling then, boy, not the way she was. Shit, I'd still settle for her any day, glue and all.

I think the hippie's got the right idea. It's a lousy government, end of story. The last president we had with any balls was Nixon and he was totally out of his mind, which just shows how impossible it is to elect the right combination of a brave liar with plenty of decency and common sense, who doesn't act paranoid even when he knows those other sons of bitches are all out to get him.

Like the hippie keeps saying, before this is over we'll have to go a lot farther. Maybe all the way. Like not only do we keep the bridge but we also get the contract to repair it. Plus we get the state to pay us a monthly rate to maintain it. Plus they lower all our property taxes for five years, better make it ten years with five years backdated and a refund check with interest, who cares, make it a ten-year grace period just for putting us to all this fucking trouble. Why?

It would make me happy.

It would at least put me in a better mood.

18

Jessica Stoddard

OVER LO THESE many months, I have often asked myself what I am doing, and why. For the truth is, truth is a handmade thing, not a sequence of blips on a screen whose wink I turn off at night, entrusting them to the safekeeping of a memory I cannot see any more than I can see and trust my own. Sometimes I find myself writing the wrong word, but time sorts out the small errors of a life. Our revolt was itself likewise a handmade thing, an early-twentieth-century revolution erupting a century late; it resembled combat incarnadine at close quarters in sultry Burmese jungles more than some political uprising in a dank Balkan square. It deserves to be remembered, I tell myself this every morning while chomping my Froot Loops, with words that have their solid existence on actual paper, and whose inky darkness justifies the errors in my poor handwriting. It may even deserve to be translated one day. (Personally, I have always wanted to be made love to through a veil.)

I will tell you what this book is. It is a history! Of whom? what? when? where? Don't bury yourself in such questions: it is an honest book, which may possibly recommend it to the world, of what passes in a woman's own mind.

It is his story too, of course. And when on my deathbed people ask me—I envision a pack of crocodiles struggling to hold back their tears—what was the most notable thing I ever did, I'll say, *Well, I knew Toby Auberon. In every sense. Now go get your own lives.*

He built his perfect machine as I am trying to build mine, but he made his to encompass the world, whereas all I hope to encompass in these pages is what I remember, what slips away incrementally every day no matter how hard I fight forgetfulness. The blue light in his eyes, the level gaze of the only one who ever saw who I really am. No wonder I keep dropping my pen this morning, no wonder I keep losing track. I must try to do better. More oxygen for the brain, this is the master plan.

Which brings me to arguably the most important meeting of all, on the first Monday in June, my house. As usual the social mountaineering was no surprise; while I bustled about fetching coffee I could observe the shifts in power. At first Roscoe was the epicenter. Installed in my biggest armchair, chortling away at his unlit pipe, he seemed an inflated version of his deft dead father (whom I once went swimming with at a Beauport quarry, a picnic in another century). Waiting in his massive way, serene in the knowledge that sooner or later everyone's septic tank backs up and they have to call him. One thing I've always liked about Roscoe is that he never needs to prove himself the largest man in the room, he's content to say nothing until absolutely necessary. If more men were like this we would have fewer wars and fewer divorces.

Yet as soon as we began to settle into War Room mode, the might shifted quite definitely toward Toby. I find in my notes that he'd brushed off the black sweater I'd seen hanging rather drably by the entry to his lighthouse. (Later I was to wash it for him.) His hair and mustache also looked well tended, even luxuriant. His jeans, with their mysterious splotches, bespoke not the casual drug smuggler among us, as so many first imagined, but the well-stropped razor intellect, ready to slice at our enemies' exposed hindquarters.

I realize this is not what is considered a responsible way to write history, and that every moment I let my opinions intrude banishes me even farther from the Thuycidean pantheon, the timeless registrars of their times. But I do not get asked very often what I think.

My lofty living room, with its embracing view, was in a way what we were all munching on cookies to protect. No, it is not full of inherited musty furniture, for I sold that off ages ago at ridiculous prices since, regrettably, my grandmother was so short she sawed two inches from the legs of her hitherto valuable antique Americana. I'd replaced them with woven armchairs and sofas from some tropical sweatshop in Asia, an airy feel in a long room which even in winter remains full of sunlight. Plus I'd framed several abstract paper collages on the walls, from a year when I spent hours cutting and gluing, mostly primary colors. It is surprising what you can accomplish if you do not care what other people say.

I had shut the large windows, as I'd kept a breeze in the room all day and even in June it can be cool at dusk. Along the opposite shore the lights were beginning to twinkle from the rocks; someday I must write about the allegorical significance of the Other Shore, of having it constantly before you as a reminder of all that is perpetually just out of reach. You could hear the sea sliding like a restless animal shifting relentlessly in sleep. People were in a festive mood, and not just because of my gingerbread cookies. The weekend had resolved certain uncertainties in our minds, we saw what was at stake, we knew we were the ringleaders. And we were sure—later we were not so sure—the entire village was behind us, though in the usual cards-to-the-chest, half-hearted, closemouthed, stingy, stiff-necked, gloomy New England way.

We few, we dyspeptic few. There were Toby Auberon, Roscoe Hughes, and Italo Simpkins. Mitch Wapping, who'd been first to arrive, with Anita in one of her yellow cardigans, and Billy Fagles, looking sheepish and carrying a six-pack, most of which he left in my refrigerator for the next meeting. There was a young couple, newcomers, Nancy and Jon Eckerman, with a baby son who slept contentedly in my guest bedroom the whole time; his mother looked ready to fall asleep herself. There was Italo's wife Myra, who can be very shy in a gathering because of her stammer, even among friends, and there were enough people here whom she'd never spent any time with to keep her incarcerated in silence. Leilia and Harold Milne trooped in, still in bold high gear despite the setbacks her oncologist had admitted to her on Friday. Or maybe because of them: I don't pretend to understand real courage.

On the unattached distaff side, heading cradlewards, there were myself, then faithful Mildred with her wispy hair in a crisp bun. Mildred had made copies of the bridge chapter from her meticulous Salt Cove history to supply "perspective," implicitly admitting that not everyone owned a copy.

The other solo woman there was Molly Mellew. That carpenter from Stilton who worked on her house swore to me she'd made pornographic movies under another name, years ago. I never reveal people's secrets without some pressing need, but since Molly no longer lives here I do not suppose it matters. I will try to do justice to her toehold on youth.

Though she wore a lumpen gray tracksuit, the eyes of most men in the room kept alighting on her. As the guest list suggests, for them it was feast or famine. She did look quite fit, and drank only bottled water she brought along. Her hair was about the honey hue mine was when I was younger, it looked as if you could spread it on buttered bread with a knife and gorge all day. At first Toby kept regarding her with puzzlement, but the more she spoke, the more I'm relieved to say he kept his attention on the matter at hand, and even cast a few sympathetic glances my way to see if I was getting it all down.

I do not want anything in the above paragraph to sound peevish. I am writing this in pen to prevent myself taking anything back, or doctoring up the historical account to my liking after setting down the events precisely as I and many others saw them. But I do feel I should explain a little.

I've noticed that whenever there's a room full of men they become, in their doggy manner, even more predictable than usual. They give way first to the most physically imposing and, after about twenty minutes, to the one they psychologically agree on as leader of the pack. This giving-way is a selfless impulse; it has created nations. They'll also pay most attention to the youngest woman in full sexual vigor, then proceed down the hierarchy to the oldest (usually me) with declining eagerness. This too is supposedly creative, a result of evolutionary efficiency, but there are plenty of healthy tribal societies where women escape that trap. Not ours, for it has been a while since I made anyone's mouth water.

When I was a young woman myself, naturally I took this attention for granted. I thought it was me they were raptly gazing at, not my youth. As a woman in her twenties and thirties I received my share of attention from men. I had my few adventures, my quick affairs and my slow affairs. I was usually looked at, occasionally even stared at. I thought it was my soul whose then scant depths they were hoping to plumb, or the individual attractions of my body, which, I see now, were sufficient. As a young woman you take it for granted that all men have eyes; as you get older you find them growing ever more blind around you until at last you reach a zone where no one really can see you anymore, your age has rendered them sightless. The more you perceive, the more invisible you become until, finally, you cast no shadow.

I have waited a long time for the beauty I finally have, the beauty of what little I uniquely saw for myself, the shred of glory I can sing as no one has sung, even if it seems only the idle whistling of a canary in a cage.

And as I've gotten older I've come to blame not the Molly Mellews of the world, who were plainly prettier than I was—I can hardly blame them for what simply did not come my way because, well, that's show biz, folks, the real show biz, and I was never a star. No, for what has been withheld I've come to blame the shadow government dominating men's minds, a nefarious conspiracy on the part of fashion magazines to present women as interesting not on the basis of their personalities but on whether their looks conform to what society agrees is attractive. This varies regionally, of course—I might've been a raging exotic beauty in Arkansas, or Rumania, or Ougadougadou—but by and large these magazines hand down dictatorial edicts, as they have all my life, which the rest of the media and society pick up on and mimic in their apelike way, and that make me, and other women like me, into third-class citizens, never the adornment of choice for a masculine arm. To pretend they cannot manipulate this when they can manipulate world hemlines and underwear designs is absurd.

It was not enough, never enough, to be the different one. To be fascinating I had to be lovely, and not being lovely I instead always seemed eccentric. Then you grow older, and really learn what it's like to be shut out; the only older women considered attractive, apart from the intolerable wives of male politicians (and never any female politicians, naturally) are the ones who were goddesses at thirty and are lucky enough to still resemble wise echoes, not harsh parodies, of their former selves.

I do not blame men for this, or the biology of natural selection. I do not blame the genes, I blame the magazines; if there were any justice they would be wiped off the face of the earth. On mornings like this I want a supermodel for breakfast, though I know it is not their fault. My only consolation lies in knowing that the true puppet masters—those tyrants, the fashion editors—are all doomed as I am, that they will each feel it more acutely than I, that growing older has been much harder for them as they have built, month by month, brick by brick, issue by issue, the walls of the tomb which they will soon lie festering in. For with every tottering, high-heeled step they take down Cemetery Road, the perpetually bright eyes and bushy tails of young beauty glimmer in satisfied mockery. And I will personally be waiting there, on a weekend visa, to welcome them to hell.

As I was saying, it was a splendid June evening by the ocean. I made everyone comfortable, took out my notes, and we got down to defending ourselves.

"Okay," said Toby Auberon, "here's where we are."

At that instant there was a titanic rap on my front door, and we all froze instantly in a group tableau of fear. *Cheese it! The cops!*

"Come in," I managed to mutter. My mind darted like a field mouse to the Bill of Rights—which my father made me memorize at eight—coming breathlessly to the right of assembly, and halted cowering beneath its leafy overhang as all my co-conspirators glanced nervously at one another.

I got up and scurried down my hallway, which I'd sensibly lined with bookcases ages ago. There was no siren flashing outside in the gravel drive; I knew from bitter experience I'd have seen it reflected on the book jackets (a hospital scare of my own a few years back, a false alarm, resulting in a waste of good money). I boldly pulled the door open, and there stood the last person I expected to see, our village's other mystery man.

I didn't even know his name. He was compact, possibly bullet-proof, with thick black hair, rather coldly handsome in a brooding way despite the smudge of an irregular nose. He looked like some olive-skinned foreign-film actor of another era, too swarthy for a leading role although he had the urgent energy of a hero, and a kind of nervous hurry even when standing still. He would be the foolhardy one who hides the explosives in the Nazi fortress but gets shot trying to make it back across the bridge. I guessed he was thirty-six, and I am a good guesser. He'd only been here for a year; Isabel, who lived catty-corner from him, said he kept odd hours and his blinds closed and was often seen carrying armloads of videocassettes into the house. Not that that's a crime, Isabel added, but it makes you wonder.

"This the right place?" I heard a city in his voice, maybe New York, though I do not keep up with accents. "You're Jessica, correct?"

"That's correct. And you must be . . ."

"I must be Scott Mahren," he said. "My friends call me Scativo."

His gaze flickered over himself in the hall mirror as I let him in, shut the door, and locked it this time. That mirror has revealed more of how people secretly think of themselves, catching their own reflections by surprise in someone else's home, than anything they ever said once they got here.

We shook hands and I mentioned that I'd been friends with old Hazel Wanderly, whose house he bought down on Shepherd Street after she went blotto and got put in a nursing home for her final docile months. I still felt a clasp of guilt, as I can rarely bring myself to visit friends in such places when I know the stay is once and for all. I told Mr. Mahren how glad I was he'd evidently been able to put the structural work needed, et cetera, into the house.

"Never knew her," he said tautly. "She bought the wooden kimono before I showed up. Her son was a creep. Acted like he was doing me a favor. Couldn't wait to spend every penny she left him. Plus all he got from me."

"I heard exactly the same thing," I said.

We stood assessing each other in the dim hallway, united by remorseless gossip. He nodded at my bookcases in grudging respect.

"Alphabetized," he said. "Only serious way to go. Find 'em in the dark."

"Otherwise it's all chaos," I agreed.

"The Scativo has no use for chaos." He grimaced. "So, I heard there was a meeting. With maybe room for one more."

"We'd be delighted," I said, and led the way, wondering what we all wondered—where his money came from. He looked like a wily pick-pocket, he did not look like a man who inherits. And he seemed too solitary and vital to be one of those electronics millionaires. He was fit: I imagined he kept a punching bag hanging in his living room. I do not need to keep one in mine.

"Everybody," I announced to the motley allies, "this is Scott Mahren—"

"Scativo will do fine," he said firmly, and held up one hand as a greeting also meant to discourage lengthy applause. "Don't let me interrupt."

He took a seat on the sofa beside Billy Fagles, nodded approvingly at my view which was rapidly being lost to darkness, and at Toby. Now I recalled seeing him in the back corner at our first fateful Village Hall meeting, in this same black turtleneck. He gave a gentle smile of appraisal at Molly Mellew, who appeared not to have noticed. You know what that means.

"Here's where we stand," said Toby. "I've met a couple of times with Bob Herbert." To explain his own legal background, that is; which was why Bob, who represented our interests in court, skipped these meetings. He didn't live here anymore, and with his own time constraints, he trusted Toby as more experienced in such battles. I suspect he also feared having to answer a lot of foolish questions, which Toby endured patiently.

"I'm sorry to say," Toby went on, "I have nothing but bad news. First, this morning we struck out with the U.S. District Court in Boston. They didn't bite on the Clean Water Act. For reasons I'll get to in a minute, the federal judge denied the writ."

"I don't get it," said Italo. "How can they pretend that pollution—"

"Hold on," said Toby. "I'm coming to that."

"So we got thrown back on the state's mercy," said Italo.

"That's right," said Toby. "Now, last week I went up to Newbury-port, to see a man named Gilmore with the Army Corps of Engineers. These guys are involved because they officially define the inner cove, the half mile enclosed by the bridge, as well as the outer cove, linking the river to the sea, as a single navigable waterway. And that's crucial. The guy did agree that during low tide there's not enough water in the inner cove to float a toy submarine. Plus the entire cove ices over during the winter. So much for navigability."

"I don't get it," said Mitch. "He's willing to do what for us?"

"Despite my arguments," said Toby gently, "he can't do anything. Our bridge gives access to both sides of a navigable waterway. He can't stop the cove being defined that way, and those two words throw us permanently under the jurisdiction of federal authorities, with the state doing the dirty work for them. We want this to be a local issue, meaning up to us; the law just won't let it be a local issue. Even if I try to take it further, the state and the feds can ultimately claim they're only protecting a navigable waterway. It's as if we're deliberately trying to block a major highway. And that's not even the really bad news."

I saw Scott Mahren shaking his head, thinking what I was: it can always get worse.

"The really bad news, which got waved in our faces in court this morning," said Toby, "is that the state already got the jump on us. A year ago they filed for what's called a declaratory judgment. It's like a preemptive strike. Giving them the right to demolish and replace the bridge whenever they see fit. They even did their own EIS back then. Which spells 'stall' to a lawyer. Environment Impact Statement. Proving that the ecosystem will be just fine, maybe even better off, with their nice new bridge. And that's why the state has taken its time sending back the lawsuit we filed on environmental grounds. They didn't bring up the declaratory judgment because they wanted to watch us go round in circles, and eat up valuable time and energy. We've just been wasting our breath."

"But we were never even informed," said Italo, scrabbling in his trousers pocket for his inhaler. "Why didn't we know? Surely we can still protest—"

Toby shook his head. "I checked into it myself this afternoon, down at city hall. The City of Leicester, as the affected party, was served the declaratory judgment. Probably some clerk just filed it away like he's supposed to and never told anybody. Figured he had no reason to. And because the city didn't do anything to respond against it within a suitable period, a default judgment was entered. It's been languishing there in the files, all this time."

"Can't we open this up again?" said Jon Eckerman. "Drag it out with another lawsuit?" He struck me as a young man entering middle age much too early from not getting enough sleep; his wide eyes had an unnatural glare from staring at a computer screen too long. This is one reason I insist on first writing every page by hand. Also, no one can unplug you when you're not looking.

"The problem is," my hero answered, "with a declaratory judgment, we can't even get in the game anymore. The state has known it all along. They did a job on us. And yes, they could've pointed out that the game was over at the first meeting. Believe me, all of this was done very, very deliberately."

Someone—it might've been me, since my notes do not say who—asked amid everyone's stunned silence, "So what can we do now?"

Toby nodded as if to himself; he'd expected every word he'd said all evening. "No legal move that I can think of—or that Bob can think of—can prevent their destroying our bridge a week from now. We've done a miserable job of exploiting the initial press coverage. Which portrayed us as a bunch of selfish yahoos anyway. Public opinion might stop their replacing our bridge with a concrete disaster later on. But for now, the only thing I can think of is to physically stop them. It's that simple. And that difficult."

"Fine with me," said Billy Fagles, "Let them know-it-alls try something Monday morning. Then we'll make it into the goddamn papers, pardon my lingua franca. Maybe they ain't never seen *Frankenstein*. With Karloff."

This is, word for word, exactly what he said.

"They'll have police with them, of course," said Toby coolly. He wanted to see who got spooked. "It'd be good to have one reporter for every policeman or engineer. Journalists go further when they don't feel outgunned. We want the state to feel overwhelmed by reporters asking tough questions."

"There's nothing wrong with getting arrested," said Mitch. "Not at my age. Anita and I, some of you know this, we get over to Spain or Portugal or Italy every winter for six weeks. Sometimes even France besides. We love it over there."

"We do," she chimed in.

"This kind of civil disobedience, heck, it goes on all the time over there. You fly into Rome or Paris, any month of the year practically, they're always on strike. Then they go get themselves a drink in some café. And just look at the Palestinians."

We all agreed that foreigners had this sort of thing well figured out.

At this point, I'm afraid, my scribbles get the better of me, because I seem to have written down what I surmised he was thinking. At least I am fairly sure Toby did not actually say what my notes say he said.

"I also should announce that I have fallen hopelessly in love with that dashing woman who sits thanklessly writing down every word everyone utters, who knows unerringly what each of us thinks, who comes like a thief in the night and steals our souls away, who sees with laser precision what joy lurks in the heart of at least one man. How could I resist such a woman? My lighthouse is hers, and I see no need to put up even the semblance of a fight."

Well, it's always remarkable what you're confronted by if you set down faithfully what people really mean. This is my true task, my calling, even if I diminish myself on these pages in the process, even if writing such a history will dissolve me. Let the lean-headed eagles of posterity yelp about what my role was: it is I who sit here with piles of detailed notes, with Toby's own treasured notebooks which I shall donate to the Library of Congress after my death. (But not before.) Be kind to my mistakes, and live happy: it was I who kept writing calmly when we were under siege and all the world was watching. The years glide away and are lost to me, but the most glowing days are still at hand, and I am still here.

"We should remember," said Toby, "that it's really stupid to smash a bridge when there are people standing on it. The best way to stop them short term is to have so many that it's impossible to move the crowd off the bridge. And pointless to arrest anyone."

At this moment I felt, frankly, disappointed. I'd been naïvely hoping for some masterstroke, a lightning bolt of tactical genius. I wasn't looking for a bunch of people squatting on the bridge hoping they wouldn't get arrested because they had plans for lunch.

Italo spoke up, as if he knew just what I was saying to myself. "That might be a good idea at first, Toby. But no one's going to want to be stuck on the bridge for very long. What if they show up every morning? I give us a week, tops, before everyone bails out."

Toby looked pained, and glanced at me as if to say: You see, Jessica? See how humanity lets you down? Yet there you sit, and I know you will never disappoint me.

No doubt he felt constrained at the inch-by-inch nature of most men's minds. He said, "You're right. We can't rely only on the village. There aren't enough of us, we aren't even a voting bloc. So we should divide up Cape Sarah into areas where each of us has a foothold, even just a friend who'll help. And put up signs explaining why we need bodies to protect the bridge next week. We'll need fifty each day. Enough to make it ugly if the state tries anything outlandish."

"That's all?" said Mildred. "Just ask people to come to the bridge?"

"I can write up a text and give it to Jessica. We'll suggest people leave their cars on the other side of the cove. We don't want either end of the bridge accessible to state equipment. And we have to promise media coverage. People will hang around for hours to get on the nightly news."

He did not know, he could not have surmised, that the time would come when the flea circus of the nation's journalists would be infesting us, leaping about, clamoring for interviews, telling the world their version of what we were doing; at first amused and making fun of Salt Cove, then mourning with us, and eventually defending our cause as the tanks rolled up. This little gathering, just we fifteen, was the last moment when any of it was under our control, was ours alone. There was a kind of innocence to the way we listened to Toby and watched the darkness envelop the sea as the lights on the far shore shimmered with the promise of many more lights once the summer people arrived. But this is hindsight. That evening we were worried we'd get nowhere, that a week hence our bridge would be destroyed, and we'd look back on these paltry efforts only with immense regret.

Billy Fagles muttered, "I still don't see what we do if them squad cars show up with megaphones. Ordering everyone off the bridge. I mean, it don't bother me, but most people aren't into that damn-the-defiant shit, excuse my French."

Toby shrugged. "We'll make sure there's always one of us in charge. So in a standoff we can urge people not to abandon the bridge. Force the police to arrest them."

"You think people round here are brave like that?" said Roscoe with disdain. "People got no backbone." For an instant the years blurred and I heard his father telling me, that time he took me swimming up at the Beauport quarry, "It was easy being brave in the war, you either grow up with a spine or you don't," then leaning over to try to kiss me. At least we'd gone swimming in daylight, I had that much sense. So much for human interest.

Toby stared hard at me, as if to say: *Stop that reminiscing, Jessica.* "What can the police do? They're not going to shoot someone for refusing to move off a bridge. And Leicester doesn't have enough squad cars to arrest a hundred people."

Never in a hundred lifetimes could I imagine being Roscoe's mother, though it might've turned out thus had my father not warned me always to consider the largest consequences of the smallest action, had we not been interrupted by a rainstorm, had I not liked better a fellow whom I'd glimpsed at a community band concert and was convinced, as you can be at eighteen, that I'd speak to him the following week. I forget his name, but I remember the tune was "Tenderly," and the band never played it again, just my luck.

I said, "I'll speak to Phyllis down at the Cove Market. She can make good money selling sandwiches to everyone on the bridge."

"The crux of it all," said Toby, "is the media. With this declaratory judgment in their pocket, the state will only back down now if the coverage makes them look awful. If it doesn't hurt enough, they won't crumple. The last thing they want is every little community ready to think for itself, defy a state edict and win. They want to make an example of us. We have to go so far that it becomes suicidal for them to continue."

"Well," said Jon Eckerman, "I've got a friend in New York at one of the networks. They probably won't be interested in the story, but if it lasts a few days they might."

All this time I'd had my eye on Scott Mahren—Scativo, or Mr. Go as I was to call him later—trying to gauge the right moment to interject. A couple of times his glance met Molly's; his gaze lingered across her torso; I figured they'd be coupling like ermine before the late evening news. This actually cheered me to think about. Contrary to what my niece might believe about me in her all-knowing way, I enjoy imagining what people look like rollicking away in bed, I enjoy mentally turning them this way and that, I enjoy seeing an alternate true nature of the persons there revealed, with all those unexamined gestures. And it struck me that once this urgent life force was in the air of a room, like the faint but unmistakable buzzing of bees, it might hover in the atmosphere even after the instigators departed. ("Can you stay for a brandy, Toby? No need to leave with the others." "Why, what a wonderful idea, Jessica.")

Roscoe said, "Who's that photographer, Billy? At the paper. The one with the sister."

Billy Fagles screwed up his brow as if trying to recover some arcane fact. (I could feel the healthy vibrations increase as I spied the guilty look on his amiable meat-locker face.) "Oh, yeah. The guy who got the picture of us before. After that first meeting. Fred somebody. Or Ed. Yeah, we could call him."

"You going to call him?"

"I can call him, you want me to call him?"

"You think it's maybe better I talk to him instead?"

"You was the center of the picture, Roscoe. Maybe you better call him."

Roscoe smiled tightly, almost wickedly, around his pipe. "But you're the friend of the family."

"Not really, Roscoe."

"Maybe his sister said something. What was her name?"

"I don't think so. Maybe. You never know."

Roscoe took several interminable seconds to relight his pipe while Billy, his best friend in all the world, fidgeted and stared at my pastel throw rug. Finally Roscoe said, "You think she remembers that far back?"

"I think," said Toby delicately, "maybe Italo should call him."

"Oh," said Billy Fagles. "That's a good idea."

"The other thing," said Roscoe, "is they might pull out some pilings. Let the bridge come down by itself. So we got to block them from the river."

"That," said Toby, "puts us in all kinds of trouble I'd like to avoid. Blocking a navigable waterway. Not quite the same as free right of assembly."

Roscoe bit on his pipe; I heard it. "Just telling you what I'd do if I was them. I'm not worried about blocking some jerk in a hard hat walking onto the bridge. We need a guy to make sure they don't set explosives from the water."

Toby nodded. "So long as we have people on the bridge they won't set them off. Or even try putting them in place. The risks are too great."

Roscoe said, "You want to be the one to defuse them?"

"Not particularly. I will if I have to."

Absolutely not! I nearly shouted. I wrote down my shout instead, and tore through the paper exclaiming with my pen.

Roscoe looked vindicated. "See? Don't worry, I understand the law. I know these bastards. They work on contract, I done that myself. Paid just to show up. We let them float around, but we make goddamn sure they don't get anything done. Not their fault. They don't have to do nothing, fine by them. All they care about is extra days they get paid to be here." He puffed away. "We send them into double overtime, they're grateful."

"I just remembered something," said Molly—and I was surprised by her mellifluous speaking voice, it suited her surname. "Something one of the surveyors said. About bringing a truck in. That they'd be around with a truck for a few days. Then a barge with a crane. To take the wood away."

"You spoke to him?" said Billy Fagles with incredulity, as if all surveyors were diseased.

"He spoke to me. I was taking a walk, he tried to dial me."

My pen paused above the paper. "Dial?"

"You know, meet me." She swallowed. "Pick me up."

"Thank you." I went on scribbling.

"Look, you're dealing with chumps here," said Scativo. He looked slightly pained, as if he were sucking on a lemon. "So you have to go with a chump approach. We need to make sure their trucks don't enter the village, right? Maybe they don't even make it to the other side of the bridge."

"Go on," said Toby.

Scativo shrugged. "Here's the scenario in slow-mo. Down toward Willowdale. Before the stone causeway. Turns out a car's backing out of the road next to that cove. Right when the state truck's coming along. So it has to stop, right? No choice. A few wily seconds, someone slashes their back tires, bingo. Buddy of mine from Jersey City showed me how you do it. They drive on, no one's the wiser. A mile later the ride feels funny, they pull over. Two flat tires, what a coincidence, that's the end of their workday."

"Someone w-will see you," said Italo's wife Myra, pushing nervously at stray strands of her black hair. She has, I always feel, a suppressed regal quality about her, like someone from a distant arm of European royalty who has inherited a title but no castle. "If they saw you, you w-would get arrested."

Our new ally looked faintly amused, as if dealing with amateurs. "So I go with the Lone Ranger approach. *Who was that masked man?* I'm in a second vehicle, I head off in the other direction. I'm gone, I'm history, no one's sure what they saw. And soon those chumps are watching their wheels go down by the side of the road. No way they're carrying more than one spare. No way they're going to work on the bridge. Not right now."

"Cool idea," said Molly Mellew.

"Well sir," said Mitch, "better you than me. I guess if they can't get here, it's harder for them to get started."

"You know what?" said Leilia Milne, as Harold squeezed her hand. "I hope they do show up. I'm seventy and dying of cancer, what do I care? I'll lie down on the road in front of their trucks. Let them run me over. With every newscaster in the Boston area watching. Don't tell me to shush. Let them put that on the evening report. News at ten, my eye. No one around here wants to stay up past eight. Like children telling themselves they deserve to be punished and sent to bed."

I said, "Stop lying, Leilia, you know you're not seventy yet." I didn't say she was not dying; that would've been an insult.

Harold, who knew better than anyone that it was not worth arguing with her, said gruffly, "I was thinking you'd be better for the tire slashing. You're quick and you're stubborn and you know how to use a blade."

"Damn right I do. I wasn't a surgeon's wife forty-seven years for nothing." Her eyes flashed.

"All right by me," said Scativo, though I guessed the last thing in the world he truly wanted was Leilia Milne, armed with a knife and a sense of vengeance, hopping alongside him. "You take the left tire, I'll take the right."

"I'm a little concerned," said Toby quietly, "that we go into this with a clear sense of alternatives. In case things turn out half wrong."

As Toby was speaking I fell into a dreaming—for a millisecond, for two minutes, who knows? I find a gap in my notes. His eyes flicked over me like a cat's tongue making its first lick into a saucer of milk, and I felt myself wondering what he kept hidden in the upper reaches of his lighthouse, up that black spiral staircase heading to the beacon. Surely he kept something crucial there. Besides his bed, I mean.

Perhaps I might actually have to break in. Did he lock his door when he went out? Many of us in the village do not. Presumably he went grocery shopping in Leicester by the cape jitney, since he owned no car. I wondered what his locks were like. We have all read stories about the phantom stranger who enters the house after midnight, cleans up the dinner plates, and eats the cake thoughtfully left out by the young widow. Maybe he'd get used to my being around, and even become enamored of this person who visited when he was asleep or away and did the washing-up for him.

We'd have a balanced relationship. He needed caring-for. I needed to know who he was so I could care for him properly, to know what he was doing all day long in there and through those interminable hours of darkness when, unable to sleep, I found myself crossing the Meadow on moonlit walks which ended at the rise above the beach, the fine upstanding body of the lighthouse illuminated even as the beacon kept flashing its solitary message, like a Miss Lonelyhearts of the Atlantic, over the sheet-metal sea. Illuminated, no doubt, because he was up most nights doing his secretive work, not merely reading, I knew that. A man does not secrete himself alone in a lighthouse in order to open a few closed books, even if he comes to resemble one himself.

Tempting as it might be, I am not flattering myself by inventing insights not earned at the time. No, I knew something electric was up with Toby Auberon, I knew he had come here not just (just!) so I might meet him, not just so he might defend us, but for motives of his own devising. Even though he appeared impenetrable, to me he carried the unmistakable aura of great forces stirring his ponytail and surging within him, he walked like a ghost on fire. I knew he was here to accomplish something immortal; I'd felt it when he greeted me, sleepy-eyed, in his bathrobe that lighthouse morning. I knew in my gut that years from now we'd be proud to say he had lived here and moved among us, and we would gladly embellish and enlarge inconsequential conversations and stray gestures to suggest he had been our friend.

"What do you mean?" Nancy Eckerman was saying to him. "Half wrong?" She was a slim redheaded creature, with a Connecticut station-wagon voice, and she held herself with a hint of bony schoolgirl tension; it was easy to imagine her worrying about tomorrow's test. (I was, by contrast, always very good at taking tests. Hence my impatience with those religions that insist on failing a student for life then finally offering a passing grade when it's too late for him to enjoy it.) I think Nancy might've been what men call pretty were she not sleeping too little—but her infant son was still dozing pacifically in the next room, which I suppose is all that matters.

Also, I'd caught her looking over my bookcases, and it occurred to me she might become my friend, if only for the volumes she pulled out; people who find time for poetry can be trusted. I remember a distinguished Italian gentleman of a certain age—he may have been one of those land-poor counts with which the continent used to be rife, I am told—telling me so while adjusting the cape draped over his bespoke shoulders. This happened one morning at a much faded hotel in Istanbul on my sole journey there, soon after my father's death, during a breakfast of goat cheese, bread, local salami, and tea you could trot mice on. He sipped thoughtfully from his cup and in his quaint Tuscan way said, "In life, my dear, one is either a poet, or—" And he added what I think was "an asshole." Because of the rapier cut of his elegant suit I did not dare ask him to repeat himself, I merely nodded and left my cold breakfast to discover the dusty Bosphorus, but I believe he might also have said *isola*: some Turk rattling a cup interfered with his imparted wisdom. Either way, I agree with him.

"If everything goes half wrong?" said Toby. "That means we turn away the wrecking crew for a few days, but we don't get the media coverage we need. It doesn't become a David-and-Goliath story on TV, in the papers, on the Web. At that point, what do we do to get the world's attention? We can't camp out on the bridge all summer."

I had a sickly feeling, writing down those words, that we'd spend the summer doing that, and more. Sometimes you describe with overwhelming assurance what you know will never come to pass, and in between thudding heartbeats the rush of your blood tells you you're wrong, it is coming as surely as the holidays.

"I tell you one thing," said Mitch. "We don't roll over and play dead."

"Right," said Toby. "They've been ahead of us every step of the way. No matter how awkward we make it, they won't be put off more than a week. They'll get a court order and send in a legion of policemen. Because once the old bridge is gone, our support will wilt."

"All right, hippie," said Roscoe. "You got something in mind?"

"I do. If all else fails, we should be ready to secede."

"From what?" said Jon Eckerman scornfully. "The City of Leicester? The Cape Sarah Chamber of Commerce?"

I heard in his voice the self-flattering disdain of the man who feels he is the most intelligent in a room, who cannot grasp why he is not a natural leader, nor why anyone else's opinion, in the end, holds as much weight as his. This scorn for other people, so unquestioned, makes it impossible to love someone else fully, which is why I saw his redheaded wife looking around the room's men like a blind person feeling for some solid object to find her way by.

"Fuck those Chamber of Commerce assholes," said Billy Fagles, unwittingly echoing my Italian count by the Bosphorus. "My buddy Arnie tried to get a permit to run a whale-watch boat, and you know what they—"

"Secede," said Toby, "from the United States. I know it sounds ridiculous. But it will definitely get us noticed."

It doesn't sound ridiculous to me, milord, I wrote in my notes, then struggled to catch up with what he was saying.

"Noticed?" said Mitch. "They'll call us crackpots."

"It'll get us on every news report in the country," Toby retorted. "In our ex-country, I should say. A small New England village, faced with having its age-old bridge destroyed by a bureaucracy that refuses to listen, finds it has no choice but to secede. Henceforth we are absolved from any allegiance to city, state, and federal governments. We are willing to open up diplomatic talks. But any attempt by them to seize any part of our territory, namely the bridge, shall be considered an invasion and an act of war."

"It's absurd," said Mitch.

"I bet it gets us on the evening news, though. I bet it gets our bridge repaired."

Harold sighed. "I can't believe there's no more legal recourse. Who'll take us seriously? Everyone will know it's a publicity stunt."

"You're not listening," Leilia snapped at him. "This is only if, if, if—"

"They'll portray us as loons. Eccentric loons," muttered Mitch just as Italo was saying bitterly to Myra, "This is all my fault, I should've resigned last year." Myra tried to quiet him; as she and I agreed over the telephone the next day, in private he was bold and scalding, in public he became a tad afraid.

Meanwhile Roscoe chortled and sucked on his pipe triumphantly, sending the scent of my father's law office—pipe tobacco has fortunately changed little in my lifetime—swirling around the room. If only my father could've lived to join forces with us, with Toby, to not be so very disappointed in my own last half century.

"Maybe the media won't take us seriously at first," said Toby. "But they'll televise shots of the bridge. And drawings of the concrete replacement. We'll say we're ready to raise the money for repairs.

They'll be merciless with someone like Chet Cairns. The governor will look like a jerk. The state will seem heartless and bullying. We'll be in the great New England tradition of fighting back against tyrants."

"We're not really going to declare war, are we?" asked Molly. "I mean, I just don't think that should ever be part of any game plan."

"I get it," said Scativo. "We let the chumps declare war on us. No need to go with the armed and dangerous approach. We're unarmed and not hurting anyone. Float like a butterfly, sting like a Stinger missile, baby." He spoke as if he did this every month. "But we need to get a cash defense happening, too. A Bridge Repair Fund. People see the news, our story breaks their hearts, tune in tomorrow. They should be able to send in twenty bucks out of sheer gratitude."

"I can take care of that," said Jon Eckerman confidently. Now I read clearly the dumpling face and receding hairline of the fellow who neglects his wife. There are so many, they are seemingly everywhere, it often makes me glad I have never been neglected. I saw from the way he and his Nancy sat together that they hadn't made love for weeks. I have always been able to read this on people, I just have never been able to verify it.

"I can set up a website for the repair fund," said Eckerman. "I'll do it tomorrow. I'll scan in photos. Then we can grow it as we move along."

"'Bridge to the past, bridge to the future,'" said Scativo. "Leave 'em with a slogan. Know what mine was? *Lift up your toilet seats, and lift up your hearts.* That's another story."

"The point is," said Toby, "it's preposterous for us to actually secede. It'll be obvious we're only trying to get our point across. But the fallout in public relations won't be worth it for the state."

"Maybe it won't ever come to this," said Mildred in her prim way, shifting a copy of her book on her knees.

"Wait a minute," said Mitch. "We're discussing this like we've got the support of the whole village. We can't go taking power and seceding from anything. We'd need to hold a Village Hall meeting and vote."

"Of course," said Toby. "But right now we need to meet with people one-on-one. So they'll want to blockade the bridge in the first place. It's easier to enlist someone's support if you can talk privately in their kitchen. And warm their cold feet."

I saw his logic; at a big meeting nothing would get resolved. Democracy could never be as wise as the wisest man in the room, and I knew Toby would be in danger of getting shouted down.

"I'm sorry to say you've convinced me," said Harold Milne, whose bedside manner as a surgeon always relied on his statuesque presence. "In a terminal situation, I don't believe in inching along." Leilia patted his knee; I could tell what doom was on his mind.

"I just want to see," said Roscoe in his deafening whisper, "some new tax rate when it's over. No right to assess us the way they been doing."

Nobody spoke, and he realized what we all thought. He nodded. "Yeah, right, they'll bleed us even more. The bastards just won't let you live."

"They won't let you live," echoed Billy, ruefully shaking his shaggy head and glancing at Nancy Eckerman. Then he frowned and I could tell he was wondering if it might be rude to crack open another beer in my kitchen.

"Right," said Toby. He stood up and smiled at me, a smile that made me feel all would yet go well. The last words of his from the evening which I have in my notes are, "I wonder if there are any more gingerbread cookies."

19

The Vultures of Justice

Subj: Don't Worry!
From: avenger101@incoming.com
To: eckermanjon@coastal.net

We are a small, lethal, hand-picked band of freedom fighters based in Missouri. For reasons we are sure you understand we are forced to keep our cover "identities" concealed. Yet the trustworthy man will find a code revealing the name of our website, and the necessary password, encrypted somewhere in this message. As you may not realize

Vultures roam
Far from home
Till kingdom come
And carrion moan

Checked out your Salt Cove Rescue site. >>>Bridge Defense Fund>>> Loud and clear you straight, we can read between the lines, we don't need weathermen to figure out the wind. And help is on the way. The forces of evil will NOT be allowed to triumph. Vultures feed on! Swoop on! Let the meek inherit zilch. If we have to bury our weapons for years and cut our way through the impenetrable rock of secret government cells hidden seven levels underground we will do so, because no force can stop the Vultures of Justice! No prison can hold a free man captive! Never fear, help and ammo are en route.

We were not surprised to learn of your plight. Some of us predicted the next government assault, intended to cripple all remaining civilian resistance, would come in California (disguised as another massive "earthquake") or else in Montana, where we maintain a network of covert allies. However, more than one of us as far back as eighteen years ago predicted an attack in New England, cradle of American liberty and riverbed of armed resistance. So comprehend that we do not intend to let you down. Blood has flowed in the streets and more blood will flow before this is done.

What part will the Vulture eat?
The Vulture will eat the head.

It may not have occurred to the brave souls of Salt Cove that you guys are the linchpin. If you let them grab your village without putting up a fight, if you let them steal whatever they want, let them run amok in your houses, let them take your guns, let them seize your bread knives since you might want to defend yourselves one day, you might as well turn over your wives and your comely daughters and let them switch on the underwater landing lights and activate the whole invasion code hidden on all the street signs. And then you've got foreign forces moving in. When you see that first wave of so-called National Guardsmen coming at Salt Cove from over the hill, you just grab the binoculars and verify the slant of their eyes, you don't need to ask if they can hum the music to Leave It to Beaver, you don't need to ask to see their phony passports, you just open fire. Take it from us—the Vultures roost in the trees, they smell what's decaying on the ground and they see what's moving across the horizon.

And to quote our handbook: In any dying society, the free

man is forced to lose standing by his very nature, which is to spit against the wind. He is condemned if he takes action and condemned if he does not. This leaves him no choice except to wait, which is why the society is in total landslide.

We will be monitoring at Code Amber priority the public "news" reports to keep an eye on the situation. You may also reply to the above e-address or, for security reasons, acknowledge by not replying. We can be there and ready to strike in two attack vehicles an estimated 27 hours after receiving any SOS.

Should you manage to secure any media attention next week, we will be watching each individual newscaster to verify if their allegiance has been compromised. As we both know, in any standoff situation the first thing they do is take control of ALL the lines of communication. Just open the damned papers, man, the daily ledger of lies, you want to see what I mean.

In other words, we expect to learn the government has "backed down," withdrawn their plans for your bridge and ordered all their foreign architects taken out back and shot. We will not be surprised immediately afterward to see no more on-the-spot coverage coming out of Salt Cove.

In the event we determine the situation has reached Code Whitewash and no news reports are filtering through, we will strike.

And in the event they decide to move in with any force, we will strike. Who is your leader / c.o., so we can prioritize tactics? (Please use encryption software provided.)

Meanwhile, as a goodwill gesture of the comradeship that exists between free men everywhere, we are sending your village a small care package which should come in very handy. We will include a translation of all instructional materials. It would be best if someone with solid military experience opens it. Don't worry, we have plenty more where that came from.

The rabbit has left the hutch. The Vulture will soon take wing. Free men, have no fear.

[No reply.]

20
Leilia Milne

I WAS READING in the Boston paper today about radiation in the soil. When are they going to discuss the more pressing problem, of radiation in the soul?

I never imagined, on all my walks over many years, that the afternoon light could hold so much sweetness, that the way the leaves shifted in a breeze could have so much meaning even if I cannot say what it might be. Perhaps the restless contentment of a dreaming mind? But I have never been a dreamer. I never imagined that the gradual shy shift of one season to the next could be trying to tell me so much, and always here I was not listening, not letting the change suffuse me, not allowing myself to give in to the inevitable.

And always knowing so much more than I admitted to myself. None of it I could hold in my short ugly fingers for any time at all. So many seasons, so many secret messages received, and all I remember is the vanishing. My body has been blasted with a medical radiation, a mediation as Harold calls it, that has seemingly done no good whatsoever, only interrupted what should have been the natural process of dying and not provided my soul with any radioactive half-life. Put that in your hospital brochure.

Yet this afternoon the tender light is here before me, the astringent river winding slowly past my front garden, I can walk over the hill and an ocean will be spread before me like an offering. The only sense I can make of it is that everything I saw and felt will soon be gone, not taken with me, not left with Harold or with the dispersed children. Everything will just evaporate. (If there were a way, for ten seconds, for the physical memory of what it's like to be made love to by a man and to give birth four times to be transferred to your mate, it would blast open his mind.)

There is, no matter what they deny, a radiation in the soul, but I see no evidence there is a posthumous half-life to the radiation. The people I've known who died were then only gone, and no amount of my missing them or thinking about them ever convinced me that their glow was still in the room.

So it will be with me. The life I lived was only mine and nothing before me now, the effervescent ping of another season awakening, will survive as I see it any longer than I will. Every single instant the world winks out everywhere except in our fossilizing brains, which try to selectively hold its imprints and fail pitifully. Imagine how different it would be, how much solace we'd have from day to day, if we could visit our pasts like a library where anything we want is available and easily found.

If I had known that near the end of my life everything I ever thought or felt would get smushed until all that matters is the here and now, the plain edge of this windowsill, the clutter of our stone wall, the rasp of Harold's voice and the steadiness of his hand, the curl of our garden hose that I told myself months ago I should replace, the uncomfortable chaise longue I have sat in for years, not wanting to find another and hurt its feelings, just as when I was a child all things around me seemed vibrant with living, fully awake and easily upset, like when I used to worry as a little girl swimming that I'd hurt the feelings of one end of the Boston city swimming pool by not touching it with both hands as I had touched the other, just as going up the steps to our house in Jamaica Plain one step often seemed friendlier to me than all the rest, I went through the day worried about the feelings of every object that I later agreed was utterly inanimate, and now at this late date I learn how very wrong I became, the child in me was correct, I learned nothing as important as what I knew from the very beginning, how every single aspect of the world is alive if you can only respond to it and you cannot count yourself entirely alive until you learn to do so, to feel it pulsing around you with many voices, and just as to a child the most miraculous thing is not to love or be loved, which one takes for granted then, but that I can grasp these bones, the bones of my arm, and they'll remind me that I am here and I am me, even though one day soon I'll feel how little life is left in the arm and in the hand trying to grasp it and keep it from disappearing, it was all like a music vanishing just as you summon it: as I thought about the music the music changed again, but even when one of us drops away the music goes on nearly as before, and when this hand begins to fall and keeps falling we will vanish as we fall, the elusive music swirling around me until I am left wrapped in a cocoon of the silence I hear more and more every day, approaching like storm clouds coming with summer behind them, but not so long as I can still look out at the salt river and touch the bones in my arm and know the sweetness of the light on my garden is real and will not be taken away from me this afternoon, not yet, not yet, not for another minute or two.

21

Toby Auberon

You call this a potato? I wouldn't feed a potato like this to a dog. It's a disgrace to serve people a lump of rubber doused with sour cream. You want to rob somebody, rob a tourist. Now bring us proper baked potatoes and pretend you're serving them to your own dear mother. I assume you like your mother.

This speech was given tonight by Ms. Stoddard, surprising a waitress as much as it surprised me, at a Leicester eatery. I was there at Jessica's invitation to discuss the volunteers-wanted posters. In this sawdust-floored joint, filled with mostly men and a few women traveling in packs, the main event was yelling at wrestling on TV, not bickering about the Salt Cove bridge smack-down.

Also here, in a back room where they didn't notice us, were the so-called Scativo and Molly, no longer wearing a tracksuit but instead some shiny Hindu goddess outfit. Eventually (I noticed on my way to the men's room) they started necking, and ended up practically throating. Lucky man. There's something familiar about her; at first I thought it was her California locutions, though her accent is midwestern. No doubt mere childhood prickings I felt at hearing a few long lost expressions. Then I realized she bears a passing resemblance—just as Italo resembles a famous marble bust of Julius Caesar—to a porn star I was fond of years ago, who went by the classical moniker of Clitemnestra. In America one must savor wit in very tiny doses.

She was, oddly enough, the subject of a legal case while I was in law school, in which her heartfelt cry of spread-eagled rapture ("This bud's for you!") provoked an unsuccessful lawsuit from a beer mogul not astute enough to realize that any context which makes a blurb memorable is good—and self-important enough to think free speech might be overturned in the courts to protect his half-wit slogan. Sadly, all that made her peal of joy so amusing is doomed to die even as her naked, vulnerable beauty lives on, for fifty years from now her line will have lost its fizz as memory of the ad vanishes.

All this ran through my mind as I sat thinking how unlikely it was that the face of a local jewelry designer should echo that of an actress from my twenties, though it's not always her face I think of first. It reminded me how desperately we need a slogan, and that bridge to the past bridge to the future crap concocted by the Makeout King in the corner won't do. I mentioned this to Jessica, sitting in apparent contentment. She seems to hang on my every word; given the chance, she'd be jotting down our entire conversation on a place mat.

"I've never been good at slogans," she said. "They remind me of those mottos you find in fortune cookies. *Starting Wednesday you will have better luck.* We used to play a game where you add the phrase *in bed* at the end. They're better that way. Then the Chinese restaurant here closed down."

Ask what you can do for your country, I thought, *in bed.* Hmm, it works.

I suggested she come up with a dozen slogans for us, the sooner the better, and discovered she has dimples.

Then I asked if she felt there was really the will in the villagers to fight back with all it might take. We have five days before they start tearing apart the bridge. The declaratory judgment only means one thing: someone has had this intention for a long time, long enough to order the Environment Impact Statement and carry a neat package quietly through the courts. My idea of a mindless bureaucracy grinding its wheels was a naïve fantasy. I couldn't stop thinking that my every effort would prove futile, that Salt Cove en masse would show less backbone than my mustache. If I put the same time into the Machina, I'd be done long before the developers got around to evicting me. Now I wouldn't be able to go back to my old life until all this was finished.

"I think you'll be surprised," she said mildly, "how much fight people have in them. There's more to some of us than meets the eye."

What meets the eye when I look at her closely? A woman in her late sixties, with pale hair the color of raw ginger, and a direct green-eyed gaze. Unlike most people, she does not look away when you talk directly to her. Dignified features; she might've been lovely once. She's taller than I am, which isn't saying much, and exudes the rangy health that comes from walking briskly every day in every weather. And pausing to wonder about what she sees, for she has a contemplative turn of mind. Different eyeglasses, which she uses when reading, would help. Her glasses flatten her face, and in fact she has strong cheekbones and a calm forehead. She probably resented her nose when young. I, whom no one would ever consider handsome, find such drawbacks endearing, since they let you focus on the personality, unswayed by the illusion.

She never wears makeup, nor should she; the soul does not require mascara. The few seams in her face are like the marks of a handmade pot that can withstand still more shaking up. Nor has she adopted the deliberate mannishness that infects many New England women, young as well as old, as if the ultimate attribute of womanhood would be to look ready to chop wood. She likes to wear a scarf knotted at her neck inside the collar of a blouse or visible over her sweater. On her it looks casual and does the job of necklaces, plus it carries the solo-aviatrix tang of pluck and daredevil glory.

Her best feature is her voice, which cracks a little in that New England way—as if strained from speaking over the howl of wind and rain, or as if she's unsure of an occasional pronunciation. This is misleading, since she isn't afraid to say what she means. The serene sarcasm of those growing old is a sublime thing, it always carries the weight of truth, and a forgiveness besides.

None of this matters, though it marks how absurd my life has become that my only date for some time has been with a woman several decades older. Who has not the foggiest notion, fortunately, what I am doing here. Carried a few steps further, this means that one day I'll be escorting one of those sturdy Central Asian shepherdesses, age 109, who smokes a long carved pipe and smears herself in yak butter to keep out the Himalayan cold. Unless the Machina Excelsior, which put me in this position, brings about a sea change in my romantic fortunes.

My years in Rio (see notebooks) were the dental-floss bikini opposite of my years here, *Obrigado a Deus.* Better not to gorge on memories; this is what comes from living alone and keeping unusual hours. I could always ask Jessica if she knows any nice women around here, meaning someone not "nice" at all. But that would violate the respect she's bestowed on me.

Given the chance, I'd be a pasha, drawing beauty from all over, with a map of the world on one wall and even those little flags on pins that get pushed around in WWII movies. I'd pursue the divine tropical paradise that few men will admit they desire: a pride of many gorgeous creatures wandering, loose limbed and barely clad, with the insouciant grace of a devoted harem girl—minus the conspiracies, the rivalries, the dagger concealed under the ottoman, naturally. It's not that I want so many because I do not really want to get to know any of them profoundly. On the contrary, I want to know all of them wisely and well. Once you understand that the world is rife, no *ripe,* with its Claudias, its Deborahs, its Vivians and Henriettes—its Luisas, Dorothys, and Moniques—its Lilians and Marikas, its Sylvies and Tanyas and Eves—how can you not wish you were everywhere at once? How can you not imagine all the many lives you never got to lead? I ask as much in wonder as in regret.

A psychiatrist, overpaid as much as a lawyer, would call all this wishful thinking a futile attempt to compensate for being short and not dashing in appearance, despite a crumb-free mustache and clean ponytail. Such an accusation implies that were I tall, dashing, and better coiffed—someone whom tailors would not sneer at but address reverently—in sum, were I attractive to women, my fantasies would be entirely different. This is ridiculous: they wouldn't change one bit.

Regret? All right, there is a darkness in me that I cannot identify and do not like. Not the darkness of being alone. Or the darkness of passing the age when men normally have children. Probably the darkness of not yet having seen something I created come to proper fruition in the garden of the world—which shows not the slightest interest or harvest need. Or it may even be a darkness that originates outside me, to which what little I do is the only answer I can give, a quiet attempt to stand up against the summit of that night, having left the noisy lower slopes of the law. If I am lucky the Machina will one day change all this, will justify me; perhaps the game best played in the dark will, *Special when lit,* banish the gathering darkness.

Or perhaps there is nothing substantial to my dream of pure radiance. And in the end I'll feel the darkness swell from inside like some orchestral cataclysm, and learn, too late, that all this time all there really was, all I really had, was nothing more than—what? Than the person staring back from the weird depths of a mirror, waiting for me to say something first.

What I said to Jessica at that moment was, "It's late. I really should get to—" I nearly said *work,* with a long night ahead trying to design the crucial third drop target, the most difficult to hit. I did manage to say *sleep,* and at this Jessica looked surprised.

"We can go if you want. But I had the impression you keep late hours."

"Me? No, early to bed, early to rise."

She shrugged. "Funny. At my age I often have trouble sleeping. So I'll go for a walk in the middle of the night. And no matter how late I'm up, your lamps are always blazing away."

I made some lame remark about falling asleep reading, too many books.

She said, "There's nothing embarrassing about being an Internet addict. I know a lot of people are."

At that I spluttered in indignation. My outburst shocked her; maybe I just have a microchip on my shoulder. But why be polite about a way of life which has killed off not just my own chosen field but an entire mode of thought? And drained dry the attention span of a civilization, painstakingly built up like a coral reef over seventy centuries? Personally, I don't see what's so great about that.

"You'd feel less cut off," she said, presuming a lot. "Living alone."

Not cut off enough, or we wouldn't be having this conversation, I thought. The easiest ploy is to admit that you too watch a lot of TV. People rarely ask what your favorite program is, they only want to know that you're part of the family of man, hooked up to the same life-support system they are.

"How can a man feel cut off," I murmured, helping her on with her jacket as we stood up to go, "with over two hundred channels at his disposal? I'm just trying my best to keep up."

We picked our way through the clamor and press of people; Leicester eats early but drinks late.

"I don't know why," said Jessica, "you're doing your damnedest to be misleading. Your secrets are safe with me. I'm sure you don't own a television. I'd bet my life on it."

"Don't be so sure." She was right, of course. I realized when I pulled the door shut that our canoodling fellow conspirators had slipped away ahead of us into a surprisingly balmy June night. It reminded me that I already had several Junes here to compare this one to, devoted to the Machina Excelsior, and that one day I would be old.

"Show me your premises, then," she said triumphantly. "Prove to me you own a television."

"All right, have it your way. I'm between sets."

"I knew it!"

"But as soon as I can figure out a way to wrap an eight-foot screen around curved walls, I'll be back in business."

She accepted this dubiously and happily, feeling she'd won. Fortunately I persuaded her not to drop me off, via the Heights, near the lighthouse. Instead I offered to walk home from her place. We drove through the exasperated Leicester streets, dense with their mood of having been heavily sedated when fishing began to die out a half century ago, now ruled by clumps of teenagers sullenly hoping to join a gang but lacking the ambition. As we roamed homeward along the tree-shaded road of dark hills, moonlit coves, and rocky villages already asleep for hours—their denizens thrashing away in voluptuous dreams full of summer people—I grew sure that Jessica had romantic ideas about me and the prospect of a nightcap at her place. If she only knew the pictures lurking in my head, if she only knew what images crowd the backglass of my imagination, the personal memories that nourish me still, she would not expose herself so, she would not allow herself to dream. It is no small thing to feel you are about to break an old lady's heart.

Or maybe all I was sensing in her voice and manner was that last glass of wine.

As we pulled into the village and trundled over her hill down toward the shore, I said I wouldn't be able to come in, I was tired and had better move along home. She seemed to accept this as inevitable and made small talk about bringing me a page of bridge slogans tomorrow. Her house is a rambling stone pile with restful verandas and a view to rival my own. Something made me ask about it; I knew from dinner that she'd had the house from her father, a lawyer who long outlived her mother. I imagined the two of them as a cozy pair, it explained Jessica waiting to marry until it was too late. My question came out rude, like a stab at the property's future, which was, after all, what I wondered. The executor in me, I guess.

She kept the car idling in her drive. I heard her breathing. She said tonelessly, "I have a niece who looks forward to owning it soon. And putting me to sleep." Then she added, almost merrily, "You know, if you come looking for me one day and I'm not here, be sure to ask what she's done with me. They took Helen of Troy away, they can kidnap me."

"Oh, I wouldn't be so sure about that," I said.

We rolled slowly toward her garage, built into a side belly of the house, and she clicked a gadget that hoisted up the groaning gray door, revealing granite innards with rakes and a mower and a wheel-barrow, picked out by her car's glaring headlights. As the door rose higher, like a curtain on some antiquated cinema screen, we saw more of the garage, which went back and back. And as we drove in, suddenly, there it was, unmistakably before me: no chance of confusing that treasure with anything else, even in an ill-lit garage at midnight, even from thirty feet. I leaned forward and swallowed. At least I had the presence of mind not to gasp or give away too much. "What's that?"

"Just some rusted fencing I took down. I should probably throw it out."

"No, over there." I pointed, felt my hand tremble.

"Oh, that. It's a pinball machine."

"It's yours?"

"Now it is. My father's pride and joy. He bought it right after the war. I think it's from the early forties."

Nope, sorry. *Contact,* from 1933, Pacific Amusement Manufacturing: the first battery-operated game and the first that featured sound. Two historic leaps. Not to be confused with Exhibit Supply's *Contact* of 1939, with ghostly airplanes that appeared on the backglass as the score mounted and the stakes rose, like a harbinger of the air war to come.

"Pinball, eh?" I said. "Neat. Does it work?"

I did my best to sound nonchalant, not too eager. But she doubtless heard something in my voice, because she looked sharply over at me and paused before replying.

"I don't honestly know," she said. "It didn't work the last time I tried. But that was years ago. Who knows, maybe it repaired itself. I always feel games like that have a life of their own. Maybe I'm crazy." She gave an honest, rueful little laugh. "Why, do you play?"

22

Mitch Wapping

"Anita," I said, and rolled over in bed, feet bare on a bare June floor to go pee, "there's more here than meets the eye."

Grunt from the other side. Grunt from me as I pad into the bathroom, should never have cut corners on the heat lamp. Older and wiser now. "What do we really know about him?" Steady trickle, still steady after all these years. "He could be anybody."

"He sounds like he's highly educated." She's talking in her sleep, not making sense.

"Education, schmeducation." Shake the governor by the hand. "Got us into a mess."

"Let me sleep."

"I should've run the Village Hall this year." Run it in the sleet, in the snow, in fog of night and gloom of day. Kiss those bridge problems away. Instead that useless science twerp got hold of it all. I guess Italo can't help being who he is, or should I say whom. A schoolteacher doesn't know what it's like to be out in the world. And now this oddball from God knows where takes over, what do we know about him that's facts on paper. Nothing, Mac. Not a thing.

Drip, drop, rain this time of night. If the Coast Guard had given me the lease on the lighthouse like I asked we wouldn't be in this mess. Then Dora could've moved back here from Nevada with my grandson, think how much a lighthouse would mean to him. Sure, Grandpappy will show you how the light works. Maybe when you're a little older we'll let you run it, if you're a good boy.

Instead the Coast Guard rents it to some drug-deranged hippie with big ideas, got everybody convinced divided we stand united we fall. We could've sorted this out six months ago. If I'd been running the village we'd have known what was on the way, we'd have seen it coming. I've got all the friends in high places you could possibly ask for. I'd have been to see the governor personally. Mitch, what can I do for you? he'd say. Are you all right? You say there's evil plans afoot? I'll scotch them right now. Honey, get me Public Works on the line. On the double. No, Mitch, you tell *me* what to do. I'm all ears.

"Are you all right?"

That's right, good to the last drop. Governor, I'm glad we had this little chat and reached an understanding. I hate to have to be so blunt . . . No, Mitch, think nothing of it. It's *my* duty to serve.

"Mitch, are you all right?"

Yes, dear, yes. Good-bye, governor.

"You're taking a long time in there."

"Go back to sleep," I say. Back to our bridge-addled dreams. Not a decent night since all this came down the river and every one of them powerless to put a stop. Especially that who knows what he is, that dopehead, that Toby, swarming around in his rat-infested lighthouse sleep, all smug in his bed. Even Jessica taken in. Poor old sap.

"Aren't you coming back to bed?"

Back to sleep with all the years together like a blanket over us. Even in June you need a blanket around here. Bare floors hold the cold, all right. When the bridge was open to cars the plank rattle kept you up the night, you could guess who it was coming home late. Dora conceived to that rattle. Go back to sleep, go back. Not if I was running the show. What a comforting bum my wife has. Yes, it would all be different. Back to where was I, that's right, all the way back. Rattle no more. Sleep till morning. Still, still. The country will survive.

23

Ed Grier

PEOPLE OFTEN SAY, how do you do it? How do you get the shots you do, Ed? And I'm tempted to say, Right, figure cause I talk like I'm from East Overshoe I don't know how to use a light meter? And the Pulitzer Prize only gets won by the staff of a great metropolitan newspaper, like they say on *Superman*? Forget it, buddy. That locomotive you hear coming down the tracks like thunder, that powerhouse is me.

Pro is pro. You go pro, you know pro. I tell that to kids in seminars at Leicester High or up the line at Dunwich State every week, and it's true. The Gospel According to Ed. They said you'll never make anything of a hobby but in six months the circle of North Shore papers offered me a contract and I took it. Now it's looking like time to move on. I made more from all those shots of the Great Salt Cove Uprising, including some that no one in this country is ever going to forget, than I made in a whole three years on contract. I mean, people bought those overseas for newspapers in places your computer can't even find on a map and nobody I know can pronounce.

A year from now I won't be working the Cape Sarah playgrounds for Halloween shots, that's for sure. Not too long ago that photo editor at *The New York Times* was talking Pulitzer as soon as he had me on the line, and those guys see it all. I might even make a book out of it, starting with that big ox breaking the bridge sign that evening back in March. They don't get handed to you like this very often, no matter how hard you work, and when a crowd gets out of control, when everything gets out of control, you got to shoot from the hip. Maybe in the old days I'd have been a sharpshooter, a lone marshal dispensing frontier justice, the Wild West man with the gun who was faster than the others. Quick Draw Grier. Cause slow is no pro. Any of the greats will tell you that. But heck, I'm just doing my job.

The reasons for the success of those shots was twofold. First, location. That unerring instinct a pro has for being in the right place for the right shot *before it has even taken shape.* Plus preparation. This means that after the guy up in Salt Cove, not the longhair who got famous but the science teacher, called me once, and then the big ox called me several times to warn me, I got the message. So I was there by 7 A.M. on what they eventually called Black Monday. I knew a real moment was going to happen, there was that hum of expectation in the air, and a kind of pulse in people, like your blood throbbing, as they started to assemble.

The total surprise for most everyone, even me, was how many turned up. If there'd been less people it would've probably been real different, that's what all the smart alecks said afterward, but there wasn't, so there you go. You pass a certain number and anything can go down. I've seen it at all kinds of sports events, I saw it in Salt Cove. And when there's someone trying to impose their will on that many, well, you know what occurs. It's like a car rolling down a hill, whoever jumps on trying to stop it is making a huge mistake. A pro knows how to look out for himself. I sure kept my head down once the shooting started, but I kept snapping pictures, as everyone knows.

Let me lay out where people were in the first place, so the events make sense. The *Leicester Daily News* did publish a chronology, practically minute by minute, of the morning the siege began, but Phil Baxter, who took credit for his eyewitness account, didn't get there till things had already started. He was late as usual, with his usual six-dollar cup of Mogambo Java blend, so I was really the source of half what he wrote and he got half what I told him wrong. The fact is it's too late for him to understand teamwork or even the basic idea of backup in that kind of an unpredictable situation. No pro is just no go.

I had mentally stationed myself in two locations, even though I was roaming, because both had advantages. The secret here was that I didn't have to scope out the bridge cause I've done it a hundred times over the years. You could stick anyone down there, I don't care who, from any rag in the country, and they'd still be playing catch-up to me. And they'll tell you the same thing.

The end of the bridge toward Leicester, down that short (approx. 45 ft.) approach off Monroe Street, which circles the entire cape, was an obvious one. Put yourself in my shoes. You get the view all the way back across the bridge to Salt Cove itself, with the boats at their moorings and all those jigsaw-puzzle houses on the shore and the hills behind, which is one of your classic great New England village shots if you ask me, call it a cliché, but put a howling mob on the bridge instead of a few kids jumping in swimming and it's sayonara cliché, hello Press Photographer of the Year award. I've done that bridge in every possible light and on a clear spring morning there's a ten-minute stretch where the thing looks made of old toothpicks or matchsticks or something. I nailed that real early, before everyone started to show, cause I figured the thing had never looked in worse shape, more frail, than right now, so why rely on a prior shot? Besides, I didn't want the paper squawking about paying a lower rate for some shot they used before. As it turned out that was the last picture anyone ever took of the bridge before it became more than a bridge, before blood got spilled and it turned into a lightning conductor for people.

About then I managed to talk to the longhaired guy, Toby. And he seemed pretty sure the state engineering truck would come down that way, off Monroe Street, to set up outside the village if possible, and just stay there, right on the incline. As we're talking, this truck for pumping out septic systems, with a big tank rusted fourteen ways from Sunday, pulls up and starts to slowly back down the incline and Toby's talking to me and ushering the thing down, directing it, grinning ear to ear like he wasn't sure it'd actually be that big.

I fired off a great shot of his grin and when he looked at me sharp I said, "Your kids'll love it," and he just shrugged. Suddenly the septic tank truck looks like it might slide and we both yelled and it inched forward uphill again and parked. Then the big ox who broke the sign in my shot in the rain back in March gets out along with some other guy I didn't really get a good look at. I says, "That truck's seen some shit, eh?" and everyone laughed. The big ox says sure, used it twenty years till it rusted out, it sure makes a good roadblock now. Then he and his crony get some chains, like snow chains but longer, and chain both sets of wheels together, and padlock the chains, and that's that.

I get a few shots, figuring the ox won't mind, I mean R. L. HUGHES is in tall letters on both sides of the truck, no mystery there. Then I move down the bridge toward the Cove. Toby Longhair is clearly in charge, he says to me, "So, what would you do if you was them and you come out to start pulling a bridge apart and see all these people on it?" Cause by now there must've been thirty people, carrying signs with *Protect Our Bridge* and *Save Salt Cove* and *No To State Arm Twisting*. I guess it takes a while to think up a great slogan. I took some shots figuring this might be it in terms of a groundswell of popular support, nothing like your classic Tiananmen Square crowd. Never guessed there'd be over a hundred fifty people out here by the end of the hour.

I says, "Well, if it was me I'd back down. Especially once they see a photographer from the press. That's just begging for hostile coverage. I mean, some of your protesters here must be older than the damn bridge. That ain't going to look too cool."

He said, "I'm hoping you'll introduce yourself to the state engineers. And photograph them right away. So they understand no one's playing games, that their reputations are at stake." Then he added, "If they make it this far."

I said, "How about a portrait for prosperity, right here?" He smiled cause he got the joke—believe me, not everyone does—grunted and said he wouldn't stop me, and that's the picture I got, three shots *boom-boom-boom*, squinting a bit like he's trying to see the future and can't quite make it out, the wooden bridge sloping off behind him to the Cove and following that little lane up to the Village Hall right at the top of the shot like some cut-rate Monticello. A pro does not go with the flow, a pro makes the flow and then rides it, just like Duke Honolulu out there on his surfboard, baby.

Anyway, so I'm doing the crowd, lot of them seem to be from right in the village, and I'm thinking the other money shot is not going to be looking back in the opposite direction but maybe tighter in to the village side. But no, turns out the money shot's from up the hill, off the steps of the Village Hall, then closing in till I get the bridge, where the engineers are now going to have to set up their truck if they set up anywhere. Plus I can still get in some of the houses on the other side to suggest the village—oh man, do I have the frigging sixth sense for location or what? This kind of eye you can hone, sure, but basically if you aren't born with it, you might as well be shooting in braille.

And now people are beginning to show up like crazy. I mean, the Cape Sarah bus stops up on Monroe Street and in no time there's maybe forty people coming down from around the septic truck. They're laughing like it's some kind of picnic, a few of the young chicks have got the bare midriff action going cause it's set to be a warm day, definitely rain would've changed everything. And I see that Toby Longhair—guy looks a little like Custer and acts a little like him too, maybe Custer after plenty of recreational drugs, same foolhardy set to his head if you check out those old Brady shots—well, even he looks surprised. Like a politician who got real lucky after the election.

Meanwhile from the village side there's more and more middle-aged or older folk, carrying the usual homemade signs. All the Sals are showing up now. They arrive not knowing what to expect, but as soon as they see all the people they don't recognize, support from outside, well some of them look downright teary. So when people get cynical about democracy in this country I say they need to shut up and stare at a few pictures I got that morning, the last of the generation that went wading in the water and died for us on Omaha Beach or over in Da Nang, you're talking to the proud son of a vet, you look at my shots you can see what true democracy looks like. And if you go through the contact sheets in order you can see what happens when other people who should know better abuse that democracy. Cause there's no excuse for what Leicester's finest allowed to happen. Christ, I'm surprised my lenses didn't shatter from what they saw that morning. That was it, all right, the beginning of what they call the Siege of Salt Cove.

The name came from Custer, not *Newsweek,* by the way. I was standing right by him, and we both heard three long steady blasts of a car horn, real methodical and intentional, from the other side of the bridge as some car went down Monroe Street. He looked at me and nodded kind of grimly and said, "That's it. That's the signal. They're on their way. Something went wrong. The siege of Salt Cove has begun. Be sure to get some good shots."

I nearly said, "Listen, dimwit, I know what I'm doing here, do you?" then realized he was only encouraging me, not criticizing. Which I always do when young photographers ask me for advice, like how did I turn pro so young? I always encourage. Cause you never know. And that was when—I remember I looked at my watch, 8:08 A.M.—three police cars come ripping down the hill from the Village Hall toward us.

I just had time to make sure both other cameras were fully loaded and ready for bear. I saw Toby Longhair grimace and move forward through the crowd, and I realized there had to be pushing a hundred fifty people milling around on the bridge, more if you included the ones arriving every minute. We was toward the village side, him and me, and he was going to go speak to the police. That was when I knew I should've taken that leak in the bushes cause I was about to get real active. I caught up to him and moved quickly ahead and to the side since the money shot was maybe going to be on his expression too when the big confrontation happened.

When I saw the orange state engineers' truck come down the hill with another police car behind, and a black sports car with dark windows scream in behind it, and trouble in uniform started to get out of the vehicles, I got busy and started shooting. There was plenty of sunlight on the faces, and kind of a human chain forming at the edge of the bridge where a few months ago they'd been laughing in the rain and angry and tearing up that sign like a flimsy overgrown weed. And though I have to admit, when I saw the shots I got later that day I felt I did just as good a job as anyone could have done, truthfully, pretty soon into that morning I didn't feel much like a pro at all.

24

Scott Mahren

You win lose, you some some. Learned that in school. But get this straight: when the Wily Scativo decides to walk the road of revenge, even on someone else's behalf, when he chooses the warpath, he walks it straight to the bitter end. The rage of mere mortals is nothing against the determination of his cold, rigorous heart. He doesn't blink, he doesn't shrink, he keeps going until the gods give up. And anyone who tries to stand in his way is a chump waiting to die. Which describes most of humanity, natch, most of the time.

Despite what you hear, the price is not right. The price of having titanic abilities is never right. What's so great about having a century to blaze alone in? All around me, the hungry sheep look up and are not fed; meanwhile the Scativo samples the rewards of the flesh and tries not to think too much about what else he might be doing to help the bleaters and the baa-baas. Until something tips the seesaw so far the wrong way that the W.S. cannot let it stand and still look himself in the mirror.

Still, where I live, when you talk about a Monday morning, early June, there's only regret, no matter how much revenge falls my way. Think I'm kidding? The Scativo does not kid.

So what happened is this. That morning I'm awake early, for the obvious reason. Newcomer, surprising repertoire, great concentration, which you'd never guess from a casual dialogue—anyway, I'm up early, and eventually en route solo to get the accomplice, Mrs. Milne, from her house. Past the bridge and harbor, nothing stirring but a few retired pedestrians and their yappy dogs, down along River Street past the curve, just before the river turns into the sea, a seriously mystical spot. One of the oldest houses in the village, blue with green shutters. Remind myself to ask who repointed her chimney.

I've got the black Z-car primed and ready. Got the plan streamlined and ready, even though I learned long ago that nothing ever follows a timetable perfectly, the most you can do is minimize wear and tear on the strategy and hope no one changes the street signs. Buddy named Whack, owes me a favor, going to meet us at Mill Cove, by the stone causeway in Willowdale. Basic plan: Whack does the blocking on the state truck while the old lady and I do the slashing. Been a sizable distance since I slashed tires professionally, but it's like riding a bicycle, you never forget, that's the beauty of having a useful skill, no matter how arcane.

And little Mrs. Milne, Leilia, is armed to the eyeballs. She buckles herself in like we're on a space launch, adjusts her wig—from the cancer radiation, I learned later—and empties onto her lap some felt sack grandma kept the family silver in. Now, she'd promised to bring her own cutlery, but I'm hardly expecting a set of weapons that would bring a tear to the eye of any serious connoisseur. She's got knives you could perform open-heart with, she's got knives you could skin a moose with. "Where'd you get all the hardware?" I ask, she just nods and says, "Professional secret," and gives a savory chuckle. Fair enough, her husband's a surgeon, or was, but this is still a woman who believes in carrying the right equipment for the job.

So we peel out of the village onto Monroe Street, curving to the causeway into Willowdale. Plenty of morning sunlight. On the right you can see way upriver to Salt Cove as far as the bridge and even the Scativo's lair, which is smack on the harbor, primo location. A ways ahead the river hooks to become a channel to the sea one way and branches toward Leicester the other. After a mile or so I hard-left into an overgrown lane, right before the stone causeway crossing the water of Mill Cove, turn the Z-car around, and park in position.

No time for chitchat with Leilia. She's got the plan straight, but I'd feel better if this were just Whack and me. I'm not saying women don't make effective agents, I've seen all the films, but I'm noticing there's a bad feeling in my gut. Learned a long time ago that when the Scativo intestines go flip-flop, things never turn out tip-top.

It's not the slashing I'm worried about, it's how fast she can get back in the Z-car when it's mission accomplished. I don't want to exactly stick around and play cards. We have to pull out and hang a left into town seconds before the state engineers get there, so Whack can pull out slow right after us in his junk van, stall, and block them and the entire road. She and I brake, jump out bang bang, right on their tails, do the deed, into the Z-car again, then we're gone toward Leicester. No one spots us in action except the cars waiting behind the engineers, but no one's going to follow us or weep for a couple of slashed back tires on a state truck. And maybe there won't be anyone close behind them at all, at this corner of the morning.

I'm going over the plan with Mrs. Milne step by step, I even make her repeat it back, and no surprise she grasps the idea quicker than Whack did on a dry run two nights before. By now it's ten of eight and we're idling by Mill Cove in some trees. I've got my driving gloves on and my own knife out, wiped it off for prints that morning in case it gets dropped. We're looking at an ETA for the pigeon of seven to ten minutes. And Whack's nowhere, it's starting to remind me of the time he was set to take the Scativo to the airport, en route to ten days of recuperation and inspiration in Acapulco, always had a soft spot for the tropical escapist cinema of the late '50s, and because of his ama-teur understanding of alarm clocks I missed my flight and got rerouted via Chicago and Denver, which is not my idea of a compro-mise. As the minutes ticked away on the Rolex submersible chronome-ter, limited edition by the way, I was forced to realize Whack just has a profound need to be screwing up. I'd made my recurrent error, of thinking people a shade better than they are, but it never fails—if you approach the world with enthusiasm and joy, you tend to get your eyebrows singed. Invent all the noble labor-saving devices you like, the columns still don't come out even.

So I was suddenly glad to have old Leilia with me. Unfortunately she didn't want to do the steering and let me do the slashing. Her excuses ranged from unfamiliarity with driving a standard (which I didn't believe) to not having her license with her (relatively minor infraction in terms of what we were about to do).

Now I have learned over the years, at substantial personal cost, that there are some women you can argue with and some you can't, just as there are benevolent dictators and then there are dictators. Maybe her age finally shut me up, maybe she reminded me a little too much of my own mother, thirteen years gone this February. Whatever the reason, I gave in. She'd slash, I'd drive. Mistake numero uno, because it put her in high gear, with dire results.

We had to fancy-footwork the plan. The new version, which I went over till she got annoyed, was this. The Scativo lies in wait in the Z-car for the engineering chumps to come along. Leilia takes a stroll on the stone causeway, pretends to be eyeballing the ducks while actually on ambush, like some cross-dressing samurai. Then I do the blocking, she does the slashing. I convince her to stash her personal arsenal under the passenger seat, lend her my knife, think better of that, we find her a switchblade in her felt sack.

By now it's a few minutes after eight, and she's hopping mad, really hopping. Armed and dangerous, too. One of those people who take it personally when they can't find a parking place; the blood pressure must be sky-high. Just let me at those sons of bitches and so on. It always worries me to hear a woman speak like this, I'd much rather someone about to walk a tightrope be chatting about the weather. I try to cool her off a bit, then push her out of the Z-car. And in the nick of time, since here comes the orange state truck with the seal of the Commonwealth of Massachusetts in blue and white on its side, like a bull's-eye from this distance, heading over the causeway.

At this point, as in so many human events, it's all a question of timing. Not only can you thread the needle, but can you do it in three seconds? Before the chumps figure out they've got a pint-size dynamo on their tail, going to the mat with cancer but hardly out for the count, and ready to shish-kebab the enemy for her own peace of mind? Not that it matters, but as a teenager in Jersey, before the fruitful activity of a unique talent enabled me to change cultural zip codes, so to speak, which is why I still love this country, let's just say before the Scativo turned Wily, I'd seen the old block-and-tackle run a few times by some true artists of the genre, not that the Scativo ever pursued such a course of action. You time it right, every move looks innocent, one of those annoying traffic misunderstandings that happen every day. And fortunately there was no car in front of the state truck, so it was easy to time perfectly.

As I pulled out, right into their path, and hit the brakes like someone scared he'd done the wrong thing but so jumpy that he'd made it much, much worse by halting middecision—and yet enough in front so there was no danger of them actually hitting the fabled black Z-car—I thought, Man, this world is filled with charlatans, just chockfull of goombahs like a quarter dispenser at the grocery store is full of gum balls, but among the multitudes, and you can carve this in stone, baby, the Wily Scativo remains the real thing, a phoenix at liftoff. Flap your wings and burn your way to glory. . . .

That thought lasted about a rapid half second, because I hadn't reckoned on three police cars just behind the state truck, separated only by some fat guy in a blue Volvo, the kind of boat-shoed idiot who'd rather run you down than spill his coffee. But even with him between the engineers and their cop escorts, at that instant I knew there was no play. The hand we'd been dealt was dead, no sense laying down chips on a sucker bet, the only thing to do was let it go.

I waved to the engineer chumps, who'd pulled up short, and shifted out of there to let them pass. My window was down, and as I straightened out on the narrow causeway toward town I shouted to Leilia, on the opposite side, "Okay, time to go! No more snapshots! Time to go!"

Only around here would three police cars think absolutely nothing, rolling blithely past, of the sight of an enraged bloodthirsty woman, the size of a hotel minibar and about the same shape, jumping up and down waving a knife—the sun kept glinting on it, sailors must've spotted her signal down in Boston—and yelling at the top of her voice, "Come back, you state bastards! Come back and fight like men! Come back and take what's coming to you! I'll carve your lungs out! I'll dice you, nerve by nerve!"

Strange what goes through your mind. I found myself thinking that the woman was not only tactless but probably a gourmet cook as well, and maybe I'd invite her and her sawbones husband over for a little cordon bleu with a date of choice for the Scativo. A core mark of a civilized man is to be able to prepare a great culinary evening, and it's even better alongside a young lady wearing an apron and nothing else—I love the way those loops look in back. This is why I find restaurants such a letdown; it always tastes better at home.

So I'm on the causeway, shouting at Leilia to get in, cars starting to back up and honk rudely behind me. By now the state truck is gone, the fat chump in the Volvo is gone, the three police gunsels are gone, and I'm blocking people late for work. At the first opportunity I make the swift U-turn, put the flashers on, leap out, grab her and shove her in the passenger seat. She's yelling at the world in fairly graphic terms. I don't even bother to try to discuss the blade she's brandishing, much less take it away. I might've been arguing at first, but then I realize the best move is to join in and yell exactly what she's yelling, which calms her down enough for me to strap on her seat belt. Then I'm quick round the other side and we're tearing out of there, back toward Salt Cove. The knife is gone now and I figure she's dropped it in the car, which is fine by me. I like my passengers disarmed.

"I could've had them!" she's still yelling. She's got her window down, she's yelling at the road, at the trees and the houses flashing past through the leaves, at some poor sap out walking his dog, at me. Mostly at me. "The police would never arrest Leilia Milne! Think I'm scared of the police? You've got another think coming, buster! I'm paying their salaries! What do I care if they arrest me? Let's see your goddamned cuffs, officer! I'm dying already, you ugly brutes, you can't hurt me! Plus I'm a doctor's wife, you just try to arrest my black ass—" and so on. She's not the slightest bit Negroid, not that I can see, as white bread as they come, which just proves my theory that most Americans who were adults in the 1960s subconsciously equate social injustice, standing up for your rights, and getting trompled on no matter what, with being black. I can't imagine why.

Anyway, once she grasps not only that we failed to stop them but that—through no fault of our own, as I do my best to communicate—they're about to attack her beloved wooden bridge, the wild battle stare comes into her eyes again. Reminds me how sometimes you're lying in bed with a lovely woman, you're both sweaty and sated, suffused with an inner glow, then she starts telling you her life story as if it's all perfectly reasonable, and you look over with trepidation and find her head spinning round and flashing like a siren. Maybe it's the unexpected police cars up ahead that made me think of this, or the fact she's yelling, "Hurry up! We've got to stop them! I marched in Washington! I marched in Boston! I'm not afraid of those cucumbers!"

Well, they don't mold them like Leilia Milne too often these days; I'm half wondering if she might have a granddaughter coming up through the ranks. So I step on it partly to oblige her and partly because I figure it might downshift her, maybe even shut her up. When we pass this end of the bridge I can see the big septic truck lodged in place, blocking any approach, and through the leaves I can just make out bodies on the bridge, but then we're gone and I'm giving the three-horn signal to let Toby know we've failed.

Of course the police chumps ahead of us, and the engineering dorks ahead of them, had stopped to regroup at the bottleneck by the church where you make the sharp turn into Salt Cove. By the time they reach the center of the village and head down that little street toward the bridge, we're tearing in right behind them—the W.S. nearly rear-ended a cop vehicle, which would not have been a wily move. Before I can stop Leilia, she's out of the Z-car and I'm trying to take in the scene through the windshield. Like one of those Japanese epics where you round the corner of the village and there's suddenly several hundred peasants shouting and thundering and waving their damned bamboo poles. Except this isn't in black and white.

Picture this: from the Village Hall looking down the hill, the bridge looks nearly full of people. Amazing what forty minutes can do to a situation. You'd think they got bussed in as paid votes for an election. People are shouting and there's that excited murmur of a waiting crowd, you can see the cop cars made an impression, like always. The same as having a stepfather in a lousy mood standing in the doorway.

I'm trying to catch up to Leilia, who's headed down the hill—you do acquire a sixth sense for when something is about to go grievously wrong. Up ahead the state engineers in their stupid blue jumpsuits are trying to look like they know what's what. They've opened up the two big doors at the back of their truck but they're not exactly doing anything, just standing around with their hands on their waists, as if they're trying to figure out how to shift the mob off the bridge so they can get to work. Really they're already thinking about lunch. Several police are lumbering around this end of the bridge, and one is talking to Toby Auberon, who even from here is looking troubled on the outside but smiling on the inside, shaking his head with what almost looks like sincere concern. ("It's not my fault, officer, it's called the right of assembly" is what he was saying, it turns out.) Another cop, with sandy hair—he took off his cap and wiped his forehead with the back of his arm—is squinting toward me, frowning. And another is loping down the hill.

That's the one Leilia goes for. Because she slowed down I thought she only wanted to join the crowd on the bridge, and maybe give the engineers a piece of her mind along the way. It also occurred to me she might try to slash their tires right now just to prove a point. I was thinking I ought to run and stop her, since it wouldn't do any good now. But then she screams at the cop's back, "You leave my bridge alone!" and she raises both fists, to pummel him I'm sure. I don't believe she intended to do anything else but whack him on the shoulders, but the other fist had her knife in it, and what happened was the sun caught the blade full. It was like this blinding dagger of steel sun, it flashed even in my eyes forty feet behind her, and seemed to explode all over the cove.

To the policeman at the edge of the bridge looking uphill this way, next to the one talking to Toby, it must've seemed like this woman screaming her head off was about to stab his partner in the back—she probably looked like one of those Apache wives in a vintage western who leaps on the horse and cuts the cavalry's throat all in one motion. And without hesitating he drew and fired, and whether he intended to hit her in the leg, as he should have, or in the shoulder, as he said he did, his shot blew her head apart.

I'm not exaggerating; I threw away a black linen shirt from Milan that had some of old Leilia's brains on it, and believe me, the Scativo tried to get it cleaned properly, with the idea of wearing it in homage to a rare woman. There was no question of an ambulance, even though one was called. There was no way that body twitching faintly on the ground, blown back a few feet uphill in my direction, was going to have any life to it, and a couple of minutes later, it didn't. By that time her husband had run over and was cooing like a gentle bird to her, or what had been her, in his arms, but she didn't hear a word of it, and pretty soon she stopped twitching.

You'd think that in a situation like this people would be fleeing in blind terror from the police, imagining there might be more shooting, but most people just stood their ground on the bridge. A few villagers came forward, including Toby, but this horrified silence descended on everyone as they realized what had happened. A bit later I saw a cop talking with one of the engineer chumps, and I saw them both nod, and when the state truck fired up and pulled away, a weird roar went up from the crowd, like it was torn out of a wounded animal's throat. As it turned out, the engineers hadn't closed the back doors of their truck properly, and some equipment fell out near the church, but we didn't know that till after. But when I heard the roar, I knew this was just the beginning, and as we all saw, Leilia's death united the village in a way it would've never been otherwise. So, in the end, she got what she wanted, and not a day goes by that the Wily Scativo does not honor her courage, and drink to her memory. Not that any of this meant squat to her husband; when they broke her they broke him.

The other thing that happened was the switchblade that Leilia had been holding, that she must've dropped when she was hit, was never found, like it got flung away from her as she fell. A couple of people said they saw it go through the air, and it certainly would've made the government side of things less complicated if they'd found the knife. But they never did, not amid all the hubbub, and they never found the rest of her arsenal hidden under the passenger seat of the Z-car, since they never searched it. Never searched me at all, come to think of it.

25

Harold Milne

. . . NOW IT'S HAPPENING now it's happening what did I just see please God get out of my way I'm a doctor I can do get out of my way something anything now it's happening to me. There she is and I can't do anything. Oh my darling.

Crowded around me in this air, ghosts of all who are and were. Staring over my shoulder at her blood seeping down into the road, no earth will ever soak it up, remember your first surprise at how much blood came out of a body, some nameless corpse more than a half century ago. And you got home and told her and she said *More fluid than ever went into it, that's for sure,* which meant a child on the way, David on the way, call him in Flagstaff and have him call the others. I should never have let you this morning, what was I thinking, who could ever argue with you, I never could. I'm a doctor and I can't do anything, this isn't even my darling anymore. Someone turned her into a thing, one of those things beyond hope they bring in so we can shake our heads and go tell the next of kin it just wasn't possible. This is my defiant darling spattered on the road, this is the hand that shook out my shirt this morning.

No don't call an ambulance, no don't speak to me, just leave us alone, go away all of you, leave us in peace, give us one more minute, no I don't want your official hand on my shoulder, I don't want your shoes in my field of vision, I just want you to leave us alone. Apologize? Apologize? Sir, you must be mad. We will all go mad. You're correct, you cannot tell me how sorry you are. God help you if you or your family ever come on my operating table. Yes, sir, that stench is the last stench of my wife, the sight of her and the stench of her may make you gag but this is what humans are, this is the last smell I will ever have of her, breathe deeply, sir, inhale a last enchantment from a woman whom your wives will never equal, not in ten generations or a hundred. And goddamn you keep that minister away from me, I don't want his wisdom or his prayers of goodwill, just leave us be, leave us alone with each other. Thank you. Thank you. See that, my darling? They heard me. Yes, that's better now. Yes, she's stopped breathing. That's her way of thanking you. No, I'll clean it up. Please don't try to lead me away. I can clean Leilia Stewart Milne off the road, she'd want it to be me, you know. All right, I'll come, I'll come. You see, my darling, that was all the time together they let us have.

26

Jessica Stoddard

I HAVE SPOKEN earlier of the unruly gyroscope of the world being so often off-kilter. It still weighs on me heavily that, had Leilia not died that day, all things would have been different: between my village and the nation, between myself and Toby Auberon. Our revolt might have gone unbloodied; my "affair"—how I loathe that word, but the language will not give me lifelong syllables worthy of all I am trying to say, the sunstruck, brazen music of a never-foreseen morning—with Toby might've remained unventured, might never have happened. (Unbloodied sheets, my niece would insinuate, thinking she knows me better than she does.)

And when I give myself godlike powers, the ability to challenge destiny and arm-wrestle it to my will—what my father, in my youth, told me lawyers sometimes refer to as *condition contrary to fact*—I am unable, candidly, to say whether I would reverse the events of the morning and of the evening to come. Look me in the eye and I will tell you that I would gladly give up a toe to have Leilia's life back, or even a few more months before the inevitable; but maybe if she'd been merely wounded in the shoulder, let's say, the rest could still have happened, I'd be giving up a digit and nothing else. The truth is, I gladly replay much of that day over and over to feel its surge again, to relish all it gave me. Perhaps I am being too honest here.

Leilia's murder changed everything. No exaggeration: from this point on every gesture, every chance remark, every whisper of intent that occurred in Salt Cove was under public scrutiny. Her memorial service three days later, in the austere old Seamen's Church in the Portuguese Hill section of downtown Leicester—Leilia had quarreled years ago with the minister at the Salt Cove church—was attended by hundreds. Toby and I sat together with Italo in the second pew, behind the immediate family. A cadre of sober policemen occupied the very back and were raggedly booed as they filed in. (An investigation of her death had already been ordered, but—no surprise—with oncoming events it got back-burnered for months, and was never concluded.) Harold drifted past us all like a sleepwalker stuck in a relentless dream, wearing a wrinkled blue suit and a crimson tie that one of their daughters had had to knot for him, his thatch of straw hair flopped messily sideways. I wondered if he'd read the editorials— the one blaming it on excessive movie violence creating a pistol-toting society, the other blaming it on "an upstart community" (that was us) and "regretfully" on Leilia herself. Words like hissing insects, nothing more; the murmur of innumerable bees.

Even the minister, a peering man with no link to our village, spoke of the "cruel crime that robbed her from us" before going on to the usual palaver about God knowing what's best and having His own laundry list of reasons for wanting her early. It was all I could do to stop myself standing up and telling him off. Only the implication that our cause was just, and Toby's shushing hand, kept me mute and inglorious. We knew Leilia was on her way out and might not have lasted another year; given the choice she'd have readily laid down her life to help our cause. But she thought the will of God was crap, and I doubt she'd have wished her husband's last moment with her to be kneeling on Drawbridge Street, trying to cradle her destroyed skull in his arms.

When my father slipped away my hand was stroking his gray unshaven cheek in a hospital room not three miles from here, a mere hundred yards from the ward where he'd been born—where I was born, too. Queer to think he went all the way through life and only shifted one floor up; the soul progressed just a stairwell higher and down the corridor a ways. I remember saying to myself, having turned forty-eight a week before, *There goes the last of the Stoddard men, like the last of the Mohicans; too late for me, now*—with a suspicion my niece would never carry on the bloodline with a child either, and doing my futile best to forget the sensation two months earlier of identifying the mangled bodies of her mother and father, sliced up by Pontiac parts and a massive elm in the wrong place by the wrong road. Not a week has gone by in the ensuing years when I have not swallowed the miserable fact that had the elm's seed come up a few feet to the left my sister would still be alive. It was even closer on Leilia's bullet, so the question of death or life is a matter of inches—or centimeters, if God has finally switched over. I watched Harold at the memorial service running down the same logic with a dull stare on his face, as if still waiting for the gorilla in the corner, the Almighty everyone kept invoking, to stop peeling another banana and change his mind, to take it back for once.

I'd been one of the many clustered on the bridge that day, interviewing people and scribbling my notes, but with no vantage point. I heard the shot and saw only the aftermath. My war time in Korea, nineteen months at a field hospital, had shown me even worse, but those were never people I'd known for many decades. At least I had the good grace not to disturb Harold, not to try to lead him away from the only place on earth he wanted to be. And I would have let him ride in that ambulance, not urged him into a police car with the colleagues of his wife's murderer.

It took two hours for everything to settle. The police dutifully taped off part of Drawbridge Street leading down to the bridge, and would've sectioned it off entirely had they not realized they'd end up with a riot on their hands. A number of older Salines wandered home in shock, but a good eighty people on the bridge weren't budging, and the Cove Market did a brisk business selling luncheon sandwiches from a few hundred yards along River Street.

After the ambulance left and a couple of city workers did their best to clean up the gore, the police drove away except for two officers who had to stoically stand there and take it for the rest of the morning while some of us came up and screamed at them. Amazing the things people say now, things no one thought of even back in the sixties. It made me realize how impoverished my imagination is; I'd personally never taunt a cop by calling him *amoeba-dick breath*, and it made it worse that she was desirably young and blonde.

Sometime that afternoon the two police gave up, after the crime investigator took photos. Once they drove off we tore the forbidding yellow police tape down, and everyone let out a cheer. Toby, who'd remained throughout the day and did a good job holding Roscoe back, went round making sure we'd have at least thirty squatters on the bridge bright and early the next morning. Then he went home without a word to me. The photographer from the *Leicester Daily News*, who'd handed off rolls and rolls of film by nine A.M. to a stable-lad assistant who drove up and delivered an infusion of more film, kept shooting for hours, but he too eventually left—his job well done, for his pictures (including ones the whole country came to know) filled the front page and an inside spread of the paper later that afternoon, along with a muddled story by the tardy reporter who'd arrived sheepishly along with the extra film. The first television crew from Boston showed up just in time for lunch.

At four I staggered home and fell asleep on my sofa until early evening, when I was jostled by a humid breeze and finally awoke to a rapping. I peered at my father's small wristwatch; it was nearly eight thirty, still barely light out. A messy sheaf of the day's notes lay on a table beside me. I couldn't remember why I felt so exhausted, then I remembered Leilia. Another determined flurry of knocks, I hadn't dreamed any of it. I went to the kitchen door, rubbing my neck, and to my surprise Toby was there, waiting like a cat to be let in.

Up till now he'd never been alone with me in my house. In shuffling to the kitchen I'd assumed it must be Mitch, or a police detective. Either way, I didn't bother to check a mirror, nor did I intend to tell them everything I knew. I opened the door, expecting someone else, anyone else, and there he stood, bathed in the supernatural glow of my amber no-insects light, which dusk turns on automatically above the kitchen door. Beyond him was the tumble of rocks that edge the Smithson property, and a blue wedge of sea rapidly turning to slate as twilight settled in.

"Jessica." The abject music of my name. Surprised at how hard he'd had to knock. "I hope I'm not disturbing you."

"Come on in, Mr. A.," I quipped feebly. "Let me show you my slogans."

He blinked, unsure how to take this. By now in our relationship he must've realized that I only ever say what I mean, one way or another.

"Not slogans we need," he muttered as I bolted the door, for the first time in years, behind him. "Not after this morning. Did you watch the news?"

"Nope. Did you?"

"How could I?"

Still between TV sets? "Well, it'll be repeated at ten."

He said, "It's my fault there weren't news teams on the bridge. If they'd caught poor Leilia on film the state wouldn't have a chance."

He was, I realized, boiling with compressed fury. He knew full well that none of this would've happened if not for him; we'd never have fought back this way, our bridge would be gone, but she would still be alive.

"It's not your fault," I said.

He shook his head and glared at me. "A woman gets murdered because of a selfish government, that ought to at least achieve something. This won't be an unavenged crime, I promise you that. I've seen too many of them."

"Have you eaten dinner, Toby?"

"I don't want to put you to any trouble. Look, I can come back in time for the news—"

Trouble? Trouble is my middle initial! I practically sang. Getting it wrong, of course. In fact I have no middle name, thanks to my father seeing too many clients saddled with the nominative weight of ancestors. And it occurred to me that, were she here to witness it, my niece Sarah would undoubtedly be jealous at seeing this man ablaze, alone, and at large in the kitchen with me; that the day might come when Molly Mellew would open her sleepy eyes to him in a way that would

be hard for any male to resist; that Mildred, had she known my sala-
cious thoughts, would utterly disapprove; that, without having to
count on either my fingers or toes, I had zero female allies. But, anyway, here he was, standing wonderfully beside my stove at the end of
a horrible day, the worst our village had ever known. Don't mind me,
I'll just manacle you to the kitchen table and get out the hot sauce.

"No trouble at all," I said. "Perfect timing, in fact. Stick around,
we'll see what those reporters did with the truth."

I took out three hamburger patties and got them started.

"I won't argue, Jessica." *Was that a promise?* I saw him wrinkle his
nose like a field mouse sniffing the wind as I added my special
touches. Despite his vegetarian appearance, I knew he was a meat
eater.

"The dash of curry makes it," I said.

He stared through me. "Did the police speak to you?"

"Not yet. If they ask, I'll tell them I was looking in the other
direction."

"They spoke to Harold. And Scativo. And me. A few others.
Everyone chose the same story, luckily. She went for a morning ride
with a friend, and that's it. Scativo was totally convincing. No one saw
a knife on her. It still hasn't turned up. All a terrible police misunderstanding."

"Tell that to Leilia's children." I saw I wasn't making it any easier
for him. "With luck the police will be stuck in a corner explaining this
for weeks."

"In L.A. her body would've been riddled with bullets. That's the
advantage of living in the country." I saw bitterness cross his face, like
someone ruefully setting foot on the foreign soil of the past.

I said, "You know, I was the first person she met when she and
Harold moved here. My father handled the purchase of their house.
They didn't know anyone, she already had one daughter and another
child on the way. We gave them an old sofa that every one of their
children used as a launching pad." The idea of that sofa unexpectedly
put me on the verge of tears; or maybe it was the curry. I turned
toward the stove and recovered my composure.

He said gently, "Perhaps I'd better come back."

"Don't be ridiculous." I thought for an instant that he was about to put his arm around me. Even for the wrong reason, an arm is an arm. "It's just not something you see every day. I haven't seen it for years."

I did not specify the war in Korea; it all seems a long time ago now and I did not want to sound dated, even though I know that is not exactly the word.

He said, "I haven't either. Not since—" He stopped himself. "Not since I did volunteer work."

(Not since he'd worked four years in Los Angeles as a public defender, having first worked a couple of years for the feds as Assistant U.S. Attorney, and gotten fed up. I found out the details of all this later, after much prying and a few phone calls, plus a look at his journals. But then again I did not turn over all my cards, either. As if it were a game between us, with someone keeping score, and a winner and a loser.)

I said, "You know, if it comes down to witnesses, I spoke to a lot of people who did see what happened. Look, come look at what I've done."

I ushered him into the dining alcove that opens out to my big living room with its view of the sea, where the computer on my dining table was asleep, not winking with its all too knowing eye. Each week it had grown more encircled by paper barricades that were mounting higher and higher, my notes like walls piled against an inevitable attack—odd scribblings on junk-mail envelopes; flipback notebooks bought in bulk at a church sale years ago, I'd filled three that day; and large red ledgers, the golden year embossed on the spine, where I kept my finished minutes of the Village Hall meetings, to be transferred into the computer. Most years these ended up barely used, so little happens. Now, for once, I was filling the pages.

He glanced at the current one, propped open beside the computer, and flipped over a few pages, not really reading, but trying to assess the me he saw in my handwriting. Even during those distant eras of the manual typewriter and the electric typewriter, followed briefly by the electronic typewriter, writing remained primarily a handmade thing for me. Touching pen to paper, the long caress of word upon word interrupted only when the nib hesitates in expectant bliss between them, is the closest thing I know to sensual rapture, even when you do not like what you just wrote.

My father, also, was an amateur graphologist. He often saw evidence of clients' personalities in their signatures, though this was informed guesswork, not sound analysis of script, since he already knew them. Curiously, Toby's attention to my handwriting reminded me of the shard of autobiography he'd let slip twice earlier: that he'd at least set out to become a lawyer.

He confirmed it by saying with approval, "You're very thorough. You'd make a good legal secretary."

"My father always said so, too. I helped him when I was a young woman. You know where his office was. In Leicester."

"Do I?"

"You've passed the building. An old sea captain's home. Across from the library. The little house in the middle."

"Right, right." He added, "Your handwriting is very difficult to read. But I see my name here and there."

Shall I describe to you, I thought, the pleasure my stroking pen takes in writing your name? Long version and short alike? I felt a stab at what he might've been about to decipher. Like all the best historians, I occasionally express more than I intend.

"It's not as simple as it looks. I try to set down exactly what people say at these meetings." I frowned. "Sometimes this leaves me in a quandary."

"I'm not surprised."

"Suppose I write word for word"—I tapped the large red ledger in which I'd fallen one significant meeting behind—"what Scativo and Leilia planned? Suppose the police subpoena my ledger? You see the danger."

"Have you written that in already?" He was turning pages, fascinated for some mysterious reason since he obviously couldn't make out what I'd written. I see now it was a sense of my doing my own work in private as he was doing his, though believe me, I could never have undertaken a serious historical account of the siege had I not seen his Machina Excelsior and realized what he was sacrificing on its behalf, for he is someone who would do well anywhere. If I have any courage these days, evidenced by the labor of these pages, it is because of his example, because I know he would want me to finish this, against all odds.

I said, "I've got my rough notes of that meeting. Here." I showed him a sheaf of papers underneath my father's heavy dictionary, 1958 ed., which I use not to look up words but to keep loose papers from rattling in a breeze.

I added, "But I haven't transferred them properly into this big red thing. So I could leave out the whole tire-slashing plan."

"I would, if I were you."

"Is that a properly considered legal opinion?"

"That's the advice of a friend. Are those hamburgers okay?"

They were sizzling so loudly in the kitchen, when he pointed it out, it was strange I hadn't noticed.

While I dealt with them and got the salad ready, Toby remained in the other room. There is nothing I can do, I told myself, if he reads what I've written so be it, if that's how he learns, via the hopeful loops and swirls of my handwriting, of all the feeling that lies behind every word I write, then so be it.

But when I went to check on him, the meal under control, he was staring out at the water. He said, so angrily it shocked me, "Can you believe those bastards? They take one look at this view and say to themselves, *What this place needs is an ugly fucking concrete bridge, that's the answer.* Beauty always scares people in power. And it's not enough to stop them. We have to punish them till they writhe in agony, or next year they'll try it again."

It was thrilling to see him so ready to explode.

I said, "You're right, they should be punished. And they mustn't be allowed to succeed."

He swallowed. "Oh, they won't succeed. Whatever it takes, they won't succeed, I promise you that. They have no idea what they're up against." I saw his Adam's apple bobbing; he was too furious to speak. The lawyer in him, aware he might utter more than was effective.

I said quietly, "You're going to need all your strength. Dinner is served, finally. We'll eat in the kitchen."

I feel I should interject an apology in what has, up till now, been a fairly cold-eyed recounting of our conversation that evening. No, we did not dissolve in a pool bubbling with illicit passion, like one of those hot tubs you see in the movies. But we did gradually find ourselves talking in a more personal way, over those curry burgers, than we ever had before. He seemed genuinely curious about who I was and what I thought; it may have been some antidote to seeing Leilia killed. Though I didn't point this out, for me exactly fifty years had passed since I'd enjoyed (there is no other word) that mixture of relief, terror, and a biting sorrow which is also sheer stunned permanent joy in knowing that death has come awful close but, for its own reasons, passed you by. No, nothing gets the juices flowing like that peculiar sensation of *not yet, not this time, at least I'll wake up tomorrow morning. Someday I won't.*

And I found myself talking more than I intended about my father. Toby started it by asking a few apparently idle questions about that broken pinball machine in the garage, questions I naïvely brushed aside. It had been a decent time since I'd spoken much of my father, but I was with someone who never knew him and was also interested. I always feel that people who talk incessantly of their parents, whether in praise or damnation, are really making excuses for something they themselves did not achieve. Falsifying the distant past by giving it too much credit for what the present has become, unloading responsibility off their own shoulders. I believe it is up to us to shape the flow of time, and thus to pretend that the world is not made new again, every day, is a way of rejecting the only offer granted us on a regular basis. Like turning down a gift, but then plenty of people I know spend their time shuttling to a mall twenty miles up the highway, standing in line to exchange what they found so excitedly the other morning, perpetually inventing excuses. Personally, I never take anything back.

I told Toby how my father had come perilously close to financial ruin by being so lax about getting clients to pay. He was a neat man except in his office finances, with a gentle mouth and inquisitive forgiving eyes. I often told him he would look dashing if he grew a mustache like those early romantic movie actors, and people would not be so inclined to take advantage of him.

"He always argued," I said, serving Toby another bowl of my

trademark salad (the usual suspects, plus avocado, Vidalia, cilantro), "that a lawyer has a responsibility, whether he likes it or not, to do his best to keep the knots of society in place. He felt people have a continental drift toward injustice, especially in cities. He thought the 'just city' was the highest ideal a civilization could accomplish, and how you build it is the great problem of mankind. To him it was remarkable that beavers can accomplish what we can't."

"Still," said Toby, "they aren't doing it on such a large scale, are they?"

"He always compared it to weaving a carpet," I went on. Oh well—the beavers were my idea, not my father's. "And the lawyer's role was making sure the knots didn't loosen and unravel. Because only he understood, better than any other profession, how the carpet got tied together. Part of what this meant for a local lawyer was not going after people who didn't pay."

I was, I admit, trying to goad him. Ever since my rueful journey to Istanbul, I always respect my instincts, and I knew one side of him wished we would all leave him alone at whatever he was doing in his lighthouse lair, even while another side was tying his ponytail and girding his loins for battle on our behalf. Like my father, this was a man who knew the minds of many men and of cities too. However, he also wished to withdraw from that knowledge, to rinse his tonsils in his private sea and let the rest of the world go hang.

And much as I respected the dreamer in his lighthouse—my God, I was ready to tie him to my kitchen table, leave him here breathlessly waiting, and go break into the place to find out what on earth he was doing on those many upstairs levels, then hurry back here and find him still tied down; perhaps I'd make him wait even more breathlessly while I tormented him by doing the dishes first, or maybe on the other hand I'd let the dishes wait—anyway, as much as I respected his purposeful solitude, I wanted him to know we were all counting on him, a village doing its best to be just. And that I personally, not to mention the lawyerly ghost of my father, felt he was doing the right thing and no less than what he must do, as a man of most uncommon ability.

Never mind that everyone else, myself included, had until three months ago thought him another unwashed hippie. You can't expect society to simply wake up and see what's obvious to the ones who aren't heavily sedated. At that first fateful meeting I had looked at him and abruptly realized there was a bridge between us; maybe it was only a lucky trick of the light that changed everything. But the world was never the same for me afterward.

By now we'd moved on to coffee ice cream, which I make in the orthodox way, by taking vanilla ice cream and mixing a teaspoon of instant coffee granules with it—thus you can have decaf ice cream if you wish to ignore your responsibility to a free society and go immediately to sleep. I was glad to see Toby was not so inclined, and I expressed my regret that I didn't have any fresh mango slices to go with the caffeinated ice cream. If I have done nothing else in life I have invented this one recipe of sheer genius.

"It's the most sensual dessert I know. Sorry I can't offer it to you tonight, Toby."

He smiled at me. "Gives me an excuse to come back for more."

I felt like hurling my seltzer glass into the fireplace and yelling *Bravo, banzai, damn the torpedoes* or whatever it is you sing out lustily when the inert crystal of your life gets joyfully shattered in the heart's smelting crucible.

He said, "I understand what your father meant." He hesitated, took another spoonful of ice cream; I watched the caffeine claw grip his features. "Don't tell anybody, but I actually practiced law for a few years."

"Don't tell anybody? Why on earth not? I guessed, by the way."

He shrugged. "Just superstitious. The less people know, the better. I was a federal prosecutor for a while. My clients were the alphabet soup. The INS, the FBI, the DEA. Lying criminals with badges, who get to fake evidence because they're the good guys. My final case was getting jerked around trying to clean up a corrupt California water board. So to wash the dirt from my soul, I became a public defender for even longer. Got sick of that, too."

"Sick of what? The lack of money?"

"The money didn't bother me. I was making more than my father ever had as an electrician." Once he got started, he seemed relieved;

no doubt he realized his secrecy had stood between us, though I also rather enjoyed it. "No, I got sick of—sick of the city not wanting to be just. Sick of working like a dog for a whole new set of clients. Clients who vomited on my shoes then told me they wanted a real lawyer. Sick of being treated like dirt by judges, and having crack dealers' wives hit on me or shit on me or fire me as soon as they found some money in a bedpost. Sick of people hating me whenever I told them they were wrong to want to bludgeon the other guy. How usually the only viable answer was for everyone to lose. Be defeated a little. Suffer a little. That's what makes a city just, but no one wants to hear it. Plus I'm selfish. I decided there were things I wanted to do more than help people who were unbearable once they stopped being the underdog. So I gave up on the idea of ever working at a law firm, and I gave up on the just city. I decided—" He pulled up short, and I knew he was about to dissimulate, having revealed too much of the truth. "I decided I'd rather be left alone out in the unjust country, and get a lot of reading done."

"Still you persist," I said, taking another spoonful for dramatic effect and wishing I could cover his chest with the glistening orange of fresh mango slices, "still you persist in this absurd charade that you spend your whole time reading. Come on."

"You don't like books?" He was teasing, but I was too on pins-and-needles to go along.

"Of course I like them! I used to want to be a writer! Haven't you seen my bookcases?" I put down my trembling spoon; perhaps I shouted, then realized he was joking. Too late to take back what I'd said; too early to admit I was writing down all that was going on in Salt Cove, interviewing everyone and keeping notes far beyond the mere minutes of a meeting—my minutes had become many hours—with a growing sense this might all come to mean much more one day, my devotion would be vindicated. And if not, at least it gave me something to do, urged me to tweeze a slim grain of meaning from each day. In retrospect, it was Leilia's death that finally made up my mind, strengthened my wavering purpose.

"Well, then," said Toby Auberon, "you can understand, of all people."

I don't understand! I nearly cried aloud. I can read people's faces the way intelligent people read a newspaper, I look in your blue eyes and all I see there is determination, unwavering purpose, a clear view all the way to the horizon and an intention that hasn't budged for years. I look at your mouth and I only wonder. And you sit here slurping my coffee ice cream and raging away about the bridge and how you used to be a lawyer, then try to persuade me you're living in that lighthouse because it's easier to turn pages there?

"Of course I understand," I said. "You're not telling me the truth and nothing but the truth. That's all right, Toby. You will, eventually." And you'll come back for more coffee ice cream, too, I nearly added. And next time, I'll have plenty of ripe mango waiting.

"Maybe I will," he said quietly. "That was delicious, Jessica. Thank you."

I had spied, during my internal typhoon, the clock on my stove: five minutes of ten.

"Time for the news," I said. "We'll have to go in the living room. That's where I keep *my* television. I wish I had an extra to loan you." Actually, I did, upstairs, in my bedroom closet. A hedge against the winter flu that could lay me up in bed for weeks; at which point, my unread books exhausted, I would turn desperately to TV game shows. Thus my annual flu shot.

"That's all right," he said. "My big wraparound set is coming in any week now." And he knew that I knew.

The coverage of Leilia's death was discombobulating. *Local politics turns deadly!* was how the severe anchorwoman, with her prim disapproving mouth and a phony semi-English accent, introduced our segment. The morning's events were peculiar enough, and to see a man who resembled a mechanical pencil—same eraser haircut—give his live-from-the-battlefield report from our bridge, clearly filmed not moments but hours after Leilia's death, was jarring. I sat in one corner of the sofa (Toby, resisting the obvious, had pulled up a chair), and numbly watched the flickering images of Salt Cove go by. A flat, bleached, alternate reality. "That's what videotape does to a place," said Toby when I stammered my reaction. Maybe it was the megapixels which unsettled me.

Our stalwart reporter interviewed a wide-eyed little boy on the bridge who was shaken up, having come from East Leicester on the bus with his mom, who was hugging herself behind him. Mildred got interviewed and put in a good plug for our side by mentioning the bridge's long history, then finished with, "Leilia Milne was part of what makes this a special village. Like many who live here for much of our lives, she felt a responsibility to protect it. Her death diminishes us all." Which I believe was a quote from Winston Churchill, and gave the reporter the lump in the throat he was looking for.

He also interviewed one of the hapless cops, who tightened his jaw and said that at this time he wasn't at liberty to make a statement. The reporter, up from Boston for the afternoon and in a foul mood by now—Leilia's body had been taken away, there was only yellow police tape to show, and Harold was "in seclusion," though they monitored the house on River Street, naturally—asked the cop if it was the policy of Leicester's finest to fire on seventy-year-old female cancer survivors, which made the cop repeat his memorized nondisclosure word for word, the humiliation our reporter was looking for. He stared grimly into the camera and promised to return with breaking developments. Then the glottal anchorwoman reiterated that Salt Cove was "in a dispute with the state" over the bridge, in case viewers thought this only another aimless case of police brutality. She handed the ball to a twinkling movie reviewer, and I shut it off. No Toby in any of it, not even a glimpse.

"That guy interviewed me for ten minutes," Toby said sourly. "I took him through it step by step. And all he had to say was 'A local protest over an old bridge turns sour.' Guess I'm not telegenic enough."

"Nonsense. They don't want a political story. Let's see how they treat it on the news at eleven."

"Those other stations were even less thorough. With me, anyway. The question is coverage in the Boston papers. Reporters should be asking why the state wants a concrete bridge so badly, when Salt Cove doesn't."

"There'll be a memorial service for Leilia," I said. "A lot of attention will be paid then."

He stood up to go. "We need the right attention. The media will exploit this for their own reasons. We need to exploit it for ours. They may not coincide. I hate to be so crude, I know she was your friend."

"No, no." I stood up myself, a bit uncertainly. "Leilia would agree with you. She'd want us to exploit it, however we could."

"I'm sure we'll have people on the bridge for the rest of the week. The state won't come back until after her memorial. That'd look awful. So it's up to us to make our case to the public in the next few days."

"I'll do anything I can to help." I added, "I'm going to make a pot of tea," thinking he might stay.

He was moving inexorably to my kitchen door. My back-door man. He said, "I'm afraid I've got to get home."

This was crap. "Back to your reading?"

"Back to my overdue taxes."

This was a lie, also.

He said, "I wanted to ask a favor. Could you write an opinion piece for the local paper? And submit it to the *Boston Globe* as well? That's what we need, and it will mean a lot coming from you. With all your family's years here."

I said, nonplussed, "You remember that Italo did write a letter a couple of months back, and Mildred is really the finest historian we've ever—"

He said firmly, "Exactly why I want you to do it. Humor me. I know you'll do a great job, Jessica."

Humor me! He might as easily have said, *Agree to do my bidding forever, wench.* I envisioned surprise visits to the lighthouse (he claimed not to have a telephone of any sort, and it turned out that was not a lie)—discussions of this paragraph or that, disputes over niceties of punctuation, petty lovers' tiffs over a word here, a word there, finally an agreed-on, finished, mutual text. . . . "When do you want it, Toby?"

"The sooner the better." He smiled, a gleam of confidence that went through me. If he'd said, *Write me a sequence of sonnets tonight, darling, I want to enjoy them during breakfast,* I'd have plunged without an instant's hesitation right into the intricacies of masculine and feminine rhyme.

"Okay," I said. "I'd love to." Then—his hand was on the doorknob, he was about to thank me for dinner—I put my palm up, stopped him, scurried to the other room, scrabbled among my sheaf of papers for a heartbeat, and returned holding a page with my original notes of the speech he'd made at that first village meeting, back in March. I could not very well ask him to sign my words in the red ledger, but I could ask him to sign his own.

I had my favorite pen with me, tortoiseshell and gold. I also had my whole soul in my voice, for once in my life. I said, "Toby, you're *very* telegenic. That's what I think. Look, I wrote down everything you said. These are your words. Would you inscribe this for me?"

Handwriting never lies.

27

Danny Adler

THE MORNING WATCH
by Danny Adler, columnist, *The Boston Globe*

People sure talk a lot about democracy in this country. In the Information Age talk is cheaper than ever, and ideas you can sink your teeth into, like a hearty steak, are few and far between. But democracy in action is what a few curious bystanders have been witnessing in a village on Cape Sarah.

Salt Cove's a quiet, unassuming spot, about five miles by road from Leicester, the city it has to answer to. Don't get me wrong, I'm a fan of Leicester from way back. We like to take the kids on summer weekends. Fried clams. Ice cream by the Fisherman's Statue. Faint Hope Beach. Even a few down-at-the-heels antique shops for my better half. New England not quite as it used to be, but darned near close enough.

Seems Salt Cove has been in a flap with the city and the state over a two-hundred-year-old wooden bridge. For pedestrians only, since the part that used to carry cars has too many holes in it. Just like my favorite suede jacket.

Seems the state wants to replace the wooden bridge with something functional . . . and modern . . . and concrete. Progress in the Information Age.

By now you've heard about the protest there last Monday. Things turned ugly. An elderly woman was shot dead by a policeman in a tragic, cruel misunderstanding. (So far her relatives haven't sued, but lawyers must be banging down their doors to get in.) The protest was to stop a state wrecking crew, and it succeeded all week.

That's democracy, folks. Why? Because it's the will of the people involved, taking responsibility. We all brag about how you can up and move anywhere in this country whenever you like, no questions asked. The sad truth is, that doesn't foster much loyalty for a place you're living in temporarily.

I met an interesting feller up in Salt Cove, guy by the name of Toby Auberon. Doesn't own a phone, so don't bother trying to call. Look at him once, you'd put your hand on your wallet and expect he'll ask you to buy him a beer. Look at him twice and you might figure he's a wee bit shrewder than he makes out. The third time, you'll *want* to buy him that brew.

Dead ringer for an old-fashioned gunslinger from a black-and-white western, only pint-size. Talks like a pretty cool customer. Or maybe even a politician in the making.

According to Toby, the loose buzz circulating about a state "compromise" would involve—and you heard it here first—a narrow pedestrian walkway set into a wide concrete monstrosity. A few dozen planks like a pull-out board on a cement cheese platter.

When I asked if that might ever be acceptable to the villagers, Toby laughed. "If the state wanted to build a highway through your living room, would it go down better with you if it were only five lanes, not six?"

Calls from this columnist to the Office of Public Works were not returned. Surprised? As Salt Cove residents know much too well, they'll have to start their defense strategy all over again Monday morning.

Says local leader Toby Auberon, "The saddest part is that even after Leilia Milne's death, the state believes it should still destroy our bridge, just to prove that it's always right. This is how a beautiful place gets ruined. This is how politicians lose elections. This is how innocent people get killed."

Amen, brother. That's not chitchat, that's democracy at work. Too little, too late. Watch this space for news of the impending collapse of the republic.

Danny Adler's column is syndicated in over thirty newspapers throughout New England.

28

Allie Teague

IRATE? YOU THINK I'm acting unjustifiably irate? Believe me, you don't know from irate.

To start with, painters like me *made* this place. Take away Hopper and Fitz Hugh Lane and Winslow Homer and Stuart Davis, Avery, Prendergast, all the rest, and what have you got here? A bunch of lobster pots and belly-up fishermen with nothing to do but talk about the good old days. This is during the three months it's not raining or snowing, right? That's your cape, kids, and it took us painters to make it into something. Think about all the postcards you sell by dead artists.

For a year now, ever since last summer, I've been planning this. One whole year. It is not, by the way, particularly convenient to save that kind of money in Manhattan as a working woman.

The idea was to hit the place running, two weeks before the season, and rent the one-story cottage above Dunster Beach. The light, as any painter will tell you, is more varied and dynamic in June than July or August. September I can't speak for, because I have to be back at the Center; the guppies in my think tank need to flex their gills after Labor Day. So for me it's June, or nada.

The whole idea was to paint only in Salt Cove. An entire series based around that incredible bridge. A still-life at rest in a landscape. Do it totally uninhabited, since in June the local kids are in school, not hollering and jumping off it. And the summer people, who don't really show up till July 4th, haven't taken possession.

Am I making myself clear? A series of canvases of the wooden bridge at all times, with no one on it? Or maybe a lone figure ambling across. Or a stray dog on patrol through the village.

You asked how I feel. So let's nix the subtitles: I feel rooked. I feel hoodwinked, I feel misled, I feel totally cheated, usurped, waylaid and taken for a ride. Like a used paper towel, that's how I feel.

The Salt Cove realty office, right there in what (they never stop telling me, like it does me any good) used to be a tiny post office in one side of the Village Hall, kept in touch with me constantly. They knew, starting from well before they received my Thanksgiving deposit, exactly why I was coming. I explained that I am not some Sunday painter. I explained who I am, that my work has hung in prestigious group shows both in New York and outside the city. I explained that for six years I've rented somewhere different on Cape Sarah every June. Over on the Neck one year, in Beauport another—two weeks of sheer amateur hour—in Teal Bay, even in Leicester with old Fitz Hugh's immortal view of breakwater islands right there, filling my window.

A dozen times at least I explained to the village's dominant-alpha realtor Martha Hanson exactly, *exactly*, why I was coming and my intentions. How this is part of a multiyear project for me, it'll be a book eventually and a show this coming February on East 11th Street, of course they'll get an invitation. And I made it clear that though I intended to cover other views in Salt Cove—Dunster Beach at dawn and dusk, for example, or Baven Rock in the Meadow, it's so buffed with those shreds of a rusted ladder halfway up the granite face—my reason for coughing up more for two weeks here than I ever paid elsewhere was to be five minutes' walk from the bridge, the austere, naked, unadorned, *empty* bridge spanning Salt Cove. So I could paint it in every light, at every time of day, even at night, with no one else around.

Let me risk repeating myself. *With no one around.*

It's not easy getting out of Manhattan. Nothing in Manhattan is ever easy. It's not like the country where people are on your side automatically. It's not even easy organizing a rental car, not that it was any easier when Adam was around. He knew how to make everything complicated, it was his way of asserting his identity. By now I know how to comprehend an identity.

And it's not easy getting loaded up without a doorman to help you. By Connecticut you're ready to collapse, then the farther you get from the city the better you feel, by the time you cross into Massachusetts you're singing. In two hours you pass the sign that says *Welcome to Cape Sarah*, you can take a deep breath and feel the sea gulp in your lungs, just coursing through the ventilated rent-a-car air, all that salt stripping away a year of city grime on your neck and eyeballs. A few miles later you're in the village and winding over the hill and finally there's the cottage waiting, just like that morning the Hanson woman showed it, a key hidden at the back of the mailbox behind a new phone book as promised, everything ready to go. One expedition to the huge new supermarket over in East Leicester—open till midnight May through Labor Day, can you imagine?—and we're in business. Done deal, as Adam used to say.

Plan for Day 1 is daybreak: my first painting of the bridge. Back to the familiar ritual of prepping my brushes, paints, and canvas before bed, so I can make coffee and be out the door by dawn's early light.

Except this once I sleep in. Call it a well-earned breakdown for the most recent escapee from all the trials and tribulations, the divorce proceedings, the legal actions of Manhattan. I gift myself with a serene breakfast, midmorning I wander down to the bridge ready to work, and what do I find, on the first of my fourteen short days here? What do I find on every subsequent day all week, every time I show up, easel and colors in hand, trying to get some work done? What do I find, essentially destroying what I worked all year to come here for? Blocking my view?

I'll spell it out, slowly. What I find is wall-to-wall people protesting away, dozens every morning, a hundred by lunch, even a few camped out through the night. Politicized kids copulating in sleeping bags. *Free the bridge,* they chant every now and then. *Save the bridge.* You really want to save it? I want to howl. Let me paint it! Art can save anything! (Even a marriage, if both sides are mature grownups, not selfish feeding-frenzy Type A manipulators.) You want to unleash some power? Get out of my goddamned paintings!

One more week here, that's all I've got. *Eight days.* "We didn't imagine it would turn into this" is their excuse at the village realty. The accents around here are like sandpaper. Why didn't you say something? I implore, practically in tears. Don't I deserve a warning? You could've given my deposit back and found another tenant in a heartbeat. Instead you've stolen my whole year from me.

"Maybe it'll be different next week," they rasp. "There's talk of some agreement. Can't you paint something else? Like the beach by the lighthouse—"

Your heads are stuffed with cloud, I say, and all the paintings on your walls, bought obediently over in Beauport, are clichés, every last one of them. No, I cannot paint a lighthouse, thank you very much. I cannot even paint the flowers on my veranda looking down to Dunster Beach because when I tried that yesterday some military jet went shrieking overhead like it was strafing the village. Followed ten minutes later by two news helicopters. Thank God I'll be somewhere peaceful, like midtown Manhattan, in nine days. At least I'll be able to hear myself think.

"There's no need," they say, "to get rude, Mrs. Teague."

Rude? It's Ms. ex-Teague now, the name is Leland again, and if you think this is rude, apple blossom, get ready to wake up and smell the coffee, because I didn't come here to go home empty-handed, I promise you. Whatever it takes to get all these people out of my paintings, if there's someone I should speak to who I haven't yet, you tell me, and make it snappy. Because I tried to reason with some long-haired clown who everyone on the bridge said was in charge, and he looked at me like I was crazy. Gave me some crap about being able to work from a postcard like Van Gogh and Millet. So find someone else for me to reason with. Or else just tell me who to sue.

29

Jack Fowler

WHEN I MARRIED RACHEL, part of the understanding was we'd continue to live here. She is old enough, at twenty-six, to know what a contract is, what an agreement means, even an unspoken one. It means you keep it. I wouldn't have been able to make a living as one of the best—no, let's face it, the very best—roofers on the cape for, well, the entire length of her lifetime if I didn't understand what it means to keep my word.

It was the long black hair that did it. Falling in love—Jimmy used to say this to me when I was fifteen, apprenticed to him, running all over these roofs like I could never fall, he'd say this to slow me down and teach me to take care—falling in love is like going out on a roof. Walking the shingle tightrope, he called it. You think you're secure, you're whistling while you work, one foot slides out, before you know it you're not kissing a dame, you're kissing sky.

Long black hair, long legs, long slate eyes. The sight of her still has me kissing clouds. When we first got serious and she told me like it was a joke that her friends in school made fun of her for dating a man in his forties, I said, Look, I understand if you want to go off somewhere like Los Angeles. I've been to Los Angeles; I thought that six weeks there would either lose her to me forever or send her running back into my arms. She had a friend out there to stay with, it was worth the price of a plane ticket to find out which it would be.

And she came back, all right. No, she didn't mind the city, I think she got her share of attention, though I know they grow them tall out there. But she missed me, missed my shack on the marsh—I'm the only one who calls it a shack—looking across to Salt Cove. Missed our happy aimless walks after work, missed having the village beaches virtually to herself eight months a year, missed going out rowing with me at dawn, the fog dispersing on the river as we moved gradually ahead, watching what we were leaving behind us. She missed me, she said; missed all the years of experience in my arms, missed what I did to her. Well, I had a lot of practice, I'd say, and she'd smile, knowing that a man on his second marriage really does know what not to do, and if he's able to admit half of it to himself, that's maybe even enough.

She knew not only would the roof over our heads always be tight, but there'd always be money, even with what I pay every month (and I am always more than generous) toward Samantha and the two girls. A man surrounded by women, as Rachel likes to tease me. What was clearly understood, so clearly we did not have to say it out loud, was that we'd stay here.

Oh, the question came up, occasionally. Yes, people do need roofs everywhere, I said, from Tulsa to Timbuktu, but I can't just move to Southern California or one of the Florida Keys—where we spent our honeymoon—and expect to make a living right away. They have names for people like that, and we don't much like them up here either. Sure, we're in a building boom, but once a roof goes up it ought to stay on for a while, and people don't fix their roof until it starts raining in the living room, that's a fact of life.

Besides, it would mean throwing away twenty-nine years of professional goodwill around here. I started full-time when I was seventeen, just out of high school, because I was smart and had talent. Then Jimmy unexpectedly kicked the big pail and his widow sold me the goodwill and the name cheap. Now I bet you everyone on Cape Sarah knows that when you need roof work done, Jack Fowler is one of three people you call first, and if he says he'll be there the first of May, he's never more than a week late even if he has to go up on a Sunday morning. No one else around here can say that, and stick by it.

Think any of this adds up to anything for Rachel? While I patiently explain away, she sits and listens—sits in a short skirt, mind you, doing her best to look attentive to every point I make—stands up slowly and goes to the window and looks out to where the marsh meets the channel, and she just puts her hands on her elbows and shivers. Then she turns back to me and says, Well, I want to be an obedient wife, you know that, sweetheart.

And at that moment I know she'd cut my throat on a dare.

Everything they tell you is wrong about women. Be nice and they roll right over you like a bulldozer. Treat them rough, handle them with a whip and a chair like some panther in the circus, and they act docile and even tame till it's feeding time and then there goes your arm at the shoulder. So it's here puss-puss but keep quiet or I'll thwack you, that's the mixture you have to give them daily, and you're so busy wondering which version you're married to at any given moment that you end up exhausted. You never know which approach will work not just today but right this very second because they'll turn on you like a jungle cat, they think faster than we do because strategy and tactics is *all* they're ever thinking about. So you wind up worn down and half asleep on a roof with a pitch on it like a frigging Alpine slope, something you ought to be rappelling down not trying to work on all day. Believe me, if I get any less sleep there's going to be an accident up there on the Matterhorn, and I sure don't want to be kissing sky and proving old Jimmy right. Lucky guy, his ticker stopped just like a clock, didn't even run down, just stopped one day at three minutes to three. That's divine symmetry for you, and on the third day of March too. After shingling all those roofs, he came out even in the end.

And now the latest ploy, and it won't be the last by any means, is my jungle cat wants us to live over in Salt Cove, in the village "proper" as she puts it. Like we're not in the village now? I say. How could we possibly be more involved? We vote in Village Hall meetings, I'm there hammering away for hours on end before the one-day summer fair to raise money for the old buildings, you're at the beaches every afternoon for half the year, we're on the Meadow Committee, we even own shares in it and those haven't been sold for years, we know everyone by name and they know us, what more do you want?

What I want, she says, is a house in the village itself. Doesn't have to have a view of the ocean. Come to think of it (as if she just thought of it) I wouldn't mind seeing this marsh from the other side of the river. Wouldn't mind a view of this very house, so I could remember where you first took me.

Well, I won't forget that night anytime soon, and she knows this. What do you want? I'd asked her, very quietly, as we lay on my former bed, where I'd been learning the flavor of her knees for the first time, and she said huskily *I want you to take me.* Now three years later here she is, saying just as huskily I want you to take me out of here, Jack, but don't take me away from all this, I've temporarily given up on that ultimatum, just take me a mile away from here by road or a half mile away from here by water, you choose, just for the sake of all you hold sacred and all that was missing from your other marriage, for the sake of how long and how strong I look to you naked, for the sake of the future of our love, not that its survival would ever be at stake, sweet Jesus, Jack, if you like the marsh light in my eyes when I wake up on the pillow next to you, take me to a totally different property tax, take me away from the house you contentedly raised two lovely daughters in, and make it quick.

Oh, all right. I'll just sell this place, cash in every penny I've ever put aside—let's throw in their college tuition funds for good measure, the courts'll never suspect till it's too late, besides, Samantha's an understanding type, she'd do the same thing in your position. Let's cash it all in and buy into the village immediately, just before they put up a new bridge and the prices drop like an idiot off a roof because they've ruined the place. Sure, let's buy at an exorbitant price what a year from now we can buy cheap *after* the location's been ruined. Good idea, honey.

Say this to your wife, you get Niagara Falls. And those aren't honeymoon tears, those are Rommel on the move, circling behind you across the desert at a speed you cannot begin to grasp until it's too late, you've been outsmarted and you're about to be machine-gunned right where you live.

You're just cynical, she says. That's all. (She murmurs this with a kind smile, as if it's the final insult—that's the optimism I fell in love with, rearing its other head.)

No, I'm not cynical, I say. And that's true. Jack Fowler always tells the truth.

You know, she says, I heard from Cynthia who works for the parking clerk in Leicester that she heard from Amy who's in the land tax office that what's really happening is some guy in Boston, some honcho, has a deal on some land past The Bight, and if a new bridge goes up across Salt Cove, then it makes The Bight the last part of Cape Sarah without any modern development. But what they were saying is it could all backfire, and in fact property values in the village would probably go up like crazy once it's easy to get in and get out on a new bridge, especially in winter, because it's a lot easier to keep a bridge plowed than the whole length of Shepherd Street leading into the Cove. That's what Cynthia said. So we should buy right now, even with all the troubles.

That's the dumbest real estate investment theory I ever heard, I say, and before I can explain why, it's Niagara again, and Cynthia's her only friend, and maybe I'm wrong just this once, this itty-bitty once, and just because I know what every house on Cape Sarah looks like from above, chimney to chimney, doesn't mean I understand the first thing about what goes on below. And it doesn't mean I understand what goes on inside a house, inside a home.

That's right. Jack Fowler always tells the truth. Look where it gets you.

30

Billy Fagles

WHAT I SAID WAS we might as well be stuck up there on the surface of the frigging moon, throwing rocks. I never said they wasn't going to start throwing them back at us. Week Two, and once the old lady is hasta la vista history, baby, them state assholes is back with a swagger, more determined than ever. We're here to take away your bridge, pal, no matter what you throw at us. You don't scare us, longhair.

Who cares, suckwad? says our hippie friend to their main engineer, more or less. *This is the moon, moron. We got an endless supply of rocks.*

In fact I didn't hear word for word exactly what Toby said, but I saw the look on the other guy's face. Like he just sat down on a plate of ice cream and he can feel it twitch all the way up to his balls. Jerk's got a yellow hard hat on like Chicken Little, the sky is falling. And the hippie's not even raising his voice, he's calm as can be. Well, not his nuts that are losing circulation. He even gives a shrug, like who'd have guessed these people would turn up again? After you guys took out an old lady a week ago? No wonder they don't show how that gunshot to the head stuff looks for real in the movies, man.

This is the next Monday, the one after what went down. We're out there on the bridge, seven thirty maybe, expecting trouble, and we already got plenty of support. Three dozen people so far and the Cape bus ain't even come by yet, so there's another load coming soon. Just shows how memorial posters get through to people. Some incredible gash out there, too—summer chicks and tank tops galore, though I'm not really into this navel-piercing thing. Also a few buddies of mine from the weight room, in muscle shirts just like I asked. So people see it's not only a bunch of retired folks in Salt Cove, we can do plenty damage if we have to. That was the Roscoe's idea, he says, *Billy, pull in some guys from the YMCA weights out here. They'll like the female talent and we can show them state bastards we grow 'em bigger than those dinks from the Crapper Squadron who the governor pays to wipe his ass.* That's what's so great about Roscoe, he sees how to take the psychological approach. And you know the guys are always ready to show up for a good cause.

When Toby gets done with the main engineer he wanders over to me and Roscoe shaking his head and says, *He asked my permission to start demolishing the bridge. You believe that? He figures he asks nicely we'll all pack up and go to the beach. Numskull doesn't get it.*

Then about eight fifteen some serious equipment shows up. Half a crane on a flatbed. Cab and wheels. No way to get it down the other side where Roscoe's got our old truck glued in place, so seems like they tried to get it past the church up at the head of the cove. Big mistake, since a flatbed won't fit around that corner, if they had any brains they'd ask us first, not that we'd help. They got traffic tied up in and out of the village for twenty minutes. Eventually they get the flatbed backed up and they try to take it through the dirt lane behind the church, the Roscoe shortcut. And big surprise, it fits.

So Roscoe and me and Toby are all standing there on the bridge waiting like the Three Musketeers, wide-screen version with Raquel, talking about who's going to go get coffee, probably me, when this flatbed comes creeping down Drawbridge Street with the bottom of a crane wobbling on it. And the police who was standing there apparently not doing anything all of a sudden go into a feeding frenzy. They got megaphones, they start the old shock tactics like in those Nazi prison camp escape flicks, yelling for everyone to get off the bridge, resistance is useless and punishment will be swift.

This is pretty stupid, it turns out, since the engineers can't do jack yet with only half of a crane till they unload it and the rest gets here. All the police did was give their game away a few hours early. And everyone ignores them and starts retorting shit back, like *Come and get us.* You got to love it when the old folks as well as the young babes in cutoffs both yell the obscene stuff, you know? At that point the hippie goes into action.

He's got a big manila envelope with him, surprise surprise, the kind with a wraparound string, and he goes over to the older policeman and undoes the string and unfolds some paper that he just keeps unfolding. Turns out he's copied this document out of a legal archive from 1956 or 1936 or somewhere and it's a something Latin forbidding vehicles of over so many tons from not only crossing the bridge but even crossing the fifty feet of pavement right before the bridge, past where Drawbridge elbows into River Street. Why? you maybe want to know. Turns out that legally this fifty feet of access road, if you want to call it that, is technically part of the bridge, legally speaking. Pay dirt, baby.

Bottom line is they can't get near enough to the bridge with a crane to actually destroy the bridge, since it's not safe for heavy vehicles. Translation: the meatheads won't be able to demo the bridge with a claw cause they aren't allowed to even approach the bridge with the fucker. Man, I love this legal paradox rigamarole. Figure if we give the hippie enough time and backup they'll be paying us taxes soon, not the other way round.

Funny thing is, I was always a Perry Mason fan, liked the office setup, the private investigator he had on retainer, that brunette secretary he had on a leash, but I never liked courtroom dramas as such. After Perry they all seemed phony. Go figure.

So then the police and the engineers and the hippie confer. I'm leaving out a certain amount of yelling back and forth and the fact that my exercise buddies and me wandered over just to be a little closer to the discussion. Along with that tubby photographer, too. (Turns out his sister was Delilah, not Denise/Darlene, and she got married and moved to New Hampshire a while back, and he basically doesn't care what I did to her, since it turns out she can't be bothered to send him a Christmas card. Me neither, I said.)

It all ends with the hippie jabbing his finger at the legal papers and then at the weight figures below the rear window of the crane cab, and the police end up shrugging at the Chicken Little hard-hat engineer guy, who's frigging apoplectic, and when the younger cop turns he gives a sly little wink at Roscoe and me and I can tell he's next door to laughing. What does he care, it's a sunny day, good weather to be out here with the tank tops. Better than standing alongside some giant pothole in Leicester directing traffic.

The state engineer finally stomps off in his yellow hard hat and starts yelling to the flatbed guy to back it up, back it up, and everyone on the bridge cheers. Fuck you, Ozzie, and fuck Harriet too. Takes them like an hour to go the half a mile out of the village, it turns out, so that's their morning.

So then the hippie comes over and confers with me and Roscoe. The old Day One by land, Day Two by sea is what we figure. The Roscoe says there's no way they're going to fart around with a team of men trying to pull it apart plank by plank. Toby says they can get round the 1956 or 1936 Latin something, I forget which, by getting another paper from a Boston judge, it might just take them a few days. So we're back to the crane, which is bad news. Or it might take them a few weeks, which is good news. Now we're back to a team of explosives experts might be coming in, like Alec Guinness next to the river Kwai falling on the dynamite handle all googly-eyed with a few Nipper bullets in him. Or else they could float a crane in by flat-bottom barge if they can get all the boats moored around here out of the way, which is another paper from a judge, says Toby. Explosives are out as long as we got live bodies on the bridge, but so isn't the crane tactic. But the real problem, I say, when it comes down to it, is the police can always clear the bridge at gunpoint. But as the hippie says, if nobody moves, they ain't exactly going to shoot. They'll just wait for nighttime, and hit the bridge then. So we got to keep people sleeping on it, no matter what. Don't worry, says Toby, that's legal too, I looked it up to be sure.

Then who should show up but that pasty computer guy married to the skinny redhead who was eyeballing me at the meeting. One with the baby. Guy's not very handy around the house lately, if you ask me.

Seems a package got delivered to Twinkletoes here from some weird militia group in Montana or Wisconsin or someplace, saw all about the bridge on the Internet and instead of sending us money they sent ammo along with detailed instructions in Baghdadian or who knows what, guy can't keep his story straight. Would've refused the package but the delivery guy just left it and moved on. Can't blame him, those drivers make twenty-three an hour plus benefits, he don't keep the truck moving he'll lose his run.

So Roscoe sends me up to get the package, which is all old Twinkletoes cares about. Guy's a little slow on the uptake, they bought the Chapman place on Baven Lane for way too much plus the filtration tank the city installed for the new sewer always backs up in the first November rains and we have to go pump it, which is an extra $375, but they'll find that out soon enough.

Anyway, the redhead's home, Nancy like Nancy Drew, Teen Detective, but looking more like Brenda Starr, Ace Reporter, and she's definitely into the whole muscle-shirt trip even though she's got enough books to open a public library. The baby starts crying and she goes to deal with it for a sec, meanwhile her husband shows me this box. There's stuff in it I've never seen before. I mean, there's a top layer of small cakes of Lifebuoy soap, dozens of them in wrappers, looks legit but don't ask what happens you try to wash with the stuff, there's a couple layers of bubble wrap underneath the soap and then this plastic stuff, in square sheets the size of some book, and kind of a pale color.

By now I'm turning pale too cause I know there's shit in that box you could blow up an army with. I don't even want to know what's underneath the plastic explosives cause so far we're only halfway down the box and there's got to be more in there than just more bubble wrap and guess what, grenades, and oh Christ, three little electronic clocks also with the full shipping & handling treatment. Probably more cakes of soap, in case you need to wash off the flying body parts.

Meanwhile Twinkletoes is breathing hard and waving some blurry papers in my face, looks to him like instructions in Iranian and Israeli and something else, and a translation all smudged on the other side in Chinese, which is really convenient since the Mandarin Duck opened last month in Leicester down by Jimmy's Auto Glass, maybe I'll wander in and order the beef with broccoli and ask if they mind translating this one little paragraph, see if that buys me a lifetime discount.

Not a bad moment to let off some tension in the air, so I ask him to please stop shoving the papers at me, foreign languages weren't my major at Harvard. Not even a smile out of old Twinkletoes. But he gets the message and tosses them in on top of all the cakes of Lifebuoy soap. Then he says, and he ain't joking either, *Maybe we should just put this out with the trash on Friday morning and get rid of it that way. I didn't think them Missouri lunatics was serious.*

Serious? You didn't think they was serious? I guess I yell at him. I'm practically pissing my pants, though I don't want the redhead to see that. *How much more goddamned serious can you get? You can't put this stuff out with the trash. They don't recycle plastic explosives along with beer bottles and newspapers. Jesus H. Christ swinging like a monkey from a tree.*

What should we do, then? Nancy the lean mean redheaded sex machine says in that husky educated way, and I think, Man, if you don't hear what I hear in your wife's voice, you really deserve to get some bad news, special delivery. I believe that too, I guess, though at that particular frigging moment all I can think about is some poor son of a bitch on a garbage truck getting his faucet blown off because genius here thinks the way to deal with a problem is put a trash sticker on it and leave it curbside Friday morning.

What we should do, I say calmly, and back out the door just like Mitchum in *El Dorado*, smiling nervously all the way, *is get a second opinion. You folks wait here, I'll be right back.*

31

Mildred Sykes

THE OTHER DAY I was down in Leicester on a little visit to the bank. And I stepped into the messy antiques shop Charlie Simmons runs, in between taking thousands of photos of high school sports teams that he gives away out of the focused generosity of his soul, while his shop looks far more cluttered, far more undiscovered, than a pharaoh's tomb. And Charlie mentioned an odd thing.

He said, "Mildred, I had someone in here earlier from out of state, and you know what they asked for? If I had any etchings of the Salt Cove bridge. Isn't that strange? So I sold him a Wainwright Harvey for a fair price, and—"

"A fair price?"

"A decent price," he said. "Fairly decent."

I was wondering what that might be, as I have a few myself; many of us veteran Sals do.

"What's so strange about that?" I asked.

"Well, it's not so strange. It's a beautiful view. And it occurred to me," he went on in his squirrel-gathering-nuts-in-May way, "you should think about consigning some copies of your history of Salt Cove. I bet I could sell them for you."

"It's been out of print for years," I said. "I only have, oh, a couple of copies left."

"That's too bad."

"It is. It's worth, and this is only what I've seen, about fifty or sixty dollars on the rare-book market."

The truth is I have several unopened boxes, of sixty-two copies each, in the attic. I got the young man who used to do my raking for me every autumn—he moved to San Francisco and I have never heard from him—to put them up there for me. I call it my pension fund. Well, not all unopened. Last winter, just as a precaution, I opened one box and signed every copy, dating them from eighteen years ago, the original year of publication. As an investment.

"Well," said Charlie, "have a look around the house. If you find any extras you can part with, I'd sell them for you. Whatever price you want."

"What would be fair?"

Not decent, fair.

He peered at me across the mayhem of his desk. A wiry grasshopper of a man, more vulnerable than he looks; I am tougher than he is, down deep, we all are. He is no cutthroat negotiator, even within his own shop, which is why we all worry about him.

"Name your price," he said quietly.

"In your professional opinion, Charlie."

He hemmed and hawed and bobbled his head. "I guess if you've really seen them listed for fifty or sixty dollars—have you actually seen them *listed* for that amount?"

"Listed, Charlie."

"Listed," he repeated to himself, like a priest saying amen. "All right, Mildred, if you'd be willing to autograph them. And we made a little display at the front of the store, with several framed collectible postcards of the bridge, people love those, I sold the out-of-state guy a couple from the twenties—"

"The side of the store, Charlie. Right over here. Not the front."

"Why not the front? Most people would kill for the front."

"The front looks like there's plenty more where that came from."

"Well, are there?"

I rolled my eyes. "Why don't we try eighty dollars to start with? One autographed copy at a time, displayed in your glass case." I tapped on it. "Among the swizzle sticks."

"One at a time?" His cheeks inflated as if he were about to blow a bubble. "Okay. Seventy-five, then. We can always come down to sixty."

"All right," I said, and when I told Jessica in her living room that night I added, "Don't worry, every penny is going to the Bridge Defense Fund. It's my contribution."

"I should go buy the first one," she said.

"But you already have a copy! I can see it from here."

"It's a present," she murmured. "For a friend."

"Uh-oh. I don't like the sound of that, Jessica."

It was dusk, this was midweek. I had already told her not to worry, I am not competitive. I'd done my share for future historians of Salt Cove years earlier—which was why I'd relinquished my position as secretary of the Village Hall Association to her. However, I pointed out judiciously, if some future publisher decided to bring out a revised edition of my book, with an epilogue recounting whatever happened to the bridge, once something does happen as we still fear it will, I would be in no position to refuse, no matter what Jessica herself might be writing. And she understood that; Jessica has always understood everything.

What I did not understand, I said, was what she thought she was doing by falling in love with a man about whom she knew very little and who was barely one·half her age. Less than six tenths, in fact.

She gasped. "Is it really so obvious?"

"To those who know you. Maybe it's not obvious to the tenderfoots."

A word I knew she loved.

She stared straight ahead in dismay. I took another sip of gin. Eventually she said, "You make me sound like an aberration. Like some gila monster."

"Not at all. I just don't like to see an old friend make a fool of herself." Thinking it better to change the subject, I said, "I hear your niece has taken up quite seriously with that developer over on the

Neck. I've never seen such a determined ambitious man. That'll be a wake-up for Sarah. Seems to have his fingers everywhere. Not that he's much older than she is."

"I don't see," said Jessica, and I thought she might snap my head off, "anything foolish in my behavior. There is nothing foolish in conceiving an affection for someone. Whether or not they return it doesn't make you into a fool for feeling the affection."

"I never said it did, Jessica."

"Suppose," she said, "I simply waited for him to make the first move? I'd wait till doomsday."

I could not argue with that.

"Anyway," she added triumphantly, "he was over here for dinner. Not once, but twice."

"That's wonderful." I took another sip.

"And I know more about him than you might surmise."

"I'm very happy for you, Jessica."

She said, "You'd be very surprised to learn exactly where he comes from. Who he was before he was one of us."

"Tell me more about him, then."

She pulled herself back in her chair—that trademark look I know all too well, Jessica pulling herself back from the world. I have seen her do it among people she's known half her life; I don't doubt she can do it just as easily among hothouse strangers in some outlandish foreign port like those she frequented back in her salad days. It's as if she is infinitely receding, an exotic bloom folding its petals before your eyes until nothing important is left visible. Even when she is staring straight at you, speaking reasonably all the while.

"I can't tell you anything," she said. "I've been sworn to secrecy."

I nodded. "He's not an escaped felon, is he?"

"Oh, no."

"Because if he were, it would be an issue of community safety."

"He's not, though."

I gave the appearance of not quite believing her, though I did, of course. You must always ask for far more than you really want in terms of hard gossip, then appear politely accepting when they won't give it to you, so you can settle for learning what you wanted in the first place.

"Is that his real name, at least?"

"Oh, yes."

"It never sounded much like a real name to me."

"I don't know what Toby is short for," she admitted. "Tobias, I suppose. I've never known a Tobias."

"Neither have I," I said. "I knew a nickname Toby once. His real handle was Leonard, I believe. His parents were Jewish. He was a bartender."

She nodded. Now it was I who'd said a great deal, though she did not know that. I spoke slowly, so she would realize the words were coming from my heart. "You know, Jessica, I am your staunchest ally. Nothing you confide is echoed outside these walls. If there's anything you want to tell me—"

"There's nothing to tell you," she said. "Yet."

"Then I'm glad to hear it." I got up to go. This sometimes works, too. The other side of people not wanting to tell you the truth is also wanting to tell you too much of it, and they often turn the coin over when they see you making for the door. I learned this writing my history of our village, and it constantly surprised me how ardently people had kept family secrets of a century ago, about relatives they'd never met, and how happy they were at last to be unburdened of that weight, the weight of the truth. And no one ever complained to me after my book appeared, not a peep.

"Why are you glad to hear it?" Jessica asked, bewildered but on the edge of furious at the same time.

Your fury is misplaced, I wanted to say. You should be ever alert, Jessica, ever vigilant, as I have known you to be for more years than I care to count. Now, especially, with your niece consorting with a man who would stop at nothing to wrest this place from your fingers and turn it back into a classic summer hotel. You should reread my book from time to time, there are all sorts of gentle implicit warnings hidden inside. A summer hotel or worse. I've mentioned this before, but I never know how much you're really listening.

"I don't want to see you made a fool of," I said. "I told you that."

"He would never make a fool of me."

"Jessica, you don't need anyone else's help."

"He was over here two nights ago for dinner!"

"And you're a wonderful cook. I'd have dined here too, if you asked me."

I wondered if she'd indeed buy him a copy of my book from Charlie.

She said defiantly, "We watched the news reports that showed them moving that . . . that crane away. It made him laugh."

"I never said he doesn't have a sense of humor. I can see it in his mustache. His ponytail."

"And," she continued, a little breathlessly, "we went downstairs, afterward. He got my father's old pinball machine going again. Not totally, not all the lights. But he opened up the back with a tiny screwdriver, and wiggled something, and it worked. He even made me play a game."

"I just don't want to see you hurt," I said quietly. "I'm not trying to pry. I'm not moralizing, you know that. I don't care what anyone does."

And it's true. I'm not judgmental, never have been. As long as no one touches a hair on the heads of my grandchildren out in Chicago, a city with a long history of graft and worse, I don't care what people do with each other. I got this from Gene, bless him: we're all just passing through the belly of a vast whale. Like plankton. I would still like to sell off some of my pension fund, however.

"What hurts," she said, "is that you're trying to deny me this. I don't see why it should matter to you."

What should I have said? That it was all too clear to me that he was not in love with her, with a woman plenty old enough to be his mother? That despite her dynamism and energy and her eyes, even her willful cheekbones which I have always admired, her independence and, all along, her capacious spirit, I could not imagine the two of them as a couple, I could never imagine their heads on a pillow together, touching?

I could not say any of this. Nor have I ever asked Jessica what she might or might not have done while abroad. Instead, not knowing what to say, I must've laughed nervously. It sounded eerie to me, and I know to her it sounded as though I were laughing at her.

She flushed. "Mildred, please leave."

"I didn't mean it that way!"

She swallowed. "Please don't laugh."

I shook my head fervently, and went over and put my hand on her shoulder, careful to avoid where she had a couple of problem spots removed a few years back; as a girl she spent so much time in the sun. I had to make something up fast.

"I won't laugh, I promise. It's just, well, you caught me remembering something funny an old fisherman told me. Back when I was researching my book. I didn't put it in because . . ." Oh, Lord. "Because there was no place it seemed to fit." I shrugged. "We both understand what that's like. You know what he told me? He said, 'Young lady—' and Jessica, you recall I wasn't young then, that just goes to show you how old and toothless he was—he said, 'Young lady, never ever fall in love with a lighthouse keeper.'"

I earned a reluctant smile with that, from my quick thinking, and she even said, "Words of wisdom from a fisherman," which meant we were still friends. But when she wanted to show me her father's pin-ball machine, humming now thanks to Toby Auberon, I begged off, and said it was late and I had to get home.

32

Gretchen Moresby

So, SHE SAYS, get a job, you're sixteen now, so just get a job finally. There's like no possible point, I point out, cause as soon as I get out of this stupid nature preserve, as soon as I get to New York where I can model clothes or act or do something useful for a change, what's the point of one slave labor summer in some dumb ice cream stand in Beauport for minimum wage? It's not even decent ice cream and the owner is wicked disgusting, I swear to God if you saw how he looks at me behind my back you'd call the Vice Squad. Tell that to your brother, she screams, when he was your age he was mowing every lawn in this village. Yeah, well, my brother's still a classic parasite, he was just hoping some frustrated hose monkey of a housewife would pull him inside and give him a lube job, that's the only reason.

Don't you get it? When I'm twenty-one I'm not even going to be in contact with him, not even through my lawyer, and when he ends up in major trouble don't ask me to help out financially cause I refuse. And I am personally going to write this down on paper and get it witnessed and notarized and sent to every single person we know. If he gets arrested you can take him his lawn mower in prison yourself cause I am so out of here, you have no idea.

So so far the summer of sweet sixteen, never been appreciated, is looking deeply potent. To start with, there's all these people around, real people, not Cape Sarah snaggletooths. A lot, and I mean a lot, like four or five, TV network crews from the Boston networks, filming a few hours every day. The camera guys have all been really friendly to me even though one is maybe a little creepy and they're all really over-weight from carrying the cameras around and eating bad food. And there's one reporter, this bitch with an ancient '80s hairdo worse than Erica's mom's, who absolutely hated me on sight, which was great, since I hate her too. Women are amazing, they look at you and they know, they just know, that in a couple of years you'll have their jobs, they know they'd give anything to be as hardbody as you are again but forget it, honey, you started the StairMaster ten years too late. And don't worry, your husband is safe, believe me, I don't want to go there. Do I look desperate? That's why women were warriors once, it's so cool.

She's not the one who interviewed me. The one who interviewed me, and they showed a whole forty-two seconds of it, a minute almost, Erica taped it and she's going to copy it for me since nothing in this house ever works, that would be too much to ask, like why buy something new that works when you can pretend you're about to repair something totally obsolete? Anyway, the one who interviewed me was this distinguished-looking older man, he looks exactly, I mean exactly like on TV and it's true, they really are a different species, I wanted to ask him if he takes hormones. He'd probably have told me the truth.

First he asked me how I felt about the whole bridge thing and I thought right, he's trying to get me to say the correct answer. Then he said no, to really tell him what I thought. And the camera guy, the nicest one, was right on top of me practically, well it seemed like it almost, and I kept thinking this was a screen test except I had to make up all my lines so I got really nervous. And I said I think there are bet-ter things to spend all that money on, like world peace or farmers or something. Honestly, it felt like one of those beauty pageant questions. Or build a big mall right outside Leicester so we don't have to drive a zillion miles up the highway just to find a few normal stores, which is where I wouldn't mind working this summer if there was some way for me to get there. And he said that was an unusual point of view. But the next day when I told him I wanted to do my interview over again, I wanted to change what I'd said, he wouldn't let me. Typical.

33

Toby Auberon

THEY SURPRISED ME. After the crane fiasco, rather than nibble and scratch at us again by way of the courts, they struck by sea. And struck more greasily, more ruthlessly, than anything I ever saw on the other coast, in even the most greedy criminal maneuverings, with absolutely no fear of consequences, no sense that we're worth taking seriously. I swallowed it in Los Angeles, in another lifetime; I saw my gentlest Brazilian neighbors swallow it daily, no matter how much a foreigner tried to help; I'm not going to swallow it here. I am going to make these dung-smeared dogs pay over and over. For Leilia, for the havoc they've loosed on an unsuspecting village, for making me abandon my vows and give up my Machina at its crescendo. They're about to find out how much concentrated force one powerless man can wield.

Their assault came late yesterday night. Which indicates a determined and strongly led bureaucracy—all that overtime pay to justify and approve beforehand. More wasted taxpayers' money.

It'll be two weeks Monday since Leilia's death. A dripping tap of Boston TV coverage has proven useless, due to paltry interest prior to summer, amid graduations, vacations, championships, etc. You have to keep spilling blood if you want to hold people's attention. Newspapers equally disappointing: the usual editorials about police incompetence, and most articles only partially sympathetic, since the bridge is more decrepit than pretty. The Leicester press little better, due to local yearnings for "efficient development." People would rather protect something natural than something man-made, even though nature is more dynamic at renewing itself. Mankind firebombs its handmade treasures and preens, proud of having successfully shut the other guy up.

Thus a certain resentment that we're standing in the inexorable way of progress. The state has hammered away at the safety issue, via terse interviews Cairns gives to Boston journalists, accusing us of wanting a footbridge to keep people out. Hardly the groundswell of media support I expected. The village is portrayed as a loony old lady screaming down a hill toward her doom.

I saw this constantly in California: unless there's some flagrant injustice wrapped around the victim, like a patriotic flag of pity and anger, it's almost impossible to get people living ten miles away interested. Now that Leilia's buried, and the police have told their side of things, at the end of it all she's seen as a kook with a blade in her hand going after a cop, even though (thanks to Scativo) they never found the knife and it might've been only her wedding ring. But so what? A week after her death, that mysterious force—*Amnesia americanus*—sweeps all her clearheaded passion into the dustbin of history. Harold Milne seems to have chosen not to sue anybody, though their children may yet, and it's not for me to insist he should.

We've still had zero coverage in a national paper. No TV footage got picked up by the networks, though a twelve-year-old claims he saw a report about the bridge on cable news at 3 A.M.

Apart from a few meager contributions to Jon Eckerman's website, we've received two boxes of snack crackers to succor the starving populace of Salt Cove, and one box of Armageddon from some Missouri wackos with more ammo in their survival bunkers than even they conceivably need. Eckerman nearly shouted with relief when I told him not to thank them, tempting as it was to suggest that good manners are good manners and a gift is still a gift. Roscoe knew where to put such matériel—under his bed.

Until last night I was worried the state plan might be to wait us out. Daily, it was getting harder to attract the volunteers whom Jessica "estimated" (counted scrupulously, of course) as half residents, half outsiders. At least the Sals are more determined than ever, having seen Leilia's head turned into a sieve. It would be a brilliant strategy for the government: let the people of Salt Cove and their motley allies sweat out those first lazy weeks of sunlight on a tattered bridge with no shade, no breeze, nothing happening, and sooner or later people would decide they'd won, the state has conceded and wandered off to bother someone else, so we can all go home.

No court order backed up by squads of policemen, no news flashes, no official statements from goons. No need. You can always count on human inertia. You let the outraged citizenry get bored and walk away. Then you make your move. That's what I'd do, having learned the hard way never to overestimate people's ability to stick to something.

But from now on we are in a different struggle, with different rules.

It was only thanks to that kid, Henry, that we found out we were under sneak attack late last night, and were able to fight back. Smart boy. I didn't think kids read Sherlock Holmes anymore, yet Henry dubbed himself one of the Shepherd Street Irregulars. I first met him by the bridge a week ago, soon after his suppertime, since a shred of napkin poked from his belt. Elementary, my dear Jessica. Ever since, he's stationed himself faithfully on the bridge long after dark, probably slipping out of his house in secret to do so.

He even made me take a walkie-talkie back to the lighthouse, some retro space-age toy made obsolete by the cell phone (naturally he owns one and I don't). I stuck it in a bookcase on my mezzanine then nearly went out of my mind last night after it started squawking and I couldn't find it. When I finally grabbed it down I was ready to blast the kid if he assured me, crackling with a dense quarter mile of static, *Wilkes here, this is only a test,* as he had several days before. But this time he said, "Come at once. This is not a test. Scativo and Hughes on the way. Bridge at once."

Three months ago I was spending days and nights on a labor of love that has galvanized me for years, an idea mighty enough to yank me out of a more syncopated residence in Rio. Now, thanks to a pack of state savages, I'm back to writing pointless writs and legal pleas. I've given up all prospect of getting any work done, to persuade people I barely know to defy a government doing its malevolent best to defy them. If this is the human condition, I prefer pinball.

On the other hand, I'd run out of toilet paper an hour earlier, and was furious out of all proportion to the basic oversight and my distaste for week-old newsprint. Which meant I was furious with myself for other reasons, larger defeats from a decade ago that normally I no longer thought about. Cases lost, agreements broken, expectations evaporated, life squandered. This is what happens once you give up the routine of regular working hours, once you lose your concentration and lose your way: you get trapped in the unalterable past. When I finally located the squawking walkie-talkie, hit the button, and got the boy's desperate message, I was glad to rush out of the lighthouse. I should've realized that if they were ready to lay siege under cover of darkness, we were entering a different kind of war.

It was a moonless night, which was why they chose it for an attack, with a many-minded salt breeze on the Meadow—how many times in my years here had I trodden this path by starlight, I reminded myself, hurrying by Baven Rock. In a few weeks I'd be hearing the mutter of teenagers who'd climbed the massive granite outcropping to drink; one night I'd even talked down a tearful, tipsy girl abandoned by friends, who then wanted to thank me.

Out of the Meadow, once that nameless little lane took me beyond the Village Hall buildings to Shepherd Street, I expected signs of life, but at eleven thirty the village was asleep. I'd assumed we still had sentries on the bridge, rutting away in sleeping bags, but as I came down the steep hill of Drawbridge Street past where Leilia met her bullet, I saw none. In the cove there was no breeze, no moon, everything was motionless under a sky infested with stars.

Nor did I see any sign of the boy, or Roscoe, or Scativo. I was about to traipse out on the bridge when a massive hand gripped my shoulder, hauling me through Dr. Hengerberg's privet then out the other side onto his scrap of hedge-enclosed lawn, across River Street from his corner house. Though we were right beside the cove, no one could see us from the water—all four of us.

"Good evening, gentlemen," I said.

"Not so loud, hippie," hissed Roscoe under his breath. "Talk carries."

I could barely make out their faces: little Henry, panting with excitement and the pre-teenage flush of a job well done; Roscoe like a satisfied smuggler from another era, in a wool shirt (I could smell it) despite the season, pipe clenched in his teeth; Scativo all in black and barefoot, impossible to discern in the darkness if he stepped back a few paces.

"What's going on here?" I whispered.

"Explosives, Mr. Auberon," gulped Henry. "See, I found them just finishing—"

"They got the bridge all wired," said Roscoe flatly. "That's them in the boat. Lying just off Fowler's dock. Listen!"

I listened and heard, faintly, two voices carried by the water, not a hundred fifty feet away, but I could not make out what they were saying.

"They're ready," muttered Scativo. "They can blow it whenever they want."

I've failed was all I could think. Failed once again. Wasn't I the cocky one? Certain they'd do this the lawyer's way, getting a kangaroo judge to sign off on a crane. Instead they were doing it the East Boston way. They had their printed permission to destroy the bridge, they weren't going to get halted by a technicality. What did it take to tear the cobwebs from my brain? No wonder I'd run out of toilet paper, I had no idea what the hell was happening before my very eyes.

"You were right, Roscoe," I said softly. "I'm sorry."

"Yeah, I was right, all right." He nodded. "Won't be the last time, neither."

"So what are they waiting for? Why don't they blow it?"

Scativo gave a slow chortle. "Overtime, baby. The game may change, but not the rules."

I heard a crack as Roscoe bit down on his stem. "Midnight. Overtime doubles after midnight. Greedy bastards." He took out his pipe.

"Now listen. I got Billy on the other side. Can't see a rat's ass tonight, but he's there. Going to take time to pull their shit and wires off them pilings." He nodded to himself. "I need you on the bridge making plenty noise." He meant me. "So they don't rush things. And I need you"—he jabbed his pipe at Scativo—"and Billy in the water. You got to get on their boat, kill their transmitter."

"And you?" said Scativo a little icily, though he can't have envisioned Roscoe silently swimming like a commando.

"I'm taking Hengerberg's skiff." He indicated the water-side part of the hedge; beyond it lay the doctor's small float. "So I can reach them bastards' explosives. If you and Billy don't screw up."

"What about me?" piped Henry.

"Stay here and keep your hands to yourself," snapped Scativo. "We make our move right now. Their watches could be fast."

I later found out the three men had arrived only a minute before, and Roscoe had immediately figured out what to do and sent Billy silently across. Sure, if we all strolled onto the bridge and made a racket, the enemy weren't about to raise the body count; but unless those wired explosives got removed, the bridge was still ready and waiting to be destroyed, once nobody was on it. Roscoe was right. And these people deserved a slow death, by water torture.

"Make sure they hear you, hippie. Not the others," he hissed as I started shoving myself back through the privet.

It did strike me, as I squeezed out of the hedge on the other side, that those engineers might even relish giving up a little overtime to send the bridge sky-high in a melee of rotted timbers and destroyed planking. Or maybe their charges would surgically bring down only the decayed pilings, and let gravity take care of the rest. Either way, as soon as I felt visible under the spread pool of illumination from the street lamp at the River Street end, I started lustily singing *Oh, one hundred bottles of beer on the wall* and strode onto the bridge.

I had the satisfaction of hearing the faint voices cease on their boat—a medium-size craft with a heavy outboard, it turned out—when they realized this clown bellowing fit to wake the village was indeed out on the bridge itself. Six minutes till double overtime and kingdom come, according to my luminous dial. Then I heard them mumbling again. The clown was only walking across, no problem, he'd be gone soon, right on schedule.

Ninety-eight bottles of beer on the wall, ninety-eight bottles. I stationed myself halfway down, where they couldn't miss me. Their voices ceased again when they realized my silhouette wasn't budging. I kept giving it both barrels, with maximum enthusiasm, and heard the gentlest splash on my right, presumably Scativo slipping into the water, though I couldn't see him—or figure out which shadowy boat was theirs.

At *ninety-seven bottles* I detected an answering splash of Billy Fagles to my left, near the opposite bank. I thought of two stealthy crocodiles closing in, letting the water drift them to the boat. I didn't hear Roscoe, but then he wouldn't want to give the game away.

At around four minutes to midnight I'd just reached *Eighty-nine bottles of beer on the wall, eighty-nine bottles of beer,* what could be taking so long, the idiotic ditty was driving me insane, when I nearly jumped out of my skin—a higher, lighter voice, even more off-pitch than mine, had joined in and was moving toward me.

"Evening, Pop," the boy called out. I nearly yelled *You fool, get off the bridge.* But of course he was correct: they weren't about to blow up a kid, and by now they must've even been cheering inwardly, blessing their extra pay. Clearly a father and son were standing out here, and that meant they'd have to wait a while longer, right? Henry wore a huge misbehaving grin as he sidled up, and put his hands on the bridge handrail just beside mine (two minutes, I saw on his lit-up digital watch—one of us was surely wrong). We stared out at the gulping darkness but there was nothing to discern, only the black artery of water down the cove past all the sleeping houses, the slow curve of River Street with its weak, unevenly spaced streetlights, the muffled shapes of a dozen boats riding their moorings like distracted animals at the truce of the water hole. Now I saw it—the tiny, winking glow of a cigarette being sucked on arrogantly in one boat, anchored farther away than I'd imagined, waiting for us to finish the damned song and move so they could press the button and shatter every one of those bottles.

Then we heard a splash, and another rapidly after it, like crocodiles surging out of the water. I saw the cigarette glow rock violently back and forth and disappear as someone yelled, "Goddamn it!" Not a voice I knew. Henry and I stopped singing and I patted him on the shoulder. I heard Billy say, very distinctly, "You're going swimming, cocksucker," then there was a scuffling, a groan, two big splashes, much wild spluttering, flailing water, and curses ("Cover your ears, young man," I said, and felt the boy smile) followed about ten seconds later by a light coming on in the boat at some control panel. It went off right away and there was a faint faraway plop upriver from the bridge, like a fish jumping. Scativo called out, "Transmitter drowned, repeat drowned. Two men overboard. Engine"—he paused; I imagined Billy yanking gratuitously at a fuel line—"disabled. We are safe to go, repeat safe to go."

"You fucking assholes," one of the schmoes in the water yelled up, treading water and no doubt wondering how he'd explain all this to his superiors. Scativo had the satisfaction of saying, "Ah, swim home and whack off, chump," and Billy added, "Yeah, don't drown, suckers," to the other, quoting some movie, I think. The two of them dived off the stern, away from the guys they'd dumped in the drink, and began stroking their way back to Dr. Hengerberg's float.

"Look there!" said Henry beside me, pointing.

Roscoe was already under way in a skiff, standing upright, using an oar to pole and paddle the brief distance until he was beneath the bridge and we had to peer over the railing. He put down the oar, switched his big flashlight on—pipe clenched in his maw—and ran the light across the pilings to reveal wires running like diseased veins all along them, taped in place, leading to packs of explosives. Grunting, he pulled a pair of clippers from his pocket and, arm-over-arming his way along, he went vengefully after the state's official handiwork, delicately snipping, snipping, snipping, then tearing the wires down piling by piling and grabbing the small packs of explosives. A few fell in the river, most wound up under his bed.

"You saved us tonight," I said to the boy. "You saved the bridge. How'd you ever spot those guys?"

"Experience."

"Aha."

Blind luck, I thought. You were playing Sherlock Holmes and noticed the men hurrying about their business once the village turned in for the night. What was it to them? Another annoying job, single overtime shifting into double, blowing up a bridge that'd stood for five generations. But someone had to do it. There was no point in reasoning with these people, no point in arguing with an ugly government that became a bully whenever it wanted, since a great unwritten amendment gave them the right to wield a cattle prod if a swagger stick wouldn't do the trick.

It was the sight of pack after pack of explosives, the noises of Roscoe swearing as he dismantled their professional handiwork, and curiously enough the scent of his pipe tobacco, that were like switching on a flashlight for me. Years ago I'd vowed to stay with the Machina Excelsior until it was done. I now made a different vow.

By this time Billy and Scativo had clambered out of the water onto the floating dock not twenty yards away. Billy gave a little exultant jump, rubbing his upper arms, and said loudly, "Hoo boy. Come to Papa. Feed that puppy. Roscoe, you want a hand over there?"

I flinched at the use of a name, since until now with the darkness we'd been difficult to identify; well, those state guys were probably out of earshot, striking out upriver for the other bank, which was sensible since Billy was just as ready to prove his point onshore. They'd have a merry time hitching a ride on Monroe Street, soaking wet, after midnight, back to wherever their orange truck was parked. On the far side of the cape, I hoped.

"Do I look like I need a frigging hand?" said Roscoe. "I don't want you guys dripping on this stuff. Christ, you made enough racket out there."

"Roscoe, we was quiet."

He snorted. "Like a herd of fucking elephants. Goddamn it, those bastards wanted to blow this bridge apart. You guys seeing how much shit those sons of bitches used? Now I am *really*"—he broke off to rip at more wires directly beneath where Henry and I stood—"really in a bad mood."

I felt, then saw, Scativo come up beside us, as black and glossy as a seal. He looked like an assassin. He scowled and pushed his hair back.

"Hey, kid," he said. "What's the big idea, playing the canary? Trying to get yourself hurt?"

"Trying to do my job," said Henry.

Scativo shook his head. "Can't argue with a hero." He said to me very softly, "Listen, where I come from, you don't wait for the third time. They might get lucky."

"Believe me, I'm convinced."

He carefully squeezed out his trousers leg by leg, as if they were expensive—a most meticulous man. Without looking up he asked, "Say, what's the, uh, legal situation regarding their boat?"

"You mean which laws did you just break?"

The trousers finished and smoothed to his satisfaction, he straightened up. "I assume we're all mutual accomplices in the whole shebang."

"Something like that." Not entirely.

"So let's hear the laundry list."

I said, "I think you'll be proud of yourself. Depending on who owns it, you and Billy either boarded, hijacked, and vandalized a private vessel, which is a state crime. Or you boarded, hijacked, and vandalized a state vessel, which is an even bigger state crime."

"That all?"

"Let's see. You also assaulted two state employees who were attempting to perform their official duties. I suppose you could be charged with assault with a deadly weapon. Your fists. Or even attempted murder by drowning—you threw two engineers in the water. Impeding state officials in their public duties. Malicious mischief. And theoretically you obstructed public safety."

"How's that?"

"Someone out for a midnight swim could've been hit by those falling engineers. What else? Reckless endangerment. Reckless indifference to human life. Piracy. You also destroyed state property."

"Destroyed? Those guys are maybe bruised a little."

"The transmitter you tossed upriver. Just like Roscoe's destroying state property right now."

We could hear him cussing and snipping away below us.

"On top of that, you also violated the Clean Water Act, by throwing a couple of corrupt engineers in an otherwise clean body of water."

"Pretty good night's work, eh?" said Scativo.

I felt like the top of my head was coming off. "I'm sick of getting pushed around by these hyenas," I said. "Tomorrow morning I'm writing out an act of secession for everyone to sign. It'll be the most damning legal document I can come up with. It'll run in every newspaper in the country. Every magazine. On every TV station. They want war, they're going to get war. Let them bomb the bridge if they want to take it out. I'm not bickering politely anymore. I'm going to destroy them."

Scativo put a sopping hand on my shoulder. "You draw up a petition, I want to sign on page one. Got that? Don't make the Scativo sign on page two."

"Don't worry."

"Okey-dokey. You were never that polite with them, by the way." He sighed. "Man, I must be slowing down. In the old days I wouldn't even need to change my threads. Now I only want shut-eye."

"You've earned it. Leilia would be proud of you." I pointed down the bridge, toward the village. "They'll all be incensed when they find out what just happened." Around us the night was calm, there was no breeze, the waves we'd stirred up had settled. Almost as if nothing had occurred, thanks to the tremendous restorative powers of the world.

"I'm not getting any sleep," said Scativo. "That's the tragedy. Not after I get back to what's waiting for me."

I did not want to hear all about his personalized version of insomnia. Luckily Roscoe hissed, "Hey!" and emerged from under the bridge, paddling the skiff along to Dr. Hengerberg's floating dock, where Billy was waiting. We three trooped back across the bridge, the boy trotting eagerly between Scativo and me, to the corner scrap of lawn, this time without having to push through the privet hedge.

I said quietly to Henry, "I know I don't have to ask you not to mention this to anyone. Not even your best friend at school."

"Oh no, sir." He added, "School's almost done, anyway."

Billy and Roscoe had the skiff roped in place by the time we reached the little dock. Roscoe ran the flashlight across the boat's innards to be sure he hadn't forgotten anything. Then he turned to us and said, "Put your hands out." From a pile at his feet he gathered up several clumps of wires with squarish pads attached in taped plastic bags. He handed a clump each to Billy and Scativo and me and kept the lion's share for himself. He muttered, "Just so they know they got to hang all of us. Except the kid. So they don't hang us separately. Ain't that the quote, hippie?"

"Close enough."

He nodded and winced. I saw he was actually shaking with rage; then I realized we all were. I had not noticed it before. Roscoe said to me, "Next village meeting, hippie, I want you to refer to that shit as Exhibit A."

"Let's call this Exhibit A," I said, surprising Jessica this morning, dumping my clump of state-sponsored explosives on a rattan table on her enclosed porch where she was doing the *New York Times* crossword in ink and admiring the view. Somehow she'd already heard what happened, though she wouldn't reveal her source—it was as if a system of bush telegraph operated, a covert code of jungle drums or smoke signals which only lifelong Salines were privy to.

"So that's what the stuff looks like," she said. "In my grandfather's day it was very different. Blowing out tons of granite in the quarries."

She was less surprised than I; years and years without a television, telephone, or computer had seeded and vitalized an unhealthy naïveté in me. (Rio, despite its reputation, enforced its own weird innocence, a purity of physical beauty at least, which I still treasured.) I certainly never expected to stumble bleary-eyed down my cast-iron spiral staircase one morning to find, on the bottom step where I'd left them a few hours earlier, a tangled mass of wires and explosives in plastic sandwich bags.

She was gazing at me oddly, I suppose because these days it was I going to her home to see her rather than she coming round to the lighthouse to pester me. The other evening, after stopping by to watch the news coverage of the crane retreat on her TV, I'd gotten her father's pinball machine going again; it took me all of three minutes. She was a little surprised that I didn't particularly want to give *Contact* a try myself—I was more interested in seeing her play. How profoundly it seemed to matter to her that it was not broken any longer, that the past could be repaired and the lights would flash and all would be as it once was and ever should be.

I'd blamed my expertise on my widowed father, the best electrician in Sierra Madre, who often repaired such machines for collectors in the area, taking his riveted son, an only child, with him on house calls. Quite a pair we'd made, I did not need to say; remarkable what you learn in life by keeping your eyes wide open, asking the right questions, listening hard because you sometimes get the right answers. Playing the game never interested my father. Only design mattered to him, the art and artifice of it, the technical problems solved at the service of beauty, but he loved watching other people's faces as they played. Funny what you inherit.

"No, I've tried this one before," I said to Jessica when she stood aside and tugged at my arm so I would take a turn. I didn't want to intrude, to break the sacred bond between her and her father's game, a bond whose lines of force she might barely sense but which I could see like comic-book zigzags of energy unleashed in the air as she hovered girlishly over the machine, hearing its remembered trilling again—as a boy I'd known collectors who could identify a game from a room away, just from the inflection a specific playfield gave a stock bell mechanism. I was content to have restored the electrified zigzags to Jessica, and sure that when I was no longer around to make her self-conscious, she'd wander down to play every now and then, and be flooded with remembrance each time. That meant a lot to me; it would've meant as much to my father.

Now I said to her, "Let's face it, the government's declared war. Can you imagine? The whole village would've been jolted awake by the roar of our bridge exploding. Who knows what they'll try next? It's like the fantasy of some crazed militia group, with their canned goods and their arms caches in the backyard. No wonder those guys are all so paranoid."

She said, "What do you expect? Look at the scum we elect. It's not the best and the brightest, it's the worst and the dullest. Most of them should be selling golf shirts at some country club. Or making license plates behind bars. But if you say this, people think you're being cranky. That's why they haven't run my guest editorial in the Leicester paper. 'We don't print negativity,' they said."

My rage last night had given way, this morning, to exhaustion from hours of lying in bed jabbering defiant phrases to myself and wondering how the villagers would react to all I knew had to be done. A part of me was even thinking: if you can't get Jessica to go along with you, just pack up quick and move on, because you'll never convince the rest of them.

I said, "We don't really have many choices left. We've been very lucky, so far. I don't want to count on luck again."

"Nonsense. You've out-thunk them."

"We broke a lot of laws last night—"

"How on earth can you say that, Toby?"

"And if they have any sense they're trying to get warrants for our arrests right now. If they can figure out which names."

"So what? I'll bail you all out. Wait till this hits the newspapers. You'll look like Greek heroes. All of you. Here on the ringing plains of windy Troy."

I said wearily, "Jessica, a box of demons has opened that I can't keep shut. I don't know why they're so determined. Maybe they think a protest here might start a domino effect everywhere. They could show up any day now and just bulldoze us. And I see only one strategy. One way out."

Standing there, bathed in the light off her airy vista of the ocean, I felt all the old anger come roiling back. I had not felt this way in years, not since I'd abandoned the law for South America, not since my umpteenth pointless job interview with some senior partner twit in private practice who hadn't gotten his hands dirty by actually going to trial a half dozen times in his life. And who still felt he had the right to virtually start me off in the fucking mail room.

She said, "Has it occurred to you that there might be other reasons why you're so deeply drawn to the idea of secession?"

What I'm deeply drawn to, I nearly said, is staying home by the ocean and keeping my door locked from the inside. And if I can't get laid at least I can get some useful work done in peace.

She went on, blithely oblivious. "Because that's what you seem to have tried by coming here. Seceded from your former life. Whatever it was. I assume there was a unity that you dissolved. So some part of you, personally, must want to pull back from the world and declare independence. And that's why you want us to secede, too. To help you prove you're right."

I could only stare wordlessly at her. Very well: she had my attention.

She said, "I don't say you're wrong. For us or for you. I'm not criticizing. I trust you wholeheartedly. And I believe that, far more than any of us, you know what's best for our village. I bring this up because I want you to tell me, really and truly, who you really are. And what you're doing here."

What did she expect? That I'd lead her back to the lighthouse and show her? It is less a matter of keeping secrets than of keeping faith, and staying sequestered in oneself. What I do is utterly private until I get it right, I am not looking for encouragement or understanding. What I needed at that moment was more toilet paper.

Still, a long time since anyone has spoken to me that way. Or since someone substantial with nothing to gain from me (I didn't see her as a lonely woman, she was far too dynamic and self-sufficient, despite evidence of pain in her face, for that) has felt I mattered. Like finding that a fortune has been anonymously conferred on you. It was still up to you to accept it or not.

She was watching me expectantly, confidingly, with what I can only call love shining in her green eyes. It made me want to pat her hand and tell her of my former lives, it made me want to retreat over by the enormous sea-stunned window, it made me want to tell her about the game beneath the game and the Mayan underworld principle, it made me want to tell her lies, it made me want to take her home and show her all I've nearly finished and what still besets me every day. It made me feel as treacherous and insidious and cold as black ice. It most of all made me want to retrace my steps and choose my words carefully, for everything I said could and would be held against me.

I said, "I trust you also. I don't trust many people. And I admire you."

She said with a hint of naked bitterness—this was not what she wanted me to say—"What a famous feeling it is to be admired."

"I need your help, too."

Hopeful again, she stared at me. "What do you need?"

"I need a pad of paper and a pen. And a quiet corner, for about an hour. Then I'll need you to read something, criticize it, and type it up for me."

"If I do all that, will you tell me all I want to know?"

"Jessica, you see far, far more here than there is to see, I promise you."

"Then," she said triumphantly, a little wickedly, and closed her eyes, "you have nothing to lose by telling me everything."

34

Henry Wilkes Jr.

As soon as the airlock hissed shut behind us, I said to Molly Mellew, my shapely first lieutenant, "That was too narrow an escape. They may not give us another chance. Let's get out of here. And make it snappy."

"Aye-aye, sir." Though her skintight vextex uniform was torn in a dozen interesting places, she had not lost her sense of humor. "Cover me, sir?" Her eyes twinkled.

"I'll lead the way. Dr. Analyd has guard scorpions prowling the corridors. Same as on the bridge. You know how deadly those pesky little robots are."

"With due respect, sir, I'm as fast a shot as you." She unconsciously drew herself up to her full height, clicking her zzz gun onto *Eradicate* mode.

"But I'm smaller. Closer to the ground. Which is the guard scorpions' battlefield. And that's an order, Mellew."

"Aye-aye, sir," she said breathlessly.

With movements as lithe as a panther back in the pre-nuclear jungles of Terra, I prowled ahead of her up the stainless-steel corridor, retracing the steps that had led us onto the computerized bridge to Dr. Analyd's lair—not that I'd make that mistake again. The scene was ghoulish, as only the emergency lights were flickering ever since I'd managed to disable the electrical system of Dr. Analyd's battleship in a previous adventure. The corridor was also littered with the bodies of countless Analyd legionnaires I'd wasted with a stolen zzz gun during our aborted escape attempt across the doom-fraught bridge. This had been in the next-to-last adventure.

We were both lucky to be alive. My first lieutenant, in a rush of emotion, had thrown her arms around my neck once I'd freed her from the computerized wall manacles, tossed her the remains of her clothing, and mown down the two Zazinas preparing to molest her biologically—all in one smooth motion. In no time the steel floor was slick with the oozing green slime that passes for blood in the Zazinas, but we were careful not to step in it on our way out, since it has a half-life longer than plutonium's.

My plan had been for us to hurry down this corridor and blast free in Dr. Analyd's own escape pod. Only those few legionnaires stood in our way, and several guard scorpions whose charred carcasses gave me thirteen seconds of target practice. But I foolishly hadn't reckoned on not knowing the encrypted password for the escape hatch. Who might have it besides the evil Dr. himself? I racked my brains. Here we were in orbit above Nocturon, hidden in the folds of tesser-space, unable to contact our own disabled vessel, the *Stellar Maiden,* where the rest of my crew were sunk in Dr. Analyd's hypno-sleep, and the fate of our entire solar system depended on my being able to stop the upcoming invasion. It had taken our battle fleet three years to get here, and it would take another three to get home unless I could discover the secret of Dr. Analyd's omni-dimensional shuttling, but if we succeeded, and saved human civilization, it would be worth it.

Without warning and almost silently, at that moment a couple of guard scorpions popped out of an air vent in the steel corridor wall and hit the floor running, tiny legs jittering like crazy and deadly tails arcing up, trying to get a good fix on us before letting loose their deadly poison darts.

"Incoming!" I yelled, dropped to one knee, and fired. Jammed!

And no time to recharge! Before she could protest I grabbed Molly's zzz gun from her hand and spun around, pulling her to the floor as two lethal darts whizzed directly through the air where our torsos had just been. In a tangle of arms and legs Molly lay on top of me, and I couldn't wrench my gun arm completely free. But, using her shoulder to steady my hand at an impossible angle, I squeezed the trigger. The guard scorpion on the right let out a little electronic squeal and went ratcheting into the wall in a shower of sparks. I saved him for later and burned the tail off the other, then blew off his carapace. Then I took out the first; he was still banging pointlessly against the wall, but his ratcheting was starting to annoy me.

From three inches away Molly swept her tawny mane back around her ears and gazed at me with those deep brown eyes drenched in adoration. "Sir," she began, then couldn't go on. She swallowed and I felt her luscious body breathing up and down my whole length. "Sir—how many times must you keep rescuing me?"

Not now, I told myself firmly, wrestling with what my hands wanted to do and every fiber of my well-honed survival instinct told me to prioritize for later. "Not till we walk out of this death tub from intergalactic hell," I told her. "And get ourselves headed back toward Terra in one piece. Battle stations, lieutenant."

"Aye-aye, sir."

As we clambered to our feet, it suddenly struck me: the utter fiendishness of Dr. Analyd's plan. Of course, I muttered to myself, of course. He *wanted* us to come looking for him. He *wanted* to lure us out here full-force to attack him. He'd known we were coming all along. (Did that mean a spy somewhere? Hmm.) No, this was all part of his master plan. Draw our best talent, our entire fleet, out here to Nocturon to try to stop him, and meanwhile leave ourselves exposed back at Jupiter Command Base, vulnerable to the worst kind of counterattack. If he could get through our defenses there, nothing would stand in his way. It was simple, it was genius, it was terrifying. It must not succeed.

"Bad news, Mellew," I said. "We've got to get our hands on that dimensional shuttling device. Or we're doomed."

"You mean—"

"That's right. Back across the bridge to Dr. Analyd's lair. And let's hope he's taking a siesta."

I saw her gulp. She'd been through plenty in the last few hours—getting stripped naked and ogled by Zazinas preparing to reorganize your DNA can't be very pleasant—but she'd held up through all of it, she was definitely promotion material if we ever got home, and if she hadn't zzzed a couple of legionnaires on our scramble to the airlock, I'd have been lunaburger meat.

But I knew the prospect of making our way back across Dr. Analyd's bridge might be too much for her. It meant taking our chances that he hadn't changed the attack codes built into every luminous, booby-trapped bridge girder, where the slightest misstep could send you plummeting to your fiery doom all the way down to the reactor core, or else vaporize you in an instant. Or snap electrified pincers around your legs so you had no choice but to wait till the guard scorpions came to cruelly sting you. Or else—worst luck of all—the perverted Dr. Analyd himself would emerge from his lair, as he'd caught us once before. And this time he wouldn't leave our demise to be bungled by underlings.

"You wait here, Molly. No sense both of us risking our lives for that bridge. It's too dangerous. If I don't return, you'll have to learn the secret of his omni-dimensional shuttling somehow, and get back to warn Jupiter Base. Don't hesitate to use any weapon you have." I paused. "Any weapon. It may be all up to you."

"But you can't make it across that bridge alone!"

"Sure I can. Dr. Analyd won't have bothered to change the codes. He may be the greatest evil mastermind in the galaxy, but even he slips up every now and then."

Her eyes were shining, and when she spoke her voice throbbed. She said in a tone I knew better than to overrule, "Lead the attack, sir. I'm coming with you."

"Mellew, you know this is our last chance." She nodded grimly. I raised my smoldering zzz gun. "Ready to go all the way, lieutenant?"

She brandished her weapon. "Cocked and ready, sir."

"Let's go, then. Let's cross that bridge."

35

We,
the Undersigned People of Salt Cove

RESOLVED:

Because the will of the people must of necessity come before the will of the government in a free, just, and democratic society, and since to render a people voiceless has a destructive effect on the very health of that society;

and

Whereas the Commonwealth of Massachusetts and its various subsidiary systems, including offices of public works, public safety, and of city, county, and court, have totally rejected on the basis of selective deafness the will of an overwhelming majority of citizens resident at Salt Cove, a village within the City of Leicester, Cape Sarah;

and

Whereas said law-abiding community, comprising about 350 souls year-round and 600 in summer, finds that all of its requests, entreaties, petitions, writs, and arguments have failed to secure a fair hearing or productive discussion with the state regarding their proposed destruction of the Salt Cove bridge;

and

Whereas the bridge is a beautiful entity which could be conveniently repaired or rebuilt to the original design, with private funds to be raised by the village over a reasonable period; and whereas the bridge is also integral to the village's personality and a long-standing part of a vulnerable ecosystem, as well as one of Cape Sarah's very loveliest public structures and a historical rarity, being one of only two uncovered all-pedestrian wooden bridges in the United States with a length of more than fifty-five yards;

furthermore

No persuasive case has been made by the state that this bridge puts Salt Cove at greater risk from fire, crime, illness, bad weather, or other emergency than it has happily endured for over three decades, since the bridge's 1969 closure to vehicular traffic;

yet

Despite these compelling arguments, the Commonwealth insists this architectural treasure must be destroyed and a bridge of unacceptable design and materials erected in its place, despite strong opposition for the last three months from the people of Salt Cove;

and

Whereas during its attempts to destroy the bridge, state employees have trespassed on private property, destroyed private property, blocked public waterways, disrupted the normal course of road traffic into and out of the village with resultant loss of benefit, disrupted the peace, put the lives and property of abutters of said bridge as well as others in the immediate vicinity in utmost peril from explosives, repeatedly threatened the public's Constitutional right of assembly, and taken one innocent life while disdaining the sacred will of the people;

thus

The village of Salt Cove now considers itself under siege from a close-minded state bureaucracy whose invidious tactics of

subterfuge and brute force are more in keeping with a dictator-
ship than a democracy;

and whereas

We, the undersigned villagers of Salt Cove, hold this truth to
be self-evident: that the rights of a village to decide its own
fate, like a microcosm of the nation as a whole, in issues per-
taining to said community's beauty, must surely prevail over the
rights of the state so long as there is no threat or damage to
other communities; and any attempt by city, state, or federal
governments to impose their will violates the most fundamental rights either implicit or designate in the U.S. Constitution,
rights which all free people enjoy;

therefore

Finding itself with no alternatives, on the stroke of midnight
tonight [date] the village of Salt Cove duly declares itself
henceforth IN SECESSION from the City of Leicester, the
County of Stilton, the Commonwealth of Massachusetts, and
the United States of America, with all sovereign rights, protec-
tions, and liberties thereof;

as a result

Any further attempt by an outside power to destroy or otherwise harm the Salt Cove bridge shall be considered an act of
war and be treated as such;

likewise

Any attempts to restrict the citizens of Salt Cove from enjoying
access to locales on Cape Sarah or beyond, such as Salt Cove
offers to outsiders without fee or hindrance, shall be considered
unfair limitations of free passage, as shall any attempts to
restrict the flow of goods, mail services, and supplies as protected under the laws of the United States, our neighbor; and

lastly

Though none of us have any desire to sunder our relationships
with our parent country, and fervently hope we may resolve this
grave matter by less disruptive means, until such time and such
a resolution, with a corollary signed document overturning the
present one, the village of Salt Cove declares itself an indepen-

dent, sovereign state, with all the rights and privileges regularly and happily granted to such by the international community of independent, sovereign nations.

(signed)

THE PEOPLE OF SALT COVE

Toby Auberon, rep.
Jessica Stoddard, scr.

36

Jessica Stoddard

HISTORY IS THE DREAM I keep trying to sleep through, that keeps waking me up. If I had more control this would be nothing but, oh, a paean to pinball, the flashing lights and ringing bells just like they always promise. Let me not stray too far, let me prevent this being merely (merely!) an ode to Toby Auberon, let me at least profess, out of a sense of historical accuracy, to mention other people. Other people are hell, man; I overheard this once in a city and never forgot it.

So forget it. Let's talk about Toby.

He sat there amid the trumpet blast of noon sunlight on a sea as blue as bottled ink, oblivious to an extravagant view behind him, one leg over the other, a yellow legal pad like my father favored on his lap, arrhythmically tapping a pencil and every now and then writing with urgent purpose, a few swift lines at a time. This is how they say Mozart composed, forming the musical idea fully, gracefully, considering it, solidifying it, then at last scribbling it down as if taking dictation from the gods. It is not how I write, but then again I've never had much chance to enjoy being divinely dictated to.

When he was done he read the document aloud, sentence by cascading sentence. I offered several helpful criticisms—I was not a lawyer's daughter and office assistant, a paralegal by inclination and *per stirpes*, for nothing. It was I who suggested "disrupting the peace," in fact; elsewhere he gently pointed out where the flaws in my thinking lay. I shall never forget his rueful smile or the way his ponytail shifted when he shook his head at failing to notice the obvious, as if acknowledging he was prone to this.

I typed it all into my computer while he waited, printed out two copies, and we both read quietly to ourselves, admiring our joint handiwork, in mute assent to a profound truth about friendship I read somewhere: two is not twice one, two is ten thousand times one.

I was done before he was. He said finally, "No one will ever sign this. No one."

I said, "Leave that to me."

I was tireless. I took it round to a printer in Leicester and ordered a master copy on superb paper, the kind used for well-written declarations of independence. I photocopied a whole stack and dropped them off that very evening at the forty households I trusted most, or distrusted least, in the village—besides us ringleaders. (I had the foresight to get Toby to sign his penciled original and date it, much to his befuddlement, not realizing this was apart from my feelings for him; the next morning I secreted it in my safety-deposit box down at Leicester Bank and Trust, the bank you can trust.)

You will find this all spelled out in whatever the publishers leave behind of my appendix. I likewise left each household a handwritten note, in large legible letters so no one would complain or make disparaging remarks about my accursed cursive style, saying *Please read this and call me. Tell no one.* I didn't need to leave behind the afternoon's front-page article in the *Leicester Daily News* trying to reconstruct—with no eyewitnesses, just detailed hearsay and a photo of the few wires Roscoe left meaningfully behind on two pilings—the dastardly attempt to blow up our bridge. Everyone around here had seen the newspaper, and many of us knew the entire story, even though no one was singing for the police.

There was also a photo of their boat turning tail in mid-morning light and putt-putting out of the cove harbor. Rented, it seems, to the state's demolition experts for double the usual rate by the Mancuzzi brothers, who own a marine shop down on the Neck, over the other side of the cape. As my father had handled their parents' will, I called Mancuzzi & Fr. to remind them to be sure to slap on a hefty surcharge for late return. It always pays to be thorough, I find.

I figured that rather than pleading our case I'd let the situation, naked as a jailbird, speak for itself. I was anticipating a few telephone calls of horrified refusal to sign such an absurd, incendiary document. But the Plot to Bomb the Bridge, as it became known (thanks to Mitch) did a lot of convincing; betrayal does have its own loud way of talking. People took the attack as an insult, a flagrant gesture of disdain for who we were and the taxes we regularly paid. It revealed not only what the state but what Leicester really thought of us; it was seen as a bullying declaration of war. People had mourned Leilia's death, but that could be construed as an accident, plus the woman had been brandishing at least a wedding ring and maybe even a knife. At least Mr. Go, as I called him—a.k.a. the Wily Scativo—all but admitted to me that very day that she was armed, if only by raising his eyebrows silently when I asked point-blank.

But there was nothing accidental about plotting to blow up our bridge on a moonless night. It got the bridge-sitters clustered back there in force, it prompted another sardonic editorial in the Boston paper, it merited a brief return of the TV crews who were hankering for more blood—viewers' appetites having been considerably enriched in recent years. Soon the incessant flapping of news helicopters came to sound like the baying of hungry hounds to me, though theoretically they were our allies.

All this took a week, we were nearly at the end of June, and the timing was perfect. The state was sitting on its hands, no doubt waiting for the patriotic holiday to pass before trying another assault. Toby was convinced an emergency court order justifying the use of force was in the works, though neither he nor Bob Herbert could ferret it out. I know Toby spent several days rummaging through old maps and city archives and the files in our Village Historical Society, in what used to be the *Firehoufe* (according to the original sign) beside the Village Hall, that Mildred unlocked for him specially on a couple of afternoons. I do not know how well they got along; I know she never took back the cruel things she said, but then who ever does?

He was looking very tired these days, getting by on practically no sleep. Several times I stopped by the lighthouse but he was never there, or never answered my knock, not once.

It took me a week, as I said, of relentlessly shepherding people along, convincing them the secession wasn't "serious"—no I was not revoking my U.S. citizenship, no I was not secretly a socialist much less an anarchist, no this was not a liberal plot nor a terrorist ruse, no this was not the hippie's idea but rather the Bridge Committee's. All we hoped to accomplish, I felt I was mowing a lawn back and forth, was to gain as much attention as possible in hopes of winning our case in the fickle tribunal, the crucial alembic, of public opinion.

I did not tell anyone how serious I knew Toby was, that he thought we no longer owed our country any allegiance.

At last we held a Sunday meeting at the Village Hall. There were no reporters present; we'd turned them away to preserve an element of surprise. First Roscoe recounted what he'd found in the way of explosives, and showed us a few batches as evidence. Italo spoke, Mildred reminded us of the bridge's history, Toby assured everyone that if there were a better approach he'd be delighted to hear it. He seemed reserved that night, holding back a little on what he'd created and abruptly found himself convincing us to do. This was partly an act, for he was ready to speak as forcefully as needed. But I saw he felt shyness played better—this wasn't a moment when a hard delivery was called for, it would've frightened people.

Personally, I was astounded, since this was a village of bickering gossips ready to argue about the territorial rights of a thorn bush in the Meadow. Yet here we were, talking about signing a resolution with real thorns. As Mildred said, it was probably the most concerted act of Salt Cove as a whole since deciding to build the first bridge across the cove back in 1817. The sorrow was that everybody was terrified of his own government, and there is nothing like fear in the belly, a rumbling and tumbling in the bowels, to make you feel friendly toward the neighbors you cheerfully resent the rest of the year.

It could've gone sour even after all that, when it came down to a voice vote, until Harold Milne stood up. I'd been surprised to see him, and a lot of people didn't know how to speak to him. But after he raised himself, put up his hand for the floor and said, very quietly, that he was grateful for our support and our prayers, and he knew what Leilia would have wished us to do, how if she'd been here she'd have spoken loudest of all for letting the world know how determined we were, to stand and never yield no matter how heavily they leaned on us—well, after that there wasn't a dry ear in the house and things were only going one direction. No one's more sentimental down deep than New Englanders, you just have to drill through several layers of inherited glacier and granite first.

The vote was a full-throated roar, and people quickly lined up to sign the resolution, which I brought down from the stage. No one would've dared protest it at that point, not after Harold. He was the first to sign, on a card table against the wall (a bridge table, as more than one wag pointed out). We made way for him silently, letting him have the honor, and afterward I noticed him shuffling toward the door by himself, once he was fully satisfied with the result. Scativo, who signed right on the line below Harold, walked him out, a hand on the big man's arm going down those treacherous nineteenth-century stairs, so he wouldn't have to shuffle home alone.

That Monday we overnighted a copy of the Act of Secession to the governor: a well-meaning, retired, Irish-extract accountant named Thrale, Dick Thrale, you can't fail with Dick Thrale, a dangling ditherer in his second term who was not going to run for another and who was already being pushed around by his lieutenant, one Spencer Rowe III, of the Nantucket and Salem Rowes, a wealthy old sea mercantile family, who was a safe bet to replace the dumfounded Dick when the election came up in a year's time.

We called a news conference for Tuesday at 10:30 A.M. on the bridge, the same moment when the governor would be receiving our signed resolution. We'd held on to the original copy for dramatic purposes, and we got a good pavane of reporters out there, the lords and ladies of the press with their footmen and cameramen and butt-boys in attendance, even the TV crews from Boston who for the past week had given up on our ever producing anything worth a slog from the city. Only one helicopter was on the wing, providing a dragonfly's view of the cove, but we had a solid dozen journalists' crews. It'd taken Harvey Wilfong, our bulky, bearded resident ad man with an office in the city, to make sure they came. He promised each the exclusive scoop of the decade, and they'd never trust him again, but it did the trick.

That morning I went to fetch Toby at the lighthouse and help him choose a tie; he'd told me he intended to wear a suit. I wasn't prepared for the dapper vision, the steely-eyed advocate, the indomitable liberator of the people who greeted me at the door. Everything brushed and snipped and pulled back in place, a charcoal suit that would not be too dark on television, a crimson tie with a tiny woven gold insignia which turned out to be a lightbulb when I peered closely— the symbol of the Electricians' Union of Sierra Madre, California. ("My father's alma mater," he said.)

"What a handsome revolutionary you make," I breathed.

Mornings make me bold, you see; by nightfall I have lost my resolve, sapped by all that didn't happen earlier. If anything were ever to arise between us, I told myself, it would have to be in daylight. Unless he were to make the first move.

He blushed at my compliment. "Just a momentary illusion." Unconsciously touching his tie. "Do you have the dingus?"

I waved the large envelope with the signed resolution, plus all fourteen pages of signatures, at him. "Know what you're going to say?"

"I'll sum it up in a few sentences. That's all they'll show."

I paused him at the door. "What about that famous rat of yours? Shouldn't we ask him to come along?"

He grinned. "The rat jumped ship. He's on his way back to Rio."

Strange, the ways people choose to express what they really mean.

As we ambled across the Meadow I said, "Toby, you promised to tell me everything. You promised to show me what you're doing in the lighthouse, all of it. And now here it is—"

"And now here we are," he said firmly. "Jessica, this is what I'm doing. It's that simple. When this is over, I'll be looking for something else to do."

"I see," I said through clenched teeth.

"You know what really interests me?" he said mildly. "The underworld."

"Organized crime?"

"No, no, the other one. When I quit being a lawyer I traveled a lot in Central America. And I got immersed in Mayan and Aztec history. Mostly the ceremonial ball game they used to play in those outdoor stone courts. But they believed there was a matching court and sacred game played in the underworld, too. No one's ever really figured out in a satisfying way how the game worked, though in some places they put on a show for tourists. Then I was living down in Rio, and I used to watch people playing foot-volleyball on the beach, hitting the ball with everything except their hands. And I said to myself, Of course, that would be a kind of training for when they had to compete against the Lords of the Underworld, since they might not be able to use their hands—" His voice trailed off; he could feel me no longer with him. "You see? You think I'm hiding something important. But everyone has their own weird little hobbies. Just like—" He paused. "Just like your father's was pinball."

I murmured, "I'm sorry, I'm not following you, I'm too keyed up." We were coming from Baven Rock out of the Meadow and down the gray road past Harry Boller's shaded house. We could faintly hear, reverberating off cove waters we couldn't see yet, an expectant hum of people on the bridge. It was ten minutes after ten by my father's watch.

I said, "Did you ever think we would end up here? Like this?" I wanted to add, *When you saw me up on the Village Hall stage, taking notes, writing down every word you uttered? I knew, my darling, even though I didn't realize what that instinct meant. And no matter where it leads, for the rest of my life whenever I make this walk I will always remember this morning with you. And someday I'll show you the tree back near the water, the rheumatic old oak that I think of as my father, the tree I go to for advice because it was the tree he used to fall asleep under when I was a child and wanted him to wake and listen to me. The tree where I learned to sit and listen happily to nothing, to all the messages that the nothing of the world was trying to send me.*

He said, "I always knew we would end up here. From the very first village meeting. I nearly left, you know."

I saw him swallow, and I felt a stab that when it came time for him to go, the only clue would be the lighthouse door swinging vapidly on its hinges and no one inside, no proof that he'd ever lived there, and no warning of his departure.

"I'm glad you didn't leave," I managed to croak.

He reached over then, just for an instant, and touched my arm, just for that instant, with his forefinger. It was not an accident. "Well, I might be glad I didn't, too," he said. "Ask me an hour from now. Or in a week."

Exactly a week from that morning they blockaded our village.

37

Spencer Hamilton Rowe III

WHO IS THIS PIPSQUEAK? I'll tell you one thing: this administration will not be made a fool of on a national holiday. If I were in charge we'd have ended it weeks ago. Not gotten stuck in some ludicrous public debate. End it the hard way, it'd be history overnight. Send some gunboats in to shell their village and take out that bridge while you're at it, if it's not too much trouble. Teach them a lesson and score big with the voters.

Yes, Jenkins, I have seen the front page of this morning's paper. Tough questions? The only tough question is why the governor has failed to respond in an effective and timely manner. And I will not be linked with his inadequacy, with his indecisiveness, with his cowardly refusal to do anything controversial for his last two years in office. Think Teddy R. worried about the polls? Think he asked himself whether the American people wanted him carrying a big stick, a so-so stick, or a tiny, shriveled-up stick? I'm not going to let this administration get cornered by a bunch of village idiots led by some conniving beach bum who smells a chance to get famous. When I'm done they'll have their own tax code. Or maybe we'll put in a drawbridge, see how these Moldy Saltines like real historical accuracy.

A year from now what the voting public will remember, Jenkins, is that I took care of business whenever a vacationing governor failed to do so. Fail with Thrale. Otherwise we'll have every nickel-and-dime road repair, every safety order, blocked by a bunch of pamphleteers whining about aesthetic considerations. They don't think Massachusetts is beautiful enough, they can move to Vermont and beautify a few milk cows.

Yes, I am aware of Chet Cairns's request for transfer to a waterways project in Lowell. I am also aware of his thinly veiled threat about how certain memos have been deleted from the database but which, being a thorough little fraidy-cat for life, he kept his own hard copies of. Does he imagine it's cute to blackmail the next governor? Someone who ought to fire him for screwing up a simple demolition problem? Bring me his transfer request, I'll okay it, then in six months you can bring me his head on a paper plate. With extra fries.

No, we do not make rash moves. We act coldly, carefully, efficiently. This is why we first took care of the situation in the courts and waited a year. We've been patient. We've watched the tide go in, we've watched the tide go out. Time is still on our side, but we've got to make every day painful for them. I'm not some terrified damage-control weasel like the governor, who doesn't understand that every hour's delay hurts us. We shouldn't have to wait till after the holiday weekend to flex our muscles. We should be humiliating them, we should have every taxpayer in the state furious at Salt Cove for every dollar this secession nonsense is costing. Bill these yokels daily, that'll shut them up.

What infuriates me is that I shouldn't even have to point out to the U.S. Attorney's office that this goes way beyond party politics. If it drags on and the crackers don't give up and go back to the beach, ultimately it can make the feds look much worse than us. One more history lesson I shouldn't have to give.

My family built this state, Jenkins. While everyone else was spinning yarn and churning butter and thumping the Bible, my family was sending whaling ships round the world, they were importing spices from heathen archipelagoes, they were risking other people's lives to construct a great New England future. Where I come from we call that having a vision, and you don't command that kind of fear and obedience with empty bravado, you've got to march out there and grip the future by its miserable throat. I'd like to see how this beachcomber feels with one of my family's harpoons embedded in his gut.

Change of plan. Call up the museum my great great grandfather started in Salem, tell them the lieutenant governor needs to borrow back some Rowe ship's property off the walls, I'll go up to Salt Cove and harpoon the runt myself. You bet I'm serious. Throw him in the water and see if he can swim as fast as he can talk.

I want you to smear that mosquito, Jenkins, but from a safe distance. You've got two whole days, so don't make excuses. Spare us all from the heartwarming village democracy crap. I don't want to see any more stories about another Declaration of Independence, and I don't want to see his ugly mustache on TV trying to upstage me for the Fourth of July. Find out who the pipsqueak really is and what he doesn't want the churchgoing public to know. Everyone's got something disgusting to hide. Sex with animals, who cares, use your imagination. Just keep our name tag off it.

The farther Salt Cove goes, the more they'll get hurt when we have to step in and punish them. And the more noise they make now, the louder they squeal, the worse they'll look when it's over. Nobody likes a spoiled brat. They'll finish with every county in Massachusetts cheering for us to pave every inch of their stupid sovereign cove. That bridge will come down in an hour.

And yes, Jenkins, I am aware you feel this is no way to endear myself to my eventual neighbors, though they don't know it yet, up in Teal Bay. You seem convinced that a diploma from a fancy school of management means you know something about human nature. You think all these Cape Sarah villages are secret allies, right? Bull. They don't even know each other, and they still hate each other. This little puppet show of solidarity won't last for long. And if we can't throttle Salt Cove slowly, we'll just shut down this fiasco with a surgical strike some morning. All we really need to worry about is the back end. Think Teal Bay is going to mourn someone else's bridge after their property values go up wildly? Think they're going to connect the dots? Don't dream.

Nobody knows how to play connect-the-dots anymore, Jenkins. Nobody knows how to draw a straight line, and that's not even the most direct route. Not if you know where to fold the paper. And not if I'm the one who put all the dots in place.

38

Wilfredo Heredia

THE HON. WILFREDO HEREDIA
United States Attorney's Office
12 Northern Avenue
Boston, Massachusetts 02210

July 3

Sidney McAdams
Special Agent in Charge
Resident Field Office
Federal Bureau of Investigation
Boston, MA 02108

Sid—

Re your note of July 1 regarding the secession uproar up in Salt Cove, and pertinent to our telephone conversation the other morning:

The U.S. Attorney's Office is likewise disinclined to pursue this matter at present. We've got no dog in this fight, and neither your office nor mine has time for a few disgruntled fishermen.

I think we can safely trust the FBI's counterterrorism unit that we do not have on our hands a serious group threat to overthrow the government, avoid paying taxes, or undermine the safety of the general population, etc., etc.

Both our staffs have better things to do, and I suggest we sit back and watch the governor's office handle with their usual grace, subtlety, and tact what should remain a purely state matter. I don't think this is even worth a meeting, and frankly, if I get one more call from the lt. governor's office asking me to issue a statement, I'll set fire to that bridge myself.

If you ever hear back from the boys at Homeland Security, would you kindly let them know what we've decided?

Sharon and I are looking forward to seeing you and Lucy at the Party clambake this weekend.

Sincerely,

Wilfredo Heredia

UNITED STATES ATTORNEY FOR THE
EASTERN DISTRICT OF MASSACHUSETTS

P.S. That's right, Auberon was Stanford all the way. About six years after me. I hear he looked even rattier in a suit and tie, without all the hair.

39

Susan Thayer

July 5

Dear Italo,

You'll understand why I've held off writing till now. I've kept hoping—not just in my official capacity as representative on the Leicester City Council for the villages of Salt Cove, The Bight, and Gibson's Cove, but also as a friend—that the village would re-think the resolution of last Sunday.

It is not for me to tell my constituents what to do. I'm just a go-between, a bridge. I argue not just for us against them, I try to explain in the other direction, too. My goal as a "politician" is two words: *Work together.*

I've told you how bad I feel that at the beginning of this whole mess I dropped the ball by not being at the first meeting. (This happens when you have two teenagers, you neglect your own agenda sometimes.) But I have been present at every Village Hall meeting since, and tried to put in my two cents' worth, even if I got shouted down.

Understand that I am totally, 110% on your side in terms of

the bridge controversy. However, I still feel there are untried diplomatic avenues that may achieve the desired result.

As the nonelected Bridge Committee, without inviting me to any of its meetings, has taken an increasingly hard line over the last six weeks, I have felt increasingly left out of the loop. As, I'm sure, some of your fellow residents must feel. We all mourn, along with Harold, Leilia's tragic loss. Nor can I condone for one second the state's attempts to ride roughshod over the boundaries of decent behavior and just playing fair!

Ditto, I applaud all the favorable exposure you've gotten on TV, in the newspapers, etc. (I thought you handled yourself marvelously, by the way, on the radio interview I heard.) We both know you cannot buy that kind of goodwill.

At the same time, as I tried to tell you over the phone a few minutes ago, I think we've reached a critical juncture. I cannot support a decision by some of my favorite constituents to secede from the United States of America. I cannot even wrap my head around such a concept.

I feel that under the present circumstances for me to explain and excuse and support your decision before the city council is simply wrong. Though I wish nothing but the very best for all of you, I cannot possibly justify your actions to myself, and it would therefore not be right to have me attempting to justify them to my fellow councilors. With regret, I must therefore resign from my responsibilities as Salt Cove's voice on the council.

I send you all good fortune at what is, I know, a trying time. And I look forward to going back to being your representative again, when the world is a better place for everyone concerned.

This has been a difficult letter for me to write.

Your friend,

Susan L. Thayer
Leicester City Council

P.S. I do want you to know that if the village ends up needing someone to act as a go-between at any meetings with state reps as may hopefully come up, or else to "monitor" or chair future discussion groups on this issue, no matter how small, I would be happy to offer my services. I always feel people should *work together.*

40

Van Chapman

SECESSIONIST PROPAGANDA
[*The New York Times*, op-ed page, July 6]

Patriotism makes strange bedfellows. "A scrappy, bantamweight prizefighter of a New England village" was how this paper referred to a tiny nuisance of a place on our nation's birthday. A few journalists even cited the Texas Rangers' motto ("*Little guy always beat a big guy, little guy keep on coming*") in praise of this apparent exercise in democracy.

News clips offered the same glycerine footage, as Salt Cove trotted out all its charm with a hypocritical July Fourth parade led by a female disguised as the Statue of Liberty. There was the obligatory speech on their toothpick bridge, whose demolition they are protesting with a featherheaded resolution to secede from the very country they were supposedly celebrating.

Offended by this propaganda offensive? You bet I was, since the parade was clearly a ploy to raise media support. Which they are attracting in droves.

Hello? Anyone awake out there? Have you noticed that whenever people mention Tocqueville (1805–1859), they're really after cash? The ringleader in Salt Cove, a former Left Coast lawyer named Toby Auberon, was careful to cite our French observer. " 'Political life originated in the townships, and it may almost be said that each formed an independent nation,' " he remarked, quoting *Democracy in America*. " 'No man would acknowledge that the state has any right to interfere in their affairs.' "

When a small man misquotes a great man I always feel a personal sense of loss—you might say I'm a dreamer, but I'm not the only one. What did Mr. Auberon slyly leave out of his Tocqueville lesson? Why, that each township "gave up a portion of their independence to the state."

Therein lies the rub. Massachusetts has ordered an unsafe bridge replaced with a safe one. This is the state's responsibility, to protect *all* its citizens, even those who prefer a dog-eared postcard. Nor should it spend a fortune repairing an old relic that will need expensive upkeep—a dangerous precedent in a state whose financial glory days are long past. Besides, surely it behooves a civic-minded Massachusetts village to build a bridge that its senators would have great difficulty driving off.

Secessionism in this country has a checkered history; no need to go into the obvious. Few recall the seventies with any clarity, but in those distant days every tiny community with a grievance wanted to secede, like children kicking and screaming to get their own way. The list was considerable, from Alaska to Long Island's South Fork to Cherokee Nation, an island in the Rio Grande, and multiple Indian protests on Martha's Vineyard, in Vermont, in Maine.

Internationally, Quebec's still itching for independence; Wales, Cornwall, Brittany, Corsica, the Kurds, the Basques, the Catalans, the Tamils, the Sikhs—need I go on? Everyone wants his own country. Few are grown-up enough to ask themselves if they'd really be better off.

Back in the sixties there was a fellow from Australia's outback with a similar idea. He declared independence for his several thousand acres in the middle of nowhere; set up his own stamps, currency, visitors' visas, parliament of one; no wife or neighbors to outvote him. He was a brief blip on the world's back pages, with a no-nonsense Down-Under accent, and the Aussies had enough sense to leave him alone till he rejoined the mainland around him. ("Long as he resists the temptation to shell Sydney," one of their government ministers remarked, "he can print all the crazy maps he likes.")

I shall thus pray for our own decision makers not to take leave of their senses. For there is nothing "democratic" happening in Salt Cove, nothing admirable. This is no disenfranchised ethnic group struggling to take back what was once theirs. These are self-ish, self-righteous reactionaries who claim they owe allegiance to no one, and everyone owes them everything.

Once every Lilliput community believes it can push the state and federal governments around—and once those governments elected by, for, and of the people start to fear the little dog yipping at their heels—we're at the mercy of any grievance, any complaint, any whining p.r. campaign. The Massachusetts Department of Public Works must never answer to the Salt Cove Minutemen.

We should adopt the unruffled ease of our Australian counter-parts decades ago, and let the little dog yip away. And if it yips a bit too long, a bit too loud, we should not hesitate to spank it. Very firmly.

41

Scott Mahren

WHEN IT COMES TIME, in the not too dim-and-distant future, for the Wily Scativo to write his memoirs—and believe me, it'll put to rest such debates as the artistic virtues of Molly on Monday, Pamela on Tuesday, that cognac-eyed Egyptian waitress on Wednesday, etc.—one question the hungry flock will want me to settle is: What's the best method around a blockade? What's step one when a SWAT team shuts down your village? Whether they're real pros or, in this case, charlatans and chumps? And even when you're surrounded, like our hero, by gullible amateurs who still believe in the letter of the law while the alphabet is being torn to tatters around them?

Say it over and over. The reason civilization is not a one-foot-next-foot march forward is because people can't think for themselves. Sorry, boys, you blew the life savings on a troop suicide off the cliff. The crux of the Scativo's philosophy, and this will be one of those gold-embossed commandments when I get round to publishing (alongside the one about how it's better to watch a woman dress than undress, since by covering it up she's saying I'm all yours, even if she doesn't mean it), goes as follows: Every self-generated problem is a solution in riddle form. People slice, dice, and liquefy themselves under subway cars when they should be levitating their way to glory, not grinding themselves into luncheon meat. But the corollary is: Any problem put on you by other people is an act of aggression, an act of war, and has to be repelled.

Repelled in a way that's not vindictive, not loose cannon, not revenge at any cost, but methodical—because baby, the rain must fall. If someone deliberately does something to you even once that no friend ever would, then they're no pal. The Wily One has watched too many poor dupes wait years to get the message they're being trampled, lulled by how nice the other guy sounds, how friendly he seems, how shocked he is that something's amiss. He's relying on your trusting, timid, terrified politeness to take it in the gut or take it under the chin, take it in the back or take it right up the highway, and the last thought you're granted before your eyes jiggle belly-up in their passive sockets is, Boy, was I slow on the uptake, now look at the obsolete Lincoln pennies on my fucking eyeballs, Ma.

(*But what about accidents?* I hear the sheep bleat as they jostle for post position in front of the rotating knives. Here's the bad news, buster—there are no accidents.)

Let's put it another way: I can appreciate war. The Scativo has seen far less efficient ways of settling a serious argument, even when the right guys go down groaning. Old Leilia understood that right from her tirade at the very first meeting. She knew it was war way back in March, when nearly everyone else thought it was paperwork. You could've bounced silver dollars off all the legal chitchat, but my bet was either they'd cave right after Leilia bought it or they wouldn't cave at all. Another bet I was winning repeatedly.

I was pointing this out to Toby Auberon, skeptical as ever on my back deck that morning in front of a cup of Joe. He wasn't visiting for the caffeine. What got him there was I'd promised to bestow on him my personal invention, the labor-saver every man can use, and not ever having owned a Mahren Pedal, naturally he came running. I gave him a deluxe three-height model, signed the back of the pedal with a special pen used for such august occasions, and let him know how few I give away. His was only #17, after nine years of record sales. He got the message—they're not all asleep out there, despite the deafening snores.

From my deck you could see the bridge with a couple of dozen people obediently guarding it on a patriotically sunny morning, and look right across the inner cove to Monroe Street, the steady hum and slow-mo blip-blip of a few cars that always reminds me of a shooting gallery I used to visit out on Coney. Call it a weakness for a great American childhood—there are worse things than growing up with no cash but good hand-eye. We'd hit the subject of pinball, since the Scativo came in at the end of that era, and the Auberon was intrigued enough to pick up a few pointers. We both started noticing something funny through the trees on the other side of the cove, how cars were getting backed up. Then we heard a few horns.

"Could be roadwork," he said. "Got to be."

"Dubious at best. Check the binocs," I said, and handed them over. All in all, a peculiar guy, odder than he seemed, okay by me as long as he stayed a step ahead of everyone else and kept smiling enigmatically while giving the people in charge a hosing. Still surprised he didn't have the chicks crawling all over him, though, since he had that commander-with-a-mysterious-past riff going, which they love. Plus no one thinks clearly when he's at the mercy of the Deadly Semen Backup. Not to put too fine a point on it, I wouldn't have been surprised if Molly herself wasn't ready to give him the lily, since she was constantly bringing his name up. Which was all right by me, too; I like to be able to tell the days of the week apart. It just proves that if you flash 'em the tip, they want the whole iceberg brooding under the surface.

He swiveled the binocs round to the head of the cove, handed them back. "Ever in the army?" he said conversationally.

"Nope. You?"

He shook his head. Got to hand it to the guy, he knows how to deny everything and make it sound like it could all go either way. He said, "There's something that looks like an armored vehicle up at the church. Kind they use to control a riot."

I looked through and had to refocus big time; the guy must wear glasses at home. There it was, a dark green blotch. Every car was stopping to gawp and dawdle past, since it wasn't budging.

I said, "Riot, sure. Or a hostage situation."

He sighed. "Feel like taking a run?"

Only a half mile through morning shade to the church, but it felt weird and wrong, since we had Shepherd Street to ourselves. No cars were coming at us from the head of the cove, which was the only entry point to our peninsula. A couple of cars did pass us on their way out.

When we got there it made sense. They were letting people leave the village, but they weren't letting anyone back in. A bunch of guys in urban commando SWAT team costumes were looking at people's IDs and forcing their cars over to the side of the road, then checking the names and license numbers on some Mission Impossible computer link.

As we came up they finally let one car through—it was Mildred the Historian, she looked like she'd just swallowed a live rat, you could see terror wriggling across her face. Enjoyed her signed book, by the way. After her they started in on some summer gringo, tall guy with a stockbroker's tan who got furious. Which didn't help with the SWAT goon, who made him turn around and face somebody's white picket fence, like the bad boy in kindergarten.

"What's going on here?" says Toby, going up to one of the SWAT guys. Cool, collected, in charge of himself, no threat but no particular respect, either. Everybody thinks you've got to treat these Johnny Commandos like they're about to defuse a nuclear device, when they're just hired hands like anyone else. But they can smell it if you don't take them seriously, when you're wondering how well they'd do in a Coney Island shooting gallery, on timing alone with their eyes closed. Funny how live ammo impresses people.

"Step back, sir," says the SWAT guy. I hate that phony slimeball routine, like you're the taxpayer and he respects you enough to call you sir while he knees you in the clappers.

"This is Salt Cove, not the United States of America," says Toby, and doesn't budge. "You do realize you're about to provoke an international incident?"

"Step back, buddy. I'm not going to ask you twice."

The SWAT goon is glaring hard at Toby. Chump thinks this ponytail guy in jeans is going to back down from a tough stare. At that point another SWAT guy, Mr. Entertainment with his helmet in his hands like he doesn't need help stopping incoming projectiles, his skull is thick enough, swaggers over and says, "Is there a problem here? I need to see some ID, sir."

"No, you don't," says Toby. "You have absolutely no authority within the independent country of Salt Cove, which is where you're standing. Either you step back thirty feet, or you're going to have to show me your passport and a visa."

"Oh, Christ," says the tough guy, and lopes back to his commando vehicle blocking most of the road. (Pretty big target, is what I was thinking.) "You want a fucking passport, I'll show you a fucking passport."

"Must be hot in those helmets," I say sympathetically. As if I'm not with the ponytail nuisance. After all, Toby arrived a few steps ahead of me. "You guys stuck out here all day?"

"Our orders," says the first guy, the crew-cut genius, "are not to let anyone drive into the village who doesn't reside there. Security reasons."

Toby nods. "You mean we might be in danger of invasion?"

The genius shakes his head. "All I know is, they want us to limit the collateral influences coming in."

"This on account of that bridge bullshit?" I ask.

The Innocent Scativo, friend of all uniformed goons following orders.

"Must be," says the genius, then as his boss appears, he adds, "I'm not at liberty."

Meanwhile the rest of the team of crack commandos, with heavy firepower slung across their shoulders just in case the residents turn on the serious resistance, have got a good dozen cars formerly on their way into Salt Cove now pulled over on both sides of Monroe Street, and the other cars just trying to get past are at a crawl, natch. You don't see this every day, not in this country, anyway, but that's the future in a nutshell: total gridlock.

"Boy, no one living here will have any friends left," I remark amiably. "Backing up traffic for half the cape."

The boss with the helmet shoves a badge at Toby, who gives it a derisive glance and barks out, "This isn't a passport. This is all crap and you know it. You're violating the U.S. Constitution, sergeant, and yes, I'm an officer of the court. You back that thing out of our country right now or believe me, you're going to star in a class action lawsuit tomorrow."

"Really?" says the boss commando. "Well, you're not going to have a dick tomorrow," and grabs Toby's arm and whirls him around to slap the cuffs on. This is the move they always practice at the training camps. They don't practice what to do when the ponytail nuisance immediately tromps hard not on your booted instep but on your unprotected lower shin ("I was aiming for the instep," he told me later) or when the accomplice, which was me, drops you with a kick to the side of the un-helmeted head followed by the same kick to the face of the genius alongside, who crumpled like a cocktail napkin. Same move I practice every morning, except heads give way a lot easier than my punching bag. For some reason the martial arts instructors in Jersey know more than the ones in the military these days; maybe we'll get lucky and the enemy will start with East Orange.

All a huge misunderstanding, of course, since in six seconds we both were looking down the snouts of several cannons I couldn't identify and being asked if we were willing to cooperate. My error, but Toby started it—once I saw he was resisting arrest, I just finished the job.

We spent the night in jail somewhere past Worcester, hours away, and dined on meat loaf just like Quasimodo used to make, and they charged me four bucks for a call to break a first date with curvaceous destiny the Scativo was looking forward to that night. So long, buttercup. Jessica bailed us out the next morning, thanks to a phone call from Bob Herbert, and drove us home, and we had to run the backed-up traffic gauntlet of those same commandos going back in, though Tweedledum and Tweedledee were off on a short medical vacation. Probably getting their pension plans raised.

By that time Toby had stopped calling me hothead and I'd learned—sworn to secrecy—that he knew more about pinball than I guessed. (Never underestimate the healing power of human intelligence, feeble solace for me.) The commandos had their blockade by land in place, and it would stay in place; they were just getting started. They couldn't really blockade the bridge, thanks to Roscoe's truck, though they did start harassing pedestrians and a couple of days later prevented non-residents from crossing, to try to lower the numbers occupying the bridge. They hadn't gone for the blockade by water yet. That would come soon enough.

Here endeth the sermon. My advice? Always have another way in, another way out, and get used to taking advantage of the infinite darkness and smuggler's delight of a summer night. Then undermine them with charm. Pretend they're *your* hostages, *your* prisoners, not the other way round. Be sure the kids play near them and the flirty cream-filled cupcakes smile and say hello. Don't act like you hate that they're there. Eventually they'll start to resent the chump on high who ordered them in and made them stay put, sweating cinder blocks.

That was one lesson I learned in the siege. Of course before the end of the summer I was a dead man, cleaning up after the elephants, so a fat lot of good an extra dollop of wisdom did for the Wily Scativo. One more gigantic American talent wasted, fallen on the field of battle, cut off in its prime, but then that's the tragedy of this country. Bang on the sides all you want, baby, despite all the love in the room you still end up with no music, no flashing lights, no extra points, *Game Over.*

42

Raymond Pratt

Now, especially, could be just the right moment to bring it up with her.

Remember, the issue is ultimately making a person feel comfortable. That's what a home should be. A place where you can become yourself. Where you can live your life the way *you* want. You've heard what I say to clients.

People change. Homes change. Lives change.

Needs change.

What I try to do is fit lives and homes together. I'm not someone who sells houses; I'm a matchmaker. People bring me their needs, and once they say *Raymond, we trust you,* I bring them the life they always wanted but could never find. Because I know every property on Cape Sarah. Every garden and every gutter, every roof and every view. Every mansion, bungalow, and two-family. Every lobsterman's shack. I know not only what it is, but what it can be.

Places change. The cape of yesteryear is not the cape of tomorrow.

This is what I tell all my clients, Sarah. This is what you need to tell your aunt. Speak to her about her *dreams*. You don't frighten people at first. Take it from somebody who understands human nature through and through. You warm them up a little, like a teapot. Then you add the scalding water.

Here's how it goes. You let her know there are dark, dark days ahead with this latest development. You ask her if she wants to wind up rattling around that huge house with no one to look after her. You remind her that nowadays nobody knows who's moving in down the hill or even next door, you can't vouch for anyone in this topsy-turvy, cockamamie world of ours. And maybe now, before it's too late, it's time for her to look around for an assisted-living situation. A place that can be a sanctuary. That'll feel like a home ten, fifteen years from today. With people who are there to help her. And a vista of the sea just as special as the one she has now. Tides she can count on.

No, Sarah, you do not ever use the D-word. Let *her* think that herself, let *her* bring it up. Nothing is farther from your mind, that's the position you take. But you still let her get frightened first, then bring her back to the world of safe, happy dreams. Someone to look after her. No hassle with meals. No fuss with medicines. No problems with reaching for an encyclopedia and pulling the bookcase down on top of her, like last year. No more fears, no more worry. A life she can *enjoy*, in a new home, that's what you have to stress. And every bit as much hers as the one she has now.

At this point you don't jeopardize the conversation unless she brings up the question herself. Keep telling her you can talk about it some other time. Let *her* be the one to insist. As her sole heir, you're there to help her make sure all her affairs are in order, as her father would've wanted. It's her needs that matter.

But at the end of the day we can't just wait around for her to drop. So you either get her to make the house over to you in increments, which'll take a few years. Or else you get power of attorney over her affairs and we hope there's a major stroke that does the job and she can't say boo, she certainly can't stop you taking over her house for the good of her estate and her future security. No court will question that, I've seen it happen plenty of times. Someone stuck in neutral can run through a lot of money drooling over their breakfast cereal.

Just don't try to twist her arm, it'll never work. You'll end up with her taking you out of the will and leaving the house to some foundation. Took me years, but in my line you learn how to read clients like a scorecard.

What we want, honey, is to keep focused on the long term. Not next year, but five years from now. When that place is a gorgeous hotel again, the most romantic on Cape Sarah. You offer the very best, your clients do the rest. Eight hundred dollars for a summer night. People will arrive, you'll greet them and wow them and soon they'll decide this cape was named after you.

Because it should've been.

43

Jessica Stoddard

Now I shall reveal how I discovered the secret hidden in the tower of Toby Auberon, and how he discovered mine.

First, though, I should say a few words about our sponsor, namely my own unwavering sense that my times have been important ones; that through the accident of my personality, diverse and unfinished, rubbing up against Toby's in the tumbling centrifuge of history, and the further accident of this sea-lapped place being where it is, location, location, location as the real estate developers chant sacrificially like pagan priests; through these accidents and more, we have lived through crucial events together.

I have written these pages, talked to everyone and even listened, out of a sense of double-pronged duty: to posterity, meaning Toby, and to Toby, meaning me. I have tried to get it right, every syllable, no matter what addled nonsense I thought I was hearing from people. There is a destiny that shapes these pages, just as a destiny shaped our rough-hewn ends. I would not want you to think I was merely sitting here—a woman accused of being past her prime—staring out at her prospect of the sea, uncapping her wine-dark pen, and juggling the alphabet with abandon, all fall down. No, I have been purposeful. There goes that foghorn again.

I find, on looking through my copious notebooks, that events now took on a more hurried momentum, and my meticulously sifting through each day's happenings and conversations before setting them down in my red ledger went awry. I did not lose touch, I just fell behind, and only recently have I been able to go through it all, correcting my memory, restoring details, adjusting the past to suit what in fact were the facts.

So even though what I most remember of July is all that emerged between Toby and me, set against the vastness of political upheavals— the lit torch being passed from my hand to his, then gripped by both at once as we climbed the shadowy steps of the stone tower together— when I look again through my good-little-schoolgirl notes I see that what I viewed as historical backdrop may seem more important than my "private" life. Not that I care any longer about such distinctions. As the Scativo used to say, baby, you came this far with me, you deserve to know everything, because I've got nothing to hide.

And very soon I shall tell all about what happened on my birthday, when I at last put on my birthday suit.

By July 13th the situation was as follows. Two armored SWAT vehicles, dark green steel-plated trucks, straddled the head of the cove, up by the church. After the incident involving Toby and Scativo and the thugs revealed the depth of the state's determination, a set of rules became daily scripture, intended to make the village wilt in the face of overwhelming opposition.

Nonresidents were now prevented from driving their cars, trucks, or bicycles into the village, though they were allowed in on foot provided they had a written invitation from a resident. Baby carriages were permitted, though they too were subjected to a thorough search.

As you'd imagine, this made the situation on Monroe Street horrendous, since the old road around the cape, widened during horse-and-buggy days for a long vanished trolley, is still barely wide enough for two cars along that stretch. With motley cars parked while their owners visited us in our blockaded misery, it became almost impassable. The weekly garbage truck stationed itself by the church for an hour every Friday morning, and we had to come to it. No private package services were permitted through; people had to walk or drive to the church to pick up their parcels and overnighted business letters. Naturally the summer people were furious—some even at us, which was the government's idea: to sow dissension in the ranks. A little later in the siege they stopped even allowing the mail truck in, with its pleasant daily echoes of the morning milk trucks of my childhood, so we all had to troop up to the church and get handed our letters. But by that time mail was the least of our worries.

The legal justification, according to Toby, was the state's right to exert "police power" against an emergency threat. ("It's not like the Code of Hammurabi," he told me. "It's not written down anywhere. They just wheel it out whenever they need it.") The moral justification to the country at large was a blanket fear of domestic terrorism, fear like a blanket that keeps you warmer than cold courage would. The logic escaped me, since we couldn't have been more open about our demands. They had declared war, not us; we were secessionists, not terrorists; we were no longer part of the United States, hence "domestic" didn't apply. Besides, we weren't the ones wiring explosives under cover of darkness or taking pot shots at bystanders.

They also stationed commandos on Monroe Street by Roscoe's massive truck, which at first they fruitlessly tried to tow away in order to destroy the bridge from that end. Then they realized he'd locked the wheels and they might as well have been trying to drag a house. The truck was, as Roscoe chortled, part of the view now. By setting commandos not only by the truck but by the hidden footpath which starts twenty yards up the street, winds down the steep, densely treed embankment, and leads muddily to the bridge, they managed to keep many nonresidents from making it onto the bridge to squat with us. Many but not all, because there are other ways onto a peninsula surrounded by water. Plus once we had a list of our most ardent supporters all over the cape we started generating daily invitations for them to come visit. Each letter acted as a *laissez-passer* until the commandos stopped letting any nonresidents in, even footlings.

Anyway, this was an enormous pain in the ass, and made simply buying groceries an ordeal of several forms of identification and rude questions.

"State your name and purpose, please."

"Jessica Stoddard, deceased. Diseased."

"What was that?"

"I'm on my way into Leicester."

"And you'll be returning at what time?"

"In an hour. I've run out of ink and Cheese Straws. Can I bring you back a coffee, Mr. Commando?"

"No, ma'am. We're not allowed to accept gifts."

"What a shame."

Sure was: I felt ready to poison those brutes. A double *latte*, sergeant, with an appoggiatura of curare in the foam, *ciao*.

We still controlled the bridge. As Toby predicted, they were hoping to make us cry Uncle Sam, and they were willing to create absurd knots of backed-up cars from Gibson's Cove or even The Bight past Salt Cove down to Willowdale and blame it on us. But they weren't ready yet to storm the bridge with tanks and pull every one of us off at gunpoint, screaming and kicking. No, they weren't about to have such dire images flashed nationwide, not the year before an election.

They knew we weren't terrorists, though Ms. State Attorney General, a Harvard prune in pearls and sensible shoes, was starting to bandy the word. But they also feared an attempt to trample us could trigger real domestic terrorism, could provoke those hidden militias fed up with the government and just itching to blow up an official building. After all, we weren't some loony cult with our own set of sacraments, hiding in Central America; we were smack in Paul Revere country.

One of Toby's great worries was that we'd attract every wacko within three thousand miles. "Maybe it's good they aren't letting anyone in," he muttered one morning as he dropped off his grocery order with me. By this time we feared he might be arrested if he went into town, so he was in effect trapped in Salt Cove—though I have never, in all these decades, seen a life here as trapped. "Maybe we should thank them for protecting us from the nuts. Like our friends in Missouri, waiting years for this one."

"The only time I'll thank those government bastards," I said, "is when they leave here for good."

My bitterness was partly a lie, for I thanked those commandos every day in the confessional of my black heart, blessed them for thrusting us into a war-footing situation, because without it there was a foreseeable end to my time with Toby, our now daily alliance (I nearly wrote dalliance). Without it the stopper would fly off the bottle and he would swirl away in customary many-colored smoke, to vanish from my daily routine. I longed for the siege to end, of course, but not just yet. Then I'd envision life if they won and we lost, and that left me feeling guilty.

We controlled the village, but one powerful effect of a blockade is that you end up turning the thumbscrew yourself, mentally one step ahead of the actual siege. They make it annoying to leave, you're already imagining what it'll be like when they don't let you leave at all. They make it hard to collect your mail, you wonder how it'll be when they make it hard to collect your electricity and water. They speak to you with a kind of surly, jack-booted politeness, you're already seeing what happens when they forget to call you *ma'am* as they slap the cuffs on and lead you away, pleading, to the heavily guarded lockdown and thence the heavily guarded nursing home. This fear factor, of seeing all too well what the next step will be, inevitably weakens the spine of some and strengthens the resolve of others.

As Toby foresaw, the declaration of independence generated attention that a plain sit-in over weeks of lustrous summer weather never would have. Radio talk shows featured professors of history, law, and political studies debating the issue, arguing our rights versus our non-rights, citing predecessors specific and far-fetched—from Native American tribes who ended up in the casino business to Toussaint L'Ouverture who ended up in the nation-building business before dying in a foreign prison, shivering within sight of the sea. One show was even hoaxed by a caller who claimed he was assessing our status as an independent country for the U.N. Apparently two professors thought it a sound idea, though I was not tuned in at the time.

Fortunately, Toby made himself available for these call-in shows, which meant he was often at my house, if on the phone—he relentlessly refused Italo's suggestion of a cellular. At first we thought the issue was money, but he made it clear he just didn't want to be at people's permanent beck and call.

And by now he'd begun to realize that I had his number, and soon, as Molly Mellew would've put it, I might even learn how to dial him.

This is what I understand true love is: a permanent homing instinct for another person's frequency, which you can always pull in with a minimum of static no matter how crowded the airwaves are with other frequencies. Perhaps this comes from growing up in the days when radio was all there was (I can remember dancing to a strident bluesy number called "TV Is the Thing This Year"), but I've also always liked the idea of tuning in from afar, of hearing what they are thinking through the crackle, the message they're broadcasting solely for me, even unknowingly. They? you ask. He, I mean—even if statistically there must be a they out there, mile upon mile of male upon male around the teeming globe, and even if I can't tune in on distant frequencies any more, or competently send messages back.

But I could spin the dial in my head and find Toby's frequency without effort. One sun-dazed July morning I told him so, after he got off my phone with a radio talk show in Colorado—one county out there had just been proclaimed a liberated Ski Nation, with lift passports and downhill visas. History repeats itself the last time as advertising.

"So you're listening to me on your own personal shortwave?" Toby asked mildly. The day was tawny. Whenever he smiled so gently I thought he must be unsure what to make of me; once he knew me better he might find less here than my bookcases and my view suggested. But he was about to prove he was so aptly tuned in he could even hear thoughts I hadn't had for years—like those emissions bleeped out to the farthest reaches of space to let everyone else in the cosmos know we exist, which keep going and going like some tireless bunny. My old thoughts must be bouncing above the clouds, bounding and rebounding for a true love to hear eventually. This way all my thoughts will outlive me, even if there is only one person listening.

"Okay," he added, apparently playing along, "then why don't you tell me what I want to know for a change?"

"I'm game, Toby. Just remember, I always tell the truth."

I felt a pang as I said this, unnecessarily exposing both flanks—still not sure he knew my exact age, with my seventy-third coming up fast on the starboard bow.

"That's a rare achievement," he murmured. "I don't."

"I've been told it's a weakness. Though never to a fellow truth-teller."

He was stroking his mustache thoughtfully, unaware that its western tip was adorably wet from my breakfast tea. Out my panoramic window the sea was motionless, in that undecided moment of high tide; the fierce dazzle of morning light made it into blue cellophane. He said, "You're always telling me about your father. You've never told me much about your mother."

"That's because there's not much to tell."

"Now that sounds like a lie."

"It's not. She was a wonderful woman. My father and I loved her very much."

"That's all?"

I could not see the tide shift, but I could feel it querying.

"We both missed her deeply after she—" No, it shouldn't be difficult, not after all these years. "After she passed on. My sister, too, I had a much younger sister. She was killed later, in a car crash."

"How old were you when your mother died?"

"How old? Well, let's see." I searched the ceiling, where all the important dates of our lives are written. "I was in my thirties, I suppose."

He nodded. For once I did not like the way he was gazing upon me, that merciless way lawyers have of taking their time, my father had it too, when you know there are more questions to come, even if their tone of voice is kind.

"And how old were you when she left your father?"

At that instant the tears began to course down my cheeks.

"Who told you that," I whispered.

"I have one ear to the ground," he said, and did not get up to come sit with me, which was all I wanted. "And one ear tuned to your frequency."

Mildred, I thought, I'll assassinate her.

"No," he said, reading my cortex, "it wasn't Mildred. It doesn't matter who it was. I'm sorry, I didn't mean to upset you. Forget I ever asked."

"I'm not upset." But it was all I could manage to say. God damn it, I thought, why should it matter to tell him what anyone could've told him—no, not anyone, because who remembers the internal blockades and sieges within families of a half century ago? Our neighbors were all different then, the only people who knew were my niece, who'd never spoken to Toby, and a few people I'd told, except I'd probably told no one, not for an awful long time.

"A great deal is public record, Jessica," he was saying, "if you know where to look. I'm sorry, I wasn't prying. But I was curious about you. You understand—" He was searching for the right thing to say, trying to stanch the awkward sight of someone he knew as a resourceful woman blubbing away. "I'm sure your father would've done the same thing."

Not the right person to bring up, I thought.

He did come over then, but instead of putting an arm around me or patting my hand or even, God forbid, throwing me over his shoulder, like a prestidigitator he pulled from his jeans a voluminous red handkerchief (I still have it) that'd seen better years and offered it to me. I didn't care what personal history was on there, it was a gesture, and I wiped my eyes and gave a rueful laugh and said, "I'm sorry. It's not something I talk about much. Or even think about."

What dried my tears was the realization that he was actually in search of the year of my birth. After all, it was public record that my parents divorced in '52, when I was away in Korea trying to heal what I saw as the world's worst wounds. While I was getting no sleep in a field hospital and thinking that at least the peace of Salt Cove and home was waiting for me even if I didn't meet an officer worth enlisting in my dreams, the family was breaking up and, to protect me, no one wrote me a word about it, not one word. If Toby knew what year my mother walked out on my father, taking my sister Jennifer, age seven, with her, to remarry swiftly and die a decade later—I guess that was public record too if you knew where to look—why, if I told him how old I was way back when, he'd be able to figure out how old I was now.

But such zigzagging was absurd: this man in front of me, seated again, could find out whatever he wanted. What was I doing with my futile little secrets? Wasting life—especially when having secrets from him was the last thing I wanted, or I'd never discover his own. Hoarded secrets are like the buried chest of buccaneer treasure which, finally unearthed, turns out to have in it only a rusted cutlass, drifts of sand, rotted silken sashes and no doubloons.

I discovered I was no longer crying; Toby's piratical red handkerchief had more than done its duty. I spread it out across my knees to help it dry.

"Keep it," he said. "I've got loads."

So I told him the works; told him also about my niece Sarah, and my few years as her guardian. Maybe everything could've been different in her life if she'd chosen to leave boarding school after her parents died, if she'd come back to live with me year-round instead of just those few summers before the fiasco of college. But Sarah made it clear she wanted to stay away at school, parents or no parents; after a year there already, the school would be her family now. For her I was always the boring aunt, another generation older than her mother and father, who'd run off together at eighteen as was the habit in 1963. (I'd thought about doing so myself, but my thought repeatedly missed coinciding with someone else, like a missed train.)

"And that was how it all happened," I finished. At my age when you recount your early life, no matter how horrible, it sounds like a children's story. As if it happened to a person in a fable, even when you can still feel the events twitch in your bone marrow.

"Your father lived another—what, twenty-five years, after they broke up," said Toby. "And you stayed with him?"

"It didn't seem right to leave him high and dry. He kept working, I was his legal secretary. In those days," I confided, "I had high hopes of becoming a writer. Even though I never found the right story to tell. And when my father died and I shut down his office, which took a year, I ended up working with books. At the library. I stopped that a few years ago." You should see the volumes, I thought, which people used to donate, that were too scandalous to put out on the shelves; I've got those alphabetized here too, Buster Brown, right up there beside the encyclopedia, where no one looks.

I felt my way into Toby might be through the written word—if all else failed I could appeal to the book lover in him, could implore him to show me what he had ranged on those circular shelves lining the lighthouse.

I added, "My one regret is that I always felt my true destiny might lie abroad. I didn't travel as much as I should have when I was younger. I didn't want to abandon my father. And then—" I swallowed; God Almighty, was I going to start singing the weeps again? But I pulled back, just in time, from the precipice. "Then it never seemed like the right time."

He said gently, "I know what you mean. Sometimes I think I should've stayed away. I lived in Rio for five years."

"But then we'd never have met!"

"No, then we'd never have met."

"And what made you come back to the States, Mr. Auberon? A tempestuous karaoke affair gone wrong?"

Now I felt well enough to tease him again.

"Carioca," he corrected me. "No, after several years in Brazil I missed this country, though right now I can't see why. When I was a boy I dreamed of being a lighthouse keeper. Because of some kids' movie. Then I found out the Coast Guard was leasing a few. So I wrote them. In those days I had excellent credentials. This lighthouse was still available, and one down near Charleston. After Rio I needed a place with no distractions."

"To catch up on your reading."

"How'd you guess?" Teasing me. "Let's say I didn't expect all these interruptions. Or all these questions."

He was on his way out, which was fine; I'd learned far more than I anticipated. All that mattered to me was that I come out ahead, in my pawn-takes-pawn way, and advance toward the inevitability of an endgame. The real question, you might argue, was how a historian of my transparency found herself in the grip of tears at turning over a little plot of family history. Well, as Sherlock Holmes used to say, eliminate the impossible and what's left, no matter how improbable, must be the truth.

I resolved then and there to get to the bottom of the man. I could not as yet manacle him to my four-poster and have my way, dip the wick end of his mustache in my strongest brew, so to speak. But I could manacle him to the phone. Another nationwide interview, a two-hour stint on a public radio program, was coming up the very next day. In another life, given more wayward circumstances, I might've been a great thief, a brilliant creator of stratagems and opportunities, stealing all the pelf I desired, even the knowing hearts of men. As it was, it took all the genius I could muster to devise a plan to learn what another woman could've got at many weeks earlier. Here I was, anyway, about to become a thief again, the way every lover must be a thief, stealing only in order to create. To create is all that matters.

The following morning Toby showed up in the nick of time, breathless, flustered at cutting it so close. The radio show's producer, down in Baltimore, had been firing anxious ultimatums at me for ten minutes over the phone, which I handed with a smirk to Toby. The instant he put it to his ear she was all over him. I made gestures at the beauty of the day, pointed at my watch, imitated the old fingers-do-the-walking and indicated I was going for a stroll.

I'd already stationed water, juice, and ginger cookies on a tray by the phone; he had everything he needed for a long nationwide media appearance. I even helped him unknot the legal file folder where he kept his reference papers—a while since I'd unknotted one of those. There came the pleasant sensation of my fingers remembering, our hands touched a couple of times, meanwhile he was muttering, "Yes, yes," into the telephone mouthpiece and raising his eyebrows in consternation at me. "Yes, I'm ready," he said finally, as I slipped out the kitchen door and returned his farewell wave.

I had him right where I wanted him, for the next two hours: all tied up.

It was one of those boastful July mornings bursting with promise. You'd never have guessed, hurrying across the Meadow, past my father's tree, then across the beach with its clustered sunbathers in their conservative swimsuits which would've been banned in Rio, the kids hollering and dogs romping, that this was a summer village under siege. There was a different poignancy in the air, though, the bite of waiting for war, a harshness to the glow of brimming ocean and tanned sand; I tasted it these days in every glass of lemonade. Except I actually knew what it was like to live through a war, even when it wasn't entirely my war, and survive—to come out the other side with an armful of regrets for the life you didn't seize when you had the chance, the sips that should've been gulps. He didn't want me to know what he was really up to, all alone in his wigwam? Too bad. I wasn't going to send my village into battle as virtually one of its commanding officers, then come out the other end if we did survive, and still not know the essentials about Toby Auberon, Esq., the only man who has ever made me want to bite.

As I've said before, and I'm not trying to brag, I am the one nobody notices. I doubt any sunbather, having braved armed blockades to buy suntan oil, thought me anything but a beachcomber picking my way along the tide wrack, every now and then stooping to finger a clump of kelp and establish an alibi, that's not what they call it, a feint, I keep fumbling this pen. I wonder what people do see when they see me; perhaps I'm totally invisible to both men and women. At that moment I needed every inch of invisibility I could muster.

I'd removed my sneakers to cross the beach barefoot. When I reached the tumbled rocks by the white lighthouse (the brightness of the morning made it seem strangely near, with all else, ocean, far shore, sailboats luffing and powerboats chuffing, very far away), I brushed my feet off carefully with a hand towel from my shoulder bag, then put my sneaks back on for the last stretch of rocks. No reason to give the game away by tramping sand across his lair: all he'd know was that I went for a walk while he was on the phone, and he'd still be on it when I returned, exhausted from my pilgrimage. Already, I must admit, I was beginning to feel triumphant, like a marauding showgirl.

This was the most perilous moment of all, because if anyone observed me crossing the wood walkway over slippery rocks islanded in eelgrass to the lighthouse itself, I had to appear expected and not a burglar. *Few would have described her as classically beautiful, but she moved like a cat.* Plus I had to break in, though that didn't worry me. There's been a spare key to the Salt Cove lighthouse kept at the Historical Society for fifteen years at least, and I'd borrowed it via Mildred and had it copied in Leicester the previous afternoon. I doubted Toby had changed the lock. It probably would've been against his lease with the Coast Guard, and he was scrupulously a man of his word, on the rare occasions he chose to give it.

Not fifteen minutes had elapsed since he'd walked into my house than I was turning the key in the lock of his.

Naturally, it has taken extraordinary self-control to not reveal all I came to learn of Toby's occupations and preoccupations before I came to learn it. This would have done a disservice to any chronological unfolding of events, and to my portrayal of how he deliberately projected himself. Plus it would be a lie. Much as I hate to admit it, Toby wanted to hold me at arm's length. He had come here to be left alone, not get involved in saving a village and falling into the embrace of a lover of stories, an amateur historian of no reputation. I believe but cannot confirm that he may have had his heart broken in Brazil; his notebooks in my possession suggest this ever so slightly. Well, that's life—first it breaks your heart, then it breaks you. Anyone reading this far has noticed I have not tried to hide what, to an inquiring general public, might be seen as eccentricities in his character. I will have more to say about this when I get to my birthday.

Thus, when I earlier described the lighthouse interior, it was as I saw it then. Now, as the tumblers of the lock clacketed and I pushed on the heavy white door, I was prepared to be disappointed, to feel I'd exaggerated the Egyptian-tomb moment of entry. But no, there it all was—the tightly packed bookshelves with their narrow galleries every seven feet, going up, around the black-iron spiral staircase; here at ground level the pharaohlike jumble of clothes, kitchen stuff, piles and piles of photocopies from law statute books, a filing cabinet (locked, key not visible), with large surveyors' maps of Salt Cove, or of just the bridge itself, taped on the wall where sweaters and a rain slicker had hung from hooks on my previous visit.

The place needed airing out, and I was tempted to leave the door open, but why risk some curiosity seeker with no right to be here? I shoved it shut, pocketing my key. I was briefly inspired to do yesterday's dishes for him, filling the tiny sink, but that would give the game away. I remembered my vows in Istanbul twenty-five years ago, never to be afraid again to be bold, afraid of what I most wanted, and where had those vows gotten me? But that wasn't being fair to myself: those vows had gotten me here, after weeks of hope and hesitation. I took a deep breath, grasped the black handrail of the spiral staircase, felt the knowledge that I was breaking Toby's trust dig into my shoulders, shook it off, and plunged upward.

I went up quicker than I'd thought possible—terrified the door might fly open and there he'd be, exclaiming *Aha! They take me off the air and now I find you breaking in, a spy in the lighthouse of love!* and ordering me down while my heart thundered and I wouldn't have seen anything, just more damned books. No, I wasn't about to risk that.

My sneakers and my healthy lungs pounding, I surged up those spiral stairs faster than Toby ever had, I'll bet. And in under a minute I understood why he'd so relentlessly kept me and everyone else out, for this place was him, this was where Toby Auberon fully existed, head to toe, could be found in all his secret glory. I knew what he was doing here, knew what was keeping him up night after night, keeping him from the rumpled, tousled bed two levels from the top—I surely had better change those sheets for him before I left, presumably he had clean sheets hidden somewhere, maybe in that locked filing cabinet. At last I knew, when I came panting to his laboratory, with hot ecstatic sunlight pouring in from the beacon level over our heads, just as if he were giving me a guided tour, explaining why he was here—at last I saw what he'd been laboring on all this time, the life's work besides saving us, besides saving me.

I have gotten ahead of myself, because I did not know his name for it at the time, or that I was the first outsider to ever set dumfounded eyes upon the Machina Excelsior. I sure knew I was looking at something. Across its silver belly, beside the slit where in another era my father might've slipped his nickel in to play, was one mystical word in fiery red letters:

XIBALBA

Forgive me if I sound carried away. It's probably easy to think: dotty old lovesick New England crank, she ain't never seen the Taj

Mahal. No, but I've seen Venice, and I've seen Istanbul, I've seen moonlight plying the Bosphorus, I've seen people I loved or never met die brutally, I've seen the handwriting of great men; and believe me, I know a fucking elephant when I see one.

If it strikes you amiss to hear me say, in this document aspiring to truth, that knowing a great achievement lay behind his secrecy made me love him more, then so be it. And, not trusting my own eyes to piece it together when I got home, knowing how unreliable memory is when it comes to detail, out of my shoulder bag I pulled a disposable $9.95 camera, twenty-four exposures with flash included, that I'd bought specially, and took pictures from all sides. Only then, having put the blinking apparatus safely away, did I dare to look seriously myself. (I need hardly add that these photographs have achieved a historical importance I did not conceive 100 percent at the time.)

When something waddles like a duck and quacks like a duck it is often a duck, but I at first couldn't be sure this was a pinball machine, even an unfinished one. It was slightly wider and much longer than usual, and shaped different, like a capital I. It stood propped up not on metal legs but on wood blocks so Toby could slide under and get at its innards easily. There was no pictorial backglass attached yet, either, though two leaned gleaming against the wall like competing contestants in a beauty pageant, amid cardboard boxes of pinball bric-a-brac and stray tools.

Both backglasses had *Xibalba*, that mysterious word, slashing across in flaming letters; empty windows for the steadily mounting scores, I guessed; and images that looked transferred from those wonderfully lurid pictorial calendars they make in Mexico, with bronzed ancient warriors and ripe busty maidens beneath glowing skies. Each backglass showed two muscled young men, brothers perhaps, chasing a head-size ball in flight across a long grassy court, in fierce competition against two other players in supernatural, horned headdress-masks. Sloping step pyramids rose alongside, holding a standing crowd of jostling eager male spectators and a few panting maidens among them. A bloody headless body lay sprawled at the summit of one pyramid, with a garish sun like a rubbery red ball above.

Yet it is easier to describe those finished pinball backglasses than the Machina Excelsior itself, which lay like a surgery patient abandoned in the operating room. I shall try to do my best.

The Machina, if you looked down into it as a player would, was open without its protective glass top (which I didn't see anywhere), elaborate guts exposed where holes and slots sprouted a myriad of color-coded wires. Even so I could discern the elegant complexity of Toby's design, every inch hand-painted in lustrous hues like a Matisse, and built to an architecture out of Dalí.

It was like gazing down onto the body of Central America. On each side were fanciful crested waves that would surely confuse the path of the ball, and several lit bumpers fashioned as stone pillars surrounded by watery drop-holes. The brown continent was like a diorama of those backglass scenes, most of the land given over to an I-shaped ball court flanked by stepped pyramids down which the ball might roll in any direction, and carved walls with holes and targets hidden in the detail work that presumably lit up when the machine was on. Amid this Mayan or Aztec or Inca temple complex (I was struggling to recall archaeology scantily learned many decades back) were zigzagging mazes of flippers to shoot the ball around mercilessly, and other lethal holes rimmed by mock stone gates that'd suck you into them, ornate platforms that the ball would dribble down unpredictably, and larger bumpers—again, resembling carved stone masks, God knows what he'd used, sculptor's clay or something—with tiny lights like torches set in mouths where the ball spewed out. Though how it'd even get inside I couldn't imagine, unless that was where the ball went sprocketing when you first shot it into play.

Now that I'd been staring for a few minutes I realized that the whole broad isthmus, the central part like an ancient ball court laid across the land, resembled an elongated mask if you tried not to notice the game's mechanisms, the labyrinthine dangers and traps. It was like a trick drawing that shows you a man's face one moment and something entirely different the next, but once you've seen the face you can never lose it.

I have made all this sound like a historical painting, but the mood was more fantastical, and the playfield (I learned the term only later) endlessly complicated. The upper and lower crossbars of its I shape were crowded with mechanisms, targets and lights and holes and bumpers in a late Mesoamerican pinball style, and it was easy to imagine a war for control between a player and such a devious machine. And at the far upper slope, near where the ball must initially spurt out, there was one well-protected and obviously ultradesirable hole, hemmed in by gates that looked impossible to get through. All the other holes seemed like traps, but this one appeared a rare prize, because I couldn't see how you might ever get a ball near it. Its rim curved in; only a direct shot would do.

Why this, of all things? I kept asking myself. Well, why not? Would a marble sculpture have been more miraculous, more useful, more beautiful?

All this time I was leaning across the machine, trying to peer in, memorize, make sense of it—as if I'd actually surprised Toby mid-idea, because tiny pliers and screwdrivers and loose miniature light-bulbs lay scattered amid the details of the game. The burnished glare from the beacon level was not making things any easier. In leaning over I must've accidentally hit a button or a switch, because suddenly the machine gave a rumble as if clearing its throat, then started humming as most of its lights sprang to life.

I nearly dropped to my knees, I was so startled—how was I going to turn it off?—and in all its illuminated glory, even faint against morning glare, other details jumped out. Those pillars in the cresting sea alongside treacherous holes were surely lighthouse beacons warning of peril, and I noticed even more mask-mouths against the temple wall, up at the head, where a ball would shoot onto the field of play.

I was too anxious about breaking something to try all the flipper buttons, for who knew what was attached properly and what wasn't? Only Toby knew. I did find one array, my fingertips counted six each side, that worked like a trumpet's keys: you got different responses from different combinations. I stopped when two paired flippers whacked a screwdriver that went rolling till I snatched it up and put it back where Toby had left it. Yet here was a silver ball, coaxed into a side corner. I couldn't see how to set it in play, but I also couldn't walk away from this humming machine, I might never get another chance. So, egging myself on, I dropped it in what I was imagining as the dark, ultimate reward hole at the head, surmounting all the obstacles by cheating.

I gave a yelp then that must've been audible miles out to sea, for instantaneously the entire central section of the game, the ball court that formed the face of the mask, slowly halved down the middle and slid ingeniously apart, receding sideways, as the machine issued a loud human groan, a guttural cry. A voice from its lower belly intoned *Welcome to Xibalba, there is no escape,* which was not exactly the welcome I wanted to hear. Revealed below, there, was a whole other subterranean level of the game, with a more treacherous ball court, this one crowded with drop-holes, gates, and bumper posts, mechanical claws and flippers, flaring torchlights, weird horned ghost-images like supernatural beasts dressed as ancient ballplayers—shimmering then disappearing from the iridescent surface of the lower playfield—except something had gone wrong, for all at once the game started going like mad, with the ball I'd dropped caroming everywhere at frantic speed. There was another mask face on this lower level, more forbidding, whose mouth kept opening and shutting, emitting a sinister roar every few seconds.

For a long, terrifying moment I jabbed away frantically at buttons on both sides, but whatever I did had no effect until at last the machine took matters into its own control. The ball dropped into the gaping maw, a cry of glee and triumph came out, the maw closed emphatically, both sides of the upper level slid swiftly together again as the lower ball court's lights winked out, the machine gave a satisfied groan at having defeated me and then, with a final, happy sigh, shut itself off. The silver ball rolled sibilantly down some interior chute and dropped out and onto my right sneaker.

In what I can only call horrified relief I picked it up and put it back *exactly* where I'd found it. Then I gulped and stumbled to the spiral stairs and gratefully, unsteadily, climbed not down but up, to the beacon level. Fortunately.

The view from there was wonderful, much like the view from my own living room, which calmed me down. Toby seemingly didn't dust up here often, except for the large hivelike mass of the Fresnel lens apparatus, but that was being hypercritical after snagging my breath.

Fewer sailboats dotted the vast ocean bay than usual, but it was a bit early for the pleasure seekers. I checked my watch: five after eleven. I still had plenty of time for snooping, as Toby's radio show had an hour left. But if that were the case, what was he doing striding swiftly across the beach toward me? Oh, Christ.

I went scrambling down the black staircase, whimpering, mewing, gasping for air as my bag flapped against my side—there was no way out, no way to get out the door without him seeing me. What to do, what to do. I could not think, my head was still ringing with the victorious groans and cries of the machine twenty, now thirty feet above me. I shot off the staircase like a ricocheting silver ball, glancing wildly around, I was caught, I was caught, I couldn't lie my way out of this one but every instinct told me I should, he'd never forgive me and never trust me again, something more intimate would never happen between us, never. This break-in would be the pinnacle, and I would regret this morning, regret all I'd learned, for the rest of my life. If I came clean—no, there'd be no reward for breaking his trust. The ball had dropped down the worst hole of all. Oh, God. He must be at the edge of the rocks now, what to do?

And that was when inspiration, the handmaiden of utter desperation, appeared in gossamer filmy undergarments. I put down my shoulder bag, slid off my sneakers to aid the illusion that I'd remained purposefully at ground level, went over to Toby's sink and started urgently doing his dishes. It was a hectic minute's work to get a pool of soapy water brimming and scrape off the encrusted first layer of spaghetti remains. When shortly he fitted his key into the lock and found, to his evident surprise, that it wasn't locked, no sir, and pushed the door open, gawping at my back in shock, as I kept singing to myself and attacking the dishes ("I'm Gonna Wash That Man Right Outa My Hair" was the tune; I've since forgotten most of the lyrics), dipping them, scouring, splashing ever more sudsy water across his floor than I already had to prepare for that moment, the inquisitive meets the inquisitor—all I said to him without turning around was, "You need to be less absent-minded, Mr. Auberon. If you leave your door unlocked, anyone can just barge in and do your dishes for you."

He stared at me in dismay, but I gave it all back in spades, a blithe wave of trustworthy unconcern, my mind focused only on cleaning those plates.

He said at last, in a strangulated voice, "How long have you been here?"

"Oh"—I shrugged, a scrub brush held up in contemplation—"I don't know, ten minutes? I was on my way home and heard the door rattling in the breeze. Trying to swing open, I couldn't get it to stay shut." Scrub-a-dub-dub.

He nodded, scrutinizing my face doubtfully, wanting to believe me. So I turned my cannon his way and fired a broadside. "I thought it was a two-hour radio show," I said. "Didn't they like you?"

"The second hour's on a different topic." He grimaced. "It's the *Mona Lisa* today."

"A fine painting. I saw it at the Louvre once, on my way back from Istanbul. They call it *La Gioconde* in Paris."

"So I've heard." He clearly did not believe me yet. He added casually, "I think they call it *Xibalba*"—he pronounced it with a frontal Z—"in Spanish."

"Do they?" If he thought to catch me with that kind of snare, he would be well advised never to play poker with the daughter of a lawyer. As if I weren't prepared for such a ruse! "I'd always thought it must be *La Joconda*."

"Maybe you're right." He put his hands in his pockets. "Look, don't do those, please, I'll do them myself. It only takes a minute."

"Not if you do them properly."

He wasn't going to argue, still on the hunt. "How do you like what I've done with the place?"

I sniffed. "I haven't seen enough of it to comment. Judging by the ground floor, if you ask me, you could keep it cleaner. It's good to see those surveyors' maps. The distances are always different than you expect."

"Yes, aren't they," he said grudgingly.

I finished with a flourish, the last spaghetti bowl plopped in the drying rack, the metal colander upended over it in the same shape as one of those fingertip-friendly flipper buttons, come to think of it; maybe that was where he'd gotten the design. Best not to push my luck. I dried my hands on my trousers—a quick frown of reproach at finding no dish towel—and looped my bag back over my shoulder, the incriminating camera like a ticking bomb inside. "I was going to offer to make you lunch at my house," I said. "I thought you'd tell me all about the show."

He said, "I really should get on with work of my own. They'll broadcast it again this evening, at eight. But thanks."

"Okay, then. I'll leave you in peace, Toby. See you tomorrow?"

"I suppose so." He winced, as if some pain whose source he couldn't identify was flitting through him. "Look, this is important to me, I'm sorry—are you sure you didn't go up those stairs?"

I was at the door, the tattletale key safely in my pocket; in ten minutes it would be back at my house, hidden under my mattress. Was the lie now between us, I wondered, the lie that was my doing, as big as any of the lies he'd told me for week upon week, as immense as all those lies put together? I said, "Toby, believe it or not, I do respect your privacy." I held up two fingers in the traditional clasp of unswerving loyalty. "Scout's honor."

I have never been a girl scout.

44

Joe Ciarimataro

Dear Committee for the Bridge,

I been a fisherman all my life. Out of Leicester. My father was a fisherman all his life out of Leicester. But not his father, who come from Siracusa, island of Sicily and learn when he get here. Was about 1901. He come down from Canada. That was the way in those days.

Please if this is the wrong address just throw away this letter. Or send it back so I know. My daughter was telling me to use the phone but people always get the wrong idea over the phone. So she writes it down for me.

I been reading the Leicester paper and watching on the television and listening to the radio all about Salt Cove for months. Bring back a lot for me. When I was just a small boy for a few years my father brung me to your bridge every Saturday morning to fish, if his boat was in. Don't forget, he goes fishing all year long way out at sea in any kind of weather, it was not as comfortable in those days. And he still wants to bring me to your bridge. Probably a hundred times, before I was old enough to work on a boat myself.

There was a nice old lady living there, a good Catholic, she always used to speak to my father about the church and the time she saw San Pietro in Roma. The two of them was always amazed because even my grandfather never seen it and he was living practically next door. Well, maybe not next door in those days. Now my daughter just buys a plane ticket.

I was hearing the radio the other night, people from all over the country talking about Salt Cove. All of it make me very angry.

I'm going to tell you a story. Back about fifteen years ago, when I was out fishing. Before they close off Saint Georges Banks to men who was only trying to make a living for their families, right before I retire and sell my stake in the boat. On account of the ecology.

One day we find a strange thing in the nets. Was so heavy it tears big holes when we brung it up. With fins like a spaceship, about ten feet long. At first we thought it was a shark that had died on the net. But it turns out it was a missile from a navy ship. The kind they fire in the air for hundreds of miles, they can hit your front door or a dog barking in Arabia.

Maybe the navy shoot it up for a training and it just doesn't explode. Or maybe they was aiming it at the Russians and it doesn't hit nothing. But we thought if we take it in instead of sinking it maybe the navy would give us a big reward money. So we sling it from a net over the deck so it can't touch nothing and brung it back, right to the Leicester fish pier. Was on a weekend so we decide to hide it in my basement not leave it on the boat where anyone can steal it. Took a few of us.

So I call the navy in Washington, D.C., I speak to about four different people. On a Monday morning. Finally I get the right one, I leave a message and wait. Then I try Wednesday. Friday we go out again only I don't let Anna Maria call nobody at the navy, but I tell her what to say when they call me back. But they don't. Ten days later we come in, still nobody has called back. I call Washington again. Speak to some more people. And I realize no one was believing me. They think I was, I don't know, some crazy guy. Like a practical joker.

I wait a couple days, because this is making me really angry. Then I try again. Because this is my country, too. I'm doing everything to be a loyal American, only they don't take me serious cause of how I talk. I'm always leaving messages in different departments, I even try the Lost and Found, but no one ever calls back. Then one navy wise guy, the last guy I finally speak to, he says you just keep your missile, Mr. Vespucci, we'll tell you when we need it. The name is Ciarimataro, I says, but he hangs up. He doesn't know nothing, that guy.

My wife says you better call the police, or the coast guard, but I tell her look, this is navy property, there's a big difference. They don't want it back, I'm not going to break my balls calling the air force and the, I don't know, the forest rangers and Smokey the Bear. The hell with them, insulting me like this. The hell with Smokey the Bear.

Anyhow, this is a long letter. All I wanted to say is, when I hear the radio about Salt Cove I get angry all over again. And I remember the missile I brung up years ago, that I keep in the basement and almost forgot about all these years. I don't need it no more. So if you want it you can have it.

Joseph Ciarimataro

45

Myra Simpkins

I TOLD ITALO at the very beginning, things will go dreadfully wrong. I don't like to be the one to say I was right, but they have.

On the twenty-first of July we became prisoners in our own village, without visiting rights. On that morning I was told that none of Becky's school friends would be allowed to visit her, invitation or no invitation. "We're talking about a ten-year-old girl," I said, "on summer vacation." "Yes, ma'am." "That doesn't change anything?" "We have orders, ma'am."

All this over a bridge. If it ruins our lives, is it really worth fighting for? Of course, says Italo, but this doesn't really spring from his heart. It springs from a conviction that it was his failure which got us here in the first place. He got this sense of automatic failure from his father, I know. That old man has a lot to answer for, and I will not permit it to be handed on to Becky, no matter what, even if it means boarding school. So Italo blames himself even when he knows he shouldn't. But in his heart he also knows we should just give up.

When I was a child I was brought up to believe you must never give up, that that's what made this country great. And I can see why it's an appealing myth, even though that's not how it happened—so much natural wealth was handed to us Americans on a plate, all we had to do was dig in and chomp away. I don't think there's anything more to be done here by resisting. What does it matter, one bridge more or less? Our village is like a bald man fighting to hold on to his comb.

After this year, I told Italo, we should think about moving away. Sell the house even if we have to take a loss. Move on. Because they're sure to make it unpleasant for us ringleaders. Maybe someone like Jessica, who's been here all her life, has nothing to fear but a nursing home one day, but not us carpetbaggers. We'll probably get audited now wherever we go. But let's move somewhere, maybe Colorado or Arizona, where we don't have any personal history. You can teach science anywhere.

But you love this place, he says.

Doesn't matter. I can leave in a week, if we have to.

He knows how frightened I am of people, of new people especially, he knows what being in a new place does to my stammer. So he knows how seriously he has to take this, coming from me.

I'll admit it, then, I told him. I don't want to hang around for the end. We're trapped in a helpless situation that none of us have even one little bit of control over. Any day now either people will get tired of roosting on the bridge to protect it, squandering their summer out there, or else the army will just overrun us. Or send military boats in by night, like those films where you see them sliding up some greasy tropical river. And they'll remove everyone from the bridge, one way or another.

They can do it any time they want, and they will. And I don't want to be around to see it. I don't want to be watching from my kitchen window when they dynamite the bridge and the shrapnel goes flying. I don't have to see that if I don't want to, Italo. I don't want Becky and Simon to see it.

And where will we be afterward? Where will you be? Under arrest, for fomenting treason? In some lawsuit for umpty-ump million dollars for the rest of our lives? What happens to us then?

You see, I was taught in school not to ever give up, but that was the wrong lesson to learn. The right lesson, which you teach in high school physics, is that there's a strong force and a weak force in the universe, and they behave the way they do, and the universe behaves the way it does, because they both know exactly what they are. That's what keeps the universe functioning, and you can't convince me otherwise. Though I wish you could.

46

Jon Eckerman

Subj: Code Firewall
From: eckermanjon@coastal.net
To: avenger101@incoming.com

Re your communiques of the 18th, 19th, and 23rd: mucho apologies for the news blackout at this end. As you surmised, I had to deal with a possible security compromise and leakage situation, averted in the nick of time. You know what happens when it starts to go down, you learn who your true friends are and whose boots weren't laced up all the way. And you find out whose lips are so loose you can hear them tremble in the wind.

In answer to your question, yes, Avenger, I am married. Wife is an expert on 16th century Spanish swords, with a side interest in martial arts. A dynamo in a black catsuit. No, she is not permitted access to my e-mail.

Here at the epicenter we have been circling the wagons and trying to figure out the next move. You and I are in the same position, Avenger—adjutants who aren't afraid of getting our hair mussed, who know what combat means, but who still don't hold the reins of command. Ours not to reason why. Estimate the odds of total meltdown as going up every day.

You know me, if I was in charge of this op we'd be taking the fight to them, with a blinding sequence of well-timed, strictly planned, perfectly executed raids designed to utterly demoralize their forces. Operation Clenched Fist. But as you see from the TV reports, we're in the worst kind of Mexican standoff, with opposition armored vehicles controlling ingress and egress except by water—or by a few secret paths through the woods that I happen to know about. Gradually, though, the noose is tightening around our necks . . . maybe.

At some point soon I may need to call in the Vultures. However, let me make it clear that you should AWAIT A SIGNAL FROM ME.

I will keep in mind a 30-hour window of transport before your men can be on hand and ready to rock. (Are you sure this is enough? How fast do you guys drive?)

You will be glad to know that, via sources I am not at liberty to divulge for reasons I am sure you understand, we have received the "loan" of a naval missile tipped with a "very significant" warhead and payload. This hombre means business! It is being kept in a secured yet highly accessible location, its own little assisted living environment, and separate from the "care package" you guys sent us some weeks ago. Thanks again, and once again, sorry for my delay in initially contacting you, but I had to verify certain issues to my own satisfaction. You understand.

It is good to have friends when you're surrounded by enemies.

At this juncture we are looking at a scenario involving total inundation of all media outlets in hopes of swaying public opinion to the point where resistance—theirs, not ours— becomes useless. The old Marxist propaganda approach, but it can work for the good guys, too, eh? As you may have noticed from our "legit" Bridge Website, I am posting daily reports and constantly flooding news carriers with press releases. Of course, we become much more newsworthy if blood flows than if it doesn't. Right, compañero?

Will keep you informed. If security is breached, the Website's daily update will start with the word *now*. (Suggest you use the same signal to me.) Otherwise we're all still in one piece here, and we are fighting back.

Clenched Fist

47

Toby Auberon

I AM GOING out of my mind. This is how it must feel to be a pinball, getting whacked from all sides. Leave aside a war of secession, leave aside an eviction notice that arrived special delivery—one more wasp to be swatted—leave aside two weeks without even a half-day of work on the Machina, it sits up there abandoned in midthought. Leave aside an infuriating radio colloquy with a panel including an old law professor of mine who at least stood up for one of his better pupils of that long lost decade, but who cares when you have op-ed columnists baying like hyenas, asserting they know more about legal precedent than "the so-called experts." Leave aside walking, immediately afterward, into this lighthouse to find not blessed solitude but Jessica standing like barefoot Liberty holding a dish scrubber, doing my plates and asking me to believe she merely walked in and what caught her eye wasn't the staircase and no one to stop her, but the remains of spaghetti and meatballs. Leave aside the sleepless night that followed and what do we still find, shoved under my door, but a folded note? And not from Jessica, for once, since I can actually read this handwriting. Some unknown correspondent, black ink on white scratch paper torn from a pad, slanting capital letters, man or woman is any-one's guess:

IT'S NOT THE BRIDGE, STUPID

Really? You could've fooled me, I intoned sleepily, thinking it was still early, too early in the day to be insulted. Which is why it's best to withdraw from the entire conversation. I poured out my vial of pre-cious, life-giving coffee and cinched my bathrobe tight against the next stranger ready to invade. And if it wasn't the bridge, what was it?

Over the next three mornings I woke to the same bitter routine: staircase, insulting note, ruined coffee. No matter how early I got up to get straight to work on the Machina, a new note was waiting for me like a chain saw biting into my concentration. My deranged pen pal was coming before dawn, or soon after I went to sleep, which was often very late—evidently this person had me under observation. Leaving my lights on all night one night when I nodded foggily off over some statute books didn't keep him away. It wasn't a handwriting I could identify from the signatures on my copy of the Act of Secession.

Three consecutive mornings, three notes, one sentence each.

YOU NEED TO BE MORE FARSIGHTED

then:

YOU NEED TO BE MORE FORESIGHTED

then:

YOU NEED TO BE MORE SITED

A pattern was emerging. Someone was trying to tell me some-thing, not just annoy me.

I took them to Jessica, who at first was jealous until she realized these were hardly missives of seduction. Nor were they tremendously informative. She didn't recognize the handwriting, either.

"They aren't from me," she said. "These aren't the message I'm trying to send you."

"I know."

By now it was like an open joke between us; I kept relentlessly racqueting the shuttlecock of her flirtation back at her.

She said, "Maybe if you weren't such a heavy sleeper, you'd hear whoever it is rustling about. Then you might catch them."

"I could set a bear trap instead. And get a good night's rest till they started screaming."

"Or," she suggested, "I could keep watch for you. I could hide out in the bushes and see who comes along."

"Jessica, please. Let me handle this."

"I wish someone were sending *me* notes. A secret admirer. You and I could both hide in the bushes. Want to try that? Listen, if you're in danger, you could always stay here for the night."

"Maybe I'll lay out some thumbtacks instead."

"Okay," she said, "I won't interfere. But what are they trying to tell us?"

"Tell me, you mean."

"Tell *us*," she said triumphantly. "They're written to you not as Toby Auberon, Esquire, but as leader of the village of Salt Cove."

"They're telling me to get my eyes examined. Then get my head examined. It's a game."

"Nope. They're telling you to look elsewhere. Or think in a different way. But they don't want to incriminate themselves by saying too much."

I can't even think one way, I muttered to myself, gazing out at Jessica's view, I can't think at all anymore. And I saw, distantly, a couple of large gray boats hugging the horizon, two smudges alongside the optical illusion of a mountainous coastline that was there only on hot hazy days. So perhaps they weren't there either. Or maybe I was being more farsighted and foresighted: maybe only I could see them.

On reflection the bear trap didn't seem such a bad idea, at least on a much smaller scale. I rummaged around the lighthouse and found the unused mousetrap I'd bought on first moving in. I'd have to be awake half that night anyway, trying to write a reply to a newsweekly's inane opinions page ("Will Salt Cove Turn into Appomattox?"), but from forty feet up you cannot hear messages being shoved across the threshold.

I set the mousetrap at about the spot outside my door where the notes were being shoved under. Presumably the person was right-handed and had to bend down on one knee. By night he wouldn't see the mousetrap, that side of the lighthouse was immersed in darkness.

Upstairs on my bed I scribbled away at my reply till long after midnight. The magazine had offered me a half page; for a full page you have to bomb New York. I rewrote it clearly for Jessica to type up and blip over to them in the morning, then fell asleep dreaming of Rio, the scents of another hemisphere and another life.

Morning: no note pushed under my door. Ah, the loyal fragrance of Brazilian coffee suffusing an undisturbed morning after a good night's sleep. As lagniappe I'd even been granted, right when I awoke, a marvelous idea for another drop target, lower level of the machine. I showered, looking forward to stealing a few hours on the Excelsior once I delivered the magazine reply to Jessica. I opened the door to retrieve the mousetrap; either it'd scared the guy, or he'd taken a night off. Either way—

No such luck. The mousetrap, its spring removed, held another note.

*I AM YOUR FRIEND. WATCH THIS SPACE
IF YOU KNOW WHAT'S GOOD FOR YOU.*

"What do I need here?" I said aloud to no one. "A moat? Trip wires?"

My morning ruined, my mousetrap ruined, I stomped over to show the latest ultimatum to Jessica, who agreed that the threat might be connected with my eviction notice, which I have ninety days to appeal and have turned over to Bob Herbert. It wouldn't be the first harassment used to encourage a tenant's departure, and after all, my landlord is a government with explosives. But why bother? They know the eviction notice is pointless, especially against someone who always pays his rent early. The state of Massachusetts is not about to relax its tenant-protection laws, even against a tenant waging a war of independence.

Meanwhile those gray blurs on the horizon looked larger. By lunchtime everybody in the village saw them much as I did through Jessica's telescope: navy ships looming, guns visible, on a "purely routine" coastal patrol. In that afternoon's Leicester newspaper was a scoffing disclaimer from one officer that the military presence had anything to do with "the incident over in Salt Bay."

They hadn't relaxed their road blockade one whit, content to make life miserable. Such constant threat may reinforce the defiant unity of the besieged if you're fighting for survival, but we weren't. Everyone was on a short fuse, sick of being pestered on an errand to buy sandwich bread, sick of losing the visitation rights of even the lowliest inmate of a prison or a nursing home. Still, we had our bridge-sitters round the clock, and I didn't think the authorities would risk any bloodshed, not in such a staring public eye.

But they hadn't caved at all on the bridge. The state offices refused to even enter into discussions with us, knowing if they waited long enough the village would crack. Neither I nor anyone else could keep people persuaded forever, and once we lost half Salt Cove's numbers after the summer residents went home in a month, people would grow heartsick. It'd start to rain, and our bedraggled bridge would no longer seem worth fighting for with winter in sight. The bridge would go down, somehow. Then, surely, the powers that be would come after me.

The next morning I found I'd run out of coffee, and there were two notes shoved inside, not one.

I snatched them up, snarling at the door that kept out fragrant breezes but let in everything else, and read in a black fury, my hands shaking, as my cup of mud from the night before turned tepid. The first note was the longest so far:

> *HOW MANY TIMES MUST I TELL YOU?*
> *LOOK FOR THE MOTIVE, AND YOU FIND THE MAN.*
> *LOOK FOR THE MAN, AND YOU FIND THE MOTIVE.*
> *(P.S. IT AIN'T THE BRIDGE, DUMMY.)*

Goddamn you, I thought, and reread it before my hand crumpled and hurled it at the survey map of the cove tacked above my filing cabinet. Do I look like I need a cowardly fucking proverb first thing in the morning?

Expecting more insults, I unfolded the second note—surprise, surprise, it seemed to come from another source. Instead of small scratch paper, a full-size sheet. And it had been typed, with an old manual machine. Trained cobras, that's what I needed around here. Just try to get through them, pal; be sure to let me know how you get along.

No, this one was definitely from someone else.

> You attract me strangely. Here's one scenario.
> First, I sit you in a chair and do a slow strip. One
> detail at a time. Then I take inventory on what kind
> of man you are. Here's another idea. You come to
> my house and find me wearing only jewelry and
> shadows. Then you vanquish the shadows with your
> own. Either way, I am going to show you no mercy.

Now that's more like it, I thought.

No signature, no return address, but who on earth—in North America, anyway—still used a manual typewriter? With my luck my two correspondents would bump into each other some night and I'd be applauded at the wedding for having introduced them.

I couldn't take this one round to show Jessica. Unless—no, that wasn't possible, was it? Yet if anyone in this village still owned a typewriter, it would be Jessica. Only she knew I was getting besieged by notes. Plus she knew I knew she used a computer, and thus might never suspect. Even the vocabulary ("vanquish") was hers. A slow strip, to jewelry and shadows? In that case she had a more unbuttoned imagination than I'd given her credit for, unexpectedly similar to mine.

Not that she could be a possibility—what was I thinking? But maybe I could worm the truth out of her without letting on what the note said. Or letting on that it even existed, for that matter.

So I took her the first note, only, after uncrumpling and refolding it.

"What happened to this?" she said, trying to smooth it out on her table.

"It got hurt being shoved under the door."

"Bullshit. You ruined it. You'd make a lousy detective. I think I should hide out in your bushes tonight."

"I'll do that myself," I said. "You don't have an old typewriter lying around, do you?"

"My father's," she said guilelessly, looking extremely innocent, and thirty years younger. "Up in the attic. Why do you ask?"

"It would save you laboring over my handwriting, next time."

She shrugged. "You can borrow it if you like. But it's way at the back. I don't know if it still works. I quite like your handwriting, by the way. I enjoy using a magnifying glass. Makes me feel like a huntress."

She wasn't saying no to the typewriter, but she wasn't handing it over. She wasn't admitting or denying anything. It couldn't be her, could it? Maybe it was best to simply wait and see what developed. If some tease wanted to send me incendiary wake-up notes, it wasn't altogether a bad thing. No matter who it was.

I said, "So what's my informant trying to tell me?"

"That you're not as bright as you think you are."

She certainly looked more knowing than she had any right to look. I tried to remember her exact expression when I'd walked in on her doing my dishes. She's been cool, collected, almost awaiting me—and I knew from experience that when someone unexpectedly pushed open that door, it made you jump. Hardly surprised to see me, even though she did ask why I wasn't still on the radio. Did she truly expect me to believe she'd have finished the dishes and left the lighthouse without snooping, thinking I'd be away another hour? Not a chance: she'd have been up my staircase like a rocket at blastoff, all the way to the very top—which must be where, it suddenly occurred to me, she'd seen me coming, across the Meadow and the beach.

So that was it. Thus her expectant look. She hadn't flinched at hearing "Xibalba." A good bluffer, even if she didn't recognize her Mesoamerican underworlds. But that meant this was all make-believe, all play-acting, since she knew now what no one else here did.

Save Scativo, but Scativo cared little, wouldn't talk, and wasn't trying to seduce me, either. Maybe it was seeing the Machina that'd made her type a different kind of note—my God, imagine if it had that sort of effect on women across the globe.

I thought all this as I gazed at her. For some weird reason—perhaps my gut instinct, perhaps the selfless, self-destructive way she'd stood by her father long after her mother walked out—it was easier to imagine her typing this mysterious other note than lying to me. And the possibility that I might not be able to trust her gave me a pang, actually hurt.

No wonder she wanted to hide out amid the rocks and scraggly bushes to find my first correspondent. She wanted an excuse to deliver another note of her own in person. No wonder she seemed so vibrant this morning, brimming with mojo. There were these odd moments when she seemed younger than anyone I knew—her eyes steadfast on lengthening each day, not using it up. As Scativo put it before we got interrupted by a jailer clanking open the door when Jessica sprang us, "Watch out, man. You have to look close, but I've seen chorus girls with less sashay."

Big gulps, that was what kept the life force moving through you.

"No doubt the notes are right," I answered. "I don't know very much." (A merest flicker of understanding at the corner of her mouth: the flick of the Machina.) "Not as much as he does. Let's assume the issue isn't the old bridge at all. The bridge is just something in the way."

"What does a new bridge do, though?" she asked. "That an old bridge doesn't? It's not like it's a giant marina. Bring in more tourists? Maybe it means someone can take over an old house like this one and turn it into a fancy hotel. I've had offers, you know."

"Don't ever sell, Jessica," I said absently. "Anyway, an ugly modern bridge wouldn't make more people come. It might be slightly easier to get here, but so what? The reason people only pass through now is there's nowhere to stay. Except the Edgemere, and that's one bathroom per floor."

"Well," she said, "why don't you leave a note asking your informant to be less cryptic? You don't like communicating openly, I know, but it might work."

You're one to talk, I thought.

"All right," I said, "I'll try a note. Smoke him out." What I meant was a note each. "Lend me some scratch paper. So he knows the note's for him."

Who else could it be for? I read in her eyes.

On my way back across the Meadow, wishing I'd accepted her offer of lunch, wishing especially I'd remembered to ask her to pick me up a pound of espresso grind in Leicester, another thought struck me. It was what I put in the note I scrawled for #1 that night: *So it's not the bridge? You're right, I am a dummy. I bet it's not even Salt Cove.*

I folded the paper, put it in the disarmed mousetrap, and kept wondering, as I had all day, if I should leave a note for #2 also. By now I'd convinced myself again that it couldn't possibly be Jessica. When I wasn't with her she receded a few paces, I saw her more clearly and, I'm sorry to say, more coldly. Whoever it was, suppose she (I hoped to heaven that #2 was a she) removed by mistake the note meant for #1? There was no way to know which of them would show up first. I couldn't address them individually; they didn't know their own numbers. I also couldn't think of any note to leave in duplicate to cover both #1 and #2, besides the lame *Tell me more.*

And something awful was brewing. On the radio I'd mercilessly taunted both Thrale, the lame-duck governor, asleep at his dacha on Cape Cod for July, and Rowe, the lieutenant governor, who was so relaxed, so sinisterly confident in all his interviews that I thought he might lie behind all this. I'd repeatedly challenged them both to come to us in a genuine way, on the basis of our grievances; I'd all but admitted that the act of secession was a plea to get us listened to. I accused them of being afraid to openly debate me on the merits of our case, I accused them of turning this into a military situation in which more people would surely get hurt. And I laid the blame for Leilia's murder on their shoulders, not those of the Leicester police—a statement that did not go unnoticed locally. "I'm happy to say," Rowe had told the press, and he didn't look very happy even though he was smiling tautly, the smiler with the knife, "we cannot and will not negotiate with terrorists."

Those warships weren't mere saber rattling. They were here by federal authority, if only as a gesture of support. For a week it'd been soporifically hot across the country; I could sense the general populace tiring of us. In terms of publicity we'd already crested, we weren't news anymore. We were the weirdo village defying the United States, daring the government to invade, but we were now a status quo, not a bristling headline—the kiss of death in a nation with a brief attention span. If the state waited another week we'd be safely back on page six, not page three, which made me fear that any day they might do something rash and irrevocable.

That night I tinkered listlessly with the Machina. I could practically smell Jessica's fingerprints on it, which didn't improve my concentration. Why did the woman bother me so? At midnight I turned out all the lights and, carrying a blanket to sit on, headed outside, down the short gangplank and across the brief stretch of rocks into a covert of bushes.

What I really needed was to get at #1 and find out how much he knew. He didn't sound like a villager, or someone involved from the very beginning. But if #2 showed up first, once I saw who she was I could stop her, or let her go on her way, depending. And if she took my note meant for #1, I had an extra ready in my pocket.

Anyway, if #2 were really Jessica, she'd grasp the situation immediately. I was leaning toward her again.

It was a balmy July night, with that midsummer sensation, rare for here, of the earth still suffused from the day's heat, as if the entire coast had been taken out of an oven and left to cool under the stars. The sea was gurgling as the tide shifted and reluctantly began to go out, chiding me for never going swimming anymore, for letting petty disturbances get the better of me and sway me from my purpose. And reminding me, unreasonably, of a few choice nights down South America way, as the vintage films put it, with a couple of particularly friendly friends on a moonlit beach many miles from the city. I know they are now building apartment blocks along that beach, death coming in faster than any tide, I would be scared to go back and look, but on nearly tropical nights like this I could close my eyes, let memory fool me and import all the missing scents, open my eyes briefly and pretend the wheeling constellations were the other hemisphere's, try to pretend I was years younger, relive the thunderous silhouettes of that coast and, licking the salt off my lips, recall how lavish their skins had tasted, accompanied by humming voices and giggles—

—then jerk myself awake, having rolled off my blanket and onto a rock, to find I'd fallen asleep on the outskirts of Rio but woken up in New England, and was it really four in the morning by my luminous dial? The past makes you groggy. My visitors had both probably been and gone, while I slept through.

I was about to pull myself up from the bushes, watching the tail ends of my memory vanish into oblivion until the next timely reverie, thinking I'd better check to see if my note were still there, when I heard the unmistakable scrape of boots on my gangplank.

There it went again. That's what had made me turn over and awaken. Now the tiny wink of a small flashlight came on by the door to the lighthouse. Whoever it was stooped, unfolded my note, then straightened up to read it. By starlight alone I could discern a large shape, a man, but the moon was hung far out to sea and the lighthouse kept the intruder in dense shadow. I didn't budge an inch; he'd hear me and skedaddle. I heard him breathing, then chuckling over my note. Undoubtedly he'd written his next note to me already. The scrape of those boots bothered me, no one wore boots in this weather.

No, that wasn't true. Those SWAT team commandos, or whatever they called themselves, were forced to.

This inching along was absurd. At this rate it might take him weeks to get to the point, and we didn't have weeks.

I spoke aloud, quietly. "It's me, Toby. Don't worry, I can't see your face."

I saw him freeze, heard him suck in his breath.

"I don't need to know who you are," I said calmly. "I appreciate what you've been trying to tell me. But I need a bit more help."

The ocean abruptly seemed very loud, only a few feet away, now that I was trying to make out a man's stealthy movements over its hubbub. I heard him shift, then clear his throat. I waited, saying nothing, since I couldn't think what else to say.

"What do you want to know?" he said finally.

A younger voice than I expected. Late twenties, maybe. His equipment clinked slightly as he adjusted his stance, and I think he crouched down, farther into the shadows, to be absolutely sure I couldn't see him.

"You read my note?" I asked.

"I read it."

"Am I right? It's not really the bridge?"

"I told you that already."

"And not really Salt Cove?"

"That's correct."

"So where do I look?"

There was a pause, then he said, "You should look in Teal Bay. You should think about . . . about what happens to property in Teal Bay. When this place gets ruined."

"You're kidding," I said, without thinking. All this was to improve someone's stake in a village a few coves away?

"I'm not kidding," he said, with a hint of anger.

"What property are we—?"

"Look for the motive, and you find the man," he said irritably, a little pompously, as if I were slow-witted. Informants often like to play king-for-a-day. "I've got to go. I want you to walk very slowly onto the beach. Don't look back for five minutes, don't try to follow me, and don't tell anyone we had this conversation."

He was smart enough to realize I could guess, from his diction alone, that he was with those special commando forces.

"Wait a minute," I said. "Is something going to happen?"

A lengthier pause this time, but he gave in.

"It is going to happen. It will only take us half an hour."

Us—one truth sometimes has a magnetizing effect on others, tugging the scattered bits of iron together across the table. He spoke flatly, as if merely telling me how long it took to get from there to here, not overpower an entire community and take possession of a bridge.

"When will it happen?"

He said, "I want you to move onto that beach. Right now. Please." Almost plaintive; I heard for the first time the fear of discovery, of dismissal and dishonorable discharge, in his voice. Kids in their twenties being sent to do the dirty work of men two generations older, men who believed that if they kept their hands clean they wouldn't soil their souls.

"When will it happen?" I asked again sharply, but I was already up and doing as he ordered, moving across the rocks carefully so as not to slip, knowing there wasn't any more to be gotten out of this informant, he wouldn't answer. And already thinking furiously about what the next step should be, knowing I was nearly out of steps.

But then he did answer, a last gift of trust as he was treading across my gangplank. It took all my self-control not to turn and see who he was, to see which of those impassive, obedient, unworldly commandos had decided to disobey orders and be our ally. He said softly, "It'll go down just when you think you're getting somewhere. And you won't have to wait much longer."

"Thank you," I said, and kept moving.

I gave him five long minutes, taking my time on the beach, trying to think methodically, trying fruitlessly to enjoy the night, shivering in the heat even with a blanket wrapped around my shoulders. When I trudged back to the lighthouse the mousetrap was still there and so was my note, laid atop it unfolded. My mouth tasted awful, my head hurt. I couldn't stop running over alternatives even though I knew the best thing for now was to climb up the black staircase forty feet and get to bed for a few hours.

I pushed open the door—gave a start as I realized I'd forgotten to lock it, maybe I'd done that the other morning too, just as Jessica said—stumbled inside, flicked on the light, and caught myself. Another note lay at my feet, I'd stepped on it. This was the typed kind.

So my mystery woman had come and gone while I was asleep in the rocks and bushes, dreaming of Rio. I unfolded the paper; if I hadn't been so terrified by what I'd just learned it'd have aroused me, as it was meant to. Instead her unintended echo of what the storm trooper had said made me gag.

Toby, how much longer will you force me to wait?

48

Rosemary Wilkes

ALL RIGHT, I can talk to you. If you're sure it'll help. Do you have to use that machine? I guess if you didn't have to you wouldn't show it to me, and I'd never find out. My son tells me they make them as small as a ladybug these days. He's very involved. This is for *Time?* I'm sorry, *Newsweek.* I always get them confused. No, we don't subscribe. I suppose we could keep up better, but there never seems to be any need.

Where do I stand? I'm, to be honest, I mean totally frank with you, I can't believe you can even sit here in my kitchen and ask me that question. We're all practically under house arrest in our own community for weeks and weeks and you want to know where I stand?

Of course I signed the act of secession. We all did. If you were bringing up your kids here and a bunch of politicians and engineers wanted to deface, to disfigure is what I'm trying to say, the beauty of your home and wouldn't listen without their minds made up, wouldn't even come to your table to talk, all out of some narrow-minded safety regulations that are just an excuse to spend taxpayer dollars, you'd take drastic steps too.

And you'd be plenty insulted when they kept blockading you and flaunting guns and the lieutenant governor calls you an unpatriotic terrorist and then each of those men has to prove his, I don't know, his masculinity, pardon me for putting it that way, you probably can't print that. Let's just say most of the trouble in the world is made by men with nothing better to do and something really sick to prove, and I believe that.

Was I what? In favor of the Civil War? You mean, whose side was I on? What a dumb question. That has nothing to do with this. Oh, I see, it's your readers' question, not yours. Sorry.

Do we feel Toby Auberon has let us down? On the contrary. He's talked sense from the beginning. And everything he said, in his worst-case scenario, turned out right. It all came true. It's very sad, for people to be forced to waste their energy like this.

I think there are a few people here who feel Toby's let us down a little. He said it might be difficult but nobody realized how difficult, because nobody here ever went through something like this before. Maybe he's made it impossible for the government to back down gracefully. Saving face means a lot to men, especially. But let's face it, they never would have. People who use brute force only understand brute force. So I think he's done the right thing, mostly. And he's been very good with my son, who can be a little complicated. In a good way. But it's been a complicated time.

Not for much longer? Well, perhaps you're right. Oh, don't worry, we've all heard all the rumors. We've been watching the navy out in the bay, we know our ships around here.

It's an insult, really. At this point you might as well give up selling any kid my son's age all the American history they ladle out in school. Because he can see it's a pack of lies. You might look at him and think his head's in the clouds but he sees exactly what's going on here, I promise you. They were discussing it all along in school. Over in Leicester. And a few of the kids called him a traitor, a Benedict Arnold who should be hanged for treason. So the teacher let them debate it, and you know what? My son convinced them. And his teacher's a Vietnam vet.

I don't think any of us imagined that the state would be this obtuse, to refuse to even discuss the possibilities with us. You figure how much this is costing them, if they put that money toward repairing our bridge we'd be halfway there and still be on speaking terms. Instead they're getting ready to invade a defenseless country. We're smaller than Monaco or Liechtenstein, I guess we must be the smallest country in the world.

If that's the way they want to do it we can't stop them. But then this country will be the laughingstock of the planet. Can you imagine what they're saying about us right now, over in Europe? Do you think in Paris they'd just knock down some old bridge without trying to save it? Of course not. And if the government squads just move in and try to take us by force it'll be much, much worse. I hope the men with their fingers on the button know this.

That's what the people in—where's your newsmagazine based? Washington? New York? That's what you people down there never realize about those of us out here in the places that don't matter. You never realize how deep the hate runs.

49

Molly Mellew

DON'T KNOW HOW LONG since it was actually me doing the dial on some guy. Because the episode with the wild and woolly Scativo wasn't going to work out, we both knew. He's at a different place in his journey—I can stay flexible, but I just don't need another guy with a busy social calendar. It's not a question of ego, it's a question of concentration.

Maybe one day when I'm in an old folks' home I'll regret not giving him a better shot at the title, as he would say. But I also got the feeling his energy was about to go intensely wrong. Not like I did the cards for him and saw it or something, more just an instinct that such a strong life force might run into a wall head-on, or get swallowed up by a bursting star, whichever.

The notes were his idea. Funny to think he was actually helping me with another man, but he's too evolved to have hard feelings. I told him I thought we'd followed our path to its end, the view was great all the way, but maybe it was time to start heading back. And he was such a gentleman, even kissed my hand and said he hoped we'd always be friends. Which is not what they usually say when it's you dropping them, and never what they mean.

Then he mentioned casually how he'd even been wondering for a couple of weeks if I wasn't interested in someone else. So I admitted sure, now that you mention it, so we played a game of twenty questions though we both knew he knew ("Is he smaller than a lighthouse?"), which almost made me want to explore the jungle with him one last time. Anyway he guessed right. He said good idea, you'd be just what Doctor Scativo ordered for the Auberon, which sort of pissed me off except I still wanted to hear what he had to say.

Regarding strategy, because basically you never know what Toby's truly thinking. I can never read guys with ponytails like his, it's not a compensation thing like those hard-ass creeps with the itsy samurai knot. The mustache looks pretty traditional gunslinger except Toby doesn't brag, ever. He talks like he's saying exactly the right thing at the right time but you know he's really also thinking something else, there's a totally different unseen level going on there. But there's no way to verify it, like in poetry. And no one, but no one, has ever seen how he lives up in his lighthouse, not even Scativo. I asked.

So he suggested leaving Toby these very alluring and mysterious notes to whet his appetite. Guy reads as much as I do, says Scativo, and you don't bump into those too often. Offer him a screenplay for the cinema of the mind. A little today, a little tomorrow. Use your imagination, it's a vast imagination. And don't do the reveal right away. Make him wonder, then make him ask outright if it's you. Then take him wherever you want, it's a beautiful journey.

It was my idea to type them, though. Not give the game away with my handwriting. And typing seemed kind of cool, too, with a whole nineteenth-century ripped-bodice flow. (It even occurred to Scativo that notes like these could wind up as an edgy marketing scheme for my jewelry.) So I slipped Toby the notes two nights running, then nothing one night, but another taste the next. Just be sure, said Scativo, you make a lasting impression.

> The question is, how long will I decide to tease?
> Yes, we know each other. Yes, I am hiding behind
> this typewriter. I will show you all the delectable
> glory of my body one day, as promised. Then,
> very soon, I am going to show you no mercy.

50

Roscoe Hughes

FINALLY THESE GOVERNMENT goombahs stop scratching themselves long enough to do something about my truck.

What's the smartest thing they can think of on overtime? Slap me with an order to move it. Like some folded piece of paper from the parking clerk's going to frighten the shit out of me. Move it yourselves, I told them right down at City Hall, count to ten, take the kumquats out of your assholes, and get ready for some seriously bad news. I got a folded piece of paper for you, too. Cause I got old Toby to write me up a contract for $1 with Carl Elkins who owns the property alongside that roadway, I paid Carl his buck which makes it legal, then we signed, legally giving me a permit to leave my truck there for a year, and since it's only a pedestrian bridge now anyway and people can walk around the truck if they can ever sneak past the Goon Squad, it means I'm not blocking any potential vehicle right-of-way, so fuck you.

Besides, from the roadway on it's not your country anymore. Try to arrest me it's an international incident and you'll find out how much of your own goddamned firepower I got stashed down cellar. Think

I'm joking? You see anyone smiling? That's what I said to them. Maybe you don't like that idea? If you had something besides landfill for brains maybe you'd try replacing the wheels loose enough to spin and tow the sucker off but that's too obvious, you might have to get your hands dirty. And we all know you guys are busy playing hide the soap with each other's interns anyway. So don't send me any more parking tickets, don't bother me unless you come up with a serious frigging threat. If there's one thing that bugs me, it's arguing with pissants.

What I was getting at was it's about time for us to alert them in a serious way i.e. somebody besides me i.e. Toby and in writing, not yelling, which is personally what I would prefer, or maybe on the TV or radio, that we are not exactly unarmed. Since now we also got that warhead by boat at night from the senile guinea fisherman, first guy I ever met who's more ticked off than me. So it's not the same roll over us whenever they want situation. Plus we can mine the road in with their own explosives. Or that stuff from the lunatics in Missouri.

I know how, trust me.

Also, we should let them know we have that missile. Even though we don't have any way to fire it. And we should announce we'll only use it if they attack first, we don't want to threaten nobody.

Though if you ask me we should threaten everybody. I'm getting really sick of showing some fly-swat punk in diapers my goddamned driver's license every time I drive past the church. No point in having this stuff if we don't let them know in advance.

Why? I'll tell you why.

No discussion is serious if somebody thinks they're the boss. You want to make them talk serious fast, you let them know you got a bomb under their chair and a missile pointed at their castanets. Not our problem if people figure out we finally turned dangerous.

51

Anita Wapping

THAT WAS WHEN I told Mitch, "Go ahead and make the call, Tiger. Walk over to the phone, and punch in the number."

He knew I wasn't kidding. He hates to ask for favors as much as I do. And he always thinks people will do the right thing automatically, that's the problem. He knows which people owe him a small favor here or a large favor there from years ago, he has an almanac mind, and he expects people to know when it's time to pay their debts. Throughout the siege he was constantly surprised that people he knows from around the cape, or from the decades he worked in Boston, weren't calling up to help. Or at least share their secret information, since he was always ready to share his for a good cause over the years.

I wasn't surprised, but then maybe I'm not as good a person as he is, down deep. He always acts like he's suspicious of everyone, but it's a mask. It took me years to realize that.

And we'd heard the "informed rumors," same as everyone else, from Toby at Jessica's house, when he asked us all to see what we could find out. By that time we were pretty desperately imprisoned here. And I remember Toby was concerned that people swimming off the bridge every day were thinking of it as a beach and wouldn't resist if the SWAT team decided to attack.

He also mentioned that a couple of used condoms were found by one of the older residents one morning and she was particularly perturbed by this. So he'd spoken to some of the teenagers who were spending nights out there and asked them to be more considerate.

Though he didn't say where he got those rumors, he trusted them. And he was particularly interested in the large tract over in Teal Bay. The one with the vast old quarry where Jessica and I used to go swimming a few years back. A few, let's leave it at that. He seemed sure it was Teal Bay, and as we know he turned out right. I think this meeting was the first time Mitch was sincerely impressed, despite the ponytail and mustache and having gone along with it all despite his better judgment. Because my husband leaned over and said to me, "Now he's learning."

That was when Toby told us he believed an attack was coming sometime soon, and there'd probably be the bribe of a conciliatory meeting first. He said we should be ready, and I felt as silently despondent, I'm sure, as everyone else. We all got very quiet and left very quiet. I didn't know what being ready meant. Sharpen the kitchen carving knives? Get the hedge clippers out of our shed?

So when we got home I said, "Tiger Wapping," which is what I called him when we first met, "you call Brian, over in Gibson's Cove. He's got cousins down in Teal Bay, they're thick as thieves. I bet he can ask around."

Mitch spoke to Brian, I don't know what he said because I was out of the room. Toby had already found out that the property got bought a year ago by a nonprofit company, not an individual, and he was trying to track down who was behind the company, whose offices were a post office box in the Caribbean somewhere. Not Bermuda, we've been to Bermuda. Some little island with a big name.

So the land, all eighteen acres including that quarry, was in the hands of a nonprofit, Strategic Enterprises, that was apparently going to use it to hold private business seminars and meetings a few times a year, once they improved the main house, where Gosling did his sculptures in the twenties and thirties as well as the smaller house where he and all those wives, back then we called them wives and no one complained because he was an artist, lived right through the war. I'm surprised the heirs could finally agree to sell it, along with those ninety adjoining acres inland that supposedly you could never develop but what does that ever mean? Marvelous view, I've always said if anywhere rivals Salt Cove for both sheer natural and man-made beauty, it's Teal Bay.

It seemed a little far-fetched to me that the company in Teal Bay might have anything to do with our bridge over here. But Mitch made the call, and Brian got right back to him the next day and said no one knew who was behind the nonprofit. But there'd been plenty of surveyors nosing around, back when the property changed hands. And I know Mitch passed that on to Toby.

Later, of course, when it all came out—about the ninety acres and the permits he shouldn't have been able to get, and the abandoned Crotty anchor factory that was going to become waterside condos— none of us were entirely surprised. Certainly not my Tiger. He said to me, "Anita, I'd hate to be the one to say I told you so. But I've learned far and wide that if you don't say it on your own behalf, no one else will."

I was still amazed, I have to admit. What kind of people set out to ruin one place to raise the value of somewhere else? All for money? As if those kinds of important people need more money. It makes me want to bring back the electric chair, because I believe I could learn to pull that handle down myself. I'd say, *Here's your last chance, your last chance to make peace with the Almighty.* And I'd wait for them to start praying, but then I wouldn't let them finish, I wouldn't even let them get very far. I'd say, *Too late, you missed it,* and yank that handle down fast. To really savor the voltage.

52

Phil Baxter

SALT COVE ARMED & DANGEROUS!
Exclusive to the *Daily News*

August 3: The *Leicester Daily News* has learned that the village of Salt Cove has obtained weapons of mass destruction and is prepared to use them.

An exclusive conversation between this reporter and a source within the Salt Cove command structure confirmed persistent rumors that the breakaway village, which so far has not been recognized by any state, federal, or foreign government in its bid for independence, is at present equipped with both warhead-tipped missiles and explosive materials of the most lethal sort.

It is not known how the village acquired the missiles.

Some of the explosives are believed to be those attached to the Salt Cove bridge pilings early this summer by state engineers in an unsuccessful midnight bid to blow up the old wooden structure at the heart of the present dispute.

It is believed that the other explosives are of the family of RDX compounds type commonly known as "plastiques" which may be set off by a detonation cap. It is not known how they were obtained. An FBI agent in Boston commented that, "There's just a lot of that stuff going around."

The exclusive source, who did not wish to be named, did confirm that many Salt Cove residents see the present embargo situation, which has resulted in unprecedented traffic problems around one stretch of the cape and a virtual blockade of the village via both land and sea by SWAT teams and Coast Guard vessels, as a "siege" and that a "siege mentality" has developed.

"If they push too hard, then we'll push back with everything we've got" was how the source put it. "No one wants a firefight. We've seen what happens in the past. But if those chumps aren't willing to sit down and talk, they'd better know what they're getting into."

Calls by this reporter to the governor's office for comment went unreturned.

[Wire services reported early this morning that a van pulled over for speeding in western Pennsylvania was found to contain a large quantity of weapons along with detailed maps of Cape Sarah. A number of arrests were made.]

53

Nancy Eckerman

WHERE WAS I WHEN I first heard the news? The baby was in day care, and I was in the back room of Hughes Septic and Land Maintenance, doing things to Billy Fagles that no one's ever done to him before, and the radio was playing so we could make all the noise we wanted. I don't care what the psychologists make of it, doing hard labor all day does give the body a certain prolific glow. He had just made a quaint breathless speech about wanting to provide a good home for me and my baby and I'd told him, "Forget it, all I want is a couple of hours of your time, twice a week, no questions asked." He was gasping for air and staring at me as if I were from another century, which in his terms I suppose I was. The radio announced a special news bulletin, and I put my finger to his lips to stop him talking over it. It'd been so long since I was with someone besides Jon, I'd forgotten that not all men want to fall asleep afterward, some want to tell you their life stories. If only that shared singular act, the hurricane of pure fire, could give them the tongues of immortal poets.

That was when the lieutenant governor's office announced they were willing to meet with representatives from Salt Cove to discuss the ongoing et cetera. And as a gesture of goodwill they were withdrawing the SWAT teams who'd been in place for weeks now, and hoped to speedily resolve all differences.

This was followed by speculation that reports of Salt Cove possessing significant arms and even missiles had prompted the federal government to order the state to back off and give in, not wanting another Waco catastrophe. The state offices were confident a meeting for the end of the week could be arranged, with a swift reconciliation from a preservationist point of view, et cetera, to enact a conclusion mutually satisfying to both sides.

"Oh, boy," said Billy, and gave a big gulp. It wasn't their grammar that bothered him. He said, "Does this mean we won't do this again?"

He must've thought I was in the temporary grip of war fever and blood lust, so if a few commandos packed up their weapons and rolled away I might not want to roll him again. In his own way he is as obtuse as Jon, just more useful in certain idioms. Right then I vowed not to bring up a son with such a scant understanding of women. Better to light one candle, I thought, than curse the darkness.

"Let us," quoth I, "try once again to enact a conclusion mutually satisfying to both sides." And reached for him.

54

Will Smithson

ONCE UPON A TIME there was a village called Quack Baven, a village like this one, my sweet daughter, in its own quiet cove. Some months it was covered in snow, other months the sun shone down with all his might and people went swimming. Every day, in every weather, all the Baveners crossed to and fro over a wooden bridge built centuries earlier by the first settlers from across the sea.

This went on for untold generations. But it so happened that one year there were evil men who had an evil idea. They came from the big city, they didn't come from the village, and they wanted to tear down the old bridge.

Why? Well, they'd secretly bought land along the same coast, in another village. And they hoped to make their place more unique. So they brought in warriors on horseback who rode back and forth at the edge of the village, ready to destroy the bridge at any moment. Yes, dumpling, just like here.

Now the folks in Quack Baven didn't know what to do. But one very smart fellow, who lived alone in the lighthouse, did. He could signal ships in danger out to sea and keep them away from the jagged rocks, he could watch the moon rise over the water, and he could count all the stars when they came on at night and turned themselves out just before morning. This clever fellow knew if he watched the moonlight's path for three nights in a row it would show him the answer. So he perched right next to the lighthouse beacon, and he waited.

The first night the moonlight only led across the water, straight to him. And the next night there were so many clouds, he couldn't see where the eyes of the moon were sending their X-ray vision. But the third night he saw, for once, the moonlight led sideways across the sea, directly to that other village. So our hero—What was his name? His name, sweetie, was . . . Mr. Moonlight. So the very next morning he let everyone know the dark secret of the evil men.

Well, as you can imagine, no one believed him at first. But soon they did. And the evil men pretended to give up. Everyone in Quack Baven felt sure they'd finally won and could keep their beloved wooden bridge. And the hordes of men on horseback seemed to be getting packed up to go away for good.

But that was when they attacked. It was a very dangerous time. But you mustn't worry, Bon Bon. Tomorrow I'll tell you how Mr. Moonlight and his best buddy, Mr. Go, called their friends from the circus and brought in a whole noisy army of jungle animals to save the village, and most of all save the beautiful princess in her castle by the sea from being abducted.

55

Jessica Stoddard

AND NOW WE COME to the lone day that I have wondered if I should or could write about, bouncing back and forth between labyrinthine walls of argument with myself. I, after all, do not know you, and can't fathom what you'll make of me. On the other hand, the role of the historian in my sensible shoes is to gather everything up and preserve it, a harvest against time. In some future epoch a greater-perspectived chronicler of Salt Cove will be glad of what I am going to reveal.

It was, I have to confess, the most acrobatic, marvel-strewn day of my life, well worth waiting seventy-three years for: a prolonged morning, afternoon, and night in which I got to play both Scheherezade and the poet who retrieved all her tales for everyone, a sequence of hours wherein treasures of the world only hitherto dreamed of became mine forever.

Think I'm exaggerating? On the contrary, I'm playing it all down. And why should it be so surprising that a genius who can invent the complex mechanisms of a silver sphere rebounding as never before, lighting up bumpers and bells as it strokes them, should also be adept at manipulating the mechanisms of joy? As long as I can accurately remember and write that day down nothing has been lost, nothing has been squandered, and there is no harm and no tomorrow.

Oddly enough, it was my birthday. Usually not a day for rejoicing, a day when even a glass of water carries a different taste, slightly bitter, slightly flat, though I still try to drink plenty of water. I heard the miraculous news before anyone else, because Bob Herbert called to say that the lieutenant governor's office had called him and promised an announcement in the afternoon, they'd be withdrawing their SWAT teams, unclamping the thumbscrew, and they were willing, even eager, to meet and bring this to a rapid, happy finish.

Toby's desperate plan had paid off. I closed my eyes and swayed with relief as Bob's calming voice drowsed on. It'd been Toby's tactic to risk having our firepower deliberately revealed by a local reporter. (I quoted him Virgil, speaking about rumor gaining swiftness as she goes.) No formal threat from Salt Cove, therefore, but Toby calculated that these rumors would force the federal government to lean hard on the governor's office to parley with us. No one wanted a bloodbath forty miles from Boston, on Winslow Homer's coast. So Toby had the usually impassive Scativo, now riled and sulking in his home like Achilles, make the call. The reporter kept his word, didn't reveal the source, and here it was a day later, my birthday, and we had our promised retreat from the enemy.

I found myself running in a delirium across the Meadow, down to the beach and past the few morning sunbathers. It was not a bright day yet, an August haze lingering on the horizon, but it would be hot by ten. The tide was just beginning to go out and I had to make my way carefully across kelped rocks still slick from the sea. I banged on his lighthouse door, banged and banged again, charged with my mission of enormous import.

"It's Jessica!" I called out. "Open up, Toby!" In my haste I hadn't done anything to make myself look presentable or ravishable, it was just me banging away, bushy eyed and bright tailed. But temptation is a curious guerrilla force: it takes its time, it gathers power almost undetected, it is beyond our stratagems to control, try as we might; neither the tempter nor the tempted is as responsible as either feels. I, who'd been both the tempted and the tormented all summer, sinning

away madly only in my imagination, was about to become the tor-
mentor, the instigator, the *allumeuse*. Jessica Stoddard, temptress at
last.

"It's Jessica, open up!" For once I wasn't afraid of what he might
think of me. Now I was the one bringing him glad tidings of a brave
new world, the—

"Great news!" I sang out as he pulled the door back, and I
thronged in. He was barefoot but fully dressed, jeans and a black T-
shirt, and he looked muddled, as if I'd disturbed him musing at his
work upstairs, which I had. Astounded at my onslaught. "Great day!"
I hurled at him, and recounted what Bob had told me, my words tumbling. No wonder I can't hold on to this pen. "You were right, you
were right!"

"Not so fast," he said. "I told you what our informant predicted.
They'll pretend to withdraw, then—"

"Are you going to believe someone's secret messages," I said gleefully, "or what's before your very eyes?"

He looked at me a trifle askance. "Did you send me those notes?"
he asked, which made utterly no sense at the time.

"Of course not!" I warbled back. "You want a note from me, here's
a note from me."

And before I knew what I'd done I grabbed the edge of his T-shirt,
ruining it, and pulled him forcefully to me. Then my mouth was on
his and I was kissing him as passionately as a woman has ever kissed a
man—for the first time, at least. And on my own initiative.

He really didn't know what was happening at first. He wasn't
expecting this, I am stronger than I look, and I had him pinned
against his own spiral staircase. Also, despite the apparent frankness
of our conversation over these many weeks, he had never realized
what a lascivious tongue I have. Nor had I. What could he do but
respond, half unwillingly, to what he hadn't yet persuaded himself he
secretly desired? For a moment I did not let him up for air, but as soon
as I felt him truly responding to me, discovering who I am, discovering how much he too wanted to go along with the kiss, admitting to
himself that a person can overflow with sensuality no matter what
vessel the liquid has seemingly been poured into—as soon as he began

to be utterly convinced and I could feel the proof of it farther south, I hesitated my lips on his and breathed into his mustache, "We won, we won, thanks to you, my darling, we won—" Then I was in his arms.

Let me write that again, to savor how it felt: *Then I was in his arms, fully, for the first time.* And in case you're wondering, contrary to all you might expect, I was not afraid of what I knew was about to happen.

I think of so many I have known who gave up hope earlier in their lives than I did; I think of those who kept hope alive in me even as I felt it flutter away like a foreigner's scarf on a wordless Istanbul night while I rode that ferry over the Bosphorus, sure I was crossing those dark waters to my inevitable grave despite the panoply of humane lights all around me. I think of the hunched dwarfish couple, he leading, she with cane, the gnarled following the gnarled, whom I saw departing a much fallen café of decrepit opulence in old Barcelona— people with little dignity or means, keeping hope alive together. I think of Muhammad Ali, who stood up for the hopes of those beaten into incoherence by the right hooks of fortune. And I think of my father, who never failed to believe my mother might come back to him one day, never understood there was no more hope of love, love had simply moved on, not like a wayfaring stranger but like a temporary boarder with plenty of cash and other places to go.

I was not thinking any of that then; I was trying to chew my way through his mouth till I got to China, or to his soul and thence the very rest of him. What to do, what to do? I knew the next move was still up to me, I couldn't think, I could barely stand, and what was coursing through my head in a rapid flurry of pages turning as if whipped by a hurricane blast were all those scenes I'd read over the decades, scenes happening to other people, scenes in books, always withheld from me. I tried to banish them from my thoughts and let my body, so much less desiccated than it perhaps looked to an outsider, tell me what to do and tell this new insider where to go. My God, his hands were roaming me like searching, tireless Odysseus trying to find the way home. I'd gotten this far by taking charge; I nudged him back onto the lower steps of the staircase.

"I'll follow you up," I said.

"Jessica, I don't—"

"Do as you're told," I murmured, and gave a healthy nibble at him as I pushed him up a couple of steps—a nibble that surprised me as much as it surprised him. "You're going to show me everything, right now."

A curious moment, then, three flights up, past the books rendered moot by what was transpiring before their unblinking eyes, when we came onto his bedroom level and he hadn't even protested once, his tousled single bed pushed to one side, characteristically unmade— who knows, a neat prim bedspread might've been enough to stop him doing what he was already doubtless having second and fifth and twelfth and twentieth thoughts about. But there was no stopping me. I pushed him onto the bunched sheets and leaned over to kiss, no, to practically strafe his chest as I sat clumsily down beside him. He bounded up suddenly, gasping like a fish caught in the suffocating air; I grabbed his belt and kissed him again, right at the center of the world, as he stood in front of me.

"Jessica, this is—"

"This is my birthday," I interrupted courageously, ignoring the thunderbolt he might hurl if he replied *How old?* "And I get to have everything I want. Spoils of war."

"Spoils of war?" he said incredulously, and stared down at me with that gaze of being about to go over a cliff and surprised at how natural it feels, the stupefaction of slowing time to a visible crawl.

Then—thank all the pagan gods I have never stopped worshiping—he actually looked straight into me, looked down a well deep inside me, as he never had before. He didn't look at my body, or my clothes, or my age, he just gazed back into my eyes, into my gaze, and saw for an instant all of who I am while I looked back up at him in reply. Except I had always only seen him this way, and he realized it. I relaxed my grip on his leg.

"Come, Toby, sit by my side." I patted his bed. "And let the world slip. We shall never be younger."

I do not know if he recognized what I'd said, but he sat back down, albeit (I must admit) a shade reluctantly—the reluctance that still not knowing what age is, or what time really means, hesitates you with even halfway through life. But as soon as he sat next to me on the bed all reluctance vanished. He reached out and took my head in both his hands, said simply, "You're right," then brought the battle ruthlessly to me as I welcomed every taste of him.

Though I was not technically, medically I mean, a virgin, having taken care of that myself and myself alone in Korea, wanting to spare sharing the pain with anyone, I was still what my avaricious niece would viciously and provincially call a virgin. I realized at that moment how it is no small thing to feel a man's blind weight on you for the first time, or—after scuffling with each other's clothing—the dense mass of him like an animal surging alongside you on a cramped and rumpled bed. Medical technicalities aside, call it the first time; I bit my lip, I bit his ear, I bit the air.

Clang, clang. He asked me if I was all right, if he should go on, I told him to go on till the last ding-dong, I didn't know what I meant but he went on, eventually it became cling, cling, I could not cling him tightly enough to me. I can read your mind, you are expecting exactly what I was expecting from him, but what was magical was what did not occur. He didn't stand up full of regret, brushing off dusty leaves, astonished to find himself in the hayloft; he kept his arms around me, we kissed more tenderly than before, we said nothing but lay motionless in the gathering heat of the day, profusely sweating and content in our sweat. And at some point, because I am a busy bee, we began again. No, I did not see stars, but I saw the white plaster wall of the lighthouse up close, I saw my fingers splayed on it, and that was enough. You pray at your shrines, and I'll pray at mine.

We talked later, as lovers do, after napping far into the afternoon. By now I had got a good look at him and memorized all I saw for future reference. We spoke admiringly of each other, as lovers will. He told me I was a heroine for what I'd done for Salt Cove, and I told him Jessica was my first name but Joan my middle name, for Joan of Arc, a favorite of my father's, who'd led the French to kick the English out of France. "But I wouldn't kick you out of bed," I said, and heard myself giggle, then laugh in a voice I didn't recognize.

Surprisingly full of energy, I got up while he rested, I made us tea down below, and soon, back upstairs, my mouth piping warm from the tea, in a trick I'd read about in one of those books from my forbidden library, I startled him: as he gazed at me with a single sullen eye I sipped, supped, sapped him of all he had to offer.

The sunlight of the day gradually faded twenty feet above us in the tower. We did not leave the new universe of his shared bed. It was not on my mind yet that this might possibly or even probably be the only time I would spend with him here, the question hadn't occurred to me. I felt that now I was here I was here forever; or rather that the time I was now inhabiting, though I could note the hours passing on his watch, appeared without limit. The older you get the more aware you become that time is what we are made from, we grow poorer every day, we begin by spending like a soldier on a spree and end by coveting like a miser on the skids. And yet as afternoon waned into evening and nightfall I felt only rich, surrounded by vast heaps of plundered pirate gold, encircled by illicit booty, with a gossiping sea lapping mere inches away from us, awash with tales of our rapacity.

He taught me games, I his willing student ready to do ever more than he suggested or the rules of the game might allow. He told me I had a beautiful mind and a beautiful body, in a voice I did not doubt for an instant. I taught him that all his procrastinated instincts about me had been right.

I also taught him Word Pong, how to take a word and alter it a letter at a time into another—even its very opposite, which is why the game has always reminded me of what I felt sure love was like. I proved to him that though you can achieve a low score and win by using the fewest possible moves (hate = have = lave = love), the ideal way to play is to move from meaning to meaning as poetically as possible. As it grew dark around us together we devised hate = late = mate = sate = save = wave = wive = live = love, our own story mostly, and we were both winners together. Then we gave up that game, because all our words did not matter as much as what the rest of us had to say.

I did bring up what he might wear on television when the moment came to announce their capitulation to us, a prediction that made him (correctly) uneasy. He agreed to try on a blue suit of my father's, though I knew it would be too large. Secretly I only wanted to get him to undress over at my house, beside my own bed. I told him, too, my deepest fear, a lingering guilt which those clues about property in

Teal Bay could not dispel: that all this had to do with someone wanting to buy my house one day and turn it into a hotel, while a modern
bridge you could drive across would make Salt Cove more accessible
to tourists. That thus somehow I was responsible.

"But you haven't sold your house."

I bit my lip. "You're right, I haven't."

"And a modern bridge would only make the village less appealing."
I felt him shake his head in the darkness. "Sometimes you don't make
sense, Jessica." But he said it fondly.

"Sometimes you don't, either."

Our evening reverie in the satisfied darkness was abruptly broken
as the automatic beacon above us clanked on, flashing its warning—a
fog had come in—and the signal, an enormous intonation like the
deep bellow of a primitive animal, went blaring out. So that was how
it sounded, up close. When he put his arm protectively around me I
put my hand possessively on him. "There goes that foghorn again,"
I said.

You're probably wondering, whether you'll admit it or not, what a
man of his age was doing with a woman of my age. I'm glad you asked
that question. You are probably wondering also what my body can
have looked like alongside his, whether I'd kept myself in fighting
trim or let myself go like so many who live alone for life. And you are
wondering what, sexually, a man six years past half my age, to be
blunt, would've seen in me, or in the corporeal manifestation of me. I
close my eyes and can barely hold this paper steady: How shall I prove
that despite your prejudices, he proved you wrong that long day, again
and again, using all his fingers, toes, mustache, and derring-do? That,
once prodded by me, as much desire as any woman could ask for was
fully awakened in him?

Well, as the poet said, the body's not the only nakedness, and all
that eternal afternoon I was not an old woman of seventy-three but a
young woman, indeed only a few hours old, thanks to him. To all you
mistresses who wish to hold a man I would say: be prepared to do
more than he ever thought possible, and age will be the last thing on
his mind.

Still, you ask, didn't he, just once, seem to flinch? To which I reply:

imagine me with a man my age—it seems utterly normal. Imagine Toby with a woman his age (or younger, as is the fashion in certain parts, I hear news reports all the time)—it seems utterly normal. I am presuming a great deal about your imagination, no doubt. Now imagine two people at large along the space-time continuum, coasting on converging winds, their conversing souls (that word again, I mean the part of you which persists long after you can no longer grip a thought) face-to-face, not even noticing the calluses left by a few years more or less. And if none of that mumbo-jumbo convinces you that we had many hours of bliss, fine upstanding bliss between us, abracadabra, then let me just say that we were each happy to do everything the other wanted, I as a wide-eyed newcomer, he as an experienced man of dual hemispheres, and it must've been enough, for there went that foghorn, again and again.

At some point in the evening, around ten perhaps, we roused ourselves and I clambered downstairs and cooked us dinner, a proper spaghetti for an improper occasion, with gobs and gobs of buttery sauce. It is marvelous to eat a messy meal naked. There are also not many times around here—due to the weather, I mean—when you can do that without catching your death. Eventually, I persuaded him to show me around; he didn't have much fight left in him at this point. He showed me the fruits of his library and I made a few suggestions for reorganization which he did not have a chance, alas, to try out. He also showed me, finally, the Machina Excelsior, lit up by night in all its powerful electric glory.

Lovers young and old will perhaps not believe me when I say that up until then I had not done the slightest bit of acting, in the sense of pretending. However, I now had to dissemble totally, to be mystified, stunned, amazed, moved to run through all the positive chromatic hues I'd already gone through alone up here a couple of weeks before.

This wasn't easy, but at least it was after dark, and we were operating only by a few discreet lamps that set, abetted rather, a very seductive atmosphere. (I suspect he previously suspected, prior to this Grand Tour, that I'd sneaked up here the day I sneaked in, but now I succeeded in convincing him otherwise.) I learned the complex splendor of his scheme, *Xibalba* meaning the Mayan underworld—as I'd already looked it up, I had to feign ignorance. He recounted an elaborate myth of brothers, fathers, twins, blood, of two heroes from the world of men playing out the sacred ball game against the immortals below. Thus his brilliant idea of an entire lower game level that revealed itself only after making that one very difficult shot on the mortal level above, which gained you acccess to the underworld. And an ultimate contest which probably never could be won, since the immortals (i.e., the Machina) raised the level of play inexorably depending on yours.

It relieved me to hear him talk about this game of death and life with such fervor, to confirm how insightful I'd been about him all along. I even proposed to him that someday, some year, when the Machina was completed, he and I collaborate on a book about it, explaining all his ideas. I could help him write the *Liber Excelsior* and even photograph it.

Naturally, I didn't let on to Toby that some pictures of the game in its unfinished state already existed. I did not want him to know that one minuscule corner of me held a liar. He grunted and I think warmed to the book idea if only because I didn't insist. I could see that though the Machina Excelsior was a *fait accompli* in his own mind, he still knew it was painful months and months away from completion.

He took me to the uppermost, beacon level too—ignoring a stricture of his lease but acknowledging the structure of his heart, for if not then, that night, then when? We stood together on the uppermost rung of the spiral staircase like a single creature at last given form, his arms around me since my legs were shaking a little, watching the beacon almost blinding above us, the rotating light with its muscular lenswork like the blinking eye of a great mind, looking out on a perfect view, flashing its persuasive message out. Very gently then, past the nape of my neck, he said, "Jessica, why did you never marry?"

"Never met the right man, I suppose."

Easy sometimes to say what's true, especially when it's simple like that, but I still swallowed hard; the reasonable part of me sat on the squirming other part of me, knowing there'd be no unexpected requests for my hand that night. Still, it meant the earth to me that he'd asked in a general way, and found that fact of my life surprising,

surprising enough to ask and get the answer he'd doubtless expected all along.

Future historians should know that by this day Toby, through sources he never revealed (some former legal colleague in California, I believe, who knew the right people in Massachusetts and whom Toby called thrice from my house that week, because a Los Angeles law office number showed up on my phone bill), had determined who was behind the mysterious property in Teal Bay and thus the motivations for our bridge being condemned. He explained, as we went slowly down the winding stairs, that he planned to hold a news conference the next afternoon and welcome the entreaties of the state to settle this dispute amicably, then give away what he'd found out in a confidential report to the journalists present, off the record, so they could reveal it themselves. All the accusations would come from them, once they verified the information, not from us—the state's hands would be tied before they even sat down to bargain.

That was Toby's plan, anyway, though the day after tomorrow would erupt molten lava on it.

It was nearly midnight, or slightly after—I can't even tell you what time it is right this second—I had realized that I should be on my way, it might be better not to spend the night. I also thought he might miss me a little in the morning. I suggested going home and he looked surprised and a tad relieved. He did say, "You can stay, you know."

"Oh, no. I know a bachelor heart when I see one. And you know where to find me."

I wonder if he sensed how new I was to all this. If he did, he was too much of a gentleman to let on. I'd certainly not lacked bravado or enthusiasm. I dressed swiftly, and at the door gave him one last delicious, impassioned kiss until he let himself go, an intaglio on my lips. I said, "You won't mind doing the dishes yourself, this time?"

He smiled. "I'll try to make you proud."

You have always made me proud, I thought, and to be able to at last call you *my darling* is the greatest and sweetest pride of my life.

I was not yet wondering (as I would on waking in my own bed at dawn) if this night perhaps might not let him sleep, might provoke strange hours of him tormenting himself over if we'd done the right thing. I was just stepping out the door—we knew we would see each other in the morning, when he'd come to my house to make a few calls to arrange a news conference—we were still suffused with that shared-body wisdom of having become lovers, I was thinking that at last I knew what this felt like, the momentary parting, having read about it so many times although no description, I realized, was adequate to the comforting sensation of passing through this mutually elastic slipstream, I tried to smile at him good night when my foot scuffed something, it skittered, a folded piece of paper.

"What's that?" I said.

"Huh." He bent to retrieve it before I could. "A note."

"So that's what it's like," I said. "More secret information?"

He shrugged. "I'll read it later." He swallowed it in one hand. He was still, by the way, quite naked.

"Maybe it's important. Don't you want to look?"

"Believe me, Jessica," he said. "It doesn't seem so important now."

I relished over and over the way he'd said that as I passed across the Meadow by charged moonlight. I paused to murmur a few private words, which shall remain private, to the elderly tree I always associate with my father—praying, if you must know, for it to bless whatever would come with the man in the lighthouse below. I took my time ambling home. There was no folded note waiting for me but I did not need one, I was full of my own secret information. *Because the world is my lobster, not my oyster, I end up with pincers, not pearls,* I always used to joke. Not anymore.

My house seemed different now. It no longer felt so full of waiting, so needlessly alert with the sense that some event, some revelation, was about to occur but hadn't yet.

It had always driven me crazy, this waiting. I'd always attributed it to the expansive view from my living room window, which seemed to indicate some gigantic arrival or departure about to be accomplished, a sunset to end all sunsets. Now I could walk through the rooms calmly and know where the waiting had come from, or at least know that henceforth the sunsets could do their vain best and I would not care, they were nothing compared to the still smoldering crepuscule within me. Or compared to all that blackness, my beloved fellow conspirator, with only a few stars glinting faintly among dense clouds that refused to fan apart for the moon—because the whole purpose was to provide a night sea and a night sky to show off the searing path of the lighthouse beacon, infinitely reliable and unafraid, just up the coast from me.

I could draw back the bedsheets to climb in deliciously nude, my feet leaving the floor so I could throw myself girlishly back; I was exhilarated, not tired, I was giddy, ready to try this again, right now in fact. I was also ready to sleep in a way I'd never slept in my life. I could just imagine the enigmatic conversation I'd have the very next day with Mildred, who'd left a message on my answering machine wondering where I was.

"And where did *you* spend yesterday evening?" she'd say.

"Oh, you know. With Toby."

That pause of hers, hoping I'd say more. She'd been so bored when I told her how he repaired my father's pinball machine. How little she knew! She'd get no secrets out of me, though.

"So, what'd he fix for you this time?"

And I would smile to myself, languorously tasting what I was about to tell her, letting the words ripen on my tongue.

"This time," I'd say loftily, "this time he showed me the lighthouse."

56

Scott Mahren

THE FEAR ISN'T DYING, of course. You know you're going to die. Fighter or fornicator, charlatan or chump, you all end up either shot down screaming in flames or else swearing at the standard-issue chute that fails to open, splat. No, in this corner the fear is what they remember, grinning idiots I wouldn't trust to get on the right train, all of them eager to be slaves, yet they're allowed to tell stories about you for years and get the punch lines wrong, or misquote you as some trick dog who agreed with them constantly. Or else forget you entirely, lost in their own fog out in the big world. My private insurance policy? Lift up your Mahren Pedal, fans of greatness in great men, and you'll see my signature molded there in deathless plastic forever. It should've been only the beginning.

Still, at the moment the predominant fear is knowing that the only person around here actually getting it all down for posterity, at least this final chapter of the Scativo Saga, is an older lady with an itchy writing hand who makes up at least as much as she gets right. Not as bad as dying in desperation or obscurity, agreed, and better than a poke in the eye with a sharp stick, but I'd prefer to see the official record lined up a little more reliably.

Just remember, not too many wake up in the morning expecting it to happen today. The Wily Scativo sure didn't, and if even he can get it wrong, the percentages are not exactly running in your favor. And don't console yourself with the thought you're going to wind up in some celestial version of Florida, riding around in golf carts bending the ears of giants. Those of us gifted with a mission are not about to spend eternity jawing with the cannon fodder.

Big talk, Scativo, but you're the one who's kaput. No kidding. A hero's death, too. Hindsight isn't always just jerk-off time for historians: the old lady will no doubt get this part correct, and the Auberon will support her thesis, that without yours truly they'd have rolled straight over us. Oh, they played it right, all right. Let Toby give his news conference the next afternoon, let everyone relax and smile, people were even taking six-packs up to those no-neck storm troopers and the girls practically asking now can I touch your bazooka, everyone waving bye-bye, all is forgiven, they were only doing their job. (I can vouch from family history one ocean away and two generations back, whenever a flathead says he's simply following orders, it means there's about to be a slaughter of the innocents.) Meanwhile we were pulling in all our defenses and going home.

It smelled as rotten to me as a paper factory, and I didn't get any disagreement from Toby or Roscoe or Billy. You didn't have to be Hannibal to figure out you were being outflanked in the desert with nowhere to hide. I'll say this for the pinball freak, he didn't let the attention go to his head, in fact he looked more focused. Which made me think a certain someone might've gone to work on him with all the higher learning she absorbed from the Scativo.

First he gave his interview on the bridge about us being willing to powwow with the government, and stood there as everybody took his picture—while I kept thinking you poor schmuck, from now on you'll need a daily shave and a napalm haircut if you ever want to vanish into the plains and cities of America, since you're scanned into the memory banks forever. Then, strictly off the record, he handed out those wind-up manila envelopes he loves, guy must buy them in bulk, telling the journalists they didn't receive the incriminating evidence from him, have a nice day.

As soon as he was done we four slipped over to Roscoe's h.q., in back. The lunk was loudly (and wisely) refusing to move his septic truck till he had more proof than the verbal assurances of those same bastards who'd made his life miserable for months and tried to blow his balls to Hong Kong. That got me remembering the Jade Princess, naturally, same part of the world and a mouthwatering civilization to meditate on while everyone was loudmouthing at once. The dumbest news of all—fatal news, but how was I to know? You don't expect a falling asteroid the size of a quarter to come looking for you—was that a second van of those amateurs from Missouri, the Liberation Army of the Angry Castrati, had made it safely past the Pennsylvania Turnpike and was camped out somewhere northwest of Boston awaiting instructions. "Tell them to invade Newfoundland and let us know how they do" was Toby's reaction, which I seconded, but somehow the message got scrambled later by Eckerman in translation.

They weren't the immediate problem, though. The problem was, as we all believed—and the Scativo had been saying this for a week, supported by whichever Deep SWAT found the guts to inform on his fellow jackboots—that they might attack before Toby's secret info did its work. Didn't make sense for them not to take a shot, after all this time, unless the newspapers stopped them by running the story first. Then they wouldn't dare. We figured all we had to worry about was tonight, and early tomorrow, before the papers hit.

The fear that this was a trap just as Deep SWAT had warned shook the hell out of all of us, so we decided to keep watch up at the church and out on the bridge ourselves, to make sure they didn't sneak in. I figured it would take a team of semicompetent National Guard only five minutes to blow the bridge if there was no one on it yelling at them to pretty please go away.

The real problem was that just because we had serious ammo on our hands, they had no reason to back down—all they had was one more cue to not provoke us and start a bloodbath. Instead convince us we've won, agree to all our terms, then pull an ambush while everyone's home congratulating themselves and alphabetizing the suppositories. Claim it was to protect the general public because, after all, we were not only threatening the national unity, we were armed and dangerous.

Nope, we wouldn't be safe until the story about manipulating the real estate market hit the fan. Not that it surprised me—my aunt gives away her three-bedroom in Tenafly for eighteen thou and two years later they decide to put an interstate through her living room, tell me someone's cousin didn't know about it first.

If they came in this time, like Deep SWAT said, they wouldn't fart around, they'd swing in hard. We knew we couldn't do squat if they attacked in force. Roscoe wanted to wait till dark then rig up explosives at the entrance to the village, ixnay on the trip wires, but personally I didn't have confidence in Septic-Man pulling it off without taking out a few spectators. We were all sore afraid, what we needed was an alternate plan, and for maybe the first and definitely the last time in his life the Wily Scativo didn't have one. So we spread out.

Stayed on the bridge all night, solo this time. Roscoe and Billy up at the church, Toby in the lighthouse watching the coast to make sure they didn't come in by the beaches—he knew how to override the automatic controls and keep the beacon flashing like a searchlight just to discourage them. So I sat out on the bridge alone, not minding one bit, a plenty clear night, thinking what a long road I'd trod to get here, thinking about what we were on the verge of winning. Not cocky, but feeling victory so close I could practically put my arms around it, knowing it was still just out of reach.

Thinking about old Jessica, too, who'd had a long talk with me early in the evening out here, writing down everything I said. Even thinking about life and death, about how I often felt I was strolling arm in arm simultaneously with both of them. Like two gorgeous sisters, each with a kind of fiery, south-of-the-border strut, and you never got to know either sister as well as you wanted, you were constantly sleeping with both yet you sometimes couldn't tell them apart, even your hands couldn't tell the difference between them because their curves seemed so tantalizingly alike. For some reason those sisters made me think maybe this year I'd teach myself Latin, always felt it was a gap that held the Scativo back slightly, knowledge is power, always room for more of each, and it made me shiver out there on a hot August night lousy with stars to find myself thinking this life, death, gorgeous sisters baloney, because usually whenever I found myself ruminating along these lines it meant something was really wrong, some door I'd forgotten to lock. But I saw nothing stirring out there, just the little cove harbor asleep, mighty far from New Jersey, baby, and we'd done a decent job protecting it. I rapped on the wood railing of the bridge for luck, which also bugged me, since what people call luck is coincidence, the statistics falling your way when you happen to be watching. And it bothered me to catch myself so superstitious in the middle of the night, alone out there.

And wide awake, awake enough to dream. Even though I couldn't come up with an alternate plan, walking back and forth on the bridge for hours, peering through the night-vision binocs and seeing nothing moving, as the darkness wore on and I could feel the day on the verge of breaking, another hour and the newspapers would hit with that first hint of a dynamite story and we'd be safe, surely, I did find myself coming up with an alternate scenario, Scativo's Dream.

It went like this. I wasn't standing out on the bridge, I was up on a hill, looking down not as lone sentry but as commander, and it wasn't now, it was twenty-two centuries ago. I heard them coming just before dawn from miles away, heard their army tramping across the land, heard their swords and shields clank in the stillness, their massed forces coming up the dusty road intent on getting across this bridge, only they had no conception of what force they were up against. They'd heard only rumors, they hadn't yet met up with me. They had many times my men but I had assembled an army of elephants, something they had never seen before, and I could bring these enormous animals out of another continent over the hills, over snow-clad mountains if I had to, and then they'd see how much thunder a bold, original idea could make. They would see, all right.

And maybe the Scativo actually *was* the Wily Hannibal in another lifetime—but I sure wasn't going to end up defeated and driven into exile far from home. That was right when the sun was coming up, over behind the church and the head of the cove, and as I gazed at it and relished the idea of leading trumpeting elephants into battle, vengefully scattering my enemies before me, a colossal roar went up exactly where I was looking and a cataclysm of flame ripped apart my dream.

At first I thought the church had caught fire, but it was much worse. We were under attack from the National Guard: so much for the power of positive thinking. Two black Humvees equipped with recoilless rifles—they can shoot through just about anything—had come in from the other side of the cape. Roscoe and Billy had tried to blow the first and mistimed it. All they did was wake up the village, wreck the road and send smoke pluming out over the cove. Both Humvees got past them. Meanwhile, approaching along the road from Leicester, I saw an armored personnel carrier with a 50-mm machine gun on top and good Christ, a gigantic Abrams tank, cannon and all.

The green personnel carrier kept going, to secure the village entry by the church, I guessed. The tank heaved up short and stationed itself here at the bridge behind Roscoe's truck, not a hundred feet away from me. I stood there asking myself if an elephant could overturn an armored personnel carrier if it really wanted to, and wondering how much more damage an Abrams tank could do to me than I could do to it—though I did have a couple of Missouri grenades on my belt, totally useless unless the tank driver poked his head out and asked me for directions. Also pondering what would happen if they blasted a shell direct into Roscoe's septic truck; maybe he'd never pumped it out and they'd cover themselves in fecal glory.

That was when the first Humvee that made it in came roaring down Shepherd Street. I heard a few people yelling and screeching futilely at it as they ran out of their houses in bathrobes. In front of the Village Hall it wheeled on a dime, reversed with a squeal, and started lumbering backward down the hill toward the bridge, the tubular gun in the rear pointing its long snout directly at me. *Come along quietly?* I thought, nearly weeping with fury. *You've got to be kidding.*

No, I've got no subsidiary regrets, besides the major one. Always thought I'd live to ninety-six, end up in a fancy home somewhere, slurping down the macaroni and pawing at the nurses who'd have the good grace to wear short white skirts and classy lingerie for my benefit, glad to pay through the nose for the privilege so I could pretend to recognize my children when they came to visit. I imagined, with all due modesty, that it would take more than the U.S. military to take down the Wily Scativo. That's where most of the blame lies, not with an ancient dream of battle-hardened pachyderms or some naïve attempt at self-sacrifice—not even with those birdbrains from Marlboro Country, who unbeknownst to us had tried to head off the first wave of assault vehicles back in Gibson's Cove and got them plenty more annoyed en route than they needed to be.

Blame the government, blame the amateurs, but never blame the man ready to act on the strength of an original idea, even if he gets crushed by the march of the barbarians. (Memo to the old lady: get this one right.) At the end of the day, all the brains in the world can't fight vastly superior forces if they don't care what posterity will make of them. I of all people should've known, but when life goes well even the best forget. Remember that, next time you find yourself enjoying the vista and believing in the smile. Remember the un-Wily Scativo, and despair.

57

Survivors' Accounts

Phil Baxter

Around 6 A.M. this morning National Guard forces acting under federal orders entered the village of Salt Cove, xxx in all. Eyewitness accounts claimed that xxx tanks and xxx armed Humvees as well as xxx personnel carriers carrying a squad each were temporarily repulsed and suffered various etc.

—or—

The village of Salt Cove was awakened this morning shortly after six to the thap-thap-thap of tanks thundering & trundling into their midst. Explosion after explosion rocked the sleepy little hamlet. Meanwhile, in Boston, forty miles away, the newspapers were filled with accusations of hanky-panky in the highest echelons of the lt. governor's office having to do with major clandestine investments in Teal Bay were rife etc.

—or—

This reporter watched, horrified, as the forbidding silhouettes of U.S. tanks shattered the dawn stillness. As the first explosions shook the Salt Cove church, while gallant villagers fought back, this reporter came under heavy fire. Shards of shrapnel went whistling overhead. . . .

Facts, facts, facts, readers want only the facts.

Raymond Pratt

Of course it's impossible to assess the "real" real estate consequences until a decade has passed.

I wasn't surprised, personally, to hear about the short-term involvement of higher state officials. The cape has been a prime orchard ripening for years, you're bound to have someone trying to use pesticide on a few of the trees.

As for the long-term view, I don't see any harm once the bridge issue has been resolved. The place has gained a certain notoriety. You'd have to look back at other historic sites and see if development values went up or down.

In the end, Salt Cove is always Salt Cove. We're customarily handling the very choicest properties there, including one on the water with major commercial potential and appeal. And we're certainly counting on all the fuss to put the Cove on the "gold coast" map once and for all.

Italo Simpkins

I was already dressed, so I saw what happened. The explosions up near the church, thanks to Roscoe, got me out of the house. I suppose their intent was to position a couple of tanks, or those Humvees that they use with huge guns riding in the rear, on both sides of our bridge and blow it to smithereens. Then have their troops deal summarily with us as secessionists, once we were demoralized. And I guess Roscoe must've used a small quantity of the explosive plastic compounds we were sent by that Missouri group. But both of those vehicles got through despite his best efforts.

We live right on Baven Lane, in the heart of the village, so I was in the street there watching when the first Humvee came tearing up to the Village Hall. It swung its barrel past me, I guess six, seven feet long. I was waving my arms and yelling at the exposed man manning the gun. They're recoilless, which is a paradox of physics and a definite advantage. He was in a helmet and full combat gear. He didn't pay a mere civilian any attention. His vehicle didn't stop, just reversed hard left and ran backward down the hill toward the bridge at surprising speed, with the muzzle leading the way.

It's incredible how those things can move. The setup seems to be two front men in an enclosed, armored cabin, one's driving, the other's turned to see where they're going. Open in back, where the gunner is. The noise was excruciating. I suppose it was around six fifteen.

I remember thinking, don't they see there's that concrete pillar in the way? There'll be an accident. Then I realized they weren't going to drive onto the bridge, they were going to blast it away from a distance of twenty feet.

My wife came out in her blue bathrobe, she took my arm. Fortunately both Becky and Simon obeyed us and kept inside. She said, with no stutter whatsoever, Stop yelling, dear, it doesn't do any good.

Rachel Fowler

I wasn't there when it happened. We didn't own our own house in the village yet, we were still living in Jack's old lobsterman's shack across the water.

I was in bed, Jack had gotten up and gone into Leicester to get his usual early breakfast and leave my car first thing down at Lasky's Garage. I heard a boom, two booms, and looked past the tide buoy toward Salt Cove and saw smoke. Then I heard the whining of a lot of tanks and those troop carriers on the road coming past here.

So Jack heard about it from me. In fact, when I opened the front page of the Boston paper I couldn't wait for him to get home so I could say, "I told you so!" Because I told him what was behind all this months and months ago. I heard it from Cynthia who heard it from Amy, and he scoffed at me way back when, at my friends. And who was right? Who was right in the end?

But then we got our cottage in Salt Cove from that woman who used to be in the adult film industry, as they say, so that's all right. It's still tragic what happened to the bridge, though. And that poor man. He was very handsome, I saw his picture.

Roscoe Hughes

Wrong. What I used was the same shit they tried to use on us, period. You want that plastic shit those guys sent us, you better show me a search warrant. Or stay the fuck away from my doorstep. Not that I'm saying I have it or not. So go subpoena someone else and leave me the fuck alone.

I wish for once they'd come crawling to you on their hands and knees and say, Sorry, we was assholes, here's what we owe you for wasting your time and being such lying sacks of scum. Instead they're talking about making us pay for the damage done to one tank and two Humvees and burn surgery and the road on top of everything else. Trying to tell us that one tank by itself costs lots more than a bridge, so funny I forgot to frigging laugh.

Now we got another couple of years in court ahead of us if we're lucky, just to defend ourselves. Bob Herbert says let's countersue, great idea, Bob, like I got extra time and money on my hands. Maybe they ought to think about dropping all charges and declaring an amnesty is what I was thinking. Or maybe they ought to figure out we didn't invade them, they invaded us, and if you stick your dick in an electric socket you might get toasted.

What they really ought to think about is recalculating our property taxes by figuring out how much of my valuable fucking year they wasted just so this pimpleshit lieutenant governor with Roman god-damned numerals after his bozo middle name can go buy up half Teal Bay with nobody noticing then crap up the rest of the cape so he comes out even richer. You tell that cocksucker if his Lexus ever gets onto Cape Sarah I got a boxload of plastic explosives with his name on it, and believe me, I ain't going to just rattle the license plate this time. First tell him to write me a refund check and start saying his prayers, then tell him to get used to changing his shorts five times a day, cause I'm not going to be happy till he's shitting barbed wire non-stop in fear. Think I don't know how to deal with human waste? Shit.

Tell that bastard the last sound he hears is going to be Roscoe laughing. Cause I'm sure the fuck not laughing now.

Allie Teague

I did read about the bridge, yes. I'm not surprised. After being there for two weeks this summer, nothing could surprise me. Fortunately, despite everyone being against me, essentially, I managed to achieve several canvases. At the time they weren't at all what I intended. Or so I thought. Now, of course, they seem remarkably prescient.

Mitch Wapping

I was having coffee. Saw the very first attack Humvee swing into my window. Called up to Anita, told her get down here on the double. Thought about calling someone, called Jessica, told her to get down here too. Then I went outside.

He was a brave young man, all right. It's peculiar how people move into this village and immediately feel a lifelong kinship even though they just got here. I guess they don't have places like this where he was from. They say his basement was filled with books, all alphabetized, which you wouldn't think of to talk with him. Which just goes to show, you can keep any basement as dry as a bone if you know what you're doing and don't cut corners.

I suppose it only took a few minutes after he won his argument with that attack vehicle before everyone came running. It burns me up that several smarty-pants commentators on the radio compared him to some radical terrorist suicide bomber. Nothing could be further from the truth. He was armed, all right, but if he hadn't been, what would've happened? That first cannon would've exploded the bridge to kingdom come before the rest of us got there.

I was coming down the hill, so I saw everything. Saw the look on his face, most of all.

Never saw a fellow move so fast. He watched their vehicle back all the way down to the cement pillar blocking the road onto the bridge and realized what they were getting close enough to do, all right. Their cannon was adjusting its aim, getting ready to fire, but he scampered on over, he pulled the pin and tossed that first pineapple gently, just ever so gently. Like he was, oh, a master candlepin bowler gracefully laying a ball in. Only he lobbed the grenade over the head of the gunner so it rolled right across the roof of the Humvee, and tumbled slowly down the front windshield, and lay there. Talk about a perfect strike. And right away, I don't think he even bothered to count one-Mississippi, he reached down and grabbed another from his belt and tore the pin off that one, too.

By now the man behind the cannon was reaching for his small arms. His mind wasn't on the bridge anymore, it was on Scativo. But he changed priorities as soon as the second grenade landed at his feet, by the mounting base of the gun. He went scrabbling for it, I wasn't counting seconds but the two guys seated in front sure were. They were already frantically ducking down to protect themselves inside that Humvee as fast as they could with a live grenade sitting pretty on their windshield. Which was smart, they were safer inside than out.

From what I saw, Scativo realized the gunner in back was going to toss the other pineapple away. So instead of saving himself, he pulled himself on board, he grabbed the guy hard by the helmet in a kind of vicious headlock and wrenched the guy over the side and onto the road. Unfortunately, he slipped and staggered and fell back in himself. I don't think the guy had hit him but you never know. I was trying to get back up the hill myself by this time, except I kept looking over my shoulder.

I guess he just couldn't get to his feet in time. I heard him yell, "Top of the world, Ma!" then the first grenade blew in front. And a second later the one by the cannon, that he must've been nearly smack on top of, blew too.

Totaled the thing. I mean, it was still there, the engine didn't catch on fire or anything, but shrapnel went all over the place, including my direction, the cannon in back was a mess, the barrel was all bashed in and bent from the heat. The two guys in front must've been afraid the whole thing might blow from the gas, even though it didn't, because immediately they got out and away on both sides, I saw them. I heard the man in the rear was burned badly but he rolled away with his life, at least. That's what you get from sending your own armed forces after your own citizens.

Do I care? I care about that young man, sure I care. He would've had a marvelous long life here with us, and he helped save our bridge. Do I care if this country's government got its makeup smeared? I don't care. They deserve worse than they got. It's a lousy government.

Billy Fagles

Almost felt like the morning went by in black and white, like that grainy war footage from the newsreels. Either real up-close or else far-off.

What happened at the church was we decided to forget the trip wires. My bad idea anyhow, not Roscoe's. Cause we'd be stuck there taking them down every time someone wanted to get in or out and if we blew up a summer guy's Volvo, you know, they never forgive you.

We went with a few packs of state explosives instead. Set them evenly spaced, all the wires hooked up, like Niven in *The Guns of Navarone*. But when those two Humvees came in from Gibson's Cove and past the church onto Shepherd Street, and the armored personnel carriers from Leicester, and at least one tank back there somewhere, we timed it wrong. Well, I timed it wrong. So the first got through with nothing happening, Roscoe's yelling at me from across the road, the second drove right over the G-spot but the explosives only damaged it in back where the big gun sits. Though we blew off a chunk of metal that ended up in the McNally yard about fifty feet away and almost took out their garage door.

Big blasts, too. We laid them in right, cause most fences on the street got blown down and there was little pieces of metal and burning junk everywhere, plus a few weird holes in the road like bomb craters. Even so that second one kept going. At first I thought they was going to use the cannon and slam away, it was pointed straight at me, but they didn't bother. Chickenshits.

So the Roscoe tells me to take a hike down Monroe Street, the other side of the cove, to hit the bridge faster. The old sneak-into-the-fort-by-the-back-stockade routine. I take off running hard only I keep passing these armored personnel carriers, like the SWAT ones but bigger, four of them. Each with a guy up top and a 50 mm, just like on them things the Krauts always drove in *The Rat Patrol.* Going maybe ten miles an hour, no other cars at all, obviously they closed the road back in Willowdale. And obviously they're waiting till the no-recoils had done their job on the bridge. Scariest sight I ever frigging see, except for the tank up ahead anyway, all four going real slow, taking their time, getting ready to show no mercy. Makes you think them lunatics in the homemade bunkers with the ammo and the piles of automatic weapons and the cyanide pills are onto something after all.

They wasn't trying to stop me, though. Probably thought I was running away. I kept moving so fast they couldn't stop me anyhow, then I figure better play it safe, so I hook it over the low stone wall by the road and keep going hard as I can through the trees on the embankment by the cove. Must have been like this centuries ago, I was thinking. Like one of the last Indians along here getting chased down by settlers to get invited for Thanksgiving, he puts his head down, let us pray, bless this bountiful feast, looks up and now he's the one holding the Bible and they've got the land.

Only this time they wasn't going to catch me, not on foot in these trees by this cove. Not Billy Fagles.

I'm nearly up to the bridge when I see the tank. I guess it's about thirty feet long maybe, eight feet tall, not high like the ones in the old Panzer movies. Low to the ground. And modern, with a real thick barrel. And none of this pull-the-door-open-and-toss-the-grenade-in crap, you know you just can't irritate this motherfucker. Looks about as heavy as a damn locomotive, seventy tons or something unbelievable. It's staying on Monroe St. to attack the bridge from this end coordinating with the Humvees from that end. Like two hunters letting a deer have it on both sides so they can collect medals for bravery when it's all over.

Except if the tank puts a shell into the bridge they'll have to shoot down onto it. Otherwise the shell goes right through and takes out some house or the Village Hall on the other side. And no way José the tank can get round Roscoe's truck for a clear shot. Best move we ever made was inching it in here permanent.

The tank backs up as I'm Indian-footing through the trees, then crawls forward a few feet like it has a better idea. Now the sucker crashes right through the stone wall been there a hundred years at least, and starts to push its way down the embankment right in front of me. I can't even move. I guess they thought they could take a shot at the bridge from above and to the side, just blow a huge piece of it away or take out some pilings easy. Probably blow a hole in the bottom of the river too. The tank was crunching up every one of them weak trees growing slantwise on the upper embankment like they was Styrofoam, be a huge piss-ugly scar till they grow back. Like those National Guard get paid to care.

Just then I see Scativo deal with their first Humvee. It's coming down the hill from the Village Hall on the other side, ass backwards, to the edge of the bridge so even they can't miss. Maybe they're counting to three, whammo. I saw him run right up onto it, like a cockroach. First a big burst of noise and flames, then smoke all over. I had a really bad feeling cause he was there one second, I saw he got lifted up by the grenade in front, I had a little hope maybe he'd been thrown clear or maybe I couldn't see him cause of a few trees. Some guys were scrambling on the ground. But I guess when he came down the other blew right where he was, there was another explosion, flames and metal plate flying everywhere, and I knew he was a goner. I didn't see him again.

The sight of that must have got to the driver in the tank on my side, kind of an unexpected distraction, or else maybe they was just too dumb-shit to see how steep the embankment got. Or realize how weak it was right in front of them, nothing but tired old earth and skinny trees propped up by a few rocks some fishermen stuck in the water a hundred years ago. I mean, it might hold those trees forever, but not something that weighs more than several dinosaurs.

Cause right across the road from me, where one of them ancient cart tracks across the cape comes out off the hill, got turned into a mud access road years ago, this old VW bus comes flying down. With feathers and beaks and claws painted on. Knocking and jouncing, raising hell with the suspension. Missouri plates. They don't even stop to look both ways, man, not like there's anything coming anyway, they just tear across Monroe St. and through that gap in the stone wall not thirty feet from where I'm standing. And they head like a frigging kamikaze right for the rear of the tank. Which is an incredibly moronic thing to do, since you could hit it from behind with a Mack truck and it wouldn't notice.

They must have just floored that old VW engine cause they bang into it once, they made contact only once, but totally mashed themselves in in front. But the other thing is at that moment the embankment starts to implode, it sort of comes apart, the granite slabs are popping into the river like wine corks and for about ten feet the earth is crumbling away. The tank starts sliding in front of them and then the bus starts too, they both keep sliding like in slow-mo, with the tank snapping trees from its weight. The tonnage of those things must be out of control. I see its treads trying to grip but by that time it's not even really on dirt, the dirt's dribbling away and collapsing into the river, with the saplings already cracked off, and with the loco VW bus behind it, practically attached.

So the tank just keeps sliding, only about twenty yards total, and falls gun first into the water, with a big slow wake kicked up all around it. Then the painted mashed-in VW slides in after it. You don't see this every day, is what I was thinking. Made me wish I had an Instamatic handy.

Fortunately for them dingleberries inside the tank there's a hatch on top, even though it's shielded. Roof of the tank was sticking about two feet above the water since the tide wasn't high. But that was it, the rest was submerged, so you could kiss that puppy so long, suckers.

Meanwhile the VW bus is floating better, like in that ad the company used to run. I can see they're probably going to make it out alive if they're not the Vultures of Complete Fuckups.

Anyway, I ain't going to throw any of those bastards a life vest, not that I have one with me. I keep running. I get out onto the bridge from that side, it's still in one piece and still standing then. I'm watching the other Humvee, also with a no-recoil gun, the one Roscoe and me wounded up at the church, come backing halfway down the hill past where Leilia bought it. It lurches to a stop when it gets to the other Humvee, which still has smoke all round it with pieces all over the road, and they realize holy shit, this is not exactly a safe parking zone. Lucky for them Scativo wasn't hiding in the bushes cause he'd have been grinning ear to ear when he burned them to hamburger too.

Then it decides fuck that, we got to go with the mission, it backs around what's left of the other Humvee to the edge of the bridge. But there's people gathering, running right next to it, all yelling. Meanwhile I now happen to be the only guy on the bridge and I'm noticing I'm not exactly armed to the eyeballs with repeater rifles and grenades and a Bowie knife, it's just me and my bare hands vs. the National fucking Guard.

I see no one is exactly eager to come to my aid neither, to stand on the bridge in front of the Porta-Cannon, which is leveling up and sideways. People are howling at the guy manipulating it in the rear but big deal, let 'em howl, he's thinking. Don't blame him one bit, this is why he signed up, after all. So I'm thinking you better jump for it, Billy, this bridge is going to be extremely recent history in about five seconds. Time to join the fishies for breakfast, son.

And at about that precise second I see Toby come running like a banshee out of hell, hair flying, mustache flying, yelling to everyone to follow him. That was what did it. He ran right in front of the cannon and starts waving his arms like he's about to do jumping jacks. At first maybe five people got behind him, directly in the line of fire between the muzzle and the part of the bridge it was pointing at, as the gunner tried to point around them. Of course you listen to the way people tell it everyone was there lining up with Toby or even in front of him, they're all heroes fighting to be the first to go. I just didn't see it that way, but then again I only happened to be the only guy who was actually in point of fact standing on the bridge before any of them arrived, Toby included.

But before you know it they really was all over the bridge, jumping up and down, people swarming round the Humvee too, and Toby's swearing top of his lungs at the gunner to go ahead, shoot, go ahead. I couldn't hear what all besides cause I'm coming up from the rear, just plenty glad not to be the only poor son of a bitch stuck out there for target practice.

Then I hear another roar, a roar I know like my own mother. What do you figure except it's Roscoe in the regular septic truck, the Big Bertha we use to pump every day. And he's there all of a sudden pushing on the Humvee's front, which is pointed uphill, blowing his horn nonstop and yelling remarks out the window except no one can hear them over the horn. The driver and the other guy in helmets are waving guns at him and he's giving them the finger through the windshield. Funny as a bastard, cause he told me later he was yelling at them to get out of the frigging way, he's got major shit to pump.

So at this point they've got a crazy motherfucker leaning on them in a huge septic truck, and a whole crowd of people gathered and screaming at them on a bridge they're supposed to blow, and the crap of a ruined Humvee next to them, and a tank going glug-glug across the cove, and a hippie right in front daring them to fire, practically begging to be the first. Well, the second. Then we hear all these armored personnel carriers they must've radioed to, full of troops, rumbling through the village. A couple appeared right in front of the Village Hall, and there was more and more people running, people on our side I mean, running onto the bridge. I never seen so many, you could hear the timbers creaking. And that was when the old bridge just gave up, and gave way.

Oliver Smith

Naturally, any experience helps prepare you for the unexpected. I go all the distance back to Flying Clipper days. That's when I first went to work for Pan American. My second flight turned out to be the famous Tagus River crash near Lisbon in '43, we hit the water awfully hard. I was only eighteen at the time.

You can bet I knew what to do when the bridge collapsed. You end up in the water, you stay afloat, and you make sure you don't get cut up by the debris. Then you look out for the fellow next to you. Still get Christmas cards from the daughter of a guy I saved back then.

In this case, we think a couple of the right-hand pilings gave way first, started to yaw out, so the bridge began to swerve and couldn't hold for more than a few seconds. It felt to most people you'll talk to like a minute, but if it'd been a minute they would've gotten off the bridge, and no one managed to get off the bridge, it swerved too much right away.

There's that brief instant—several seconds really—before a crash when you no longer feel the presence of people around you even though they're screaming, it's just you and the Almighty. I felt it before, in '43, but I didn't feel it this time, so I thought I probably wasn't going to die.

Then the bridge started to tilt and luckily for everyone it kind of snapped in two and buckled downward. Most of us were pitched into the water directly, ass over teakettle as they used to say. A few tried to hang on, which was more risky. They're the ones who got banged up. Little water never hurt anyone, and no one who lives here doesn't know how to swim. We were only in about eight feet of water, forty feet from land.

I think the bridge let us off nicely, just before it died, because it knew who its friends were. We were all floundering in the water slightly dazed—one minute you're expecting to be fired on by your very own armed forces, whose soldiers and buildup you've paid for over the years, don't get me started on that one, a few seconds later you've been tossed into the water. Believe me, more people were hurt than ever let on because of stoic pride, not wanting to admit it. More by crashing into each other as they slid off than by the impact itself. It's a kind of postcrash toughness. I know that syndrome well.

What did it feel like? The actual event? Well, you're confused. Behind us, from underneath us too, there came a loud ripping sound, almost what I remember from the '43 crash too, which is strange in itself. First a creak, then a harsh systematic shearing like nothing you've ever heard. In this case, a wooden bridge curling and tearing and collapsing, just pulling itself apart by the sheer torque of its own wrong motion. It'd had more people on it at different times in the summer, that's true, but more evenly distributed, not bunched in one place like that morning. And obviously the summer had weakened it, the strain of all those people depending on it, day in, day out.

We're lucky it broke pretty clean. It more or less stayed in one piece, two pieces rather, as it kind of distorted itself and swung sideways into the river. Because think of all those planks of wood and the thousands of nails and the jagged splinters, potentially. No, we weren't *lucky*. No luck involved—that bridge gave us a final nod when she went down and treated her people right. Now I could tell you a thing or two about the Tagus River crash, that's for sure. Comparatively speaking, I was much less worn out when they pulled me out of the drink here, and I'm sixty years older. I told Estelle, Hang on to my arm for dear life, honey, you're with a survivor.

Harvey Wilfong

Their mistake. In an ad campaign you're not allowed any mistakes. They made a major boo-boo, they got stuck in major doo-doo. I expect his eminence the lieutenant governor was tearing his hair out and calling everyone to the carpet as soon as he saw the newspapers, but by that point it was long out of his hands and in the federal government's.

Result: you have a double spectacle on the special news bulletins that morning. First, the wooden bridge lying every which way in the river, already beginning to break apart, people walking back and forth trying to dry themselves out, a hundred soldiers wondering whether to arrest these dripping secessionists so they can take over ... what? A village of sopping wet, bedraggled New Englanders who just got attacked by assorted military vehicles, three of which are now irrelevant? I mean, none of that looks very American, you shouldn't attack people who fall off a bridge and lose the very thing they've been suffering for for months. Sorry, Mr. President, I don't think so.

Meanwhile, you've got the next gubernatorial shoo-in for the Commonwealth of Massachusetts, or so he thought at the time, also lying every which way, being asked to explain the massive coincidence of how a year ago he bought up 108 acres of land five miles up the road in another village, including woods he should never have been granted development rights to in the first place. Not to mention the anchor-factory-into-condos scam. And who would clearly stand to benefit more than anyone by the ruination of Salt Cove, while managing to hide his ownership all this time under a shadow corporation behind another shadow corporation sheltering under a palm tree somewhere south of Cuba. Some coincidences are almost a religious experience.

I called up Mike Donergan, the smart aleck who was running

Rowe's campaign, I said, Mike, when you need a job next week, you can always come make coffee for me. He was apoplectic—his own client holding out on him, imagine that. People are pathetic. One minute Salt Cove is breakfast cereal, the next minute everyone else has fatally misfired. The best part is that kid got it all on film. Not film, you know what I mean. Does the lieutenant governor hate that kid or what? Loved every digitized minute of it, myself.

Chet Cairns

Vindicated? I suppose I feel vindicated. I'm certainly glad I lost my job and joined the private sector two weeks before this fiasco. We did argue the bridge was unsafe, and I'm sure you'll agree that it was. Under special circumstances? If you want to put it like that.

Of course we were told to determine it unsafe from the beginning, so we did. But that's the nature of public service. And we did turn out correct.

Now, personally, I don't like being accused of blackmail, and I suspect that sometime very soon the lieutenant governor will withdraw those accusations. I only hope it doesn't cost me an arm and a leg in lawyers' fees to get him to retract. No one likes to be fired, it's a blemish on the record.

Do I feel I should apologize? That's not a very polite question. No, I don't. I said the bridge would eventually collapse, and it did. Salt Cove should do the apologizing. I understand their attachment to the bridge, but if they'd listened to me, none of this would've happened.

Their old bridge might've looked cuter, or more familiar, than our first stab at a design, but it was still fundamentally obsolete. You can't hold back progress. You can't hold back the future. And that's all you'll get from me without my lawyer present.

Harold Milne

As a medical man, I'd have to say the human damage could've been far greater. There were dozens of injuries, none of them serious. Three broken arms, a broken clavicle, the rest minor. Besides the one fatality, of course.

On their side two serious burns, but I've seen much, much worse. They were lucky.

The bridge only killed a couple of people, all in all.

I've seen their figures for damage to military vehicles, equipment, etc. They don't know how to count.

I would like to take back what I just said. The damage is incalculable.

Molly Mellew

As it turned out, I was standing right behind Toby. He was yelling at them. Luckily we're both good swimmers, we were able to help some of the others who were shocked to be in the water. You could feel this great wave of energy unleashed by the bridge. Years and years of it. Or maybe it was Scativo's energy, still watching us. It had only been maybe ten minutes, I think. A part of me wasn't surprised at all, even then, with what had just happened to him. The cracking noise went on and on but it felt more like this vast sigh to me.

When we came crawling up out of the water finally and Toby said, "I'd better speak to those soldiers, I guess this is when we have to surrender," I saw so much bitterness fall across his face, I couldn't tell where it came from. Not only from here. It made me want to take his hand, but I didn't.

He did look hard at me for a second, like a different man seeing me for the first time. And I said—I wasn't really thinking—I said, "You're not afraid of me, I know why you're looking at me that way." He just said sorry, he had to get on with surrendering. And he walked away to go speak with an officer.

Jessica was right there waiting for him. She never ended up in the water. She must've seen everything, we didn't see very much.

Nancy Eckerman

I took the baby inside. My son doesn't need to see real tanks. It's bad enough he'll probably be playing with toy ones soon. But not in this house, not under my roof.

Jon came home with a strained back, soaked to the skin. He said,

"You won't believe what I just saw." I've never seen him so animated. He told me we were all under house arrest until further notice, we were now under the control of the National Guard. Prisoners of war. I told him to get out of his clothes and check the answering machine. Seven creepy messages from some nutcase with a weird drawl and plenty of static, talking about having received the code word, awaiting further instructions, making their move anyway, over and out. All in the course of a half hour. After I heard the first one on replay when I brought Jeb in, I didn't answer the phone each time it rang.

Jon erased all those messages before he even let me peel him out of his clothes. We never heard from them again, not after they got arrested. Their code of honor or loyalty or something. He's actually not a bad-looking man, my husband. He's just not terribly imaginative.

Mildred Sykes

One result is I've had offers, several serious offers, in fact, to update my history of Salt Cove. And simultaneously the price has risen for copies of the rare first edition. Thus I've been forced by pressures of the marketplace, you might say, to adjust my own personal prices, especially for a signed copy.

I'm not sure yet what I'll do. First I've got to wait for this arm to mend. Then we'll see. Things don't mend quite so easily at my age.

Ed Grier

When I got there mere minutes had elapsed since the bridge went kapowie. Still people in the water, which was fine with me. I only live a mile away, see. Yeah, the pros always get lucky, I wonder why that is.

I got across the cove the old-fashioned way, swimming with one hand and holding my camera bag over my head with the other. Betting I wouldn't be allowed in otherwise. Got the shots everyone saw, taken at water level, of the last people crawling out, helping each other. Then the troops, dozens and dozens, taking down people's names and informing them to go back to their houses and not leave until they were given direct permission. Resistance is useless, where have I heard that before. No one tried to stop me, either, which was beautiful. That's the advantage of a dopey trustworthy face.

They started to shove Toby Longhair into an open jeep, they had him in those special cuffs, and then there was some urgent radio message and they said never mind, you can go home too. He looked over at me, or past me, with this faraway gaze like he was already somewhere else. That's when I got the money shot of him, the close-up, his hair all pushed back and glistening from being in the cove. I bet he wanted to laugh, once that order to release him came through, because he knew what it meant. He asked the officer in the jeep if he'd seen the morning papers yet. The officer said no, was Toby a crossword freak or something? Some joke. And Toby shook his head and said nope, he was just a crime freak.

Was I deliberately echoing that famous portrait of Che? Like El Toby or something? With the halo of hair? No way. That Guevara guy was a pinko. I'm not echoing anybody.

The Vultures of Justice

Ran interference / delaying action in neighboring sector with limited remaining manpower. Came under fire. Feathers ruffled.

Withdrew and approached via alternate route.

Subsequently encountered enemy. Tactical success against vastly superior forces using adjacent body of water. Entire squad taken prisoner.

Mission accomplished.

Gretchen Moresby

Hi! My name's Gretchen. Thanks for visiting the talking website of our Bridge Reconstruction Fund.

As you may know, the Commonwealth of Massachusetts has given the village of Salt Cove permission to reconstruct, as accurately as possible, the historic wooden bridge that was destroyed last week.

To do this, we need to raise three million dollars in the coming calendar year. We hope you'll contribute. Even the tiniest donation helps. Plus, the state government has promised to match all donations dollar for dollar. So every dollar you give really turns into two!

Our new bridge will be made entirely of wood and closely resemble the bridge as it stood from the late nineteenth century through the early twentieth century. It'll have a single road lane for vehicular traffic leaving the village only, and a raised walkway with handrails for pedestrians. There'll also be plaques honoring the two residents who died during the recent controversy.

Be sure to tour this website, which we'll be adding to as the months go by. Soon you'll be able to have fun comparing an <u>architect's plan</u> of the new wooden bridge to a series of old <u>antique postcards</u>. And be sure to come for a simulated <u>walk</u> with me across the cove on our bridge. Let's take a virtual stroll together, shall we?

You can also click on our <u>Legal Defense Fund</u>. During an extended dispute over the fate of our bridge, certain legal issues were raised. A number of cases are pending that involve many loyal members of the Salt Cove community, who all acted selflessly. The ongoing legal bills are sure to be enormous. Any contribution you can make will help.

Daniel Stoddard

There's nothing to regret or apologize for, Jessica. Trust me: you mustn't let regret poison your soul. Finish what you've started, and historians of future generations will thank you. "Don't overpersonalize" would be my only paternal suggestion.

I knew, I never stopped telling you, that my beautiful daughter would have important work in her one day. There was always more in your head than you could keep contained. A family failing, I'm proud to admit.

Besides what happens with the house, please make sure my old pinball machine finds its way into good hands. That humdinger's a keeper!

Justice? In the end? Don't expect miracles, daughter mine. No one gets exactly what they deserve. They either get more, or less.

And don't worry. At some point the judge hands down a decision, and lets you out of the courtroom. Sooner or later, we're all allowed to move on.

58

Time Magazine

BRIDGE OUT

"We never thought it would end like this," says Mitch Wapping, a retired, longtime householder in Salt Cove, the scrappy little secessionist village north of Boston whose residents—known locally as Saltines—have endured "storm, shipwreck, and finally a siege from the government itself" in the four centuries since it was founded.

An eight-week standoff ended, a day after SWAT teams withdrew, with a surprise assault by Massachusetts National Guard troops acting on "reliable information" that the village had radically upgraded its weapons capabilities.

The invasion came on the heels of a state verbal agreement—meant to buy time—to meet with village leaders and hammer out a mutually acceptable design for a new bridge. Yet soon after dawn last Wednesday, on the orders of Governor Richard Thrale and reportedly after considerable pressure from the White House, two hundred soldiers stormed the village, which had formally declared independence from the United States since June 30.

In the ensuing melee, one fully armed tank slid into the cove and a smaller attack vehicle was destroyed ("severely neutralized" in military parlance) by an angry, possibly suicidal villager armed with grenades, who died in the explosion. Another vehicle chose not to fire upon villagers protesting en masse on the decrepit old bridge, which buckled unexpectedly under their combined weight. A state engineers' report had declared the bridge unsafe back in March.

Claims recent village transplant Mary Jane Mellew—formerly an adult-film actress on the West Coast, TIME has learned—who was protesting on the bridge at the time: "No one expected it to collapse. The government's just lucky their tank didn't blow it up. They'd have had a revolution in the streets."

Ironically, that morning Boston newspapers and TV stations all carried reports linking the lieutenant governor, Spencer Rowe III, to land purchases totalling over one hundred acres in another Cape Sarah village. From one of New England's most prominent families, Rowe was also linked to the state's determination this spring to demolish the original bridge and rebuild it as "a concrete horror," in the words of one Boston architect and local summer resident.

Though Lt. Governor Rowe refused to comment, extensive documents later made available by a disgruntled state engineer whose job was recently terminated appear to confirm the allegations in detail.

Behind-the-scenes sources suggest a deal to reconstruct the bridge along historic lines and at partly public expense is in the works. However, Washington may press charges against at least several villagers. "The lawsuits will pile up like pancakes," sourly commented Bob Herbert, a counsel for Salt Cove.

In Boston, local wisdom around the State House suggests that Rowe's own expected bid for the governor's seat next year has struck a jagged reef. "Man overboard" is how one veteran observer put it. "Circling sharks." Though Rowe himself has not yet issued a statement, a spokesman told reporters, "The Rowe family has served the people of Massachusetts with honor for many generations and has no involvement with or knowledge of the present accusations."

Still, the U.S. Attorney's office in Boston is said to be "enthusiastically investigating" what an inside source called "Rowe's multiple sweetheart deals" and an indictment may be in the works.

Inquiries from top military brass are also expected into why U.S. forces fared so badly, allowing themselves to be disabled or destroyed in a routine operation. A few political cartoonists have even sarcastically blamed a lack of air cover. ("*Where were the B-52s?*")

The village attracted popular attention this summer partly due to the determined defiance of its charismatic leader, Toby Auberon, who remains unavailable for comment. A former L.A. federal prosecutor turned California public defender, Auberon is expected to bear the brunt of coming legal attacks.

"Face it, we can't just have people randomly declaring independence left and right," said one prominent Washington prosecutor. A Harvard Law School professor, Jerome Gilbert, was more sanguine. "Why not? Auberon could easily argue that everything he did is protected under free speech. It will be an unusual case, as a jury may likely see Salt Cove as the victim, not some incompetent platoon. They can win, if they're prepared for a series of lengthy trials."

Villagers strongly denied any links with an underground militia group from Missouri whose van was stopped in Pennsylvania three days before the invasion and found to contain assault rifles, explosives, and detailed maps of Cape Sarah. In a related incident, the FBI has detained occupants of another Missouri van used to attack a National Guard tank at Salt Cove.

Meanwhile, the cove itself is full of the floating remnants of the destroyed wooden bridge, parts of which date back to the early 1800s. Souvenir hunters have been busy all week making off with stray planks that have drifted as much as twelve miles away.

"They'd better hurry," said one bitter Saltine. "Two more strong tides, and the story of Salt Cove will be far out to sea."

Reported by Whit Simpson in Boston, Ada Needle in Washington, H. V. Malayalam in Leicester, and Josh McGraw in Salt Cove, with additional reporting by Lisa Green in New York.

59

Toby Auberon

TIME TO ADMIT the obvious. I lost.

I lost us the bridge, I lost Scativo, I lost Leilia. I lost the so-called war for independence because they trampled right over us.

They should be made to pay for those deaths. But they never will; I know the system too well. Never, never, never. If it were the other way round, Scativo wouldn't leave my death an unavenged crime.

What's been won? A rebuilt wooden bridge, which they could've agreed to back in March. Just what the village wanted me to win all along. But after two corpses, after all these weeks, it still falls like the most miserable defeat.

What else have I won? The heart of Jessica Stoddard, no small thing but not a victory I ever sought. Not that I had any regrets waking up the morning after, even though I could pretend our tenderness had been unwise; yet nothing felt amiss in those tangled sheets, even when I couldn't begin to contemplate the next step with her. Or what I'd do the next time we were together.

Which only proves that, at the end of the day, I am a fuckup and a fool.

All I came here for, all I wanted, was to be left alone. Quietly working away in my lighthouse, scraping by on a little money thrown off by savvy investments. And wads of sheer peaceful concentration, the truest cash of all. Now that's utterly gone too, and it will never come back. Not here.

I should've listened to my better instincts, I should never have gotten involved, never gotten intertwined. Not with her, not with them. Because I don't end up improving these situations for anyone. I ought to know this by now. Too much gets destroyed along the way, and as the years go by I can't put it out of my mind.

I nearly said as much, nearly took all the blame, at the memorial service we held for Scativo a couple of days later. Not at the church, but at the Village Hall—he'd never struck me as an interfaith kind of guy except where women were concerned. No, I stood up in front of everyone and said what they all expected me to say, that we'd been lucky to have such a heroic person in our midst for even a short time, ready to sacrifice himself for what he believed in without a moment's hesitation; that I saw him as a deeply brave man, defiant to the last, determined to be his own master no matter what the cost; and that clearly he'd loved this place, to be ready to arm-wrestle the devil to save it. I mentioned that Bob Herbert hadn't been able to locate a next of kin though he was still trying. I saved the coup de grâce, Scativo's final surprise, until last—for he'd had a will, in which he left all future royalties from his invention to public libraries across the nation. And I quoted the final line of his testament: "See, that's real immortality. I put a book in your hands. Now go ahead, just open your eyes."

They listened quietly, in a respectful hush, and I talked about how unusual it was that he'd come into the community as an outsider, yet been willing to give up his life for theirs. They thought I was also talking about me, but I was really only talking about Scativo—little did they know, my mind was virtually made up. I didn't set them straight, nor add what else I was thinking, namely: I have inadvertently caused the death of a rare man.

So much for my contribution. A week after the invasion, Salt Cove's legal status is as follows:

Reconstructed (meaning new) wooden bridge, promised to us in writing. Conforming to nineteenth-century design. Supposedly.

Salt Cove rips up declaration of independence via nullifying document. I drafted it, Jessica typed, took less than a minute. *The Act of Secession of June 29th is no longer in force. Signed, etc.* The villagers all signed, I forgot to.

We are now no longer under house arrest. Garbage trucks arrive at our doorsteps. As does junk mail, *Deo gratias.*

We were about to get sued plurally by the vengeful state, but someone told the Massachusetts attorney general to stop leaning on us, and at my strenuous insistence they included a blanket village amnesty as a clause of the bridge reconstruction agreement. They also dropped my feeble eviction shakedown. Big deal: the federal government is still furious. As they should be, since—having carefully avoided getting politically involved for months—they look ridiculous after being militarily involved for mere hours.

The feds may indict us and are certainly going to make us pay one way or another for destruction of military property, injury to National Guardsmen, etc. By their accounting methods, we owe them three times the cost of a bridge. This may force us into arcane corners of international law (i.e., were we really a separate country when the tank slid into the river, and if so, did it slide from U.S. territory or from Salt Cove territory? Into U.S. waters, Salt Cove waters, or disputed international waters?). Not to mention the various suits the National Guard themselves, collectively and individually, may bring.

We can argue that Scativo was acting independently with his grenades, we can argue all we like, but we're now under their jurisdiction again. And I cannot imagine this ever going to trial in The Hague. No doubt they'll extract as much in damages from S.C. as possible. I might even get indicted for treason—but since the Constitution requires two witnesses for that, maybe we'll just all be treated as military combatants and tried in a secret military tribunal.

They will in any event especially come after me. I was the ringleader, I even look suspicious, plus I did all the talking. Amid the usual brouhaha they're considering launching a whole host of charges in my direction, from terrorism on down. Fortunately I have an old school pal named Marcus, one of the best criminal lawyers in the country, who'd like nothing better than to go to the mat with those people on my behalf, for the sole pleasure of ruining their lives.

This presumes I have time and energy to spare, when what I need is to fade from view and go back to my routine existence of six months ago. So much for not listening to that pipsqueak of a voice which always knows better. Instead I'm now facing years of legal crap, whirlpools within whirlpools that will spin out of control forever, the nightmare of maybe one day regurgitating every inch of this in court merely to defend what I should never have given up—the chance to finish my Machina.

To say nothing of the fact that mail is already pouring in from dingdongs across the giddy land.

Meanwhile this place is swarming with FBI agents whipping their Ray-Bans off and on, interviewing people left and right, and saving the best for last so they have the maximum to question me about. There's always the possibility that at some point they'll decide I'm a dangerous person who should be locked up. Which leaves me a very narrow window of time to operate in freely.

The only sensible course of action is clearly to disappear for a few years. Charges might be dropped, or a federal amnesty declared, in the meantime; the media may even forget. It'd also deflect legal attention away from my fellow Sals if the guilty chicken flies the coop.

The feds would probably like it. They can't want to bring me to trial and risk embarrassing themselves further. After one eviscerating conversation with Marcus, they'll undoubtedly prefer me as fugitive from justice than as witness on my own behalf. We may even be able to extract a verbal hide-and-no-seek agreement from them. Three or four years would give me time to finish both the Machina Excelsior and the Mesoamerican ball game book. I can live cheaply anywhere; I've learned that much. Brazil still has no extradition treaty, though getting the Machina down there intact would be a huge nuisance. Maybe California is the best bet, after all. Lose the mustache and ponytail and I'm not so easy to locate. Another defeat, but I can swallow that one. Scativo, a man of many guises, would approve.

I'd thought out all the above over several days, trying to face the situation, when I found myself out for a late night walk—unable to sleep and unable to work. This time I traipsed across the Meadow in another direction than usual, and left it down a subsidiary lane that

eventually descends to Shepherd Street. The houses there are surrounded by the remains of once thick woods, squabbling for postage-
stamp views of the sea when winter strips away the intervening leaves.

One of the smallest houses, it turned out, belongs to Molly.
Whom I'd thought of all summer as Clitemnestra's older sister, until a
national newsmagazine, in their lust for truth, revealed all. Another
person whose hard-won privacy got violated; I meant to commiserate
the next time I ran into her.

That night I was seemingly the only person out walking or even
awake so late, on that lane. I passed her shuttered house, though I
didn't know it was hers, set amid pines. Surprisingly, a few lights were
on. I caught a rustling somewhere, like an animal in the darkness.
More light leaked from around the back; I heard the creak of a car
trunk, maybe the rear door of one of those personal vans. Then a
woman spoke.

"Hi, there," she said easily, from somewhere close by in the night,
and I realized who it was.

"Hi there, yourself." But I couldn't locate her.

She paused. "It's Toby, right?"

I went off the lane, following her voice and an earthen driveway.
There was a kind of lean-to garage behind the house, with a streamlined blue van. She was barefoot, a weary goddess clad only in red
shorts and a white T-shirt, carrying a big cardboard box. Overhead
light spilled generously across her. All I could think was: what a long,
long way to this place, from a sweaty movie house near the law school
in Palo Alto to a balmy August night on another coast seventeen,
eighteen years later. Now I felt like a fugitive from the law—how little, in the end, I'd been able to learn.

She was struggling with the box so I went swiftly over and took it
from her, noticing once again as she thanked me how much taller she
was. I am so sick of being reminded of this by women. The back of
her van was open and as I slid the box deep inside I gained a curious
peek, through an open handhold on the side, since the box seemed to
weigh nearly as much as I do. Sitting atop piles of dossiers, tax records
maybe, with foam rubber wrapped around its carriage, was an old
manual typewriter, a black Royal, vintage 1960.

Yikes. I did not need to compare typefaces.

I couldn't think fast enough. My head, despite the pine- and sea-laden air, felt packed in mud. Did she realize what I'd seen? I shoved the box in and glanced at her but her face gave nothing away, not the slightest inkling of the intention in her notes. She'd said something significant to me when we were both clambering out of the river, but now I couldn't remember what it was. I said clumsily, "What are you doing, Molly?"

She bit her lower lip. "What does it look like I'm doing?"

"You're packing to go. You're leaving. Why?"

But I knew why.

She shrugged. "I can't live here anymore. I've been through this other places. People learn a shred about your past, then misjudge you on the basis of their own corny ideas. They don't have any genuine interest—" She broke off, and took a deep decisive breath. "I just need to vanish. I can do my jewelry anywhere. All my equipment's portable. I'll sell this little house, make a profit. And move on."

I just need to vanish.

She tilted her head—ready to smile in my direction, I thought. Her stare was resigned, but confident. "Listen, Toby," she murmured, "do you want to come in? I'm going to make myself a cold drink." Then she did smile.

But at that moment I didn't have the courage, or whatever it is, to say yes, to step inside. Or to mention that I'd glimpsed her type-writer—imagine, her fantasizing about me. I begged off, saying I was exhausted, kicking myself for being a coward. It's too late, I added, but what I felt like saying was, *It's too late for me, lady, too late in this life.*

Nevertheless, we did stay out there another twenty minutes or so, our talk roaming the rest of the country and beyond; I told her I was thinking of leaving too. And gradually a plan formed that would involve sharing the gasoline expenses, the map-reading chores, the driving en route west. There'd be space for a disassembled Machina and a few of my boxes in her van, as most of her stuff was getting shipped to a cousin in San Diego to be picked up later. She wanted to leave in a few days, she wasn't sure how many, the sooner the better. I was to tell no one. I made her promise the same.

I told myself I could bring up her notes once we knew each other better, once I was behind the wheel. But the feds certainly intended to keep an eye on me, assuming I could even manage to slip out of here. The two of us in that blue van would be incredibly easy to track; I could vanish much more easily alone. And she had a right to leave here unencumbered by me. Anyway, I could always find her in California, take back the Machina, go from there. She could be trusted with it, surely.

A plan of separate departures, then: I sketched out another plan to her. Was she willing to do all this for me? I asked. A bit stunned, she was willing, all right, though from the way her eyes wavered she was wondering if I really understood the offer I was turning down—tempered by the knowledge that since she was transporting the only material objects I cared deeply about, she'd probably see me again. But I saw she wanted to say: Man, are you crazy?

Well, are you? Or just afraid? No, neither, I realized on my walk home—my footsteps perishing behind me like my years here perishing behind me. No, I couldn't do anything with Molly. Not now, not here. And not because of this place, and not because of me. Because of Jessica.

I went round to see her the next morning, the hottest morning of the summer. I hadn't slept at all. My intention was to tell her everything, or most everything, at least of my plan to escape. In my bones I had known all along that she'd climbed up to see the Machina that day I found her in the lighthouse, she'd broken in somehow, she'd lied to me. I didn't care anymore, except that if she had lied to me it gave me the right to lie to her, or leave out part of the truth. This argument would not stand in my mind for more than thirty seconds at a stretch, yet I kept coming back to it as a way of justifying what I was about to do. It still amazed me how cruel and self-serving my morals could become when they served to extricate me from a tight spot; I always hoped I might've become a better person than that, somewhere along the way. Just as it had amazed me, at daybreak, to see how cruelly all the effortless, permanent magic seemed drained out of my lighthouse, out of the surrounding sea and sky. And how the empty dawn beach, my daily miracle, looked drugged and dull.

I did not want to tell Jessica anything because I did not want to admit anything, and I did not want to see her cry, though I knew she would be sobbing herself to sleep long after I left, long after I vanished into the great gaping maw of America.

I could try telling myself all kinds of lies, though. I could tell myself that I'd given in to her, gone along with her, gone to bed with her—no, not that, admit it, *made love with her* for the better part of a day and night because I felt sorry for her. Or even because I felt sorry for myself. Or because, in the heady confusion of war or the closest I'd ever come to it, I let temptation get the better of foolhardy, horny little me. Or because I didn't care and it felt like eons since I'd been with a woman, and perhaps I even persuaded myself that those racy notes had come from her despite her apparent ignorance of them. And maybe I'd stayed abed with her not because she turned out to be, surprise of surprises, a fantastically diverse lover, but out of sympathy for what she'd given up—I now saw it so clearly—for how her mother walking off had kept her always her father's daughter, his eldest child and protector, and had kept her relentlessly from becoming her own woman in her own life.

I could tell myself every explanation, crossing the edge of the beach for the umpteenth time, my back to my lighthouse, thinking how all of a sudden my times doing this walk were numbered, because I could not envision ever returning. I could tell myself anything I wanted, and head along one of those hidden, enclosed, nearly secret paths that keep Salt Cove ever mysterious, coming over the rise and down again, to find her house there above the pearly expanse of Dunster Beach at low tide, my favorite—but it was all guff, all reasonable argument, all noise.

The truth was, I loved her deeply and I knew she loved me—she loved me despite the fact that she knew me better than anybody had in many years, and with perhaps fewer illusions than I hoped. I loved her despite the cold fact that I'd never harbored any illusions about her, for almost against my will I had come to understand her—I now saw only an infinitely capacious person before me. And after hours with her in bed I could no longer assign any age to this woman; what'd surprised me at first was how young her touch was, it was my touch that seemed old, then I swear her body got younger and younger with every passing hour, as what I saw quickly changed because of all we were doing to each other. Love isn't blind, it's only the most persuasive lawyer I've ever met.

But no love I could conceive of could spite the fact that I had no more future here, and there was little future possible with her. We'd simply been born at the wrong times, or one of us had at least, in a staggered, deadly way that made me stagger from the brute force of it. Nothing wallops you as hard as time when you come face-to-face with its sheer insidious might, and no persuasive talk from me, rapidly trying to fool myself, was going to sway it from its dull, impersonal task.

And then there she was at the side door, letting me in as usual through her kitchen—only she was not alone this morning, as I'd imagined she must be. And she looked jumpy, she was trembling. An uncertain Jessica I'd never seen before. She said shakily, "Just in time. I'm so glad to see you. Toby, they want me to sign something. A—a document. Maybe you could look at it for me."

She faltered, and I gripped her arm. "Don't worry, Jessica, you don't have to sign anything. You've got your lawyer present now." And we walked together into her big room with that embracing view, a view not nearly as much like mine as she seems to think, a wider view, a higher vantage.

There were two of them, waiting patiently for her but not for me: Jessica's niece, an angular woman about my age with long, nearly red hair and a sexiness that was mere sizzle, like meat frying, concealed by a businesslike charade. She was better dressed than you need to be in Salt Cove at your aunt's house on a summer morning, which increased my suspicions. The other was a blank-faced, sandy-haired man wearing a jacket and pressed jeans, a weekend sports fan, one of the guys, a carnival barker in a previous life, lived off his charm but looked younger than I because he slept more and read little. They were obviously having an affair, she was not as smart as he but she didn't realize it yet, and I smelled danger, danger to my Jessica, coming off both of them like a sickly vapor.

"Toby," she said, and nearly stammered—I had never heard her do this before—"you know Sarah, I think. This is Raymond, Raymond Pratt. Her friend." She picked up several typed pages from beside a pen on her glass-top table and passed them to me. "You should have a look at this before I sign."

"Naturally," said the smooth man, the Raymond, "we'd need to get a lawyer to look it over eventually. It's more a preliminary agreement, statement-of-intention kind of thing. Just to be on the safe side. Jessica's idea, really, because as you may not know, she's—"

"She's been having spells lately," said her faithful niece. "Feeling very faint. Imagining things at night. And then there was that mild stroke a couple of years back."

"Right, right," I said unconcernedly, though I hadn't known about any of it. Imagining things? I thought. I can't believe it. What's next, Jessica? Learning to fly?

The document was apparently casual, friendly, but meticulously thought out. She'd be giving up all rights to her house, indeed to decide its fate, the next time she was ill enough to spend the night in a hospital, even if she came home the very next day under her own steam. It presumed that the house had already been willed to her niece; this document was intended to get it out of her control as soon as possible, through a myriad of forking clauses. It wasn't put that baldly, of course, or she wouldn't have been staring at me so very desperately, ready to crack from trying to decide what to do. Wanting above all to do the right thing, protect the property. That dangerous, age-old confusion in her: to not let her father down. Actually—I scanned page two and flipped to page three—it gave them the right to find a suitable home for her if she caught a bad chill or sneezed too often. Reading this point by point was a waste of time.

I said sharply, "Jessica, do you trust me? As your lawyer?"

"Of course I trust you, Toby." She was over by the window, caught in bleaching sunlight, looking wearily out at the view, rubbing her elbows as if the skin might flake off.

I tore the papers in half, then did it once again, and tossed the pieces in the wastebasket. "You ought to be ashamed of yourselves."

The niece flushed and I saw this slightly aroused her, though she wanted to claw my face off—strong fingernails, too. Little other genetic resemblance that I could see. The guy, still one of the guys in his deck shoes, said quite calmly, his feelings hurt, "You're really mis-judging us, and you had no right to do that. You're only hurting her. And I'm not sure I trust your motives."

I said sweetly, "Do you really want to discuss this at your lawyer's office? I'll be glad to rip you to pieces in the presence of counsel."

You're only hurting her.

"You heard my lawyer," said Jessica softly. "You'd better leave."

Better leave, I kept mouthing the words to myself as they went sullenly trudging off, down the hall corridor and out the front door like shameless assassins, proud of their work. My good deed for the decade, I told myself, thinking it might assuage what I was about to tell her. But it only made her seem older, more vulnerable than I'd ever imagined her to be, more at the mercy of whatever catastrophes the years had lying in wait for her. She did not belong anywhere except in front of this enormous view, and anyone who contemplated removing her from it was evil.

"Thank you, Toby," she said when they'd gone, embarrassed imme-diately at having been nearly taken in, but not too embarrassed to come directly into my arms. I hugged her, too on edge myself from the disaster averted to entirely return the romantic embrace as she wanted—though eventually I gave in and just held her, which was all she needed. I said into her hair, "Don't ever sign any document these two bring you, ever. Not ever. Will you promise me that?"

She nodded, her head against my shoulder.

It should be we stayed that way a long time, or that we made love again. Or that I told her everything and she heard me out, nodding seriously, asking the right questions, understanding the gravity of my position. But I couldn't tell her. Anything I told her would hurt—that I was leaving, or who I was in some sense leaving with, or that I would have to vanish for some time, and if I vanished I'd never come back. That did not necessarily mean silence between us. It occurred to me that if I were to entrust her with the problem of looking after my remaining belongings it might be better not just for me but for her, would give us still some connection. Even that felt awful to me, but there was no way to have that discussion with her without having all the others as well.

So we didn't stay that way a long time. I told her I had to get back to my work, I'd only stopped by for a cup of tea because it'd been a couple of days since I'd seen her. I was incredibly busy trying to organize a plan of my own defense in light of what was to come, so she shouldn't be surprised if I dropped from sight for another few days. And there was the Machina Excelsior calling me, too. I had promised to let her be the first to play it one day.

That is how I like to remember her, my final sight of her: nodding happily in the streaming sunlight, the ocean past her head, talking a little about Scativo and who his next of kin might be, remembering how we'd written what she called the declaration of independence together right here, with me chewing on her pencil, seated in the wicker armchair where she was now. In retrospect it was almost as if she knew I might be going, but I was sure she did not, she suspected nothing, she was merely enjoying remembering, and hearing about it from my point of view because then I knew she would keep writing, would write it down for posterity's sake as well as for her own, because we all need something besides love to justify us to ourselves, and her love was about to walk out the door. In a matter of minutes I'd be one of those figures crossing the beach below her to disappear among the tumbled rocks, then she'd imagine me crossing the Meadow and the other beach and entering my lighthouse, and from that point on I would exist here only in her mind's eye.

This is how I would rather remember her: sitting astride me that other afternoon, in full possession of me and of the shared lighthouse, glowing with pleasure, with realized youth, with so much life and possibility still in her. Not because of anything I'd done to her but because of everything she'd done for me. And how steady her voice had sounded that day, a secret voice she disclosed which I realized I had been hearing all along without being aware of it. I'd written down so little of what she'd said to me in my notebooks but my memory is excellent, I remember nearly all of it.

No, she didn't suspect I might be leaving, because if she had she would've insisted on a second cup of tea, not let me be on my way. I had been trying to think rigorously, to think it all through, every step, like a good lawyer should. But the only thing clear to me was that I needed to leave her my spare key to the lighthouse, because she would need to take possession of it one day very soon, whenever it was I left her a note of my own, a dossier formally tying all the loose ends, a good-bye.

"What's this you're giving me?" she said with a gleeful smile. It tore into me, how happy the key made her, on a scuffed yellow plastic key ring from a beach bar outside Rio. "What's this? The key to your heart?"

The key to your hurt, I thought, but I couldn't say that.

"A safe place to hide, Jessica," I said, and nearly added *when the birds of prey come looking for you*. Was that the thought I was going to leave her with? "A place," I corrected myself, "with winding stairs, leading up to a perfect view. For the pilgrim whose words cast no shadow."

"The view is already perfect from here," she said, gazing straight at me.

What I learned, what will never leave me, is the sensation of doing something and knowing it is for the last time. Seeing her, above all, but also climbing my lighthouse staircase and turning on the Machina Excelsior in the high tower where it was conceived and built, taking it apart for safe transport, hearing the foghorn bellow and wishing I had a machine to tape it with but willing to entrust it to memory. Seeing my books ranged so cunningly about the shelves I'd constructed—I'd leave them in place because I knew the librarian in Jessica would enjoy taking them down to put into boxes via her own system—even suggesting a few odd paperbacks for the edification of that boy Henry. Deciding which notebooks to leave her, which to send off to myself in Molly's van, and which few to keep with me. Deciding which walks to take by night and in which order because there were so few nights left, knowing nothing was stopping me from going to see Jessica again, realizing how lightly I could travel alone, last of all pulling shut the lighthouse door deep in darkness and turning that always uncooperative key. Pocketing it, if only as a perpetual talisman.

It never leaves me, that sensation, of knowing it is for the last time: the last time with a place or a person you have come to love beyond all reckoning, knowing how little changed they are from your first encounter and yet how different it all is, both the place and you. Both she and you. It confirmed how right I'd been in my conception of the Machina, that the underworld is always there beneath us, waiting for us to play, ready to open for us if only we play well enough. And only the flimsy mistaken belief that the stakes are not life and death all along, that each time is not for the last time, keeps us in the surface world, the surface game above.

I had never been wrong about how much was at stake, that wasn't the problem. I knew the game would go on, would even go on without me one day, and when it did the preserved, remembered light in her eyes would have already sunk into the earth forever. I had just never expected losing her, and this very last time with her, to matter so much.

60

Jessica Stoddard

DID I KNOW he was leaving? I am often asked. Well, I answer easily, looking like I know far, far more than I'm prepared to say, it didn't come as a total shock. And (waxing philosophical for a change, an old lady offering a snack of wisdom to the eager pups) after all, none of us know for sure when we're leaving, do we?

I found out the hard way, a couple of days after his final notebook entry, when I found I needed to consult with him on a matter of historical detail. I'd been writing up a storm.

It was late morning, a good time to pin Toby down for a romp, at least it'd worked once before and men presumably have their cycles too. I went frothing across the landscape, his key with its yellow keepsake of Rio clicking away in my pocket, I kept it with me at all times now. Even the flat, senile ocean seemed to have its turbulent undercurrents at that hour. A hot day, I remember; soon the year would start turning, the months start to wheel in their usual disconsolate axis.

A few short, sharp raps on the lighthouse door. No answer, no movement within. What that boy needs is a few sharp raps on his knuckles. Once again, still no reply. Maybe he needed a few dishes washed, plus I wanted to change those sheets of his. I fitted the rasping key in that old lock, pushed on the door, stepped in, called out his name.

"Toby! To-by! It's Jessica!"

I give this in full, for sentimental reasons, because it was the last time I called his name and expected him to answer.

Then my glance fell on a large legal dossier on the black spiral stairs, with my name scrawled large in his very firmest handwriting, and before it a small white envelope, marked *Personal,* with only my first name, in his most personal handwriting.

I felt my knees go weak. I knew what the two envelopes meant; no, he was not a suicide, in case you were worried. I sat down dumbfounded, unsure what to think or what to say or whom to say it to, sat down with trembling legs on the next-to-lowest step, the one that seemed friendliest to me at that moment. I put both envelopes neatly on my knees and even found myself pressing them to my face to see if I could smell him on them or if perhaps—this sometimes happens with me, and no doubt with you—by accident a stray hair had caught underneath the envelope's seal, a memento no one expects and no one treasures until it is too late.

What was there to do? There was nothing to do except read them. I did not want to read them, and I could barely catch my breath. I think I must've said, "Oh, no," to myself several times, since I could hear someone in that echoey chamber saying this, and it certainly wasn't he. Or was it? In a flash I knew I'd accurately assimilated from the air inside the lighthouse all his feelings, how much he must've regretted doing it this way but realizing it was for the best, for both of us and especially for me, to make a hard thing less hard; and once I saw that he was right it made it a lot easier. A little, anyway. I am not a lawyer's daughter, and a lawyer's lover, for nothing.

I opened the small envelope as carefully, as harmlessly, as intactly as I could.

He'd used good paper, dug up from some crevice in the lighthouse I wasn't aware of, and black ink, the black indelible handwriting I find only rarely in his notebooks. Etched firmly into the paper, utterly sure of himself.

Jessica—

 Please forgive my departure. And thank you for all you have given me over these last months.

 Sorry for the mess I'm leaving you with. Keep anything you like, and look after the rest for me. I hope to send for my notebooks, and some of my books, one day. Maybe then we can continue what we started.

My love,
Toby

A brief note, you say, full of affection, of muffled heartbreak no doubt, but to the point. That afternoon I was to find, crumpled in a wastebasket he forgot to empty on a higher level of the lighthouse, multiple versions of that letter, in some of which he said much, much more to me, things that made my heart soar (*My darling* etc.). In some he was even terser, and left out that last sentence, which he seems to have put in only the letter he left me.

I will not quote the alternates, though they are among my papers. I should probably be coming to a close pretty soon. Actually, I was going to put in an appendix, but more and more these days I don't see the need.

The large dossier contained not, as you might surmise, secret personal pictures of Toby and me together (there are none, though in some news photographs of the siege we appear side by side, and I did get that shutterbug Ed Grier to enlarge part of one that shows us both laughing and which is now on my wall somewhere, if I turn my head I can see it, on the bedside table rather). No, it contained legal papers, duly notarized in Leicester by a photocopyist and package shipper I may use sometime in the future.

Toby had, it seemed, paid four months' advance rent on the lighthouse, taking him to the next renewal stage of his lease, and giving me sole use of it in a formal document I shall not quote here. In another he gave me sole custody of all his belongings, etc., until such time as he or his next of kin (unnamed) or appointed representative etc. could take them off my hands. There was no forwarding address; he gave his mail address as c/o me, a nice touch, I thought. It turned out he had similarly paid his electric bill in advance.

I wasn't sure what I should do, but I felt I should do something. I went up the staircase sluggishly, all the way to the top. This time no amorphous creature nudging me toward the perfect was at my heels, and the moans came only from my throat. The view seemed surreal, an abomination of my feelings, which is what I often find the outside world to be. I thought: I have seen this view twice before. On the next lower level the Machina Excelsior was missing, as was all the bric-a-brac connected with it, the tools, diagrams, stray parts, design note-books, the two backglasses, the cardboard boxes of pinball bits and pieces. Later, a week later, I was to find a journeying silver ball that had rolled under a work trolley of emptied plastic shelves.

Apart from that escaped silver ball, a stray denizen of Xibalba, apart from my vouching for its existence and my bevy of surreptitious snapshots, until such time as Toby finishes it and offers it to the world, there is no evidence that the Machina was not a figment of my own imagination. As if I could invent such a thing! This and this alone makes me laugh; I love to think of the Excelsior out there some-where, in one hemisphere or another, with him bent over it, tinkering away like a brilliant neurosurgeon, modifying, adjusting, perfecting, tightening—I still have one fantasy that involves laying him across it and making all the bells thrill and lights flash. I like to imagine it growing in power, getting ready to send its force inexorably out into the world. One day, one day.

But only that level of the lighthouse had been, as it were, stripped. One level down his bed lay as he'd last slept in it, the night before or the night before that; the sheets still smelled of Toby. I buried my head in his pillows and indeed spent many nights there, embraced by his presence, until at a certain point I could no longer do this and look myself in the eye. This was still a couple of weeks away yet, in the meantime I had no one to tell me not to, and I wouldn't have cared anyway. Even though I knew there'd be a last time for this, I didn't want to hurry it along. But the more I packed up the rest of his pos-sessions the less the lighthouse seemed his, and eventually they just became bedsheets, without his imprint on them any more than my own. They were now *our* sheets, as they had been that one day and night, and that was for the best.

On his pillows I did find a few errant hairs that he'd neglected to capture for me in the gummed seal of his personal envelope. I put them in with the letter.

He'd left virtually all his books behind, and it was these that afforded me the most hours. I learned how vast and diverse the array of his curiosity really was, and I wasn't surprised to find we had many areas if not actual volumes or even editions in common. Parallel minds, parallel souls, you say; a shame we did not have the leisure, amid the siege, to get to these common infinities of interest.

Of course, what meant the most to me were his notebooks. He clearly took a number with him (I have only a few from the Rio years, and none with the notes to his oft referred-to prospective Mesoamerican ball game work), though he left behind—thoughtful man, thoughtful gift—complete photocopies of two notebooks recording his own impressions of the siege, knowing I'd find and make use of them, knowing one day I would attempt what I have all but completed here. It has taken me longer than I thought it might.

My fellow Sals were not surprised Toby was gone, though there was a disappointing amount of tittle-tattle I need not dignify by reproducing here. (Mildred especially could be rather vicious in private, but then that reprinting of her book has never materialized, alas.) At the next Village Hall meeting, in September, there was some initial consternation at how he'd disappeared without a trace, amid all the talk of lawsuits and criminal charges to come—until Roscoe said, "Damn hippie's got the right idea. Better those bastards is out there trying to piss on him than in here trying to piss on us," which was not an argument anyone wanted to gainsay.

Toby's legal steps on my behalf stirred me to action, too, for the very next week I walked into Bob Herbert's office in Leicester, above his wife's The World Is Enough travel agency, and altered my will, leaving my house, books, pinball machine, etc., etc. to one Toby Auberon, address at present unknown, being of sound mind and body, etc., of my own free act and will, etc.—instead of to my niece Sarah. The last laugh, as Bob put it, though he wasn't smiling when I told him what she and her crony had tried to do. I did not tell her about this transformation of my will, it is none of her business, and if I were to attempt to tell her now, the way things have shaken down, she would not believe me.

I was not prepared for all the truly malicious accusations bruited about regarding Salt Cove, and especially Toby, by bargain-basement hired skulls in the media and cogs of the political machinery. This country is very hard on its originals. Some of it went beyond slander to outright calumny (lawyers make a distinction, at least my dear departed father used to) and I was forced, reluctantly because I always hate to sink my boots deep in the primordial slime, to do research in a Salem archive and dig up some hitherto little-known archaeological tidbits about Lt. Gov. Rowe's family, inspiring me to write a guest column or two for the Leicester paper. This time they printed every word, a Boston newspaper even paid me $200 to use one column for their op-ed page, and a Worcester editorial quoted me without attribution, which in many parts of New England is the highest form of praise.

At this point, I am sorry to say, things get a little muddled. And they come and go even now. I went to work on my book, determined to write down all that happened. It was like a voyage of discovery for me to delve back into my copious notes, many of them almost illegible, to talk with other people to fill in gaps even though I'd been talking with them all along. It was rejuvenating, it was like being given other eyes and other voices, being able to experience the universe as they did, or many universes, and trying to assemble and interknot them all. It made me realize they had not seen events remotely as I had, or else they had known other pieces of the puzzle, and I was doing them (and me!) a disservice to not acknowledge this. As I wrote and rewrote I came to realize it was also an excuse to relive my time with Toby Auberon, to make that half a year, so ruthlessly cut short, be prolonged by another half year, and perhaps even another year after that.

You will understand how, quite naturally, my sense of time got a little confused here and there, it would happen to anyone, staring out at the puckered ocean and the beach below my house—the lighthouse now totally emptied out, his arsenal of books moved to their own special place of honor on more corridor shelves I'd had constructed, his bed there stripped, his remaining clothes packed away, mothballed in boxes, the lighthouse now turned back over to the Coast Guard as if no Toby had ever lived there or ever existed—anyway, sitting there, writing away, remembering, staring out as the winter sea grew by turns more angry or more sedated, the beach (your favorite, my darling) crusted with ice and yet with me here above it living vicariously from months before, in brazen summer grandeur, reviving and revisiting that heat, those intense months of knowing we were at no one's mercy, for once in our lives we were safe in Toby's hands—you can see how, lost in what I was writing, searching among all those scraps of paper for the right one on which might be scribbled someone else's thoughts, or an apparently idle scrap of conversation overheard and preserved for a reason, why, anyone would get confused. Confused, even, about where they are, for there are seaside solutions, and then there's Seaside Solutions. And, naturally, I sense gaps.

They may even be significant gaps, if I am to believe everything I've been told. However, now is the time to mention a somewhat unpleasant development. Helen of Troy would say she knows exactly how I feel, and I can say that I now know exactly how she must have felt. You can consult her for verification if you like.

It all has to do with location, location, location, since if you're not sure where you are, why, then, you just can't be sure where you are, you could be anywhere at all. I seem to have lost a thicket of time there, for my impression is that at some odd moment those two, my niece and that healthy man who's a special friend of hers, came back to see me with that very same document, only I wasn't in my own house this time, I was in this other antiseptic place, and Toby wasn't around to dissect the clauses in detail when I told them what was what. So I signed. You can see how complicated it gets. But then again I have also considered from time to time a nightmare I had, that when they came to see me for the first time we carried on without Toby ever walking in on us, and I signed then instead. But I know that's not true, because I remember exactly what he said, that above all, no matter what strokes of ill fortune befell, what dark and dismal fate, I should never let myself be kidnapped like talkative glorious Helen to one of those prison-style homes where they keep goddesses. And Toby's one man who would never let his imagination be shackled behind bars: he took that machine with him, obsolete and aged as the whole idea might seem to an outsider. Yes, he and I know better.

Any day now I'll be able to resolve this a little more definitively—I suppose I should just be able to call up Bob Herbert—and we can make sure the paperwork is in order.

This is why, once and for all, I have written this down from the beginning: to make myself understood. Because I get the feeling occasionally that, like a beached whale, no one really understands where I'm going from here, or what I am trying to say, that the words as they come out do not entirely mean what I believe they mean. I have had this instinct repeatedly of late, and perhaps so have you. Then I close my eyes and remember the beach below my house, and I am back there again, not imprisoned in this medical fortress, and all is as it should be once more.

That beach means the world to me, I remember it so well.

Here I sit in this alien place, sans taste, sans clothes, sans voice, sans house, sans everything, but my mind is calm, calm like the waters of that distant cove in which the actual world is reflected, wavering but doubled nonetheless. And that wavery shimmer of life which is not quite life goes on even after darkness falls and surrounds me. In the country of the speechless but all-seeing, my darling, in the hospice of the forgotten, you will always be my king, and I will always happily be your thief, I will be with you slyly in the night's silences.

And where is he now? you ask.

I see him in my mind's eye laughing somewhere, solitary, safe—I don't see him with that young woman beside him, nice as she was—what would they ever have to say to each other? No, he is living alone somewhere under an assumed name, less identifiable without his adorable ponytail and beloved mustachios—I would know him anyhow, anyway, anywhere—in some other, sequestered equivalent of our peninsula, constructing a new private lair, altering the daily world for his needs, going back to work on the Machina Excelsior. He changed the geography of a place, that's a rare achievement. And one of these months, before too long, I hope, I may even hear from him again. Undoubtedly he will send for his possessions, so he might also send for me to go somewhere and join him. Who knows? He promised as much. He is well aware I am ready to travel, ready for any distance, and they would probably let me leave.

Or instead maybe this engulfing silence will persist, and one day I shall become, alas, a stroke-ridden old lady, a gentle discarded thing, whom they allow to sit drooling on stage at village meetings, writing her unreadable loops and squiggles for hours, filling every line of one notebook page many times over until it's a labyrinthine mass of ink, making sense to no one but her. So much for posterity! But therein she can read, even if no one else can decipher it at this late date, her entire life and loves, she can hear every voice, she can see into every soul, the swami no one notices. Scant solace: people will say I spoke too much for others, but they have their genius and I have mine.

Or maybe I will hear from him again soon—the most hopeful word in the language—and he will return for me.

Because, indeed, I have learned that to see something for the last time is like seeing it, really, for the first time. If those are shadows they ought to learn to behave. If all I can see is the four walls of this cell, the four walls inside my mind, that is splendor enough. I'll settle everything else in the morning. Memory sustains me, which is to say a pinball machine, a work of my imagination, that alters endlessly the expected outcome of what happens and will happen and tells me every bounce is right, this is the way the world was, the way the game went, these are the voices I heard, the adventures I lived, the love I ventured.

Perhaps one day I will end up that doddering old lady, landless but not lifeless or loveless, her mind blurred by the vagaries of age, no longer able to hear or be heard, to understand or be understood, yet somehow spooling it all back to herself in a process of illumination like time unreeling across all that she thinks happened, even as they wheel her around and turn her over lopsided in the clinical sheets without a grunt of protest, and feed her with a spoon or worse. Thank you, I like water except when it's wet.

Then I'll just lie awake here amid beauty, propped up by the dwindling remains of all my striving, and live it all over again and again, in a vast rush of many voices, and forget what I remember, and close my eyes, and try once more. And then maybe he will come back to take me with him, to leave this place and sail us far beyond the baths of all the eastern stars until we die. It may be we shall touch the Happy Isles, and see the Wily Scativo, whom we knew. Or maybe not, maybe never. And if not, perhaps I'll just sit here a while longer, and wait for a dream to come.
